Praise for the novels of Julie Gerstenblatt

The Stargazer of Nantucket

"I was spellbound by this novel. . . . Filled with tension, excitement, and brilliant plot twists, the story moves at a breakneck pace against the backdrop of Gerstenblatt's meticulous research. Luminous."

—Fiona Davis, *New York Times* bestselling author of *The Stolen Queen*

"Julie Gerstenblatt's extraordinary new novel. . .is both intimate and worldly, brilliant with love, loss, humor, and pirates, too. Julie Gerstenblatt is our female James Michener, our American Ken Follett, and I can't wait to see what she does next."

—Nancy Thayer, *New York Times* bestselling author of *Summer Light on Nantucket*

"A starry-eyed and gripping ocean adventure about a young Nantucket woman who must prove herself to her doubting father, *The Stargazer of Nantucket* is a sweeping story of love, fortune and how far we'll travel to discover who we're meant to be. An absolute delight!"

—Brooke Lea Foster, author of *Our Last Vineyard Summer*

"A bold transcendent love story of adventure, shifting loyalties and secrets, and a heart-pounding race for treasure and trade. . . . A gorgeous sweeping novel of a mother's fierce commitment to her daughter and her passion for the freedom of the sea."

—Dawn Tripp, nationally bestselling author of *Jackie*

"Authentic and impeccably researched, packed with colorful characters and a narrative that surprises you at every turn, until you land at last on a satisfying shore. This is masterful storytelling from a gifted writer."

—Beatriz Williams, *New York Times* bestselling author of *Husbands & Lovers*

Daughters of Nantucket

"Gerstenblatt's distinctive tale, a triumph in storytelling, celebrates the courage and tenacity of women."

—*Booklist*, starred review

"A memorable story of friendship and courage."

—Pam Jenoff, *New York Times* bestselling author of *Last Twilight in Paris*

"Julie Gerstenblatt brings a 19th-century New England coastal town to life in this dramatic, meticulously researched, beautifully paced novel. A moving story of hope, loss, perseverance, and survival."

—Christina Baker Kline, #1 *New York Times* bestselling author of *Orphan Train* and *The Exiles*

THE STARGAZER OF NANTUCKET

JULIE GERSTENBLATT

PARK
ROW
BOOKS

Also by Julie Gerstenblatt

Daughters of Nantucket

Recycling programs for this product may not exist in your area.

ISBN-13: 978-0-7783-0589-7

The Stargazer of Nantucket

Park Row Books
22 Adelaide St. West, 41st Floor
Toronto, Ontario M5H 4E3, Canada
ParkRowBooks.com

HarperCollins Publishers
Macken House, 39/40 Mayor Street
Upper, Dublin 1, D01 C9W8, Ireland
www.HarperCollins.com

Printed in U.S.A.

26 27 28 29 30 LBC 5 4 3 2 1

To Andrew and Arthur

PROLOGUE

Aboard the Shooting Star
May 18, 1838

This is the story of a mother, a father, a daughter, and a ship.

The ship set sail from Nantucket and navigated the seas in search of fortune. The husband captained the vessel with skill and speed. In China, the merchant wife purchased tea and silk and porcelain and carpets and furniture and more and more tea to sell in America for incredible profits.

When they departed from the harbor at Canton, the mother, the father, and the daughter were happy. The father had shown off his beautiful ship and family to the other sea captains and merchants. The mother had found a superior supplier for ginger and had procured the lowest price for the freshest tea of the season. The daughter, having just that very day turned from four fingers old to five—a whole hand! So big!—was happy because she was on an adventure with her parents. She was happy because she was always happy at sea.

The ship, too, was happy, weighed down as she was with rare and prized commodities from the far side of the world, her sails filled with wind, the American flag proudly waving from her stern. While spending several months in port as the merchant wife bartered and made her deals, the ship had been caulked and tarred and mended, her sails repaired and her hull tended to by the captain husband

and his crew. Together, they had survived typhoons, hurricanes, and the doldrums. Together, they would head home.

Only, sometimes, a happy story gets interrupted. Sometimes, even on a happy ship, a sailor goes mad, losing his mind from a potent combination of drink and opium and isolation, and it drives him to a deranged act.

"Get me off this ship!" the madman cried, his eyes bloodshot and face hollow in the moonlight.

It was a calm and balmy night. The ship had recently passed Sumatra and was charting its course through the Java Sea. After dinner, the mother, father, and daughter had joined the crew of thirty men on the deck. There had been revelry, with the redheaded steward teaching the golden-haired daughter yet another shanty, and the daughter telling a spooky ghost tale, delighting the crew more than frightening them with her lisp and her innocent emerald eyes.

A sailor with wild black hair and a tiny black dog danced a jig, and the girl and her mother danced with them. Her father played the fiddle.

And then the madman had demanded to disembark. "Now!" he said, and "I must go *now*!" And when the redheaded steward and the cook named Cook and even the nasty third mate who nobody liked tried to subdue the sailor and lock him in the brig, he fended off their grasp and pulled a knife from his sleeve. "Now, you bastards, now!"

As the crew decided what to do to rid themselves of this madman—Head back to Jakarta? Push on to Bali? Let him go adrift in a lifeboat?—the crazed sailor grabbed ahold of the daughter and disappeared into the belly of the ship, the girl's screams echoing through the night.

The madman jiggered open the iron lock on the door of the ship's hold using the tip of his knife and slipped inside. He dropped the daughter to the hay-covered floor and barricaded them in with crates of potatoes, bags of flour and grain, and a giant wooden desk commissioned especially for the governor of Massachusetts. "Be quiet!" he yelled at the daughter. "Stop crying!"

But now he wanted to cry, too, confused and maniacal as he

was. He inhaled and exhaled deeply, trying to make his addled mind *think*. For what had he gotten himself into? Locked in the hold with the captain's little girl? It would be the death of him.

There were shouts from the hallway outside, attempts to break down the door. The girl's cries turned to whimpers. She crawled away on hands and knees and the mad sailor lost sight of her in the dark room.

No matter. What he needed now was a gun. Ammunition. Feeling his way with his hands, he began to search for the right crate. He knew the captain kept a cache of weapons here, should the ship ever be attacked by pirates or mutineers. Was he a mutineer? No, he wasn't trying to take over control of the ship. He just wanted to leave. But maybe, by causing this chaos, he was indeed a mutineer? He would save that question for another time. Ah! He found it. The crate with munitions. Although he couldn't read, he had helped load this crate onto the ship many months ago and recognized the black markings on top.

Hiding behind some wooden chests on the other side of the room, the daughter started to hum, the tune of the new shanty fresh in her mind, the humming soothing. It wasn't one of her mother's lullabies, but it would have to do. Her song echoed through the high-ceilinged chamber, bouncing off the crates of exported tea and exotic fruits, elaborately carved lacquered furniture and beautiful, hand-woven textiles. The Chinese goods hid the daughter from view and further confounded the madman.

"Stop your singing, child!" the madman yelled.

And the daughter did stop singing. But not because she wished to obey him. Rather because, through the grated skylight above, she could see her mother looking down at her, a lantern in her hand. *Mother!* she almost called out.

But her mother pressed her pointer finger to her lips. *Shhh.*

Shhh, the girl pantomimed back.

Stay put, the mother mouthed, her palm out flat. *Don't move.*

The daughter nodded. She would stay put. She wouldn't move. She would listen to her mother.

And then, someone broke a small hole in the wall using a wooden beam like a battering ram. The madman loaded a bullet into the pistol and cocked the handle. Maybe he could beat this. Maybe he could be free.

But it was a small hole, only big enough for a tiny dog to jump through. The man laughed as the pup yipped away and tried to bite his ankles. From the other side of the wall, the men kept striking the wood until the hole enlarged enough for one man to snake his way in and rush toward the madman.

The madman shot at the sailor, the one with the wild black hair, the owner of the annoyingly yippy pup, but his aim was off, and he ended up shooting the sailor in the leg.

The sailor fell to the floor and groaned, bleeding.

"Open the door for us, you lucky son of a bitch!" another sailor shouted to the injured crew member.

The sailor crawled toward the door, removing the barricade as quickly as possible so that his mates could enter and end this.

Knowing that a swarm of sailors would arrive any moment, the madman tried to grab more bullets, but his hands were shaking badly and he ended up dropping the gun. He dashed to the other side of the room and slid into a corner behind a case of kumquats, almost bumping into the little girl.

Now the daughter was unsure what to do. Stay put? Listen to her mother, even still?

And then, from above, another sound: the hatch with its grated skylight was yanked from its metal hinges. Both the madman and the daughter looked up.

"Mama!" the girl cheered, reverting back to the babyish name she had called her mother before turning five fingers old.

"My darling," the mother said, jumping onto a stack of crates piled high. She stepped down and reached out her arms.

But before the two could embrace, the madman stepped between them and once again procured his knife. He wasn't so mad as to kill the child, no. But kill the mother? Why not?

The mother, having so very much to live for, would not die tonight.

She reached into the right-hand pocket of her beautiful, fine silk dress, pulled out a small pistol, and shot the madman in the heart.

Did the mother, the father, the daughter, and the ship live happily ever after?

You'll have to read on to find out.

PART I

Around Cape Horn

Fair Winds and Following Seas

CHAPTER 1

Sunday, June 1, 1851
Nantucket Island, Massachusetts

A new journey held so much promise. Nell Starbuck, excited for the adventure that lay ahead, had just one problem to contend with before boarding the clipper ship: she had to decide what to pack.

The tortured indecision was a surprise to no one, least of all to Nell's eighteen-year-old daughter, Winnie. For as long as Winnie could remember, her mother had been decisive, stalwart, and steady, and afraid of absolutely nothing. Nell Starbuck was a well-respected female entrepreneur, a community leader, and a shrewd global merchant. The one task in the entire world that seemed to incapacitate her was deciding which petticoat to fold into a sea chest.

Mother and daughter stood side by side and surveyed the entire contents of Nell's wardrobe, which had been emptied from her dresser and piled in haphazard heaps on the Starbucks' giant four-poster mahogany bed. Two large trunks waiting to be stuffed with Nell's clothing sat empty by their feet.

"Mother, you must be reasonable," Winnie said, lifting something from the pile. "You could leave this behind and not even miss it." The item was a navy silk jacket with pearl buttons and crocheted detail at the neck that her mother had brought back from Italy just last year. Upon closer inspection, Winnie found it rather fetching. Maybe she could sneak off with it while her mother distracted herself with the petticoats.

"The weather conditions, the climates, the cold ship—for the better part of a year!" Nell said. How could she possibly know if San Francisco would be warm or chilly, balmy or crisp? If the winds came from the east, she'd need one kind of jacket over her woolen dresses, and if it came from the west, wouldn't she need another type entirely? And once they reached China? Temperatures in Canton could approach close to one hundred degrees depending on the season, especially right before the monsoons arrived. She'd melt in anything but her thinnest cotton shift.

Even after twenty years of going to sea with her husband, famed sea captain Peter Starbuck, Nell had not figured out how to organize her wardrobe efficiently. But once she got through this, the rest would be smooth sailing. "You do not understand how difficult this is, having never had to pack for such a trip," Nell barked at Winnie.

Winnie raised an eyebrow. "And whose fault is that?"

Immediately, Nell wished she could take her words back. Being only five years old at the time, Winnie didn't remember going to sea with her parents, and the last thing Nell wanted to do was jog the girl's memory of that awful return passage aboard the *Shooting Star*. She busied herself with bonnets, hoping not to have to answer the question, which was both rhetorical and straightforward in nature.

"Do you prefer this hat or this one?" Nell asked, holding up two for her daughter's inspection.

Winnie sighed. "Both are adorned with blue ribbon."

They were not similar in the least, Nell thought, inspecting them more closely.

Her daughter leveled her green eyes at her. "You didn't answer my question," she said.

"That's because your father and I have already answered that question many times over and are tired of answering you. As our only child and heir to the Starbuck fortune, you are to remain safely on shore at all times. You are not coming along on the ship, no matter how you try to persuade us."

As grateful as she was that Winnie did not remember that tragic voyage, Nell almost wished that she did. Because then her daughter would know to be scared of the sea and would stop begging to come along.

Nell heard her husband's footsteps on the stairs and sighed from relief. Peter to the rescue.

Winnie heard him, too. "Father!" she said, her tone immediately softening.

"Ah, my loves," he said. "Dutiful daughter, thank you for trying to help your mother, who is as organized as ever, I see." Peter's tone was playful, his brown eyes teasing. "And packing light as a feather!"

He was a beautiful man. Every time Nell looked at him, she thought this. Handsome by any standard of the word, Peter had a classically chiseled jaw, a strong nose, warm eyes, and thick, black hair that swept back from his face and brushed his collar. Perhaps his hairline was receding just a bit, but that was to be expected in one's late forties. She had fallen for him in grammar school and still fell for him daily.

"Some people make lists, others—piles." Nell smiled. "I'm sure Winnie and I can get it all to fit into these two trunks." Although when she glanced at the wooden travel chests by her feet, Nell was not at all certain about this.

"We are not headed to the ballrooms of Paris, my dear. Rounding Cape Horn is a matter of survival, not one of high fashion." His smart, capable wife was often distracted by beautiful clothing and other finery. This made her an outstanding merchant, for she understood style in a way the other merchants—who were almost all male—did not. But it also meant she carried a lot of baggage.

"I know that, Peter! I've traveled with you many times," Nell said.

"I haven't, and I desperately wish to! Father, I can be packed and ready to leave in ten minutes." Winnie knew she sounded pathetic, begging as she was, but her parents were leaving tomorrow. This was the last chance she'd have to convince them to bring her along.

Her parents exchanged a look.

"Fred," Peter said, using the masculine nickname he'd been calling his daughter, Winifred, since the day of her birth, as if wishing she had been born a boy. "This is a beast of a journey. We are traversing the globe in a brand-new clipper ship, one that's never been tested at sea. And on a route we've never before traveled in order to make the stop in California. Aboard a ship, life is always a game of chance. And in this case, the stakes are the highest they've ever been. We cannot risk bringing you along."

"I promise not to be a bother. I'll be helpful!" Winnie said.

"Not another word about it," Nell said. "Tomorrow, you will move across the street and stay with your Aunt Lydia and Uncle William until we return. You will continue teaching at the grammar school, a job that I believe you love and enjoy. And when we return in a year's time, when your father and I make enough money to retire, we will discuss finding you a suitable husband. And then we can all enjoy life on Nantucket together."

Her father nodded along with her mother's words.

There was nothing worse than when Winnie's parents completely agreed on something. Particularly when that something was her.

"Now, go help Maisie set the table for our last night at home," her mother added. "She and the cook have made a going-away feast with some of your favorites."

Winnie clomped down the stairs like a horse, hoping her parents could hear her anger in every step. Not that they cared at all about her feelings.

She needed to calm herself lest she explode at the cook, her frustration boiling over like a pot kept too long on an unwatched stove. Winnie imagined the scene in which her anger met the kitchen: throwing a fresh loaf of bread into the fire and watching it burn, upturning a tureen of soup and burning her skin, ruining a rhubarb pie with a knife to its heart as she roared her rage. Thus, before heading into the kitchen as ordered, she paused in front of the dining room, gripping the back of a Chippendale chair for support.

Of all the lavishly decorated rooms in the Starbuck home, the dining room was Winnie's favorite. The walls were covered in handmade wallpaper from China, depicting the harbor at Canton. It was like living inside a painting. At the top, a pale blue sky was dotted with lazy clouds hovering over soft mossy mountains. And in the foreground, the harbor was a sea of calm, the artist having painted mint and lemon waters touched with pink, suggesting sunrise over the ships and sampans. Factories with French, Dutch, American, and British flags lined the shore. Workers had hung the paper painstakingly and meticulously, panel by panel, when Winnie was about eight or so. She remembered the day perfectly.

As the craftsmen worked around them and the scene began to grow, Winnie's father had explained the inner workings of the family business, how he and Winnie's mother traveled to Canton to purchase tea and other goods to sell back in America. "Like the plates we eat off of every day with the Starbuck crest—you know the ones, Fred—and this hand-knotted silk carpet that we are standing on right here and the lacquerware and porcelain urns that flank the fireplace."

Winnie had nodded, her gaze transfixed, her mind floating in a sampan along the Pearl River.

"I brought back this wallpaper to remind anyone who dined with us exactly how we Starbucks made our hard-earned fortune," her father said, his eyes dark and filled with pride. "A fortune that shall someday be yours."

But Winnie didn't care about the fortune. Something else was awakened in her that day, something far more interesting than an inheritance of riches. As a little girl, hearing her father talk about the challenging work he and her mother did, Winnie was moved by the sense of adventure, traveling around the globe, sailing and selling. How brave her parents were! How singular her mother was, in particular, to succeed as she had in a world dominated by men. How bold.

Her anger giving way to longing now, Winnie ran her hand over the exquisite paper scene, her fingers tracing the harbor, caressing the sampans and junks, and fluttering over the mountains in the distance. How cruel of her parents to show her a glimpse of this world and not allow her to fully experience it for herself.

While her parents were at sea, Winnie lived at a boarding school outside Boston called the Cambridge School for Girls. Winnie spent her time there learning mathematics and chemistry and horticulture, and reading Shakespeare, yes, but she also used the time to ensure a proper education for her future life as a sea merchant. Winnie read everything she could about sailing written by actual mariners, from Richard Dana's *Two Years Before the Mast* to essays and stories in *The Sailor's Magazine* printed in New York City. Unbeknownst to her parents, Winnie subscribed to the publication with money from her allowance and received monthly installments to her mailbox at the Cambridge School.

Winnie Starbuck was certain that, one day, her parents would realize how foolish they had been and invite her along on their travels. And when they did, she'd be ready.

For, ever since first glancing at that wallpaper, all Winnie had wanted was to go to sea. To travel on a merchant ship, to voyage from the Atlantic to the Pacific, to feel the ocean under her feet and the wind in her curls. To curse with the other sailors and sing shanties and watch the moon and stars light the waves and guide the way to China.

This was to be her parents' final voyage, which meant Winifred Starbuck was out of time. And she was eighteen now, no longer a child who had to abide by the whims and demands of her elders. She was old enough to make her own decisions. And so, as she stood in the dining room of the Starbuck home, she decided: nothing would stop her from getting on that clipper ship tomorrow, not even her own parents.

All she needed now was a plan.

CHAPTER 2

June 2

It was a day of beginnings, summer awakening. The perfect day to launch a new boat, with all the pomp surrounding it. Nell Starbuck had packed late into the night, and although exhausted, she had found herself tossing and turning, worried not about their impending voyage but rather about Winnie. The hurt look on Winnie's face haunted Nell. She and Peter could not allow their daughter to travel with them, but, by denying her this, they had created a rift in the relationship that felt cavernous. Nell could only hope that, someday, her daughter would understand and forgive them.

As daylight broke and the birds began to chirp, Nell finally dozed off for an hour or two, but a noise from downstairs startled her awake at 6:00 a.m. It sounded like a door banging shut, and she silently cursed her servants for being so prompt on their last day of work. She had told them not to arrive until seven, but a heightened anticipation was in the air and they must have been as eager to get the day started as Nell was.

Peter had met his crew after supper and slept on board the ship. Loading in the cargo was a long and tedious process that had begun several days earlier, and Peter wanted to oversee all of it.

"Winnie!" Nell called up the stairs from the front hall. "Time to go!" She tied her bonnet and watched through the windows flanking the front door as the driver hitched his horse to a post and readied the cart for their belongings. Winnie's school trunk would make the first stop, a quick journey across the street to Hadwen House, and then the driver would bring Nell's sea chests down to the harbor.

Upstairs, Winnie rubbed her bloodshot eyes and tried not to smile too broadly at her reflection in the mirror over her dresser. She quickly plaited her golden curls into a thick rope and quieted the butterflies beating against her rib cage.

Her plan would work. It had to work.

She wanted to slide down the banister like she had done as a little girl, for the curved wooden handrail was delightfully slick and the newel post at the bottom marvelous for launching off of, but she had to pretend to be in a foul mood—and nobody slid down a banister in a foul mood. Plus, she was no longer a silly little girl.

Winnie plodded into the foyer, her face drawn and pale. Nell realized the poor girl must have been up all night crying, her green eyes tired looking and red. She longed to grab her into an embrace and give in to whatever her daughter wanted, just to make her sadness disappear. But, no, Nell could not let herself be swayed by emotional weakness. She must stay the course. Light conversation that avoided all confrontation was Nell's goal.

"Did you sleep well, darling?" Nell asked.

"No," Winnie replied flatly.

"Neither did I!" Nell said gayly.

They said goodbye to the cook and to Maisie, who had both found temporary employment at Eliza and Henry Macy's booming bed-and-breakfast down the street. The two would close up the house over the next day or so and then work for the Macys until the Starbucks returned.

"We'll see you around town, Miss Winifred!" the cook said.

"Hmm?" Winnie asked, momentarily confused.

"Maybe you can come by Macy House for tea one day after teaching, and catch up with the twins? And say hi to your old cook and maid?" Maisie added.

"Oh! Yes! Certainly," Winnie agreed. "I would love to do that." *Except that I will be long gone from Nantucket by then—thanks in large part to the help of those very same Macy twins!* Winnie had to bite her tongue to keep herself from laughing. Had she known how much fun it would be to sneak around behind her parents' backs in the middle of the night, plotting with her childhood friends Rachel and Mattie Macy, Winnie would have done so long ago.

Nell and Winnie stood on the front stoop and watched as their chests were hoisted into the calash's cart and the driver secured the load as best he could with twine before mounting his black mare.

Only Winnie was aware that her chest—*that* one at any rate—was empty.

"I'll avoid the cobbles on Main Street and take some of the side roads down to the harbor and will meet you at the dock in a bit," he said, tipping his hat and clicking his tongue, signaling the horse to start moving.

Winnie and her parents lived at 93 Main Street, in one of three matching brick homes built by her grandfather, Joseph Starbuck, for her father and his two brothers. Since the facades were identical, they were known by their placement more than by their house number: West Brick, Middle Brick, and then her family's home, East Brick. One large, classical brick house was impressive. Three of such grandeur built neatly in a row made quite a statement about the Starbuck name—and their legacy on Nantucket.

Winnie's grandfather, who lived around the corner on New Dollar Lane and would meet them down at the harbor this morning, had made his fortune as a whaling merchant, turning oil into candles in his large factory on the wharf and becoming perhaps the most successful businessman of his time. Winnie's parents, who could have just lived off their inherited wealth, chose instead to chart their own course in the China trade, risking life and limb in the name of American innovation and commerce. Winnie was proud to be part of such a distinct and well-respected family. Most of the time, anyway. When they weren't too busy to include her in their important lives.

"Walk with me to the harbor," Nell said, smiling. Winnie hooked her arm with her mother's.

A veritable party would be greeting them when they got to the docks, and Nell wanted to exude confidence and make certain that the town of Nantucket viewed the Starbuck women as an unflappable team, even if they were privately squabbling. "It might be very crowded on the wharves for our send-off, and I don't want to lose you," Nell joked.

Winnie nodded and again had to bite her tongue to keep herself in check. She was *counting* on it being quite crowded down at the docks. Last night, when creating their strategy, Rachel and Mattie Macy had joyfully used the words "chaotic" and "a perfect mess" to describe the harbor on the day a new ship launched. Over a thousand people were expected to attend, and the schools had been closed for the occasion. Winnie had never seen such a send-off, always tucked away in her dorm at the Cambridge School, but the Macy girls had witnessed many, including some with their own father as the ship's captain.

People were shopping on Main Street, well-dressed men and women ambling into and out of storefronts. Five years had passed since the Great Fire of 1846 had razed the entire downtown, leaving almost every building on Main Street in ashes. Both the Macys' home and the Starbucks' on upper Main Street were spared from disaster, but three hundred other buildings had not been as lucky.

And although Nantucket had rebuilt quickly, with two hundred of the lost structures replaced within the year, not all the original businesses had come back. Add to that a decline in whaling and a migration west for the California Gold Rush, which also drained the local commerce, and you ended up with a somewhat lethargic downtown center. Her father put it this way: "good thing we Starbucks rely on global trade for our daily tea." In other words, the Starbuck fortune wasn't going anywhere, whale or no whale, gold or no gold, for it was based on an insatiable market, supplying New Englanders with the most important commodity in the world: tea from China.

If everything worked out according to her plan, this would be the last time Winnie would walk along Main Street for almost a year, and when she came back, she would be a different person entirely. The notion made her suddenly nostalgic, and so she decided to store the images of Nantucket away for safekeeping on the journey.

After the fire, on the site of the former Main Street a central roadway was created that was much wider than the previous one. The town planners had reasoned that, should a fire ever encroach on one side of town again, even the fiercest wind would not be able to spread a conflagration to the other side of town, as it did in 1846. This illustrious Main Street was beautifully cobbled to drain off rainwater and thus prevent typical mud and ruts in the dirt, complemented by smooth brick sidewalks for the pedestrians. And, with the knowledge brought about by hindsight, the buildings flanking Main Street were remade of brick instead of wood, a material which had easily fed the hungry blaze five years earlier.

Winnie and her mother passed the same-but-different rebuilt grocer's, apothecary, jewelry store, and William Geary's hat shop. They passed the same-but-different office of *The Inquirer* and then ambled down the rest of Main.

Sure enough, the crowds were waiting for them. A bandstand covered with red, white, and blue bunting had been erected between New North Wharf and Straight Wharf. As Nell and Winnie approached, a murmur rose up through the crowd and someone alerted the band's conductor, who started playing a very enthusiastic "Yankee Doodle."

"It's like the Fourth of July," Winnie said, her excitement palpable. The Macy girls had been right.

Nell tried to state the truth without boasting, but it was difficult to keep the pride from her voice. "The first extreme clipper ship to launch from Nantucket Harbor—and with your father at the helm? It's more historic than the Fourth, which happens annually. This moment occurs only once in a lifetime."

"Once in *your* lifetime," Winnie scoffed. But Nell noticed that her daughter didn't seem nearly as upset as she had been the night before. In fact, she seemed almost distracted, like she was looking for a particular person in the melee. Maybe she had a secret beau?

"I know this is hard for you, Winnie dear. But I think it's true what my mother always used to say: 'Time heals all wounds.'"

"Agreed, Mother. I believe that time and distance will heal us all." *Like a year at sea*, she didn't add.

"That's the Starbuck spirit," Nell added, feeling much calmer indeed.

"Oh, look! The Macys are here!" Winnie said, perking up significantly and pushing her way toward them with a lot of *excuse me*'s. Nell knew Winnie had grown close with the twins, who were only two years older than her, but she'd never seen her quite so enthusiastic about greeting them before. The three young women stood together in a tight cluster, bonnets practically touching.

Captain Henry Macy came toward Nell, carrying his youngest daughter, Jane, in his arms, his wife, Eliza, following. The Macys had four daughters—twenty-six-year-old Alice, the town's midwife with a daughter of her own; twenty-one-year-old twins Rachel and Mattie; and five-year-old Jane, born nine months after Captain Macy returned from sea, just after Nantucket's Great Fire of 1846.

"This is quite a send-off!" the captain said to Nell in greeting. Henry Macy was well over six feet, a bit of an anomaly for the men of Nantucket, and broad, too, but it was more than that: he had a commanding presence. The whole town of Nantucket was still impressed by this sixty-year-old retired whaling captain, now a man of leisure who attended whist games with his wife. "And that ship! Peter gave me a tour of her yesterday. She makes me want to come out of retirement and join you."

Eliza Macy slapped her husband playfully on the arm. "Henry! You wouldn't dare!"

"Daddy dare!" five-year-old Jane mimicked, poking her father in the chest and laughing.

"I would never," the captain said, smiling fondly at Eliza and kissing Jane on the temple. The little girl was clearly enamored with her father, although she didn't resemble him at all. Jane had her mother's brown hair and pinky-peach complexion, but the rest of her face was decidedly her own, with a deep dimple in one chubby cheek and eyes a mesmerizing cobalt. "Nothing on earth could make me leave my girls again," Captain Macy added. "Not even the fastest clipper ship in the world."

"Do you really think she'll be the fastest?" Nell asked. The faster the ship reached its destination, the faster it made money—and the more money it made. This had always been the goal when returning from China, for the faster ships brought the freshest tea leaves, thereby earning top dollar. But since gold had been discovered a year earlier in California, there was a new race to win, and a new ship to do it: an extreme clipper ship like their own.

It would be grand to reach San Francisco in record time, for both the profits that could be made by selling goods and even more so for the glory of captaining such a fine vessel.

Peter had remarked on this possibility a few times, but Nell wasn't sure if he was being honest in his assessment of the ship's capabilities, or just making Nell feel better about how much he had spent on it.

"I have no doubt," Henry Macy said. "That's why I bet a hundred dollars on it. Just don't tell my wife," he added, winking at Eliza.

"Henry! We need that money for the twins' weddings," Eliza said.

"We'll double our money for double the ceremonies," Henry said. He waved to another man in the crowd, who tipped his hat in acknowledgment. "Ah! Mr. Geary wants to get in on the action. So, if you'll excuse me, I've got another bet to arrange."

It felt most odd to have people betting on her and Peter, on her family's success, but Nell tried to enjoy the grand send-off without worry as the band segued into a rousing rendition of "Oh! Susanna."

"Mother," Winnie said, pulling on the sleeve of Nell's dress and raising her voice to be heard over the fanfare. "Would it be okay if I say goodbye to you now? The Macy twins and I would like to see the ship off from Brant Point!"

"Brant Point?" Nell felt conflicted. On the one hand, she wanted to keep Winnie as close as she could before departing, and on the other, she wanted to keep Winnie as content as possible, so her daughter would think of her fondly over the next year. "But—don't you want to say a proper farewell to your father first?" She scanned the harbor for his small skiff. They couldn't see the ship from where they were on the wharves because Peter had to dock her out farther in the harbor where the water was deep. "He's coming to get me at any moment."

Winnie tried to hide her impatience. "I said goodbye to him last night at East Brick, at dinner. Before he boarded the ship."

"But he's prepared a brief speech. Don't you want to hear him address the town?"

"I heard him practicing it aloud the other day in his study," Winnie said. "So I know what he's preparing to say." And she knew just how pompous he would sound while saying it.

"And what about your grandfather? Wouldn't you like to see him?"

"Since I'll be *home*, Mother, I can visit with him every Sunday after church!" *Or, rather, send him letters from San Francisco!* she thought.

"Winnie!" Mattie—or Rachel—called. Nell could never tell them apart, with their matching pale blue eyes and silky light brown hair styled in the exact same fashion. "Come on!"

"Mother! Please!" Winnie said, her tone growing anxious.

"Don't you want to know the ship's name?"

"Star-something-or-other," Winnie said. Every ship her father had ever captained included the word *star* in it, for Starbuck. A portrait of his favorite ship, *The Starboard*, hung over the mantel in his study. "And I'll get to see the ship from Brant Point, so I'll know soon enough for myself what she's called."

"But Pastor Smith is going to bless us," Nell said.

"Amen!" Winnie said. "There. I've blessed you, too."

"What has gotten into you?" Nell wondered, scanning the crowd. "Are you smitten with a boy? It must be a boy."

Winnie paused. Could it really be that easy to hoodwink her mother? "Fine, Mother. You caught me. It's a boy."

Nell knew it. She smiled triumphantly. A mother's intuition was not to be meddled with. "And, let me guess: the Macy girls have arranged for you to meet him at Brant Point this morning, during our send-off?"

"Yes," Winnie said, lowering her head to hide her smile. At least she didn't have to lie. A boy—with a boat—was waiting for her.

"Oh, darling." Nell pulled Winnie to her, a tight embrace. Winnie could feel her mother's heart beating, smell the familiar rosewater cologne on her skin, and felt momentary remorse about her duplicity. "You are growing up so fast." Nell pulled back from her daughter. "Let me just look at you one more time." Her emerald eyes matched Winnie's own, except Nell's were filled with tears. "You promise to follow all of your aunt and uncle's rules? And to remain chaste with that boy?" Suddenly, Nell looked confused. "Wait a minute . . ."

"What?" Winnie said, on high alert. "What's wrong?"

Nell scanned Winnie suspiciously. "Is that my navy jacket you're wearing? The one from Italy?"

Winnie smiled. "I told you that you didn't need it on the voyage!"

"Winnie! Winifred Starbuck!" the Macy girls called out, jumping up and down in the crowd. Winnie turned to her mother, her expression open and hopeful. All Nell had ever wanted was for her daughter to be safe and happy on Nantucket. And with these friends, and a fledgling romance, and a good job as a schoolteacher, she would be.

"Oh, fine, just go," Nell said.

"Thank you!" Winnie kissed her mother on the cheek. "Wishing you fair winds and following seas!" she called over her shoulder, uttering the sailor's prayer before disappearing into the crowd. Several townspeople, hearing the familiar prayer, echoed it back in cheers. *Fair winds and following seas!*

Nell Starbuck watched her daughter go, never wondering why her landlocked daughter would know the sailor's prayer.

***"FINALLY!"* RACHEL AND** Mattie Macy said in tandem. Rachel grabbed Winnie's hand and pulled her with them through the throng of townsfolk who'd come to the wharf for the festivities and the drunk sailors and loose women who always frequented the port. The crowd thinned out at the top of Straight Wharf, where they paused to catch their breath.

"Are you sure he's meeting me?" Winnie asked.

"Yes!" they said.

"And your father's old sea chest, with my clothing packed inside?" Winnie asked.

"On the ship!" they cheered.

"And the letter explaining to the headmistress why I won't be turning up to teach tomorrow at the grammar school?"

"On her desk!"

As they walked briskly along North Water Street, the Macy girls and Winnie discussed their scheme. Last night, after dinner, Winnie had sneaked out of East Brick and gone to see the twins. Since their home was also a bed-and-breakfast, the door was always unlocked for guests to come and go. Winnie had just let herself in and gone up to the twins' shared bedroom, where she confessed her desire to go to sea and the need for their help—and their discretion.

Being from a seafaring family, the twins had not batted an eye as to why someone—specifically a girl like themselves—might want to go to sea: for the adventure, and the fortune, but mostly for the adventure. And so, although they were perfectly content to live more conventional lives themselves, to marry and have children here on Nantucket, they had immediately gotten to work to help their intrepid friend.

First, Mattie had crawled under her bed and pulled out an old sea chest of her father's, brushing the dust off the top with her dress sleeve. It was a large, dark mahogany box with a lighter wood inlay of the captain's initials and forged metal handles on each side. "After his last voyage, he gave it to me for storage, but I've never needed it. I thought I might use it to carry my wardrobe to our new house after our wedding, but since Bartholemew is moving in here with us instead, to help run the inn, that won't be necessary!"

And Alastair Coffin, Rachel's fiancé, who lived just around the corner on Fair Street, was able to get a message to his cousin Marcus on Orange Street, who knew a fellow who knew another fellow who was a crew member on the new Starbuck clipper.

When time was of the essence, it was wonderful to live on a small island such as theirs, for everyone knew someone who could get the job (whatever it might be) done quickly and well.

After the twins arranged plans to secretly move both the sea chest and Winnie on board in the morning, the three young women crept over to East Brick and gathered Winnie's belongings as quietly as possible. Then they returned to the twins' home to pack the chest, laughing and talking until dawn. When Winnie saw the sky lighten, she snuck back into her home, the wind slamming the front door shut behind her at just about 6:00 a.m.

Now, instead of continuing on toward Easton Street and Brant Point, the trio turned right on Broad Street and headed down to New North Wharf. It had that same-but-different quality of the rest of downtown, having been rebuilt after the Great Fire, a new version of the original northernmost wharf. Although this pier wasn't as busy as the Straight Wharf today, it was still crowded with boats big and small. Several shops and alehouses lined the top of the pier, and cargo was being loaded and unloaded on boats coming to and fro. A fishmonger hung his morning's catch on a line, Nantucket bluefish drying open-mouthed and flat eyed in the sun, scales shining.

With this much hubbub, Winnie could sneak onto a boat without being noticed. Not so at Brant Point, where, with just a strip of sand and a lighthouse jutting out into the harbor, she would have been spotted immediately. As good sailors knew, sometimes a decoy was necessary.

The twins scanned the length of the wooden pier. "There he is!" Mattie said, pointing out a small rowboat tied up on the left side of the pier, dwarfed by a large cargo ship next to it.

Rachel nodded. "Red neckerchief! See?" She raised her hand in greeting and the sailor waved back.

The three raced to the boat. It was practically full with sacks of food, but one girl-sized spot remained open. "We've got goods for the Starbuck clipper!" Mattie said.

He nodded. "That's me."

"He's the cabin boy. He'll make sure you get food while you hide."

"This is really happening," Winnie said, her eyes welling up with emotion as she turned to the Macy twins.

"It is!" the twins said in unison, hugging her as one. Winnie thanked them and promised to write. As they stepped apart, this group of conniving, wonderful, spirited young women clutched one another's hands tight.

"What a journey you'll have!" Rachel said.

"This is going to be the best year of my life," Winnie agreed. Trepidation and jubilation mixed powerfully in her gut. She said a final farewell to her friends and turned her attention to the rowboat.

"Hop aboard!" the sailor said, smiling and extending a hand for the step down. He was young, no more than twelve or thirteen, with straight black hair and glossy black bangs that fell into his eyes.

Winnie took his hand and smiled at the sailor. "But—you're—" Winnie stammered with excitement.

"Chin from Canton!" he said, using the moment to shake Winnie's hand. He had found that this greeting was the easiest way to explain who he was and where he came from to every dumbfounded American he met.

"You're Chinese!" Winnie smiled, finding a place to sit amid the sacks. "And you speak English!"

"Do you speak Cantonese?" he asked, furrowing his brow. He spoke with an unusual accent but was easy enough to understand.

"No," she said apologetically.

"Then it's very good that I speak English!" he joked, tossing her an empty cloth sack and picking up his oars. "Now, cover yourself and blend in with the potatoes."

Winnie ducked down in the small skiff and did as she was told.

CHAPTER 3

After Winnie left to sneak off with some boy, Nell said goodbye to her friend Eliza. Nell had spent a portion of almost every day during the last year visiting with Eliza, ever since she and Peter returned from their trip last year to attend Winnie's high school graduation and welcome their daughter back to Nantucket. Nell and Eliza played whist and gossiped and shopped together just like they had when they were young. They had grown as close as sisters.

"Dear Nell," Eliza said, clasping both of Nell's hands with her own. Although they had of course both aged with time, Nell could still see the fresh-faced brown-eyed beauty of Eliza Cowan Macy. Without warning, a pull of emotion grabbed Nell. Tears sprang to her eyes, which then made Eliza cry, too.

"Oh!" Nell said. "I cannot believe it's almost time to go!" The idea of this trip had been real, yes, but only in the abstract until this moment. The warmth of Eliza's hands in her own made it very real indeed.

Eliza nodded. "We will write. All the time."

"Promise you'll send along every detail of the twins' wedding!" Nell said.

"Every last detail! I promise."

Nell and Eliza embraced, and Nell took in the scent of her friend, who wore a fine silk dress and emerald earrings but whose hair always smelled like pan-fried bacon, a clear mark of running a successful bed-and-breakfast.

Nell had spent so much of her adult life at sea, so much of her marriage on the water. And she had never regretted one minute of it, this exciting, roving life that she had chosen to live with her husband turned business partner. So why did this farewell feel different? Harder?

"Here comes your commander," Eliza said, pointing her chin up and out. Nell followed it and saw Peter in a small rowboat heading toward the pier to deliver Nell and her trunks to the clipper ship.

Peter waved from the rowboat, and Nell pulled herself away from the Macys and moved to the edge of the pier. She spotted her father-in-law, Joseph Starbuck, near the bandstand and waved.

"I've prepared some remarks," Peter said. Nell extended a hand to him, and he disembarked to much cheering. The band stopped playing and a hush fell over the crowd.

It had been over a year since Nell had seen Peter dressed in his captain's uniform, and it was like viewing him anew. Peter shook one little boy's hand and saluted a bunch of others, even signing the day's newspaper for a local bartender who had wandered out of his alehouse to take part in the festivities, raising his pewter mug in a toast. The backdrop of Nantucket Harbor, with boats big and small sailing in the calm waters, framed him perfectly, as if he had hired an artist to paint his portrait.

Peter Starbuck was made for this role. Of course he loved the sea as much as, if not more than, any man could, but he also loved the pomp. The ritual of a Nantucket send-off. To be venerated by one's whole town was extraordinary. It filled Peter with a sense of power he could almost smell, a heady mix of salt air and brackish seawater and the trade winds that propelled his ships. In this way, Peter Starbuck felt like a captain of not just a ship, but of an entire industry, an entire way of life. Anything was possible when you were at the helm.

Peter's long navy jacket was fastened with a double line of gold buttons over navy pants. His black patent leather shoes were polished to a high shine, and a black-and-white sailor's cap sat jauntily over his black hair.

"Thank you for being with us on this historic day. This two-hundred-and-twenty-five-foot clipper ship out in the harbor is one of the largest and finest sailing vessels in the world." Peter paused here as men outside the tavern on the wharf began whistling and cheering. "Her mainmast is just over two hundred feet high, and she carries ten thousand yards of canvas on twenty-four sails." More whistles followed, lewd-sounding ones this time, as if Peter were discussing a woman's buxomness and the men answering with heckling agreement.

Peter raised a palm to silence the crowd once more. "Many of you are placing bets on this ship breaking the world record, to which I warn you . . ." Here Peter's tone grew wary, as if planning on disciplining the town, and a heavy hush enveloped the crowd. "I'm aiming to make it around Cape Horn and to San Francisco in fewer than ninety-six days, fifteen hours, to beat the time set in March by the clipper *Surprise*, when she beat the *Sea Witch* by one day and set a new world record! So you better make those bets robust, both for yourself and for the honor of Nantucket!"

Drunk men may have started the hooting and hollering, but within seconds, housewives and schoolteachers, farmers and store clerks were clapping and calling out cheers, too—for Peter and this new ship, yes, but even moreso for their island home. Joseph Starbuck emerged from the crowd to shake his son's hand and wish him and Nell well.

Next, journalists from *The Inquirer* and several papers in Boston asked questions and then Pastor Smith from the Unitarian Church on Orange Street came forward to bless the family and the ship. He had married Nell and Peter twenty years earlier and had blessed every voyage they'd ever been on. The pastor spoke quietly to Peter, then read aloud part of Psalm 104, Nell's personal favorite, beginning with "O Lord, how manifold are thy works; in wisdom hast thou made them all: the earth is full of thy riches," before transitioning into his own Nantucket sailor's traveling prayer that contained the melodic line "There the ships go, to and fro," at which point Nell always rocked back and forth on her heels a little bit, to and fro. "Wishing you fair winds and following seas," the pastor concluded.

"Fair winds and following seas," Nell—and the town—responded. Winnie had uttered that same prayer not more than fifteen minutes earlier. Nell wondered where her daughter was now. Had the boy shown up? Were they holding hands and talking in the shade of the lighthouse, waiting for the ship to launch? Which family did he belong to? A Mitchell or a Coffin would be nice. Someone with island heritage like their own. Nell sent up her own little extra prayer, hoping that whatever her daughter wished for today—and every day after—it would come true.

"My wife and I shall now christen the ship. Please join us!" Peter said, and his words were met with a resounding cheer. The band started playing "The Star-Spangled Banner" as Peter hopped aboard the small boat and helped Nell into it, her trunks already there.

How long had Peter imagined this day? For a year at least, ever since he had decided to go into business with Mr. Forbes, together commissioning a new clipper ship to be built by renowned shipbuilder Donald McKay of East Boston.

Several weeks ago, Peter had traveled to the shipbuilder's on Border Street to oversee the final details with Mr. Forbes and Mr. McKay and to make sure the ship was built exactly to their specifications, before launching it at Boston Harbor and sailing straight to Nantucket with most of the crew already on board.

Peter needed the clipper to be true to her name and sail at a fast clip. For, of all the people betting on this ship's speed, none had risked more than Peter Starbuck himself. In order to get the deal done with entrepreneur Robert Forbes for part ownership of the *Stargazer*, Peter had leveraged all of their assets and put East Brick up as collateral. Peter had not asked Nell's advice, nor his father Joseph's, hoping that all would go as planned and, victorious and profitable in the end, he would never need to reveal the potential risks of owning such a fine vessel. The greater the risks, the greater the rewards.

Nell glanced at her husband as she settled into the small skiff. Peter refused to sit but rather stood with arms crossed in front of his chest as the boat rowed away. Two oarsmen pulled them, with Peter resembling Washington crossing the Delaware. Nell almost laughed at the absurdity of such a pose. She imagined him losing his balance and falling into the water, emerging wet and hatless, and had to stifle a laugh.

And this was when Nell remembered that her dear husband, the love of her life at home, was a different man when he captained a ship. Confidence on land turned to swagger at sea, a quality that Nell did not find completely appealing, although she knew it was necessary to keep the crew in order. And as he became more focused on sailing safely and fast, Peter became less accessible to her.

Small sailboats, dories, and other rowboats began to fill the harbor, the town taking to the water to witness the ship's christening from as close as possible. Even the tuba player had found his way into a boat, sending out a staccato of low notes.

North of them, Chin rowed his small skiff around Brant Point and into deeper water. From under her cloth sack, Winnie could feel the boat respond with every stroke of the oars. She could hear Chin breathing as he pulled. In the distance, she could hear the band play and then stop, and then the town cheering. Her father must have made his speech, then. No time to waste.

"Are we there yet?" Winnie asked from under the tarp.

"Almost, miss. This is a good place to have a look at her," Chin said.

Winnie peeked her head out from under the muslin tarp. "Oh!" she exclaimed. For there she was, an enormous, three-masted, square-rigged clipper, with a hull designed to slice through waves and a remarkable reputation for speed: the most glorious ship Winnie Starbuck had ever seen.

CHAPTER 4

Chin's small rowboat was dwarfed by the mass of the clipper's wooden hull, painted a shiny black, the bottom half sheathed in bright new copper that glowed pink gold in the sun. As they approached, her bow faced them, nose toward the harbor, as if she had turned directly toward Winnie, as curious to meet her as Winnie was to greet the ship.

The carved figurehead set at the prow was a sculpture of a woman, painted with a long blue gown floating out behind her. Coils of golden curls pushed back from her face as if moved by the wind. Blue and gold, the Starbuck family colors. Her lips were glossed with a berry stain and her eyes glowed green. In her outstretched right hand sat a gilded star. Winnie was certain that the figurehead was fashioned after herself, helping confirm that she belonged on this ship.

Townspeople were not just crowding around the clipper ship in their small rowboats and sailboats; some were climbing aboard her to see the marvel for themselves. Even the tuba player was now climbing the rope ladder. How would Winnie sneak on with the entire town watching? But Chin rowed around to the far side of the ship, facing the sound, thus out of view to anyone on land as well as those who chose to see the clipper off from sea. A lone, unoccupied ladder waited for her there.

"The boat is very crowded right now," Chin said, his dark eyes meeting hers. "This can help you hide. Up you go!" he said, pushing Winnie quite indelicately from her bottom onto the first rung.

Winnie scrambled up the ladder as quickly as possible and was met at the top by a tall, thin man with red hair that stood up in spikes, as though perpetually surprised. Indeed, upon seeing Winnie, his eyes grew wide with shock that bordered on fear.

"Welcome aboard, miss?" the redheaded sailor said, his eyes darting sideways and then back to her.

"Why, hello!" Winnie said in a loud whisper. "My arrival is a bit of a surprise. Best not to tell the captain." She moved them toward a large pen of barnyard animals that hid them both from view. A cow chewing cud stared at them while several pigs fought over the best placement at a small trough. Winnie glanced around the sides of the pen, trying to take in what she could of her first moments on the ship.

Chin was right: the boat was a hub of activity. Packed with people, the deck felt like a continuation of the send-off at the wharf, with men and women chugging drinks in celebration, and everyone talking and laughing. Some couples were even kissing quite passionately right out in the open! The tuba player had found a fiddler and the two started up a jaunty tune, which led to spirited dancing.

"The ship—she's so big!" she said to the cows and the pigs and the sailor beside her, who kept gaping, open-mouthed, like he'd seen a ghost. But she was too busy looking around to care much about him at the moment.

Winnie had thought the deck would be one continuous, unobstructed entity where you could see from one side of the ship to the other, but it was actually filled with structures, including one right next to where she stood. "That's the deckhouse with the galley, where some of us bunk," the redhead explained.

Winnie didn't answer. Instead she looked at the three tall masts and watched sailors climb up and untie gigantic square sails, men hanging along the yards and unfurling the canvas, singing a shanty that Winnie recognized as "Hanging Johnny."

Ah, life aboard a ship was wondrous! She *knew* it!

"Red! Put her with the potatoes!" Chin called up from the water.

"With the—" Red said, leaning over the deck rail, his question unfinished.

"Just trust me!" Chin called.

Red groaned.

"I know you trust me!" Chin added.

And of course Red did. Red would trust Chin with his life. Just a year prior, in the waters off Canton, a squall had come up suddenly along the Pearl River, almost capsizing the small junk that Red and the crew were trying to navigate, filled with expensive cargo. Seeing them foundering next to his family's sampan, Chin had jumped aboard the junk, and without knowing a word of English, had helped the American sailors right the ship. After they successfully delivered the precious porcelain and tea to their large merchant ship waiting in Macao, the captain had offered Chin a dollar—and the opportunity to work on his ship all the way back to America. Chin decided to accept the offer, make as much money as possible, head back to China on another merchant ship, and return to Canton—and his family—rich.

"I need to hide," Winnie explained. Her parents would be arriving by rowboat any minute, which meant Winnie's brief time above deck was up, for the meanwhile anyway. According to the Macy girls, Winnie would have to find a hiding spot in the hold and stay put for the better part of a week, with Chin bringing her food and only a chamber pot for company. Should she be discovered any earlier than that, her parents might decide to turn the ship right around and deliver Winnie back to Nantucket. But after seven days, a change in direction like that would cost the captain and crew too much time—and thus, money.

Once the clipper was well out into the ocean, Winnie's parents would be stuck with her. Hooray!

Red felt himself sweating all over even though the New England breeze was chilly, even in June. "You mean you're *staying*? For the *journey*?" He glanced around as if searching for help. But he was a man without a lifeboat. "As a *stowaway*?"

"Just temporarily as a stowaway. I shall make myself known in due course, at which point everyone shall be happy to see me!"

Red sincerely doubted that.

"Do you have a name?" Winnie asked the redhead.

The sailor swallowed and nodded. "They call me Red," he said. "I'm the steward. Help out with the cook in the galley."

Red's panic was well called for and growing exponentially by the second, because this girl was no ordinary passenger/stowaway. This girl, with the blond curls and the spunky attitude and the mischievous green eyes, was instantly recognizable to Red as Winifred Starbuck. For starters, she looked just like her mother. And secondly, she looked just like herself, only now in the mostly grown version instead of as the spirited five-year-old he remembered. And that meant Red might as well change his name to Trouble, because whatever happened from here on out, he was deep in it.

"Well, Red, you look like a man who can keep a secret," Winnie said, handing him a dollar bill. "Thank you in advance for your silence."

A dollar! Now in addition to hiding Miss Winnie, he had to hide a dollar bill somewhere safe amid his few belongings. Red's burdens were multiplying by the minute.

At least Miss Winnie was right about one thing: Red *was* darned good at keeping secrets. After all, he had kept Winifred's parents' secret for the past thirteen years. Although he'd never gotten paid for keeping his mouth shut until today. To think, he'd been silent for free all these years.

Was Chin getting a payment, too? Obviously, he was. And handsomely at that, Red had to guess. Because before Chin had even learned to speak English, he had become fluent in the language of commerce. Chin was an honest and hardworking kid, and Red loved him like a little brother. But he was a shrewd budding businessman, too, who would gladly take all of Miss Winnie's money without pesky scruples getting in the way, and without much forethought to the consequences of his actions. Hopefully Miss Winnie had enough cash to bribe everyone on board, including her own parents.

"Hurry!" Chin called from below.

"Hurry indeed!" Winnie echoed.

"So," Red thought aloud, resigning himself to his fate as an accomplice to this most unusual crime. He couldn't—and wouldn't—tattle on Chin, so here he was, aiding and abetting. "We need to get you over there," Red said, pocketing the cash and pointing to a large hatch about ten feet in front of them, toward the middle of the main deck. "It's just past the galley. That leads to the hold." But just as Winnie and Red were about to make a dash for it, a man whistled loud and clear, instantly summoning everyone's attention and silencing them, the small band included.

"Ladies and gentlemen!" a stocky sailor called out.

"That's Sully. He's just been promoted to first mate," Red whispered.

"Captain Starbuck and his wife are a-comin' up!" Sully announced, with a hint of an Irish lilt. Much cheering followed.

"Oh no," Winnie sighed, ducking back behind the oinking pigs, her heart beating loudly in her ears. She couldn't let her parents discover her now and throw her off the boat before the anchor was even raised.

"Um, we'll just stay put for a moment or two," Red said. "There's another entrance to the hold behind us, at the back of the poop deck. It's probably better to go that way." The pair watched as Mrs. Starbuck and then the captain stepped onto the deck, a handsome and powerful couple that Red had always much admired, both for their work ethic and their kindness.

Some of the crew members stood at attention, but others went about doing their work as intended, no matter the interruption. One old sailor, with thin gray wisps of hair over his mostly bald head, walked with a limp and carried a tiny gray dog in the crook of his arm. Sully kicked the limping man in the shin to get him to move faster, and the man visibly winced.

"And what do we make of this Sully?" Winnie asked.

"You can decide that for yourself, miss," Red said. He wasn't foolish enough to speak out against the first mate, even if Sully was a scoundrel.

"Captain, missus," Sully said, taking off his sweaty cap and practically bowing to the Starbucks with a self-satisfied smile. "Welcome aboard. Our crew's mostly a good 'un. Some are a little slow and a little slovenly, but I'll get 'em into shape in no time."

"I've decided what I think of him," Winnie whispered. Red pretended to study the lambs in the pen.

Nell smiled tightly. She had never liked this Sully, who had sailed with them for twenty years. She kept hoping that Sully would find a new position under a different captain, but he kept turning up for the Starbucks like a bad penny. Peter had promised Nell that he would never promote Sully to a position with too much power. And now look: here stood Sully, second-in-command! And sullying her first moments on board the brand-new beautiful clipper, everything gleaming, the railings glossy with varnish and brass fittings shining in the sunlight.

"Thank you to my first mate," Peter said. He had promoted Sully to first mate because the Irishman was tough but fair. Also, Sully really knew how to blackmail a captain whose wife had murdered a sailor thirteen years back. "Now, before I ask all visitors to depart the ship so that we can set sail, let's head to the prow and christen her, my gorgeous *Stargazer*!"

"And that's our cue," Red said. Everyone turned their backs on Winnie and Red as they moved to the front of the ship, climbing the few steps and crowding onto the raised deck known as the forecastle.

The ship's name was *Stargazer*! And that's what Winnie felt like! An ambitious scholar and dreamer who gazed skyward and let the stars chart her destiny. A perfect name for a perfect journey on a glorious new ship! Winnie so wanted to grab the bottle of champagne from her father's left hand and behead it with the small saber he carried in his right.

Instead, Winnie took a deep breath and lowered the brim on her bonnet as much as possible, until her eyes were completely hidden and she was only able to look down at her brown leather boots. Then Red hooked his elbow with hers and led Winifred Starbuck onto the poop deck and then down the rear companionway stairs into the cool, dark hold of the ship, the entire time thinking what an absolute fool he was to knowingly and willingly place the captain's daughter into the ship's locked cargo hold.

CHAPTER 5

The boat was moving! After getting settled in her temporary—and quite dim—home amid the dry goods storage in the ship's hold, where giant bags of rice and flour and dried beans would serve as mattress and couch and settee, Winnie had heard the metallic churning of the anchors being raised, and now she felt the ship begin to sail.

The *Stargazer* moved slowly at first. Winnie imagined the crew setting one sail after another as the boat drifted past Coatue and then picked up speed as the wind blew over the newly constructed Sankaty Head Light. And now, perhaps, they were passing the Great Point Lighthouse on their starboard side. Winnie could hear Sully calling for the men to set not only the top, t'gallant, and royal sails on the mizzen, main and foremasts, but the studding sails, too, which extended out from the ends of the yards like wings propelling the clipper forward at top speed as they reached the edge of 'Sconset and the open Atlantic Ocean.

Oh, how she longed to see it! Winnie shut her eyes tight and wished herself there, above deck. Climbing the crow's nest, taking it all in from a bird's-eye view.

Seven days. That was all she had to endure.

Before leaving her alone, Red had lit the wick of an oil lamp encased in a glass lantern. He then attached the lamp to a gimbal along the rafter beam above Winnie's head, where it swayed gently back and forth, back and forth. He provided matchsticks, and told her only to use the lamp during daylight hours. Except for a few feet of space near the front of the hold where Winnie would wait out the week, the giant room was crammed with cargo bound for San Francisco, boxes piled high almost to the rafters. Red pointed to the ceiling, where a grated hatch, used for loading and unloading cargo when docked, let in air and light from the deck above. From that hatched square, Winnie could see men's boots walking above them across the deck. "At night, someone on deck could spy the oil light below and worry the ship was on fire. Then you'd be discovered immediately. And doused mightily with water."

Winnie nodded her understanding. "Lantern only during the day."

"Chin's in charge? Feeding you and cleaning the chamberpot?"

"Yes," Winnie had said.

Red had given a stiff nod. This meant that, when Winnie was discovered, Chin would be the most severely punished. Sully would flog him with the cat-o-nines and make the whole crew—all sixty men—watch. And then, with the whip still bloody, Sully would beat Red next.

"Well, then, I guess this is goodbye for now. Mayhaps you can read a good book?" Red had asked, a pained look on his face. "Or write to someone to pass the time?"

"Mayhaps," Winnie had said, acting much more nonchalant than she felt, seated on the straw-covered floor in this overcrowded room with her back up against her sea chest. Winnie did not want to worry the steward any more than he already was, but the hold was darker and creepier than she had anticipated. She also had this strange sense of having been in a ship's belly before, which of course made no sense whatsoever. But there was something familiar in the cold, woodsy, dry-hay smell now surrounding her. Something familiar in the rolling of the boat, and something familiar even in the presence of this steward, Red.

Perhaps she was hallucinating, like a sailor sick with scurvy. But Winnie talked herself into being fine, because she was stubborn and headstrong and determined to succeed.

"I apologize for locking you in like this, but the captain and Sully'll be suspicious if they find the room open. Sometimes the crew likes to take more than what they're rationed, and with a long trip like this, we've got to make the food last, at least until we can restock in California. Only a few of us have keys."

"I understand. And I appreciate your help," she had said, stretching out her legs in front of her and pretending she was relaxed, like there was nowhere else in the world she'd rather be, though her body was tense and her heart was beating fast, as if someone was chasing her. "Bye, Red," she added.

Bye, Fred, she thought she heard him say as he shut the wooden door behind him, a chorus of jangling metal keys subsiding when he found the right one for the lock.

But it must have been only an echo.

ABOVE DECK, PETER Starbuck was basking in the glory of his new ship. The wind ruffled the sails as they unfurled one after another, each one catching air and snapping and billowing. Crew members on the deck tightened the lines as the sails filled.

Those glorious, magnificent sails.

The wind picked up nicely off 'Sconset, and Nantucket was now a small dot off the bow of the *Stargazer*, the Great Point lighthouse visible only through a spyglass.

Peter stood on the poop deck with the helmsman, Zander, a former slave who had escaped from Charleston, South Carolina, on a whaleship a decade ago and had not left the water since, moving from boat to boat and job to job. Zander had sailed with the Starbucks on their last journey two years prior and was extremely capable at the wheel, but Peter liked to be on deck with his crew as much as possible, especially given that this was the ship's first time out in the Atlantic.

"She's a dream, Captain," Zander said, his eyes fixed on the horizon as he spoke, his hands confidently gripping the giant helm. "Already moving along at a nice clip."

"That's my *Stargazer*." Peter smiled. "Let's see if we can get her up past eight knots as we get further out today, with full canvas sailing close to the wind."

"Yessir," Zander said.

Of all the magnificent aspects of his life as a sea captain, from visiting far-flung ports around the globe to helping his wife negotiate the best prices for goods and ensuring the highest profits, this was what Peter loved most: the sound and feel of the sea. He was out on the open ocean with nothing surrounding him but sky and more sky. Small whitecaps ruffled the indigo water, and the sails snapped gloriously in the wind. The metal rigging clanged, the wooden masts creaked slightly, and gulls squawked overhead. Sully had finally stopped barking at the crew and a companionable hush had fallen over the sailors as they let the ship and nature do the talking. His men had sore muscles and high spirits on this first day out on a ship that they all hoped would make history.

Peter knew it would indeed be a historic adventure. All of Peter Starbuck's dreams were coming true. The *Stargazer* would become legendary, and, as captain, Peter Starbuck would become a legend in his own time.

ON THE MAIN deck outside the galley, Red ran into Chin, the scent of Cook's clam chowder wafting on the breeze, briny like the sea. "Just what exactly do you think you're doing with that girl?" he whispered, pulling Chin by his red neckerchief into the small pantry next to the kitchen. Red could hardly contain his anger—or fear.

"She—she—" Chin stuttered, his eyes wide with shock.

"She *what*?" Red asked, letting go of Chin, his rage giving way to frustration. Red reminded himself that Chin was only a twelve-year-old boy, living half a world away from his family. While he could be naive and impulsive, Chin wasn't deserving of physical intimidation, so instead Red folded his hands across his chest to keep himself from pummeling the dumb kid. "She bribed you? Paid you a ton of money?"

"She said she wanted an adventure!" Chin said. "To go on a ship, like me! To travel the world, like me! To see China, like—"

"You." Red nodded. "Understood." Red paced back and forth in the small space. How would they get out of this mess?

"And also, she gave me two dollars." Chin shrugged and smiled sheepishly.

"Aha," Red said, almost smiling back. "You'll hand that over to me now for safekeeping."

"But—" Chin said, his hand digging deep into his right pants pocket to make sure the money was still there. It was. These were the first bills he'd ever gotten and he was loath to let go of them so quickly. Chin wanted to add the dollars to his growing stash of coins, which he kept in a secret compartment on the bottom of an old sea chest inherited from another sailor on the trip to America from Canton. That man, who Chin had liked quite a bit, had accidentally lost his footing while climbing the rigging in a squall and had fallen overboard, drowning somewhere in the Indian Ocean. His loss had been Chin's gain.

And now, each month when he was paid, Chin put all the money away, not spending it on tobacco or new socks. Whenever he was tempted to gamble on a potentially lucrative card game with the crew, he instead imagined the look on his mother's face when he delivered the cash to her and his little sisters in Canton and rescued them from poverty. After a year apart, he'd see them in just about six months.

And then he was going to buy them a house.

"I'll put the money away," Chin said. "Promise."

"And when the captain comes around, opening everyone's belongings and looking for evidence of bribery, hoping to figure out who helped sneak his precious daughter on board the ship, what are you going to do then, Chin?"

Red had never seen Chin speechless before, but the gregarious youngster was suddenly at a loss for words.

"What?" Red asked.

"She's *the captain's daughter*?"

"Yes, Chin. You just brought Winifred Starbuck onto this ship."

"But, *Winifred Starbuck*! She's supposed to be bad luck!" Chin said, now mildly panicking.

"So I've heard," Red said.

"Bad luck is not good!"

Cook opened the door to the pantry, letting in bright sunlight that stung their eyes and startled them both. "What the hell are ya both doin' in here?" he bellowed, his Cockney accent most pronounced when he shouted.

Red pulled Cook inside and shut the door behind him. "We have a bit of a situation," he said.

"Oh Lord above, give me strength," Cook said, understanding from the looks on these two faces that he was about to learn some very bad news indeed. He dropped the two buckets of empty clam shells he was holding and raised his eyes to look through the small skylight above to the heavens.

IN THE SHIP'S hold, Winifred Starbuck reached for a bucket and vomited, retching until her throat was sore and her body stopped shaking, retching until there was absolutely nothing left. She curled her torso into a question mark on the hay-covered floor and tried to calm her galloping heart.

Because there was no turning back now.

CHAPTER 6

Although the hull of a clipper ship was built to slice through waves instead of bounce on top of them, thus ensuring a faster and smoother trip for its passengers, after about an hour or so, the rolling of the boat was starting to disturb Nell's equilibrium. She had been enjoying the sun and sea and salt air, meeting the few passengers who had booked passage with them to San Francisco, and familiarizing herself with the new ship, but now it was time to locate the ginger candies in her cabin and get control of her nausea. No one wanted to see the captain's wife—and head merchant on the ship—vomit into the wind. She'd feel shipshape after a few days, once she found her sea legs . . . and after sucking on a boatload of ginger candies that she'd herself imported from China.

Nell headed to the staterooms and captain's quarters at the rear of the ship. The shipbuilder had created cabins for the Starbucks, their officers, and their passengers tucked under the poop deck, a structure with beautiful windows along the side of its two glass-paned doors, letting in much natural light along a front portico. Once inside, a small landing led to the companionway, a set of steps leading down to the three consecutive cabins.

First, Nell passed through the forward cabin, an enclosed space where the first and second mates, carpenter, sailmaker, and ship's navigator slept. The center of the room held a wooden table where Peter could meet with his officers, and doors on either side of the room led to the officers' small staterooms, each with an individual berth. Decorative filigree wood cutouts above each door were more than just ornamental touches, for they acted as vents to let fresh air flow through the stateroom windows and into the public dining area.

Nell moved to the next room, known as the great cabin, a large, bright room where passengers would eat their meals and could gather throughout the day to read and play games when not in their stateroom or out on deck. On rainy or windy and cold days, this space would be a welcome—and social—respite from the weather and the isolation of one's stateroom.

Nell absolutely loved the great cabin. And how could she not, since she'd decorated the place herself, sight unseen? Nell's goal had been to replicate East Brick in miniature, in shades of blue and yellow gold, the design based on the dining room and living room parlor from home.

Nell slowly took it all in: the wood-paneled open room with a large skylight above and portholes on each side wall, making the space much more inviting than the dark forward cabin. Navy blue tufted settees were built in under the portholes on both sides of the room, each adorned with gold silk accent pillows. Like in the forward cabin, the great cabin had a rectangular wooden table bolted to the floor in the center of the room, although this one was larger and made of a beautiful dark mahogany. A large built-in sideboard held the Starbuck insignia china dishes and English cut-glass goblets that would be used for meals. The wooden floor was covered with an ornate Oriental rug, just like the one they had at home, and an iron brazier stove was both decorative and served as an informal fireplace to heat the room.

The four passenger staterooms were located here, one in each corner of the great cabin. Curious to see the decor, Nell peeked into one room whose door was open slightly. She was happy to see that, though the room was sparsely furnished, the thematic color scheme was replicated here in the berth's navy-and-yellow coverlet as well as on the curtains that flanked the porthole. Simple but lovely. Pleased, she headed toward the final cabin, passing two private wash closets along the way, to see her and Peter's staterooms and to fill her dress pockets with the ginger candies she came in for.

The after cabin was the most private parlor on the ship, a jewel box of a room where Peter and Nell could be alone to talk and to entertain other merchants while in port. An upright piano stood against the front wall and a built-in rolltop desk and chair for Peter was tucked against the far wall, with his logbook, collection of charts, sextant, compass, and other tools at the ready. In the center of the room, under a skylight and a pretty gimbaled oil lamp, a small table was surrounded by four armchairs upholstered in blue-and-gold damask, a perfect place for Nell to make her daily notations in the ship's log. A small blue velvet sofa under the starboard side porthole would provide comfort should Nell find the time to knit or read.

And wrapping the entire space like an elaborate gift was East Brick's dining room wallpaper. Nell had commissioned the same artists from China to re-create the view of Canton harbor in a reduced scale, and it was just as impressive a statement here on the *Stargazer* as it was at home in East Brick. The sunlight above brought the colorful harbor scene to life, a reminder that, in about six months, Nell and Peter would sail their gorgeous new *Stargazer* up the Pearl River.

Nell opened the door to a private apartment on the right and found her and Peter's cabin, the wood walls whitewashed to reflect back the light from the side porthole. Vents that could open and close let in a cool breeze. The room was large by ship standards, bright and neat and decorated as the other spaces in navy blue and gold. It provided a comfortable place to sleep, and, with a large mirror on the wall, Nell could make sure to look her best at all times.

Nell located her traveling apothecary chest, carrying remedies for most of the major ailments seen on a ship, from nausea to a cut or burn. The vials and concoctions of medicines included morphine for pain, calomel as a laxative, quinine for malaria, ipecac to induce vomiting, and camphor for coughs as well as bites, for it soothed itches. Nell scooped up a handful of soft ginger candies from a large jar, popped one into her mouth, and stuffed the rest into her dress pockets. She could hand them out like party favors at dinner to whoever might be feeling a bit under the weather. The candies were tangy and chewy and spicy sweet and instantly soothed Nell's churning gut.

Being seasick was an inescapable wretchedness that tortured the mind as well as the body. Nell had fallen sick for weeks on her first journey with Peter when they were newly married, and how she had endured it was really nobody's guess. It was not a feeling she would wish on her worst enemy.

Nell opened what she assumed was a closet, finding a private lavatory instead, with small steps leading up to a platform with a hole cut out in the middle. Long gone were the days when they had to go outside to use a much more precarious setup, where wind direction had always been top of mind. But now she had her own indoor privy in her suite! How far she and Peter had come up in the world.

Behind the door on the other side of the after cabin, Nell found a room built for a child, with a single gimbaled bed tucked under one corner and a built-in dresser along the other wall. A blue-and-yellow rug in the middle of the room provided an inviting space for a little girl—or boy—to sit and play with a toy.

There had been a bedroom just like this next to their own on the *Shooting Star*, the ship she and Peter had sailed thirteen years ago, the one and only time they had traveled with Winnie. The one and only disastrous time.

Her daughter had been so small then, with chubby fingers and chubby knees and chubby cheeks. At four, she was a peach of a person, appealing in every way. She had enchanted the entire crew by singing shanties and making up stories to tell on the deck on those rare soft-winded nights, the ocean serene like a bathtub. Winnie still pronounced her *s*'s more like *th*'s—a "lithp," she would have called it—which added to her charm.

In retrospect, of course she had been the perfect target for a mad sailor's rage. Of course, as the sailor's mind became increasingly unhinged, he had grown more and more obsessed with Winnie, eventually taking her as a hostage in the ship's hold.

In retrospect, everything made sense. At the time, none of it had.

Had Nell not been eating ginger, she most assuredly would have thrown up right there. Instead, she took a deep breath and composed herself. That day was long past. Winnie was safe. And, despite the continual fear of punishment from the United States Navy or divine retribution of some kind, whether by fate or God or another mystical force, the Starbuck family—Nell in particular—had not suffered any consequences in the aftermath of the incident. Their business continued to thrive, their fortune grew, and their professional connections in China and Europe strengthened. Lucky had earned his nickname. And Cook and Red had kept their silence as promised.

Cook and Red! Nell had been dillydallying. It was approaching the dinner hour and she needed to check on preparations for the first night's feast.

IN THE GALLEY, Cook stirred soup in a giant pot atop a cast-iron stove. He tasted a spoonful and was happy with the chowder. It had the desired creamy consistency, spiked with bits of fresh cod and clams. Carrots, corn, and potatoes floated merrily in the thick liquid. If only everything in life were as trouble-free as a good chowder.

They all ate best on the first night at sea, when food was the freshest. Every night after felt a little less special, although, over the years, Cook had become skilled enough to creatively stretch a pantry's staples until the day before they arrived in port, when he created a meal out of whatever was left. Hodgepodge, he called it.

At the small wooden table in the center of the room, Red sliced apples for a cobbler and Chin counted the cutlery to bring down to the great cabin. Supper would begin right after eight bells, which signified the end of the day's main shift for most of the sailors, who worked in four-hour shifts throughout the day and night.

Chin would also now have to find a moment to slip some dinner to Winnie without being noticed—or missed. Meals were his busiest time of day. *Four spoons, five spoons, six spoons.*

"I don't know when I'm going to visit her," Chin said, feeling overwhelmed. "And now I don't really even want to." If he hadn't gone to that pub on Nantucket's Straight Wharf last night, he would not have met that guy who needed a favor—and had then showed that five-dollar bill to Chin, the incentive that started this whole thing.

"We'll figure it out," Red said.

"Figure what out?" Nell asked, quietly entering the galley.

Chin almost jumped out of his skin. A knife he had been polishing clattered to the floor.

Something about the tone in the kitchen felt rather peculiar to Nell. The galley was usually a jovial place on the Starbuck ships, a buzzy hive of activity, with Cook and Red cracking (sometimes rather dirty) jokes as they chopped and stirred.

"Hello, missus," Cook said, clearing his throat. "Sorry, I didn't see ya there." He rested the curved ladle handle on the lip of the pot and dried his hands on his apron. "You're looking well."

"Thank you, Cook. You are as well." Although in truth, Cook looked pale, his forehead deeply creased with worry.

Red greeted her warmly, although his smile was tight, and then introduced the new cabin boy, a young fellow called Chin from Canton, who spoke English, of all things! Chin said hello but seemed shy, never quite looking Nell in the eye.

"There's no need for you to be nervous in front of me, Chin from Canton," Nell said, hoping to put the boy at ease. "I like to work in the galley whenever I have free time, so you and I are going to get to know each other well."

"Yessir." Chin nodded. "Ma'am."

"I think that knife is good and polished now," Nell laughed. Chin nodded seriously and began to aggressively attack a set of spoons with his cloth.

"Well, dinner smells absolutely heavenly. I'll leave you to it."

"Thank you, missus," Cook said, staring at a clove of garlic like he didn't know what he was supposed to do with it.

Nell hesitated at the door to the galley. "Why are you all acting so . . . strange?"

"Just . . . getting used to the new ship, is all," Red said, his ginger hair sticking up every which way as always, although his eyes seemed a bit more bulbous than usual.

"Did everything we ordered get delivered?" Nell usually took a tour of the hold and the icehouse when she boarded a ship, using a checklist to go over all the supplies and ensure they had what they needed to get to their first port of call and perhaps beyond. But she hadn't done that today, too swept up in the festivities of christening the *Stargazer*. She chided herself for neglecting her work. "Are you sure we have enough potatoes?"

"Yes!" all three said at once, their heads snapping to attention. Chin looked as if he might cry. She had overstepped, though she didn't know how. Perhaps there was a Chinese custom surrounding potatoes that she was unaware of?

"Maybe I should just investigate the dry storage myself," Nell said.

"No!" all three declared. Red even reached his hands out as if to stop her from across the room with an invisible willpower.

"I'll go double-check," Red said, removing the set of keys from his pocket and walking out. "Why don't you get ready for supper, Mrs. Starbuck?" he said, passing her on his way out. "I know the passengers are looking forward to breaking bread with you."

Nell needed to at least pretend to trust him. "Yes, excellent idea. I shall see you all at eight bells."

Instead of returning to her cabin, Nell walked the length of the *Stargazer* hoping to quell an odd sensation stirring inside her. A group of sailors were covering the standing rigging with black tar to protect those thick ropes from weathering. Sully barked at them to make sure they didn't accidentally get any of the sticky tar on the beautiful new wood decking.

Seeing her, Sully softened his voice and tipped his cap. "Good evening, Mrs. Starbuck," he said.

"Good evening," she said. "Good work, men. Cook's preparing a feast for tonight for you all to enjoy." The crew's typical food wasn't nearly as appetizing as the meals given to the officers and passengers, except on the first night out from port, on holidays, and every Sunday, when Cook prepared a sweet, doughy pudding known as duff.

The men mumbled their thanks as they continued tarring. Nell hoped there was some sailor's secret remedy for how to remove that mess off their hands before dinner.

Peter waved her over to his perch by the helm, where Nell greeted Zander. The helmsman then excused himself to use the head, giving Peter control of the wheel and allowing the Starbucks a moment alone.

Together from the raised poop deck, they admired their *Stargazer* at full sail, all twenty-four sails plus the six studding sails proudly puffed up with wind, as if showing off for the sea. The orange orb of the sun hung low, lighting up the sky with a hazy, golden hue.

"She's gorgeous," Nell said.

"The clipper, the sunset, or you, my dear?" Peter smiled.

"All of us," Nell sighed, linking an arm with her husband and nestling into his side.

She'd had her doubts about Peter purchasing this clipper with Robert Forbes as partner. There were always risks in their business—from whether the price of tea would drop to the inordinate financial and physical toll taken when sailing around the world just to procure the product—but they paled in comparison to the risks taken by owing someone money. The Starbucks had always worked independently, never before giving up any financial control to an outsider. But, without a business partner, they never could have bought such a superior vessel.

"I must concede: you were right," Nell said, her eyes locking with Peter's.

"About what? The clipper, the sunset, or you, my dear?" he joked, his dark eyes dancing with the light reflected from the sun.

"All of us, naturally," Nell laughed, "but in particular, the clipper." The only way for Starbuck & Starbuck to advance their merchant business after twenty years was to stay ahead of the rest. And to stay ahead, a merchant had to sail on the fastest ship in the world, thereby literally beating the competition in a never-ending race to import and sell and do it all again.

Peter was satisfied with both Nell's appreciation for this ship and her understanding of the cost—and potential benefits—it could bring them. Perhaps now was a good moment to admit that he had pledged East Brick as part of the deal with Forbes—but then he thought better of it. Why ruin a perfect moment on this perfect vessel with his perfect wife?

Instead, as his wife admired the sunset, Peter admired Nell. His wife was stunning and strong. Twenty years ago, when he had asked Nell Congdon for her hand in marriage, Peter Starbuck had hoped Nell would have the adventurous spirit required of a successful sea merchant couple. Oh, he had no doubt that Nell, who had grown up the daughter of Nantucket's preeminent sailmaker, appreciated the finer things in life. She wore new dresses every season and put tortoiseshell combs in her hair—in the third grade! Nell had a natural sense of style that Peter knew could easily lead to her edification as a merchant of quality goods from across the globe. And he knew he loved her, deeply and fully. But, would Nell prove to be the right choice of partner not just in marriage, but in business, as well?

Yes, and she would prove it time and time again. Her skills of negotiation were both subtle and bold, she had a discerning eye for quality, and—after a rocky start—she proved to be a seaworthy sailor to boot. Nell had fallen so ill on that first trip! The thought of her crumpled into a ball on the floor of their bedchamber, so weak that he thought she might die, stung Peter's eyes. But his wife had not succumbed to her plight—rather, she rose above it with renewed vigor.

And, perhaps most importantly, for all of these years at sea, Nell had never once cowed at being one of the only women in a man's world.

Zander returned and took the helm from Peter.

"Of course, the *Stargazer* is on her maiden voyage and hasn't yet presented to us any problems she might have, in either her construction or her sailing capabilities. Zander and the rest of the crew and I need to sail with her for a bit to really know her." He pointed up and out. "That mainmast is the tallest McKay has ever built, with the most modern rigging, none of it tested at sea."

None of it tested at sea? Nell held her tongue from asking the obvious question: *Doesn't that seem foolhardy and dangerous?*

Zander nodded, praying silently that this McKay fellow knew what he was doing when he built this ship. For, even after a decade at sea, Zander still had never learned to swim. Although, even the best swimmer would likely die if he fell overboard.

"Sailing from Boston to Nantucket gave us a good basic sense of her. There wasn't time for more days out at sea before loading her up for our trip."

Nell shrugged as if it didn't matter to her in the least. The shipbuilder could be blind, for all she cared. But in truth, she didn't want to question her husband in front of a ship's officer.

She invited Peter to stroll the deck with her and check on her chickens. The clipper's first stop was to deliver supplies to San Francisco, where, thanks to the Gold Rush bringing thousands of people to a desolate outpost on the edge of America, demand was high. Rumor had it that in California you could sell a single egg for three dollars. When Nell read that in *The Inquirer* several weeks ago, she went out to Bartlett's to personally handpick twenty robust, healthy-looking hens.

"Well, hello, my chickadees!" Nell cooed, leaning down over one of the two mesh-fronted coops on the main deck. "I hope you make us a lot of money!"

Peter laughed. "And feed us, too, along the way, although I do appreciate your business acumen."

"I know you do." She lowered her voice. "But, about the new clipper. Certainly, we could have spared a few days for you to take her out and test her, no?" Nell asked.

Peter's voice was quiet but strained. "Now that we've got business partners, you cannot even imagine the pressure I am under to get to China and back for Robert Forbes and sell all of that freight for Grinnell & Minturn."

Nell did not like Peter's use of the singular pronoun *I* when she was surely under the same amount of financial pressure as Peter. But when her husband had a lot on his mind, Nell just let him speak it. A captain could trust very few people on board a ship, and Nell valued her position as one of the individuals he could confide everything to.

Sully worked nearby, looking rather suspiciously as if he was trying to listen in on their conversation.

"Everything all right, Sully?" Peter asked.

"Aye-aye, sir," the first mate said. "Just checking the bungs on these other water casks. Make sure they're not gonna leak on us." He quickly hurried off.

Red appeared from the hold, holding a bucket of something and looking rather repulsed. Seeing the captain and Nell, he quickly did an about-face and walked toward the bow, as if having changed his mind about something.

"Have you noticed anything odd with certain members of the crew?" Nell asked.

Peter's expression grew dark. "With Sully, you mean?" Nell couldn't possibly know that he was paying the first mate a few dollars extra a month for his sworn silence, could she? "He's just exerting his dominance. Showing who's boss. We need a strong first mate, to dole out discipline when necessary. I think this will be the perfect role for him. You'll see."

Nell raised her eyebrows. Peter had never before been a champion of Sully. Why now?

And here came Red, scampering as if on a mission, the bucket now empty of whatever had been in it, and a pewter mug in his other hand. He looked around him and then disappeared back down into the hold.

Peter excused himself and kissed Nell on the cheek. "See you at dinner, my love."

"Yes, see you then," Nell said, somewhat distractedly. Dusk was descending, her thoughts a jumble. Stopping by the livestock pen, she admired the piglets, who were cute now but would be dinner later. Then she locked eyes with a cow, who chewed hay thoughtfully. *I'll call you Bess,* Nell decided.

First, there had been the strained and awkward conversation with Cook, Red, and that new cabin boy, Chin, in the galley. And Sully snooping around was nothing new, perhaps. But Peter's reaction to Sully—that was indeed new.

Bess chewed as if she had all day, as if inviting Nell to share her innermost thoughts. So she did. "Bess, listen here. These men, whom I know better than almost anyone else in the world, are definitely up to something."

CHAPTER 7

Belowdecks, Winnie wanted to die. Couldn't she just die already? "Just leave me here to die!" she said to Red when he returned to the hold with a clean bucket. No doubt she'd fill it again in a few minutes, if she even had anything left in her to vomit up.

"Miss, drink some water. Here's a cup full. Also, I think it would help if you sit up. Lying on the floor only makes the motion sickness worse, in my experience."

"No!" Winnie said to Red's boots, that being the only part of him that she could see from her place on the floor. "You can't make me."

Red laughed. She was so very much like the little girl he remembered.

"What's so funny?" Winnie asked, insulted. She tried to get a better look at him, but her head felt like lead.

Red sank to the ground and sat beside her.

"You've got fire in you, all right," he said. "Just like your mother."

"My—" Winnie asked, slowly finding her way to an upright position. Red moved a bale of hay toward her to support her back, and she leaned against it. "So you know who I am."

Red couldn't very well admit that they'd met before when Winnie was four, turning five, since that was a story about which Winnie appeared unaware. So Red stuck to other pieces of truth. "It is kind of obvious, miss. I'm no scholar, and certainly no wizard. But you look just like Mrs. Starbuck, and you are a spitting image of the figurehead under the bowsprit to boot."

"I *knew* my father had fashioned that figure after me!" Winnie exclaimed. "Which *proves* that I'm supposed to be here, don't you think?" she asked, smiling. But before Red could respond, Winnie's face went slack, and her green eyes turned wide and watery.

Red passed her the bucket and waited.

ALTHOUGH NO ONE was expected to dress for dinner while the ship was actively sailing, as the captain's wife and chief merchant on this voyage, Nell liked to keep up appearances. Just because her cabin felt like it was moving under her feet didn't mean she couldn't change out of one elaborate ensemble and into another.

Nell preferred life at sea for several reasons, most of which had to do with freedoms. She was free to travel the world, free to barter and haggle like a man, free to sleep under the stars aboard deck on a tropical eve, and free to dress without cumbersome petticoats.

It was not an easy task to button up the back of one's own dress on terra firma, much less on the *Stargazer*, but with determination, a hand mirror, the mirror affixed over the bureau, and her mother's heirloom buttonhook, she managed to get the job done in only twenty minutes. The added concentration needed to tackle such a task had the extra benefit of wiping the worry from her mind about the crew's various and strange behaviors.

"What a sight!" Peter said as he entered their cabin, his hair windblown and his dark eyes glowing in the lamplight.

Nell was still a bit cross at her husband after his slight of her when discussing "his" stress and "his" important relationship with Robert Forbes, but a compliment could help her move past her agitation. Nell had the dress made specially for this voyage, and she was certain that Peter would comment on how the color matched the green in her eyes. And then maybe even pull her into a warm embrace.

"This gorgeous ship! Nell, she's cutting through the water at speeds I never thought possible. We've already got her up to ten knots at full canvas sailing close to the wind. Leo, our new navigator, is beside himself. Zander, too. We all are."

Nell hid her embarrassment at being slighted by a boat. Although, of course Peter would care more about "her" in this moment, the first day out on the *Stargazer,* than "her," his shining star of a wife. "That's wonderful, Peter. I'm so happy for you. For *us,*" she added.

"If all goes as planned, we'll have no trouble breaking the world record to San Francisco. We'll take that port by storm and then on to China, where we'll make our final fortune. Forbes will be pleased. Then we'll retire as wealthy and well-respected as any Nantucketer who ever sailed the seas."

"You're putting an enormous amount of pressure on this trip. And on us." Each previous trip had come with its own set of demands, but none—except for that one on the *Shooting Star*—had felt as fraught and with stakes as high as this. Why was it so very critical to be the *fastest*? The *best*? Hadn't they always succeeded?

Nell admired Peter's competitive spirit, for she saw it in herself, too: a fierce determination to win. But, since stepping on this vessel, Peter's drive seemed to go beyond what was necessary, filling Nell with trepidation. "Should something go wrong on this trip, Peter, I'm not certain I could withstand it."

Her husband looked at her with unwavering confidence, his dark brown eyes steady. "If anyone can withstand the pressure, it's you, my dear Nell."

RED HEARD EIGHT bells and knew he had to get above deck to help Cook and Chin serve dinner.

"Sorry, miss," he said, feeling bad for having to leave Winnie alone again in this dim cave. His concern was not eased by the knowledge that this—stowing away in the hold—was exactly what she had signed up for. Eighteen-year-olds really had no idea what they wanted. "I'll send Chin down later with some food."

"Food?" Winnie said, the word alone upsetting her stomach. "You dislike me that much?"

Red laughed. "I understand. How about . . .?" he said, getting up and moving around the room, checking in one large food crate and then another. "Ah," he said, locating what he wanted.

"Hardtack?" Winnie scoffed at the cracker. "You can't be serious."

"It's the least tasty item in the room—and the best for filling a sailor's belly with sustenance." By calling Miss Starbuck a sailor, he hoped to entice her into feeling—and acting—more like one.

"Fine," she said, taking a small bite. "Ouch."

"They call it hardtack for a reason," he said. "You might want to dip it into the mug first. And trust me: it's much better now than it will be once the worms get at it." He stood. "And with that, I shall bid you adieu."

Winnie grimaced and dipped the corner of the biscuit into her mug of water. "Thank you. Bye, Red," she mumbled.

And this time, over the jangling of keys, she distinctly heard the steward call back to her, using her father's pet name.

"Bye, Fred."

DINNER WAS FESTIVE, the passengers and ship's officers making introductions all around, while Red poured brandy and wine into cut-glass goblets and handed them out, trying to keep his hands from shaking as he did.

As a general rule, Captain Starbuck didn't allow the crew to drink while at sea, but a little bit of liquor for the officers was a nice way to celebrate the first night out, and it also helped the passengers appreciate the Starbuck hospitality. At least, that's what the captain had told Red, so he helped himself to a sip from the brandy bottle while no one was looking.

The room's skylight kept it bright during the day. Now, at night, the lanterns reflected a blue-and-gold glow as a pleasantly cool breeze came through the open vents.

Cook had prepared fresh beef tonight along with the chowder. The room filled with a warm and inviting scent and Peter welcomed everyone to the dining table as they arrived from their individual cabins.

"Good evening, Mrs. Starbuck," a well-dressed man said, taking the seat to Nell's right.

"Mr. Mortimer!" Nell said, greeting the journalist who had joined the voyage. "And how has your first day been aboard the *Stargazer*?" Charles Mortimer was going to write a series of articles for a newspaper called *The Boston Pilot*. Nell had never heard of the paper, but Peter thought it important to have someone document the trip and publicize it for all the world—or at least most of New England—to read about.

"Wonderful, just wonderful," he said, placing his cloth napkin into his lap. "I'll have my first article ready in a day or so, and would love to send it back to Boston on a passing ship, if we should see one."

Amid the celebrations as they set sail, Nell had seen the journalist scribbling in his notebook, interviewing the few crew members who were comfortable enough to talk to him and not suspicious that he had other motives, like perhaps trying to find out whether this or that sailor had skipped out on his wife and child or had left a substantial bill outstanding at the local pub. Without his notebook at the dinner table, Mr. Mortimer listened intently with his eyes, as if trying to remember every word of every conversation to record later.

"Maybe you can write about *me*, Mr. Mortimer," a young woman said from across the table. "My name is Lily Bird and I'm an *actress* from London."

Lily was dressed elegantly in a brown silk gown. Her long hair was held back with a large matching silk bow, the style allowing a few tendrils of black hair to frame her face. Her large brown eyes held kindness and were matched by a wide and open smile.

"Are you famous, Miss Bird?" Peter asked. Chin served bowls of chowder while Red placed two loaves of warm bread in the center of the table and everyone began to eat.

She laughed indulgently. "Not *yet*," she said, her British voice rich with allure, winking. With her shiny black hair and dark eyes and skin the color of porcelain, Miss Lily Bird had the entire table of ten entranced. "But I *will* be when I *get* to San Francisco! That's why I've been *practicing* lines from a *variety* of plays," she said, waving a small bound script that sat in her lap during the meal. Lily's voice was not only accented but pleasantly raspy. She'd certainly make for an alluring stage performer.

"Are you already cast in a performance there?" Nell asked.

"No, but I read a newspaper article about a man named Tom

Macguire from New York who just opened an eight-hundred–seat theater called the Jenny Lind and is looking for talent. The settlers *crave* entertainment. I'm already twenty-two and the theater is *made* for the young, so this could be my last chance."

It seemed unlikely that a single woman of high station and good breeding would be allowed by her parents to go off alone, especially given that her chosen profession was so closely aligned with impropriety, at least in the circles that the Starbucks traveled in. Acting was akin to prostitution, almost. At least that's what Nell had always told Winnie when she begged to see theatricals in Boston.

"Well, I shall certainly make mention of you in my column, Miss Bird," Charles Mortimer said, pointing his fork at her. "How does 'San Francisco's newest star will arrive fresh off the *Stargazer*' sound to you?"

"That sounds fabulous!" Lily clapped.

"Just make sure to say, 'fresh off *the world's fastest clipper ship*, the *Stargazer*,'" Peter added, and the entire table broke out into applause.

"More brandy for her captain, I say!" Sully said, summoning Red with a snap of his fingers and then motioning for his own glass to be topped off as well. Nell smiled tightly. Peter never usually drank so much on their first night out. In fact, he never drank much liquor at all. The Starbucks were loyal to tea. She took a very small sip of her red wine and turned her attention to the other guests.

Seated across from Nell was Jessie Lindquist, who introduced herself and the maid she had brought along. That woman apparently had no name, as in "This is my maid." Nell would find a moment to pull the woman aside and inquire tomorrow. Everyone on board a ship was known to her, and this woman, even if her station was below that of a regular passenger, was no exception.

Jessie Lindquist's husband had arrived in San Francisco the year prior, promptly made a fortune, and was now sending for Jessie. She was a rather large and imposing woman, with a strong voice to match. In response to this fate of hers, all she did was shrug, as if that summarized everything. "My husband, Bernard, survived as an overlander despite the most *wretched* conditions, and then this. Gold!

I didn't marry him for the money, since I already had plenty of my own from my father, but one simply can't overlook an unexpected windfall." Another shrug, as if the origins of her many riches were a mystery even to her. Nell found it rather audacious of the woman to mention her wealth in such an obvious way, in front of mixed company no less. It was uncouth to talk of such things in the open. That's why people wrote letters.

"In summary," Jessie Lindquist stated, "my Mr. Lindquist has built me a large home on Rincon Hill, where the weather is warmer and sunnier than the rest of the foggy city, overlooking Yerba Buena Cove and Mission Bay. But he's having trouble finding any servants, even for good pay. No one wants to work for a business in San Francisco proper; they all want to head out thirty miles for the hills!" Jessie turned to her maid and shook a finger in her face. "You better not do that to me, Beatrice!"

Beatrice! Mystery solved.

The diners, with the exclusion of Beatrice, laughed good-naturedly as they complimented the meal, the hospitality, the ship, the Starbucks. Peter sat at the head of the table, with Sully at his right elbow and Doc, the carpenter, to his left, mouth grinning and belly full, enjoying this rare moment instead of trying to predict—and outrun—the future.

The novelty of life aboard a ship was as fresh as the last coat of black paint along the *Stargazer*'s hull. Neither passenger nor crew member had yet grown tired of the food, the ocean, or one another. The beginning of a voyage was like a blossoming romance, that precious and fleeting time before you learned that your beloved had flaws.

As a merchant on business trips, Nell had never before traveled with ordinary passengers. These were a lively bunch, and she could sense already that she'd enjoy this journey more than she did most. Of course, her companions would be disembarking in California, but even so, the presence of others besides the crew and her husband for the better part of three months would do much to help pass the time.

Winnie would have enjoyed this evening, Nell thought. Winnie would have enjoyed this whole adventure. Filled suddenly with a sense of regret, Nell scanned the table and felt acutely the absence of her daughter.

Had it not been for a rogue madman many years ago, the trajectory of their lives would have been so much different. Winnie would have been seated at her rightful place beside Nell at this dinner table tonight. And, with Nell's guidance, Winnie would have become a remarkable sea merchant.

But, as sailors knew better than anyone, looking back at the ship's wake didn't help you move forward.

CHAPTER 8

Making several trips up and down and up the companionway stairs to the galley, Chin cleared the table in the great cabin in record-breaking time. Captain Starbuck liked tasks done quickly and well, saying that not only should his clipper ship be the fastest in the world, but that his crew should be swift and nimble, too. From the captain, Chin's work ethic and English vocabulary were both growing exponentially. Like him quickly learning the words *swift*, *nimble*, and *exponentially*.

Chin's shirt was soaked through with sweat and his hair was plastered to the sides of his face, but there was no stopping him now. While the dinner guests were chatting away amicably in the great cabin, seated in the settees or standing near the lit brazier and enjoying their after-dinner drinks, Chin sneaked off to the hold.

He found Winnie in a slightly better state than he had anticipated based on Red's warning about her seasickness. She was sitting up, for one. Secondly, she smiled at him, although her complexion was not the rosy one that had met him that morning at the harbor.

He presented her with two of Cook's biscuits slathered in butter, which she ate greedily.

Chin sank down beside her. "Why didn't you tell me who you were?" he asked.

She wiped her mouth clean with the back of her hand. "Why didn't you ask?"

Chin shook his head and smiled. He felt like he had just been beaten at checkers by a formidable opponent. At home, Chin had four shrewd and sharp-witted sisters of his own, but none of them were quite a match for Miss Starbuck. He found it hard to believe that a girl so confident and amusing could bring bad luck to the ship.

"Here," he said, his palm outstretched toward her, sticky with sugar. "From your mother. I snuck some for you."

Winnie brightened considerably and placed one into her mouth, her whole face softening in delight. "Mother does have the best remedies." But thinking of this only made tears spring to Winnie's eyes, seasickness replaced with homesickness. How she missed her mother!

"What's wrong?" Chin asked. "Does the candy burn your tongue? Sometimes ginger can be too spicy for me." He scrunched up his face and Winnie laughed. He lived a big life here on this ship, but really, he was just a little boy.

"I miss my mother," she admitted, rolling her eyes. "I know that sounds stupid."

Chin shook his head. "That's not stupid at all. I ran away, too, and yet I miss my mother all the time." He was quiet for a moment and then added, "What's stupid is that you ran away *with* your parents!"

Her green eyes went wide and he thought she might slap him for his rudeness. Instead, Winnie laughed. "Oh no! You're right! Who *does* that?"

Chin laughed, too. And then both of them chortled until tears rolled down their cheeks.

ON DECK, NELL smelled the ocean air and heard the lapping of the waves against the hull. She loved being on deck at night, even on a chilly one such as this. It was quiet and serene. With only a skeleton crew working the evening shift, and nothing to light the way but the moon's shimmer on the water, the atmosphere felt mystical. The white sails glowed like paper lanterns.

"Good evening, missus," Zander said, manning the helm alone. Peter usually liked to spend the first night of a new journey on deck with his helmsman, but he had consumed so much brandy at the celebratory dinner that he was no use tonight to any fellow sailor. With Sully's help, Peter had wobbled off to bed. "Beautiful night."

Nell agreed that it was, and inquired about whether the helmsman had been granted enough time for dinner before getting back to work. He nodded and said that he had been off for the last shift and had eaten very well. "Captain Starbuck treats us decently," he said. "An honorable and honest captain. And a role model to us sailors."

"He most certainly is all of those things," Nell said. She was glad Zander had not seen his beloved captain in his current state of inebriation.

"If I may speak candidly, ma'am?" Zander asked.

"Go right ahead," Nell said, her interest piqued. Zander was a man of few words. Perhaps that was why, when he chose to speak, Nell—and others—always listened.

He looked sheepish, like a little boy admitting a secret to a schoolteacher. "I hope to be just like him."

"Like Captain Starbuck?"

"Yes, ma'am." He nodded at the sky and the water and the wind. "I want to captain my own ship someday."

"An admirable goal. And I think an attainable one, too," Nell said, believing it as soon as she said it. "Just don't let Sully catch wind of your aspirations." As first mate, Sully was next in line to step into the role of captain should something ever happen to Peter. Sully wouldn't like knowing that someone else—a man capable and experienced and well respected like Zander—was interested in the job.

Zander smiled, a slow and shy grin. "Understood, ma'am."

As a boy growing up enslaved on a plantation, Zander had learned from his father how to chart the stars and read the sky. And, in the ten years since escaping from the South, others had taught Zander how to read and write. In the several years since joining the Starbucks, Zander had learned about leadership by observing others, often playing out scenes in his head of how *he* would have handled a particular situation with a belligerent crew member or a nervous novice. And, in every case, he would not have handled it at all like Sully.

"Well, as much as I hate for this wonderful first day to end, I must be off," Nell said.

"Good night, ma'am," Zander said. "Thanks for listening."

"Fair winds and following seas, Zander," Nell said.

Back in her cabin, Nell spent a good ten minutes unbuttoning the back of her dress. She wriggled out of it and hung it on a peg on the wall. Although she had a silk nightgown with her, she was happy to sleep tonight in just her cotton chemise. Without even bothering to comb out her hair, she snuggled under the warm sheets in her new bed with her loudly snoring husband, the brave and noble Captain Starbuck.

CHAPTER 9

Peter woke early, the light of dawn streaming in through the skylight above. He winced. His eyes were dry, his head throbbed dully, and his mouth was coated in cotton. *Some captain I am*, he thought.

"Here," Nell said, already dressed for the day. Looking rather irritated, she handed him a pewter mug of something steaming hot and foul smelling. "Cabbage soup should cure what ails you," she said.

He propped a pillow behind him, queasy. "Am I supposed to drink it down or use it to induce vomiting?" He was aiming for humor to reduce the tension between them, but his wife did not smile.

Nell shrugged. "Whichever you prefer," she said.

He took a small sip of the bitter stuff, trying not to smell it as he drank. "Sully and I got a little too high-spirited last night."

Nell raised her eyebrows but said nothing. Peter didn't gamble, he held his liquor, and he told her absolutely everything. They were partners in the bedroom and in the business world. But ever since stepping onto this ship, she had felt a growing distance between them.

"It was just a way to celebrate the *Stargazer*'s send-off," he added.

She sat on the edge of the bed and put her hand on Peter's arm. "In the future, I just think—" she began.

"I don't require a lecture from my wife," Peter said, jerking his arm away from her and accidentally spilling hot liquid onto their new coverlet.

"And I don't deserve hostility from my husband," Nell said. "Especially when he's acting like a child." She turned on her heels and left.

"Nell," Peter called. But once his headstrong wife had made up her mind about something, even something as simple as exiting a room, she didn't waver. "I'm sorry," he said to his mug of pond water scum. "And I promise it won't happen again."

The concoction did make Peter feel better, although the row with Nell made him feel worse. To add insult to injury, he saw that his lovely and caring wife had filled his shaving bowl with warm water, assuming Peter might want to look like the ship's captain, even if he didn't feel like one. He relieved himself in the private head behind their cabin and then returned to clean himself up and get ready for the day.

He felt bad for having snapped at Nell and would apologize at lunch. She just didn't understand that, sometimes, a man in business was forced to make decisions alone, without the many strong opinions of a woman like Nell. Sometimes, in order to get ahead, a man had to gamble, perhaps all the way to China.

Peter had told no one about what awaited them there, not Sully, and not even Nell. He absolutely *had* to offset the costs of the ship and ensure that East Brick would not be sold off, and there was only one way to do that: by trading in a particularly lucrative, and currently illegal, product. Which was why, at dinner last night, thinking about the extent of his plan to turn a profit in Canton with opium, a product he and Nell swore they would never trade in, Peter had drowned his worries in brandy.

But, instead of making things better, imbibing like that had done him only harm. And of course Sully had egged Peter on, happy to see his captain loosen up and thus grow uninhibited. The more Peter drank, the more Sully had peppered him with questions. Questions about the course the ship was taking, questions about their plans once in San Francisco, and most notably, questions about what they'd be doing once in China.

Luckily, Peter hadn't told Sully anything of note. Mostly, the two had slurred congratulations and good tidings. Sully had shared a story of a certain kind of woman he had met at a pub on the Straight Wharf and then described in lurid detail exactly what he had done to her behind the pub. Doc and the second mate, a young pimple-faced man named Jonathan, had cackled and mimed some lewd movements while Peter had smiled tightly and pretended to be amused. It was not a night he was proud of, but perhaps it had served him well to seem convivial with these officers. The fact that the journalist, Mr. Mortimer, was also listening in on their conversation only dawned on him now, and he groaned.

Ah, well. He invoked the Latin phrase he used as a personal motto: *semper porro*, ever forward. There was no good in looking back now, for what was done—last night, and in the deal he had made months ago with Jardine Matheson, the famed Scottish foreign trade company based in China—was now done.

Peter buttoned his white dress shirt and donned his captain's jacket, grabbing a chart as he went, and headed on deck to meet with Leo, the navigator. He wanted to take the morning's navigational readings based on the sun's position and to discuss the plans for the fastest course through the Atlantic and down toward the equator.

It was just past seven in the morning, and several of the crew were swabbing the deck, the first chore every day, mopping and scrubbing the hardwood until it gleamed. It was not unlike beginning the day with a morning shave, he thought, smiling at the comparison and feeling much better now, amid the wind and the sun and the sky and his crew.

The oldest sailor on board the *Stargazer* hobbled toward him, thin gray hair flying about his head in the breeze, tiny gray dog tucked under his arm. "Good morning, sir," he said.

"Good morning, Lucky," Peter said. "And how is Yip enjoying life aboard the *Stargazer*?" he asked, scratching the tiny dog behind one of his pointy ears.

"He likes it just fine, sir, just fine," Lucky said, and the captain moved on.

In actuality, Yip had been acting strangely since yesterday, shaking more than usual, his beady little eyes darting to and fro as if aware of something amiss. He was always a nervous dog, but this behavior showed more distress than usual. Perhaps he was just getting old, like Lucky, whose hands also shook more than usual these days. The Starbucks planned on retiring after this trip, which was good, because although Lucky loved the sea and was loyal to the Starbucks, he feared that his body couldn't take much more. He'd retire with Yip to the Sailors' Snug Harbor in Staten Island, New York. He heard it was a nice place for a sailor to live out his days, God willing. He'd been Lucky before, earning his nickname on the *Shooting Star*, and he'd sure as heck like to remain so on the *Stargazer*.

On the poop deck, Peter greeted the navigator. With his bushy blond eyebrows and thick hair, he looked a bit like a lion, and Peter wondered if Leo was his real name or a nickname given because it suited him so well. The navigator was new to the Starbuck crew, but was interested in two things: one, testing out some new theories in nautical science recently written by the US naval officer Matthew Fontaine Maury; and two, seeing California.

"Captain," Leo said, looking up from his calculations. "It seems that we have traveled two hundred and forty miles from Nantucket in just under twenty hours."

"Well, that's fantastic news," Peter said.

"Yes, so far, she's averaging twelve knots an hour. We'll just have to keep her on course based on Maury's recent recommendations. The plan he devised is to head out much farther east than usual before turning south for Brazil."

Peter unrolled the chart he was carrying and the two plotted the first point, a black dot on the blue of the Atlantic. It felt like progress. Peter had used Maury's *Wind and Currents Charts* to his great advantage since it came out in '47. But Leo had something even better: a copy of Maury's newly published *Explanations and Sailing Directions to Accompany the Wind and Current Charts*, a companion guide to the original that Peter hoped would propel the *Stargazer* to greatness.

Leo rolled up the chart and handed it to Peter, putting the sextant away in its brass case. "I believe you're our secret weapon." Peter grinned.

"The sea keeps all of the secrets, sir," Leo said. "I'll do my best to uncover them, one storm at a time."

CHAPTER 10

June 7

Boredom. That was what Winnie was fighting now that she had vanquished seasickness and homesickness. The other two had proved formidable opponents, true, but it was this third battle on the third, fourth, fifth, and now sixth day that seemed like it might truly lead to her undoing. How many times could one pace back and forth before feeling like a tiger in a cage? Before going mad?

Nights were the worst. The silence of the crew above amplified the squeaks of rats and mice scampering in dark corners, their nocturnal activity making sleep almost impossible. And then, when Winnie did eventually fall into slumber, her mind imagined other sinister creatures: giant dogs with sharp teeth and maniacal men with guns and knives. And her mother, for some reason. Always, the dream ended with her mother in a beautiful and bloodied dress, a look of horror on her face.

Winnie screamed in her sleep with her mouth closed, the sound muted and strangled in a way that was almost worse than an actual cry of terror. It woke her every night.

She couldn't survive down here much longer. She had to get out of the hold.

But then, with the weak morning light filtering in from above, she reminded herself of how far she had come and pulled herself back from the brink of the abyss. Day six! Hooray! She had journeyed successfully through the first five lonely, desolate, harder-than-hard days of the trip, and now she had almost arrived at her final destination, her long-awaited port of call: above deck on the *Stargazer*!

At least with the light from the above grated skylight and the occasional use of a lantern, Winnie had been able to entertain herself daily with Shakespeare and Chaucer. In addition to inhaling the entire tragedy of *The Tempest*, she had read many sonnets and had even committed Sonnet 29—*"When, in disgrace with fortune and men's eyes"*—to memory, along with the entire prologue to *The Canterbury Tales.* She recited the first aloud with a faux British accent and the second with what she imagined to be Middle English pronunciation, waiting for Chin to arrive with her breakfast.

Day six!

The metallic clang of Chin working the lock made Winnie nearly rapturous. Yay! Breakfast on day six!

Chin closed the door behind him and rushed toward Winnie with a bowl of porridge swirled with cinnamon and studded with raisins. "Sorry, miss, I'm too busy to talk today," he said, handing over a mug of tea as well. He also removed a wooden bucket hanging from its handle in the crook of his arm and placed it on the floor. "Your mother is helping us in the kitchen!"

"Is she being quite annoying?"

Chin looked at her with confusion. Once Winnie explained the meaning of *annoying*, Chin heartily agreed. "Very much so, miss."

"Wait!" Winnie called. "Just one game of marbles?" On the third day, once everyone on board had found their rhythms and routines, Chin had been able to come down and keep Winnie company for over an hour. It was then they had discovered their shared love for marbles, Chin's eyes growing wide in delight when Winnie removed a satin sack of them from her trunk and drew a chalk circle on the floor between them.

"I can't! Your annoying mother!" Chin said.

"I'll let you win," Winnie pleaded.

"I win when I win—because I win! Simple as that. And your mother keeps *talking* to me! Asking me this and that! So *nosy*!" He smiled.

"Another new word?" Winnie asked.

"Yes! And I know I used it right." Then he disappeared, locking the door behind him.

Winnie sighed. She couldn't wait to hug her nosy, exasperating mother.

She ate her breakfast slowly, for the longer each activity took, the fewer tasks she'd have to find to fill the hours. Also, Chin was often very slow to deliver her lunch, which was everyone's biggest meal of the day. According to Chin, the passengers gathered for hours in the great cabin during the midday, playing whist and reading and telling stories, filling the time as best they could, and asking Chin for more tea and cookies every other minute. Winnie supposed she wasn't the only one who felt the time pass slowly on a ship.

How she wished she could chat with the other passengers *now*. She had grown tired of her own company, and she had written at least two letters to everyone she could think of, including her aunt and uncle, both Macy girls, librarian Maria Mitchell, and her friends from the Cambridge School. Oh—she could write to her friend Samuel Allen! Winnie hadn't seen him in ages, but they had played together on Nantucket as children and then became pen pals when Winnie left for boarding school.

About two years ago, Samuel had written to Winnie, boasting proudly that he had just signed on as a mate on the whaleship *Chase* with his older brother Joseph. Joseph had trained as an Atheneum Boy, learning astronomy and navigation at the library so he could go out to sea. Samuel had no formal training for life aboard a whaleship, but he said his brother knew enough for both of them. They were a year apart in age but looked almost like twins, with their upturned Allen nose, soft brown eyes and sandy cowlicks. According to the hastily penned note, Joseph, gregarious and a natural-born leader, had persuaded his shy and more reserved younger brother to come along for the adventure of a lifetime. Winnie, jealous of Samuel getting to go on an oceanic adventure while she was stuck back in Cambridge, landlocked and learning the latest in horticultural science, hadn't written back.

And then, Samuel wrote once more, months later from sea, saying that the *Chase* had successfully rounded Cape Horn and was hunting whales along its journey in the Pacific: "The work is hard and the days are long, but there's nowhere I'd rather be than on this ship with my brother."

Out of a silly sense of spite, Winnie still hadn't written to him. But just look at her now: a stowaway on her parents' clipper ship! *Now* she had something fun and daring and important to say. She would write to Samuel at once.

Winnie cleared the breakfast dishes from the sea chest, wiping Captain Henry Macy's initials clean on the top. She'd already used the entire folio of pages she had stashed at the top of the trunk, so she dug inside for more stationery. Not feeling any papers among her clothing, she removed everything from the trunk and set the items aside. Out came her jackets, blouses, skirts, dresses, books, and letters to mail. Out came her hairbrush and tortoiseshell clips and the rags she would use when her monthlies came. Her boots were already on her feet and she hadn't thought to bring dress shoes, as the life of a sailor was hardly a glamorous one. The chest was now empty, only the green silk lining staring back at her. No writing paper. Except.

What was that? Winnie noticed a small bulge in the side of the trunk's lining. Her fingers traced a seam, which opened to reveal a secret pocket along the right-hand side. She reached in and extracted a stack of old letters bound together in red ribbon, yellowed a bit at the edges with age, and addressed from Eliza Macy to Captain Henry Macy, captain of the *Ithaca.*

Well! Winnie carefully extracted the first letter from its envelope and unfolded the paper, leaning her back against the trunk and stretching her legs out in front of her. Her day had suddenly gotten much more interesting indeed.

AZURE SKIES WERE dotted with soft clouds today, like the pictures that Fred used to paint as a child. Peter stood on deck with Leo and Doc the carpenter, the trio poring over Maury's book and discussing the next part of the journey. In her first five days at sea, the

Stargazer had traveled over eight hundred miles east-southeast. They were now close to Bermuda.

"And, in just the last two days, we've gone faster than the newest transatlantic steamships," Leo added.

"Did you hear that, Zander?" Peter called out cheerfully.

The helmsman whistled enthusiastically from his place at the wheel. "That's quite a feat, sir. Happy to be a part of it," he said.

But the wind was picking up now in a way that did not make Zander happy, not one bit. Blustery and intense, the gale was arriving from seemingly every direction, which was odd, because the blue sky foretold of no storms on the horizon. The air lacked that wet scent of rain. And yet, something felt like it was brewing. Zander alerted his captain.

"Yes, we feel it, too," Peter said, nodding for the trio of them and rolling up his chart, which now had five coordinates dotting their progress. They'd add the next, for day six, after Leo took his noontime reading and completed those complicated calculations. Peter looked to the sky and shrugged. Red walked the main deck precariously, his arms carrying trays of food toward the companionway, weaving and bobbing like a drunken sailor as he tried to balance the crew's lunch in the wind and deliver it safely belowdecks.

Peter was looking forward to a hearty meal. He decided to follow the steward down the companionway, steadying the other man with his right hand, and waiting out the strong gusts below in the great cabin.

THE BOAT WAS rolling a bit more than usual, but Winnie wasn't concerned about seasickness getting the best of her now that those first bad days had passed. In fact, for the past hour, she had hardly even noticed her surroundings at all, lost as she was in the pages of the letters opened on the floor in front of her. She had only put them down once, when she had stuffed all of her belongings back in the trunk.

It was probably wrong of Winnie to read these personal letters from Eliza Macy to her husband. Chin would certainly call her *nosy* for doing so, but who would ever know? There were fifteen letters in all, kept in chronological order from 1843–1846, while Captain Macy was out at sea on his final voyage.

The letters began with mundane news about the Macy girls, but grew increasingly desperate sounding as the years went on. In two letters from 1846, Eliza complained about the leaky roof and family illness and the girls' need for new dresses and not having enough money to pay for it all until Henry came home from sea. *When will you return, Henry?* Winnie could hear the petulance in Eliza's tone. She sounded like a child begging her father for attention. She sounded lonely.

Winnie could understand loneliness.

Reading Eliza Macy's loopy, loose script was like finding an old friend—or a new one, maybe. Winnie felt like she had just spent several years inside their long-distance marriage, a marriage very different from the one her own parents enjoyed by choosing to spend their lives together at sea.

Winnie reached for the final letter in the stack, which, based on timing, must have been written right around Nantucket's Great Fire of 1846. *Maybe it holds details about the fire itself!* Winnie thought, her spine tingling with excitement.

But the envelope was empty.

Henry must have read it and—what? Left it somewhere? Destroyed it?

"Look out!" a sailor cried from above. Other shouts followed. The ship jerked quickly to the starboard side, then heeled sideways, listing as if in trouble. Winnie dropped the envelope and grabbed ahold of Henry Macy's sea chest, trying not to get pulled by force toward the right wall like many of the objects in the hold.

Winnie strained to see anything clearly through the skylight—a skylight that was now located behind her as opposed to above her. Men's boots ran past and more shouts followed. What would make the ship heel like this?

"Lower those yards and pull up 'er sails! Careful, men! Care-ful!" She recognized the voice of Sully, the first mate, shouting out orders, and felt slightly better knowing the crew was trying to fix whatever had happened above.

Unless what had happened *above* had been caused by something occurring *below*. Had the *Stargazer* hit something and sprung a leak? That could explain the sideways slant of the boat, which still hadn't righted itself. Winnie heard others barking commands and frantic instructions back and forth but couldn't make out exactly what was being said.

Winnie sat locked in the hold, imagining water pouring in from a gash in the hull just beyond her reach. She feared that the ship was sinking and that she would die alone, lost to the sea with only Eliza Macy for company.

IN THE GREAT cabin, everything was fine one moment and then it wasn't. Lunch had been served by Red and Chin, with Nell helping, and everyone had enjoyed the cold pork and potatoes. Then shouts from above were followed almost instantly by a sideways motion, the china and glasses sliding clear across the dining table, some items crashing to the floor while others were stopped by the table's fiddles, raised wooden edges designed precisely for this reason.

Peter, with a look of shock on his face, raced out of the cabin with Doc and the other officers close behind him. Sully had the afternoon watch and was already above deck with the rest of the crew. Nell could hear the first mate's distinctive shouting above.

"Oh, no!" Jessie Lindquist cried out, for her chair had toppled straight backward with her in it, head over feet. "Beatrice, do something!" she added, but her maid was busy extracting herself from a similar predicament. Mr. Mortimer rushed to help, holding out a hand and bringing Mrs. Lindquist to her feet beside her maid.

Nell quickly scanned the room and determined that all of the passengers were present and accounted for and unhurt. Then she dashed out to the portico at the top of the companionway stairs to see what had happened, the others right behind her.

Nell looked up. But the sight was impossible to make sense of. The force of the wind had caused the upper masts on the main and mizzen to break, along with the main topsail yards. Hanging precariously, the wooden spars were caught in the lines and tangled in the sails, much like bodies swaying in giant hammocks. Somehow, by luck or chance, neither of the masts nor the broken yard had crashed all the way down onto the deck, where they certainly would have crushed anyone underneath.

"All hands on deck!" Peter called, addressing his crew through a speaking trumpet that projected his voice. The call was perhaps superfluous, since everyone had surely been alerted by the event itself. Nell found it hard to believe that anyone would remain belowdecks or in their cabin after having heard and felt what they just did. Not even an exhausted sailor snoring in his cabin could have slept through it.

Slowly but surely, men started climbing the masts and inching out on the yards, trying to balance themselves while cutting loose the broken masts first in order to bring them down to the deck for repairs. They also had to control sails that had become dangerous, the canvas still attached to the broken masts and blowing about, pulling wildly and erratically with the force of the wind. Once immobilized and secured, they could bring the beam down to the deck for repairs. Then they would have to do the same with the main topgallant mast and yards.

"Stay alert! That one mast there weighs over a ton!"

CHIN JOINED THE group from the great cabin on deck, curious to see what possibly could have happened to make the ship tilt in such a dangerous way. Standing on tiptoes behind several people, including Miss Lily Bird, the very tall actress, he made sense of the scene.

It looked like they weren't going to die. Not right now, anyway. So, while everyone's eyes were skyward, Chin tried to push his way through the crowd and toward the stairs leading to the hold. Winnie must be scared. He had to tell her what had happened.

Then the captain called for all hands on deck. "That means you, too, cabin boy," Sully said to Chin.

That man must have eyes on the back of his head, Chin thought, nodding to his commanding officer and retreating from that first step into the hold. Chin noticed that Red, too, had been stopped by the first mate, and the two exchanged a look. Both were concerned about Winnie. Both were unable to help.

Sully handed Chin a line. "Now, hold that tight and don't move."

NO ONE WAS coming for her. Winnie was going to die. And wouldn't that be a fitting end to her, the ironic conclusion of a ridiculous plan to live life to the fullest? Served her right to drown at sea, stowing away on her own parents' ship! What a fool she had been.

If she survived this catastrophe, whatever it was exactly, Winnie promised herself never to act in such a rash and impulsive manner again. She would grow up. Listen to her elders. Do only what she was told. No more of this childish nonsense of impetuous action and hopeful emotion that led her into danger and chaos.

Through the hatch above, Winnie saw a flash of her mother's distinctive navy silk dress and her brown boots. Her mother was standing just above her.

"HELP!" NELL HEARD a girl's voice call out. Nell looked left and right and aloft, searching, searching. There was a familiarity to the sound, a tug at Nell's heart. Had she lost her mind? Or had she just heard an echo of her daughter's voice from a thousand miles out in the Atlantic Ocean?

But Nell wasn't hearing things; others craned their necks at the sound. The deck had gone silent in the wake of the accident, everyone quiet on deck and above in order to hear the commands and instructions from the captain and first mate. Concentration of this magnitude required collective silence. Even the wind had stopped gusting loudly.

The crew and passengers were pensive and on alert in the shocking aftermath, wondering if their ship—and they—were now doomed. How could they sail a maimed, incapacitated clipper? Would they have to abandon ship and take to the lifeboats, hoping to be found by a passing ship headed back to America? Could they make it to Bermuda, the closest island to their current position?

"Help!" the voice said again. And then, finally, the girl shouted the one word Nell would have to respond to. "Mother!"

Nell looked down. And there, peering up at her from the hold like a ghost of Nell's past, present, and future, was her daughter.

"Winnie?" Nell whispered. She knelt down and placed her fingers through the openings in the wooden skylight.

"Mother!" Winnie cheered, reaching her hands up and out like a toddler asking to be picked up.

A dog started barking, a high-pitched and incessant yipping. Winnie turned her head at the sound, and then smiled up at her mother. "I think someone's coming to let me out!"

"Fred!" Peter exclaimed, coming to stand beside Nell and looking down toward his shoes. But Winnie had moved away from view, so he turned to his wife for clarification. "Was that really her? Is she here, on our ship?"

"Yes," Nell said, her tone a mix of disbelief and awe. "Our daughter appears to have stowed away aboard the *Stargazer*."

"We've been cursed by that damned girl again," Sully said aloud, not even trying to hide his animosity. Several crew members working nearby wrinkled their brows, not understanding what was happening. The poor sods hadn't been on the *Shooting Star* all those years ago. They didn't know what this girl could do, would do, just with her presence and her bad luck. But they had experienced the damage with their own eyes, hadn't they? And now here they were, cleaning up *her* mess and hoping and praying to God that this beautiful ship could still sail.

So Sully picked up the speaking trumpet that Captain Starbuck had dropped in his haste to see his beloved, cursed daughter and addressed the crew directly himself. The sailors needed to know what they were dealing with. They needed someone in charge who could command the clipper without emotion or bias. "The captain's daughter is a stowaway on this ship!"

His announcement was met with a robust grumbling and murmurs of disapproval and disbelief from the crew. Captain Starbuck flashed Sully a look of scornful warning, but said nothing. The response was adequate, but not nearly what Sully had hoped for, what he needed. So he put the trumpet to his lips and spoke again. "Do you *understand*? Winifred Starbuck is the reason why this ship is in shambles! It's her fault that we are in this mess. If we hope to sail on safely, I recommend that she be removed immediately, lest she be the death of us all."

"That's enough!" Zander called out.

Sully turned and faced the helmsman. The man stood proudly at the giant wheel from above them all on the poop deck, acting like he was better than they were, greater than them all. But, despite his air of superiority, Zander was just a runaway slave, and a man like that was in no position to tell Sully what to do.

Sully used his naturally gruff voice, loud and plain and simple. "Zander, you don't know about that which I'm speakin'. So I advise you to keep your mouth shut."

But the helmsman did know the story. Of course he did. Hearing the tale of the madman and the mother was a rite of passage for any sailor joining up with the Starbucks. But who could really believe it as absolute truth? Over the years, the story had probably grown exponentially in its retelling. More like lore, passed down as a warning for anyone brave or dumb enough to go to sea.

"I know that I don't believe in curses and devilment," Zander responded. "And I think it's downright silly that a grown man like you does."

Unlike Zander's older sister, Artemis, who had been named for the Greek goddess of the hunt, Zander had been named after a real live warrior, Alexander the Great. His father had raised him on the rational heroics of men, of making one's own destiny through action and risk. And then, after his father and sister were murdered in front of his own eyes, Zander ran. And he was still running. So he didn't need to believe in stories about curses and monsters, because he believed in men and knew how monstrous they could be.

Sully narrowed his eyes at the helmsman but said nothing. Zander felt like he had been marked. He knew he'd have to watch himself—even more than he usually did around the nasty first mate—from now on.

CONSTANT BARKING WAS coming from the other side of the hold's locked door, a tiny but fierce yip, yip, yipping that sounded strangely familiar to Winnie.

"Enough with you, Yip!" Lucky said. "You've done your job. Hush up now!"

"Hello!" Winnie called out, her hand pressed against the door. "Is somebody there?"

"Just hold your horses," Lucky said, scrambling to find the right key with his tremoring right hand and his rheumy eyes and this gloomy darkness. There!

As soon as Lucky removed the chunky metal lock, the door swung outward toward him and a fair-haired girl sprung out from behind it. "Hi!" she said, her green eyes wide, her curls bouncy around her quite recognizable face. "Thanks so very much for rescuing me! Now if you'll excuse me, I must go see my parents!"

Lucky was at a loss for words. Even Yip had been stunned into silence. Lucky scooped up the little dog and carried him up the narrow stairs and into the light, shaking his head the whole way. The dog licked his hand in comfort.

"We're really getting too old for this job, Yip," Lucky said, a sentiment with which the dog definitely agreed.

CHAPTER 11

Winnie dashed, breathless, to the top of the steps, as quickly as she could with the boat still listing sideways. She was free! Alive and well! Saved from the hold by an old man with a little dog! She could hardly contain her excitement. The ship, her mother, her father: how she longed to see them all. Mostly the ship, if she was being honest. The *Stargazer* had filled her mind's eye for the past six days, and now she would get to see the glorious thing for herself, a day earlier than expected.

She exited through a small door at the back of the poop deck, the same one Red had sneaked her through when they launched from Nantucket Harbor. She had entered that portal as a naive girl, and now here she emerged, tougher and wiser and ready to claim a spot as a sailor.

The sunlight was so strong it temporarily blinded Winnie. She squinted against it and shielded her eyes with her hand, trying to make sense of what she was seeing. The ship at an angle, masts cracked in half and caught in the lines and sheeting, and a stunned silence from onlookers with only the hollow wind behind them. She made her way down to the crew and her parents on the main deck.

"Oh, darling," her mother said, embracing Winnie, her voice a whisper of disbelief. "My brave and foolish girl." Winnie closed her eyes then, feeling safe in her mother's arms like she had as a child. Her mother could make everything in Winnie's world better, particularly when she wasn't the one making things worse.

"Fred, is that really you?" her father asked, his hand tentative on her elbow.

"Yes, Father," she said, her eyes adjusting to the white-hot sun against the glaring blue sky.

"A stowaway must be punished, sir," she heard the nasty first mate say. It felt like the ship was holding its breath, with all hands on deck and all eyes on Winnie and her parents.

"You have more important things to worry about right now, Sully. Or would you rather let the ship drift aimlessly in the Atlantic while we debate what to do with my daughter?"

Winnie saw Chin then, holding on to one of the lines as if his life depended on it. He did not meet her gaze.

So that's how this is going to be, Winnie realized. She was free, yes, but she was also very much on her own.

Sully cleared his throat, but said nothing in response to Captain Starbuck. He had made his point, and had done so in front of every single sailor. That way, should things turn even more foul than they already were, with a stowaway daughter and a crippled ship, at least no one would question where exactly *he* stood on the matter. The girl had to go, and the sooner the better. And Sully would right this ship—and lead it, too, before long. After all, who could trust a captain who couldn't even control the whims and wills of his own child?

Sully turned to the crew and shouted, "Back to work, men! Let's get those broken pieces of each mast down safely so Doc can have a look. Careful as can be. Then we can repair the sails, too."

Winnie was ushered quietly away by her mother and father, feeling a bit like a criminal heading to the gallows.

"SIT," HER FATHER ordered once they were alone inside her parents' private staterooms.

Winnie sat on the blue velvet banquette anchored to one wall. She knew she should feel cowed, but instead she was overwhelmed by the splendor around her—and pleased by the comfort of a tufted cushion under her. Her mother sat next to her, knees angled toward her daughter as if showing solidarity. Winnie's father stood, pacing in front of the small upright piano.

"How could you do this?" her father asked, his voice low and cold.

"How could I not?" Winnie replied. Six days in the hold of a ship had made her bold. Her father raised his chin slightly as if acknowledging this change in her. She had never talked back to him quite so directly on land.

"I'm not saying that to be impudent, Father. I'm saying it because it's true." She gestured to the wallpaper surrounding them. "Here is all the proof I need to justify my actions: the harbor at Canton, of which you are so very proud. So proud that you even use the same image to decorate your ship! How could you keep this wondrous life from me? I have to see China for myself, Father. It's my destiny. I want to be a successful sailor and merchant like you and Mother."

"You were wrong to sneak onto our ship," her father said.

"Yes, I was. And for that I sincerely apologize. But you were wrong not to allow me on legitimately." Winnie swallowed.

"Sneaking aboard was an act of desperation," her mother added, her green eyes understanding.

"Yes," Winnie sighed, sinking deeper into the cushions. Her mother already forgave her. Perhaps, being a woman in a man's world, her mother understood why someone would be compelled to act out against her best instinct, against all that society's rules would allow.

It was more complicated with her father, who was shaking in quiet rage. "This is madness! I should be *captaining* this ship, overseeing the dangerous removal of those broken masts. Not disciplining my reckless daughter."

"It was not my intention to make myself known in the middle of a crisis, Father," Winnie said.

"And yet, here we are. Did you think that, when you emerged from the hold, we would all just—what? Applaud and cheer? Hug you?"

"Not cheer, exactly, but—"

"Imagine if the ship had been going down or had been swept with fire?"

Winnie had imagined it, not that she would admit it now.

"I *have* to win this, Fred. There is much at stake—and I can't have my own daughter getting in the way of that. Your presence has caused an unnecessary commotion and a distraction, to say the least. And you must have had help from a crew member, as it is impossible to lock oneself inside the hold and magically have food and drink brought to you."

Nell, listening to her husband, suddenly had a flash of memory: Red carrying a dirty bucket up from the hold, and then, moments later, going back down the rear companionway with an empty one. And then another memory, of Red, Chin, and Cook acting strangely that first day together in the galley. And immediately, Nell knew who the culprits were.

"Traditionally, the punishment for stowing away on a ship is . . ." Peter said.

Don't say flogging, Nell prayed.

"To work on that ship," Winnie stated.

Her father glanced up at her, looking almost impressed, his temper beginning to wane. "Yes."

Winnie nodded. "I've read everything I can about ships and sailing them, Father. To get ready for a life at sea."

"I see," he said.

"And I know that ships require constant maintenance and oversight. So, while one might be compelled to keep the stowaway in irons in the brig, it makes much more sense for a captain to put her to work on deck."

Her father nodded. "However, Bermuda is not far. Should we need to stop for repairs, then you shall disembark there."

"But you need to keep going, Father. You just said so yourself. For the glory of being the fastest clipper ship in the world! And—dismastings are not uncommon. I just read about one happening recently." She searched her mind, flipping invisibly through newspapers arriving on Nantucket from Boston and New York. "*Sea Serpent*! She sprung her bowsprit only four days after launching from Manhattan just this past January. They mended her at sea."

Peter raised his eyebrows in surprise. Of course he knew about the *Sea Serpent*. But for Fred to be aware of it? For his daughter to be here, lecturing to him about seaworthiness and the art and craft of carpentering while afloat? That was indeed a surprise.

"Upper masts like the topmast and t'gallant sometimes crack from the strain and force of the wind, sails, and heavy rigging against them," Winnie said. "And those broken top sections are almost always repaired at sea. Either with the salvaged timber or with new logs kept below."

"In most cases, yes," Peter said, pretending not to be moved by his daughter's nautical knowledge—and correct pronunciation. It was, in fact, one of those extra spars that was used to break into the hold where Winnie was held prisoner all those years ago on the *Shooting Star*. "But those spars are not yet measured or carved precisely for use as a mast or yard, and I don't have the time to make them so. I need the originals to work."

"They shall," Winnie said. "You are the best captain the world has ever seen. You can't possibly be intimidated by a broken mast—or even two."

"Winnie! Don't be disrespectful," her mother said.

But Fred was right; Peter was loath to stop in Bermuda for repairs. They would never win if they pulled into port. Not that he would admit this to Fred. "Your mother and I will discuss the details of your punishment further over dinner. And we'll know more by tomorrow, about the conditions of the masts, yards, and sails and how extensive our repairs will be, and whether we'll need to dock somewhere. There must be consequences for your actions, Fred. You are an adult now. You know that."

"Yes, Father," Winnie said. "I do."

"For the meanwhile, perhaps Winnie can move into the empty stateroom across from ours?" Nell suggested, looking back and forth between her husband and child. To Winnie she explained with a half smile, "It was made for a child smaller than you, but I think you'll find it more comfortable than your *previous* accommodations."

Winnie and her mother followed Peter from the sitting area to the small, bright bedroom. "Your mother will take it from here. I must see what's happening above deck," Peter said.

"Thank you, Father," Winnie said.

"Don't thank me yet, Fred. I haven't decided whether to forgive you or not."

"I understand," she said as he disappeared from view. Because she did. And because Winnie knew she had time—a year around the globe, if he let her stay—to prove to her father that she was worth forgiving.

"You're quite something," Nell said, alone now with her daughter. She gave Winnie another tight squeeze, knowing she should be furious with her and yet unable to keep from smiling.

"Is that good or bad?" Winnie asked. "To be *something*?"

Nell considered Winnie. Her daughter's hair needed brushing and her face was smeared with grime and she was still wearing that same navy blue jacket of Nell's from the day they launched. But her jade eyes were clear and bright, her posture tall and strong. "Oh, darling. As a woman, it's always good to be something."

AFTER NELL GAVE Winnie a tour of the captain's staterooms, including her parents' bedchamber and the wonderful, remarkable indoor privies, Red and Chin brought Winnie's sea chest up from the hold. They squeezed it through the slim doorway and into her new room, panting slightly from the effort.

"Your dad didn't put you in irons," Chin said. "Some captain."

Winnie shoved him playfully on the arm. "I'm to work on deck. Maybe even in the galley with you. Only . . . how are we going to act around one another now?" Winnie asked, thinking about the way Chin had—rightfully—ignored her in front of the rest of the crew.

They could speak openly here. Winnie's mother had gone to help Cook prepare a special meal to boost the crew's morale. The sailors could be making repairs well through the night, and everyone needed nourishment for the work ahead. "We're supposed to be strangers, but you've become my friends." Winnie blinked back tears. Silly. She didn't mean to get sentimental, but now that she had emerged above deck, Winnie realized just how much these two had risked to keep her safe and fed belowdecks. She felt grateful and a bit overwhelmed.

"I don't know you, and you don't know me. Simple." Chin shrugged.

"You're not very sentimental, are you?" Winnie asked. And once she explained the meaning of the word *sentimental* to Chin, he agreed that he was not in the least bit at all that word.

Red nodded, although he was more sentimental in general. "I think we have to behave like strangers." The more he and Chin could act like they didn't know Winnie, the safer they would all be. Having already pretended that he didn't know who Winnie was six days ago, he felt prepared for the challenge.

Winnie sighed. She felt the loss of Red and Chin acutely, even though they were standing right there.

"No need to look so sad, Miss Winnie. We can become friends now." Chin stuck out his hand and Winnie clutched it. "Chin from Canton. Nice to meet you."

The warmth from Chin's small hand radiated up Winnie's arm and all the way to her heart.

CHAPTER 12

Up on deck, the men had managed to bring down almost all the broken spars, including the mizzen and main topgallant masts, lowering them safely to the deck somehow without crushing any of the men below. The last spar to secure was the seventy-four-foot main topsail yard, which weighed over two tons. Sully called out orders as Peter grabbed ahold of the lines with everyone else to aid in the careful, heavy, deliberate work of bringing the spar down without it punching through a sail or causing further damage on its way down.

There. All the broken spars were now on deck.

Peter exhaled for the first time in two hours. Once the giant wooden timbers were laid across the deck, their weight no longer pulling the ship to one side, the boat straightened out and stopped heeling to port.

FEELING THE SHIFT in the ship, everyone else on board the *Stargazer* visibly relaxed, including the passengers who had gathered in the great cabin to wait out the long hours of nervous anticipation together. From the damaged ship to the stowed-away Starbuck daughter, there was much for them to discuss.

"I heard several of the crew say that it might take a few days to get the beams repaired and back up," Mr. Mortimer, the journalist, said. In the past two hours, the universe had delivered into his lap much more story aboard this vessel than he ever could have anticipated. And while excited about having so much interesting content to write up and send back to the newspaper, he was also deeply disturbed by the dismasted ship.

He had taken on the assignment willingly, as a man interested in global travel and America's expanding economic reach—from the other side of the country to the other side of the world—but those interests had been largely cerebral and philosophical until today. Only today did Charles Mortimer, an intrepid journalist who had written about bloody, gruesome murders in Boston's back alleys, realize he had put himself in mortal danger by agreeing to this assignment.

Up on that deck, with everything around him in shambles, he had wanted to scream. To call out for his mother. To make sure his brother knew that he loved him—and those rambunctious nieces and nephews of his. Did no one else in this great cabin fear for their lives? Only that girl—*Fred*, Captain Starbuck had called her—seemed to greet the moment with the shock and awe and horror it deserved, screaming and calling for her mother like any rational person might. Locked in the hold, she must have thought she was going to die. But now it occurred to Charles, it didn't really matter if you were in a locked room or not: the entire ship was a giant floating death trap.

"Do you think they'll send the girl home?" Jessie Lindquist asked the group, her knitting needles clanging together. "I'd send her home, if I were them," she quickly answered before anyone could offer their opinion. "Unload her onto the first ship we see heading in the opposite direction." She pulled more yarn from the ball in the basket by her feet and continued to loop the needles around and through the cornflower-colored slack.

"But she's their *daughter*," Beatrice said. "How could they do that to their own child?"

"And what do you know about raising a child?" Jessie snapped, pointing a needle in her maid's face. "Don't go giving opinions about which you have no experience, Beatrice!"

"Yes'm," Beatrice said. "Sorry."

"Do you have children, Mrs. Lindquist?" Lily Bird asked.

"No," Jessie replied. "God never granted them to me and Bernard. But I know about these things."

Over the week, Lily Bird had noticed that Jessie Lindquist never agreed with anything her maid said. Maybe she thought that being contrary was an important part of being in charge. If so, it would behoove Beatrice to learn this about her employer—and to keep quiet.

"I, for one, hope Miss Starbuck stays," Lily Bird said. She was shuffling a deck of cards for Patience, a game played solo and with little stakes. Lily conversed with the group while casually laying some cards in neat rows, but where was the fun in that? She needed a partner to play gin rummy with, a game with hopes of discarding one card in order to pick up something of higher worth, a playing card that would make her hand a winner. And a young, courageous woman of means like Winnie Starbuck, who had stolen away upon her parents' ship? That person had the potential to become an ace of a friend.

ON DECK, PETER and Doc, the carpenter, investigated the broken wooden spars. Doc asked for any volunteers with a knowledge of carpentry to work with him, and several sailors came forward. Next, the sailmaker, aptly nicknamed Rip, assessed the condition of the torn sails. Some holes could be repaired and the canvas reused, but in a few cases, the gashes were just too wide or the canvas had shredded, and new canvas would be required. Several sailors went below to fetch new canvas while others made patches for the sails that could be salvaged.

"Father, how can I assist?" Winnie asked, trying to be as nonchalant and unobtrusive as a former-stowaway daughter with sixty sailors staring at her could be. Her father sighed and rubbed his face. He had never thought of what a grown child of his could do on one of his ships, and now, with his mind trying to focus on repairs and getting her back up to full sail, he was at a loss for ideas.

"You can do nuthin' for me, my men, nor my ship," Sully barked from behind them. "Men, don't let this cursed girl near ya. You doan wanna catch it."

"Cursed?" Winnie asked, looking hurt and confused. She searched Sully's tough, cold eyes for answers, and when there were none, she looked to her father.

"Because you stowed away," he said as an explanation, not meeting her gaze.

Winnie had never heard that lore before, but, with the crew's absolute attention on her, she decided no reaction was the best reaction. A gull overheard squawked. The wind carried the bird's echo through the broken masts and tattered sails and onto the deck.

"D'you know how to sew?" Rip, the sailmaker, asked, crouching low over a pile of canvas. He squinted up at Winnie. Rip was a compact man, his face weathered from years at sea and his arms sinewy as if made of rope.

"Yessir, I do," she said, her face lighting up. "And my mother brought her sewing table. I'll gather some needles and thread and be right back!"

Through the galley window, Cook and Nell watched as Winnie ran off. The galley was centrally located, so both of them could keep one eye on the activities unfurling on deck and one eye on the potatoes they were roasting for a simple but hearty meal, served with cold ham leftovers. "All grown up now, your girl," Cook said. "And she looks so much like you, missus. Acts like you, too, if I may be so bold."

Nell nodded. She knew Cook meant it as a compliment. She wanted to ask Cook about his role in helping Winnie hide, but she didn't feel like dealing with another confrontation today, and didn't know how she'd react if Cook lied to her face. So she asked a question only a wizened sailor could answer. "Do you think my daughter is bad luck? That she's . . . cursed?"

Cook pulled his mouth into a thin line and considered the question. With large tongs, he began to turn the potatoes, their skins crackling over the flames. "I can think what I think, but it really is no matter. Only time will tell us if it's true, missus."

CHAPTER 13

June 9

It took two full days for the crew to repair the sails and mend the broken spars. The men hardly slept, working through the night and into the next day and the day after that to fix the *Stargazer* as quickly and effectively as possible. Some men went below to sleep in their bunks for a few hours on and off, while others just drifted off and slept where they sat on deck, roused back awake by a nudge from a neighbor passing along a shared cup of water. Red and Chin had been assisting with chores on deck, leaving Cook and Nell in the galley to feed everyone, with Winnie joining in once Rip released her from sewing duties.

With Leo and Zander's help, Peter had been able to navigate the ship and sail her slowly but steadily back on course, using half her sail power. "She's moving like an old woman with a cane," Sully complained. "And I only like to ride a young filly, boys."

This, with accompanying gesturing, got the sailors laughing that first night. It was followed by lots of other lewd grumbling and jeers as a group of men worked on stitching canvas in the moonlight, their backs against the hull, or sitting on barrels, or lying on their stomachs or backs, hands raised, lanterns aglow. But the jokes and innuendo grew tired as the men did, and before long, no one wanted to talk, much less sing a bawdy ballad about going a-rovin' with the maid from Amsterdam.

Now, in the light of morning, Peter watched as the last of the repaired yards—the seventy-four-foot main topsail yard—was hoisted up and onto its rightful place. It felt like poetic justice for the last one down to be the last one up. A balance in the universe that was his *Stargazer*. He scratched the black stubble on his cheek and realized he hadn't shaved in three days.

The masts and yards seemed secure, and before long, they were rigged and moving again under full sail. "You are all dismissed for breakfast!" Peter exclaimed. "Cook has prepared Sunday duff, since you missed it yesterday." The crew cheered; the steamed pudding made with suet and raisins was a welcome surprise and a fitting end to three difficult days. The sailors thanked him and quickly disappeared while Peter and a skeleton crew stayed above deck.

Winnie, who had been working in the galley all morning and was now feeding the chickens, was as delighted as the rest of the crew, but she wanted to show she didn't need a special breakfast, that she could work harder and longer than any of them. "Can I stay and help you, Father?" Winnie asked. In the past two days, she had learned a great deal about repairing sails. She was ready now to learn about navigation and seamanship—and whatever else her father would allow.

"No, Fred." He turned back to Leo, who was unfolding a chart over a barrel. The ship had lost a good deal of time since being dismasted. Now that she was fully restored, Peter needed to ensure their navigation made up for lost time, with not a single moment wasted, sailing not a single degree off course.

"Are you certain?" Winnie asked.

Peter sighed. He hadn't spoken much to his daughter since she'd emerged from hiding, trying to quell his anger toward her and also, if he was being honest, trying to forget about her. Because Fred was a problem. She had been reckless and had acted selfishly—and on a ship, you had to work for the good of the whole, not just doing what *you* wanted when *you* wanted. A mind that worked as a single entity, putting individual will above group strength, could not be trusted at sea. And trust was everything at sea. Why, his daughter was so capable and cunning as to sneak onto his own ship undetected for days! What else could she do? Could she—would she—either unwittingly or perhaps even intentionally—discover things Peter didn't want known? That would most certainly be a problem.

And now, here she stood, trying to prove her worth after lying to him. No, he wouldn't stand for it.

He pulled her aside. "Fred, your persistence is as admirable as it is exasperating. I know what you are really asking, now that the ship is sailing safely and well. You want to know your punishment for stowing away. So my answer is this: we shall keep you with us on the *Stargazer* until we reach San Francisco. You may stay with us while we dock and help your mother deliver the goods to merchants waiting at that port. And when we disembark for China, you instead shall board a steamer and head right back home."

"Back... home?" Winnie echoed. "But what about China?"

"That is your punishment. That is what your disobedience cost you. Yes, you shall get to round Cape Horn with us and see California and have the experience of sailing aboard a renowned clipper ship. You may even learn a thing or two about being a merchant while in port. But you will not get to see China. Not with me, anyway."

"But—" Winnie started. "You can't— I must—" She began each sentence declaring *something*, only the rest of the sentence burned out before she could figure out how to argue it succinctly or clearly.

"No, Fred. I am the captain of this vessel and the head of this family. So actually, I very much *can* and you very well *will not*."

Her father's eyes were like fixed points in the sky; Winnie could use them to navigate directly from the here and now to then and there, to his Californian conclusion. Captain Starbuck's mind was made up. The sails of Winnie's hopes collapsed, defeated and deflated.

Peter Starbuck spoke with a softer tone as he put an arm around his daughter's shoulder. "Go enjoy breakfast, Fred. In the great cabin. You no longer have to stay in your room alone for meals."

For that had been her initial punishment: banished from socializing with the passengers. Her father now released her from that, thinking she might be pleased. After all, this had been what she wanted two days prior, but now that she was free to dine with the others, it didn't feel like absolution at all.

Instead of heading belowdecks to eat, she watched the whitecaps ruffle the waves, temporarily too shocked to move.

Breakfast in the great cabin, meanwhile, was a jovial affair. The passengers' spirits were lifted knowing the ship was repaired and back to full sail. Charles Mortimer, for one, was relieved to be alive. He knew it was silly, but he felt newly invigorated by the idea that life was so precious and here he was, pushing his existence to the fullest. He went up on deck to admire the huge, steady beams of timber and the sails proudly puffed up with air, and he, too, felt proud—even though he hadn't lifted a finger to help make these repairs. He saw the captain's daughter staring at the sea deep in thought and didn't disturb her.

Charles returned to the great cabin, the scent of the ocean air still around him, and discovered he was the first to breakfast. He found a basket of warm brown bread, sticky with molasses. *And isn't that just delicious,* he thought. After feeling too nervous to eat for the past several days, his appetite was back. *Even better than Sunday duff.*

Charles had heard about Sunday duff, and, as a journalist, felt it was his responsibility to taste it and report on the traditional seafaring treat for the masses back on land. Cook had given him a taste that morning in the galley before the crew got at it, knowing nothing would be left over after. Charles had liked the cakey interior, but he had a hard time getting past the outside, which was too gummy and wet for his personal liking. But he had made a show of enjoyment for Cook, *mmm*-ing as he chewed, raising his eyebrows in theatrical delight, and telling the chef how impressed his readers would be when they made the dish at home. He planned to print the full recipe, should his editor give him the space. Maybe if he put it next to a paying advertisement for flour, saying to use Baxter's Best for best results. Yes. The editor would agree to that. Anything to make an extra buck.

And to add to the excitement of this day, here came that very same captain's daughter, the young woman he had just seen on deck! Miss Winifred Starbuck, joining them for breakfast!

"Miss Starbuck," Charles said, scooting back in his chair and standing. "Welcome."

As the young woman thanked him and looked around the lovely room, Charles longed to ask her a thousand personal questions. How did she manage to sneak on the ship? What was her intention now that she had revealed herself? And those were only the first two! He didn't see anything wrong with asking. Why had he even been brought on this journey, if not to probe and extract the best stories?

Although, perhaps it was rude to jump right into his journalistic tendencies. Charles sometimes forgot that the subjects of his articles were people first, stories second. So, in this instance, he would treat this Miss Starbuck as just another passenger on this clipper ship. Relax, a bit. Act natural. There was plenty of time to get to know her and ask indelicate questions. It wasn't like she was going anywhere. Unless her father decided to kick her off the ship, that is. In which case, she really *was* going somewhere, and the sooner he could get cracking, the better.

"Well. This room is certainly comfortable," Winnie said. "I can see why everyone spends so much time here." She smiled half-heartedly, as if the beauty of the room somehow made her sad.

Winnie could tell that the great cabin was obviously also decorated by her mother, as it was luxurious and lovely, with the color palette of blues and golds always, always as a reminder of the Starbuck colors. Her mother was nothing if not consistent.

Now that she was here, Winnie's curiosity about the passengers was piqued. So she smiled nervously and took a seat at the long, polished wood table, waiting for the others to arrive.

This man welcomed her warmly, but also without question or comment. Good breeding had no doubt taught him to behave well. Unlike with the sailors above deck, here there were no snide remarks, no odd side glances, and no outright accusations of having cursed the ship. Just "please pass the eggs" and other polite and measured conversation. Winnie knew she should appreciate the man's unobtrusive demeanor, but instead she felt almost more unsettled by the silence. In her experience as a boarding school girl, she had discovered that, when people didn't speak frankly in front of you, they most certainly were doing so behind your back.

Winnie sighed, eating her breakfast but not really tasting any of it. She didn't fit in with the crew and she didn't quite fit in here, either, with the passengers. She had baked the bread they were now eating and fixed the sails they were now using to move along the Atlantic, but she had no true place to belong and no companion. Winnie was straddling two worlds, not quite accepted by either.

"Good morning, Miss Winifred," Chin said, pouring water into a cut-glass goblet next to her plate.

"Good morning, Chin," she said, perking up. He always seemed to appear just when Winnie needed him most. "Please, call me Winnie."

"Yes, sir, Fred," he replied, moving on to pour water into Mr. Mortimer's glass.

"Would you care for more bread?" Winnie asked. "I helped prepare it at dawn and was hoping the passengers would enjoy it."

"I would love another slice, but if I took a second helping before Mrs. Lindquist had taken her first, she'd no doubt scold me. But, the women this morning appear to be running late. So, since she isn't here yet to witness it . . ." Charles shrugged.

But just as he reached out, a woman's bejeweled arm came from behind them and slapped Charles on the wrist. "Oh no, you don't!"

"Ow!" Charles said, cradling his right hand in his left. "That was unnecessary, Mrs. Lindquist!"

"I thought it was most necessary indeed! Beatrice, don't you agree?"

"Completely necessary, ma'am."

Delighted to see someone other than her get reprimanded, Winnie turned around in her chair to take in the full scene. A rather tall woman with a wide girth stood behind them, wearing a peacock-blue silk dress and several strands of enormous pearls. Her face was dusted in powder and her cheeks painted with pink rouge, and she smelled heavily of lilacs. Next to her stood a woman half her age and half her size.

The larger woman smiled at Winnie and extended her hand and introduced herself. "Why, if it isn't the famous stowaway!"

Winnie laughed. "In the flesh," she said, pretending to bow in her chair.

Just then, another woman appeared at the doorway and, upon seeing Winnie, gasped. "Oh! *Hooray!* They've finally set you *free* to dine with us!" she said in a pronounced British accent. She was young and beautiful, with long black hair and dark eyes to match. "I'm Lily Bird, and I've been *dying* to meet you. I've *decided* we're to become the *best* of friends."

Jessie Lindquist sank into the empty chair next to Winnie, just as Lily practically leaped across the room to sit in a chair directly opposite her. Lily leaned her torso across the table, elbows resting on her chin.

"Now," Jessie said, taking both of Winnie's hands into her own and staring into her eyes. "Tell us absolutely everything."

"Yes! Don't leave out a single detail!" Lily added.

Charles Mortimer couldn't believe it! For, with that bit of enthusiastic encouragement, the young woman began to talk. Oh, she couldn't possibly reveal who had helped her get on board, or if she had bribed them, but she could, she supposed, share some of the story about why she felt it was crucial for her to take this potentially historic voyage with her parents on the *Stargazer*.

The Starbuck daughter chatted easily and amicably, talking all through breakfast and beyond, as Chin and Red cleared the dirty dishes around them and brought a pot of tea with several cups and saucers clanging merrily, and lit the fire in the brazier.

"And what have your parents decided to do with you?" Jessie Lindquist asked, most indelicately, in Charles's estimation. He would *never*.

The young woman's bright eyes darkened, and she looked to her lap and paused. A funereal stillness fell over the room, and Charles thought, *That's it, we've lost her. She'll never speak aloud again.*

"My father decided that I shall be disembarking with all of you," she said, looking now at Lily Bird and blinking back tears.

"Oh!" Lily said, squeezing Winnie's hand from across the table. "How wonderful for me!"

"And for me!" Jessie added.

"I'm happy for myself, too, ma'am," Beatrice added. "If I may."

"And how pleasant that will be for the whole new state of California," Charles added, for good measure.

"You can stay with us in San Francisco!" Jessie exclaimed. "My husband has built a huge house!"

Winnie smiled wide and laughed along with them, their shared destination a trait that now linked them to one another. "I'll probably only stay for a week or so," she explained. "My father is sending me back to the East Coast once the *Stargazer* departs."

"And what does your mother have to say on the matter?" Jessie Lindquist asked.

Winnie paused. What *did* her mother have to say on the matter? Had her father consulted her, or just made the pronouncement in the moment, without discussing it with his wife first? But Winnie couldn't express her uncertainty with the passengers, so she said, simply, "My mother and father agree on everything."

"Well. A week or so in port. That's still enough time for you to see the sights," Lily added. "Now," she said, seeming to want to change the direction of this conversation if not the entire journey for Miss Winifred, "tell us all about life on Nantucket!"

And Lily, Jessie Lindquist, and Winnie chatted on and on.

Charles listened in, sipping his tea. He supposed the girl was starved for social connection. After all, she had spent the better part of a week alone in the hold. Brave girl. Foolish, but bold. Maybe that was the combination of traits needed to go out to sea. Maybe that's how they all were, come to think of it. The crew and passengers alike, foolish and bold enough to undertake a trip like this one.

Yes. He could see a story forming in his mind's eye. Not just about the activities and calamities aboard the *Stargazer*, but containing all the personalities on board as well. A profile that got under the obvious, the *what* of the thing, into something deeper that probed the *why* of it all. Charles reached for his notebook and a pencil nub, which he always kept in his jacket pocket, and began scribbling away. He jotted notes based on the ideas for his next piece, but also listened intently to Winnie's story, making sure to capture it all on the page.

He had to hand it to these ladies, for they certainly knew how to get a source to open up. Mrs. Lindquist and Miss Bird showed natural curiosity and peppered the newcomer with question after question, oohing and aahing as she answered. Miss Starbuck told them about getting very seasick and about reading Chaucer and Shakespeare to pass the time. After Winnie recited a line she had memorized from *The Tempest*, Miss Bird instantly recited the next line of dialogue from the play and Jessie Lindquist—and Beatrice—applauded.

Charles's right hand raced across the page to keep up with their chatter. It was almost as if he was interviewing Miss Starbuck himself. And then he thought, as the women laughed and shared other stories, maybe being an observer was the best way to gather information.

WINNIE LAUGHED HER way through breakfast, making light of every tale she told, pretending that her seasickness on the first few days stowed away in the ship's hold had been funny, really, only a minor incident in the greater scheme of life. At no point had she actually thought she was going to die, heavens no! *Ha, ha, ha*, she pantomimed, while Lily the actress and Jessie Lindquist and her maid chuckled alongside her. They seemed quite nice, but during the entire conversation, which felt more like a performance, Winnie was too busy holding back tears of anger and frustration to truly enjoy their company.

How could her father discipline her in this way? Wasn't he being a tad harsh, not letting Winnie continue on to China? And finally she wondered, over the noise of her own incessant chatter: was her mother truly aware of—and in perfect agreement with—what her father had just declared?

Winnie excused herself from the great cabin, promising to chat more at luncheon. She found her mother in their shared stateroom, where Nell was inputting notes to the daily log.

"Did you know?" Winnie asked.

"About what, darling?" Nell asked. Three sailors had requested tobacco and another had asked for a pencil. She had to write these notes down immediately or she might forget to dock it from their pay.

"About my punishment! Father has told me I am to disembark in San Francisco and head home via steamer ship!" Winnie wailed.

"Hmmm?" Nell asked, buying herself a moment of time to think—for no, she hadn't known this at all.

Employing motherly tactics learned during Winnie's toddler years, Nell remained calm in the face of her daughter's rage—which was now, too, her own. Her heart thrummed, both with anger at Peter's decision as well as his choice to exclude her from making it with him. A large dot of ink marred the open page in her logbook. She dropped the fountain pen and raised her eyebrows at her daughter's pronouncement and said, as mildly as possible, "Why, of course."

"But! How could you?" Winnie whined. "It is a cruel decision, really," she added. "After all I did to get here!" On and on Winnie spiraled, her complaints and protestations growing louder with each declaration, mirroring Nell's own growing list of complaints and protestations at her husband, which she kept quietly bound in her mind.

The more her daughter wailed, the less Nell engaged. This, too, was part of her motherly training. All self-taught, she might add. No one had helped Nell figure out how best to discipline a feisty four-year-old, because she'd raised her daughter on a ship, the only woman in a sea of men. In the face of incessant crying, Nell had tried bribes of ginger candies, talking rationally to the little girl, yelling at her, and once even striking her behind. But eventually, she'd discovered that a wall of silence worked best.

As Winnie carried on, Nell picked up her pen and returned to the logbook.

Finally, Winnie went off to mourn this tremendous loss alone in her room. Nell waited five minutes. Then she quickly walked out onto the deck, where she sought out Peter and cornered him by the pen of animals for privacy. "How could you decide this without me?" she asked in a raised whisper. "About our child?"

"You're letting your heart get in the way, Nell," he said. "While I—as the ship's *captain*," he reminded her unnecessarily, "remain rational, always. And only a rational, levelheaded person is in the right frame of mind to make consequential decisions. And so I went ahead and made one."

His explanation was dismissive. A simple shrug of the shoulders, which felt to Nell like a masculine response to a woman's supposed hysterics. Hadn't Nell just minutes ago exhibited extreme rationality when met with Winnie's arguments in their stateroom? And hadn't she, this girl's mother, stayed calm for the entirety of her daughter's life, responding rationally to every tantrum, and eventually saving her from a madman during childhood? But Peter did not see it this way.

"In fact, you should be thanking me, Nell, for being so decisive and taking the burden off of you."

Nell was stunned into silence. She had never before lost her words in the face of this man—this *captain*. She had never before not been invited to be her husband's full partner in all decision-making, both about their child and their business. "Peter, something about this trip has altered you. And I don't like it. I don't recognize you."

That night, Peter made advances toward Nell, his hand gliding up her nightgown in the dark, the moon's light shining down on them through the skylight. Nell feigned a headache and rolled away toward the wall.

CHAPTER 14

June 16

Peter awoke in the gray dawn to the sounds of shouting on deck. He sat up in bed, listening. Nell, lying beside him, sat up as well. "It's not Sully," she said.

"Sounds like Zander," Peter said, standing and reaching for his dress clothes.

And then, through the speaking trumpet, they both heard the call much more clearly. "Sail, ho!"

"He's spotted a ship," Nell said, putting a robe over her dressing gown. She would use the head and then get dressed quickly, too. She and Peter still moved like a married couple, and lay in bed side by side, but Nell noticed a subtle distance between them. They had not made love for a week.

Nell opened the door and found Winnie there, about to knock. "A ship!" she said, sounding as excited as a five-year-old. "Who do you think it is?" she added, already dressed and frantically tying her shoes.

Peter pushed past them. "We'll know by their colors," he said, exiting through the stateroom with Winnie following close behind.

DAWN WAS JUST breaking, the sky a hazy pink. Light winds came from the southeast. A sailor on watch in the crow's nest had seen movement on the water from that same direction about an hour prior and had alerted Zander, but neither man could make out much until the sky lightened. The first part of a ship that could be detected on the horizon was a sail, and so, once verified, the call was made to alert the others: "Sail, ho!"

The second week on board the *Stargazer* had gone by quickly and without incident. She sailed on an even keel down toward the coast of South America, the sun growing stronger and the days longer, with mild temperatures by day and soft, cooling breezes at night.

Lily came on deck just as Winnie did, and Lily turned so her friend could quickly button up the back of her dress. Lily's black hair still hung in a long braid for sleeping. "I just heard the call and raced out of my cabin!" she said. "And now I realize I'm nervous. Why am I nervous?"

Winnie understood the feeling. A passing ship was usually cause for excitement, as long as it wasn't during wartime when they feared coming across enemies on the seas. And as long as the ship heading toward them wasn't a pirate ship. But those were largely relics from the past century, more lore now than fact. The oceans were much safer now than they had been a hundred years prior when piracy was at its height.

"Have we detected who they are yet? Or where they're from?" Nell asked the group, emerging from the captain's staterooms. Winnie shook her head no, along with several others. This was the first ship the *Stargazer* had come across so far on this voyage. Everyone felt the anticipation as they gathered near the starboard side railing.

Winnie watched as the journalist Charles Mortimer folded several handwritten pages into a large envelope that was already addressed to the attention of Jeremiah Wilkes at *The Boston Pilot*.

"I'm sorry, but we aren't going to be holding a gam with it like a whaleship," Winnie said, motioning to his papers.

"No?" Charles asked. "Whyever not? I thought I'd be able to send mail from passing ships. That we'd stop and send a rowboat down and visit with them a bit. That's what I told my editor. The stories need to get out quickly."

"Clippers need to get to their destinations even quicker than your stories do, Mr. Mortimer," Nell explained. "We don't sail aimlessly around the world searching for whales, meeting up with other ships for company to pass the time. We have a clear course and we won't be pausing today for anything more than a passing exchange of news."

Charles Mortimer's face fell. "But Captain Starbuck assured me—"

"I assured you of what?" Peter asked, passing by the group on his way to the poop deck.

"That I could hand my stories off to passing ships, thereby spreading word of the *Stargazer*'s progress quickly."

Peter knitted his brow. Originally, yes, he *had* agreed to such terms as a negotiation tool for getting the journalist to agree to joining the trip. But those had been vague promises at best, utterances never signed onto paper, about quickly handing off mail to other ships and the like. Now that the journey was underway, Peter wasn't about to waste even a second to off-load this man's stories. Without reading the articles first, Peter had no way of knowing what information the journalist was planning to publish about *his* ship. Imagine if Mortimer wrote about Winifred, the stowaway daughter! Or the ship's dismasting! The only way Peter could control the narrative of the story was by preventing Mortimer from divulging any of it until the *Stargazer* arrived in San Francisco, victorious. Then nothing else Mortimer said could possibly matter, except to prove how very many obstacles the captain and vessel had overcome to achieve such laurels.

"I'm afraid you're mistaken, Mr. Mortimer," Peter said, feigning confusion and walking away briskly before the journalist could offer a rebuttal.

"Why don't you share with us what you're telling readers about the journey so far, Mr. Mortimer?" Lily asked. "We can be your audience!"

"I'm sworn to secrecy," he said.

"But who are we going to tell?" Chin asked as he rolled a barrel of fresh drinking water past them, replacing the one that had all but run out. Red and Jonathan, the second mate, took it from Chin and hoisted it into place on a rack above the chicken coop. Fresh drinking water was a precious commodity. The extra barrels were locked in the hold and a new one only brought out when necessary.

Charles Mortimer laughed as the group stepped aside to let Chin pass by. "I do see your point!" he called out. "But sorry, those are the rules. You'll have to read all about it in the newspaper."

Chin rolled the empty barrel back the way he had come. "But I cannot read English!"

"Another good point," Charles said. "Chin, I promise to tell you—and only you—just before we reach California."

"And I'll tell Winnie, and only Winnie," Chin said, smiling as he left.

"And I'll tell Lily, and only Lily," Winnie added.

"Your articles will be the best-kept secret on the *Stargazer*," Nell added as Charles Mortimer rolled his eyes.

UP ON THE poop deck, Zander passed his spyglass to Captain Starbuck. "She's an American ship. Looks like a clipper."

"Then we won't need to shoot them," Peter joked. Although these were calm waters, generally speaking, a clipper ship like the *Stargazer* with much cargo to protect was always armed, the captain always at the ready to defend her. But there would be no need to worry about such violence with a ship from one's home country.

Through the glass, Peter saw the distinctive colors of an American flag waving at her stern. Flying from her topmast was a blue-and-red house flag with a bold letter *B* in a white center circle, denoting that the ship was sailing for the freight company of S. Broom out of New York. "Yes. A clipper. Returning from a run to San Francisco." The other ship would see their American flag, too, plus their swallowtailed tricolor house flag of blue, red, and white from Grinnell, Minturn, & Co. This would signal a friendly vessel—albeit one competing for dominance in the marketplace, based on profits brought about by both business dealings and speed.

Heading on steadily toward the equator, the *Stargazer* had sailed just over 1,590 nautical miles in the past week, delighting the captain, crew, and passengers, who now all fervently wished to say they had sailed on the fastest ship in the world. If the weather conditions stayed as they were, and if Leo's navigation remained accurate, and if the masts remained intact, and if and if and if—

then maybe. *Just maybe*, Peter Starbuck thought, not wanting to get ahead of himself.

Peter couldn't spare much time communicating with the passing ship, as mere minutes could make the difference between winning the world record or losing out. Although, he did think it a fortuitous meeting, for he wanted to hear about the trip around Cape Horn from a captain who had just done it—twice—while also learning news from California.

While the appearance of this passing ship from America was positive for the captain, it was not so for Zander, who nodded once to Peter and Leo. "Now, if you'll excuse me," he said, letting another sailor take the helm.

Zander slipped past the rest of the crew and disappeared into the staterooms, where he planned to wait out the visit in the safety of his cabin.

Sully tsked loudly. "An embarrassment is what that is, to have a helmsman who has to hide on a proud ship like this."

"Sully, slow her down," Peter said, choosing to ignore the slight and redirect the first mate toward his actual job. Sully turned to the crew and gave the orders to clew up the sails and turn her toward the approaching clipper.

Once they were about a hundred yards away from one another, Peter stood on the poop deck and brought the speaking trumpet to his lips. "This is Captain Peter Starbuck of the *Stargazer* from Nantucket, Massachusetts. What news have you of California?"

The other captain identified himself as Thomas Cole of the *Conquest* out of New York City. The two men shouted over the wind and the space between their hulls, neither ship fully stopping. Each clipper captain understood what motivated the other, like-minded in their drive and always in a race with time. The *Conquest*, having just been to San Francisco, now was to return home and quickly prepare to go back, filling her hold with more profitable freight needed desperately by the rushers in California.

"Good profits, great speed!" Captain Cole yelled. The best way to be heard clearly, Peter knew, was with short bursts of declarative sentences. "But we bring bad news as well."

"Bad news out of San Francisco?" Lily asked, turning to Winnie and the rest of the group, her face filled with concern and confusion.

Winnie shrugged. "That's what I heard, yes."

They all seemed to lean closer to the railing and one another, waiting to hear more. Even the crew stood still.

"What's that?" Peter called out over the ocean. "Please explain."

"The whaleship *Chase*, from Nantucket. Went down! In the San Francisco Bay. Last Thanksgiving."

"*Chase* went down?" Peter called, clarifying.

"No survivors," Captain Cole yelled.

His pronouncement carried ominously across the cavern between the clippers. The wind and sea and sky caught the two words and spread them like ashes upon the waves.

"No survivors?" Winnie whispered it to herself as a question, for it couldn't be fact. Samuel Allen was on the *Chase*. With his older brother Joseph.

No one from either ship spoke. The sails flapped noisily around them, eager to catch the wind and sail on. But it was a moment of silence for the dead, and a moment of understanding—and mourning.

"Thirty-two souls!" Captain Cole added. "God bless."

"God bless," Peter called back through the trumpet.

Winnie let go a sob. Lily reached out a hand, but Winnie pulled away and ran from the deck.

As the *Conquest* unfurled her sails and pulled away, their captain made one final announcement. "One hundred and two days to San Francisco! I dare you to beat us!"

And without hesitation, and fueled, perhaps, by the anguish felt concerning the terrible fate of his fellow sailors, Peter put the speaking trumpet to his lips and called, "We'll take the world record!"

Sully gave the order for all sails to be unfurled and off they raced. The skies opened up and it began to rain, mildly at first, and then thunderous and heavy, the first downpour they'd experienced on this trip. Chin went belowdecks with Cook and Red, fetching the empty water casks and filling them with fresh rainwater. Peter commanded the crew to stay on course without trimming the sails, and they drove on south through the slashing wind and rain.

AT BREAKFAST, SEEKING solace from both the bad news and the bad weather, the passengers were quiet around the long wooden table. Nell sipped her tea and chewed a ginger candy, trying to quell the onset of nausea caused by the news of the *Chase*. She wasn't entirely sure which men from Nantucket had been on that whaleship, but she knew without needing names that she would have recognized them had she seen them walking in town or out celebrating on July Fourth at the harbor. She knew that her daughter had sensed the same thing, causing her to dash off.

"Ah, there you are," Nell said when Winnie joined the group a little while later. Her eyes were puffy and red. "Come, sit with me." But Winnie walked over to the port side wall, where she put a hand to the small round window above the settee and peered out at the blue expanse. Nell continued on, "I know how you feel, dear. Unfortunately, I truly do. Losing sailors to the sea is as much a part of our Nantucket legacy as whaling is."

"What a terrible loss for the entire island," Jessie Lindquist added. She had her knitting beside her but wasn't happy with the progress of the blanket she was making. "Beatrice, please undo the whole of it so I can start again."

"Yes, ma'am," Beatrice said, unweaving the yarn.

"You don't understand," Winnie said. "You couldn't possibly." She turned from the window to address her mother. "Samuel Allen was on that ship."

Nell's brow furrowed and then she sat up straight. "Not one of the Allen boys from that sheep farm out on the Madaket Road? Cecily and Jed's boy?"

"Not *one*," Winnie said, and her mother visibly relaxed, misunderstanding. "*Two* of them! Samuel and his brother Joseph Allen both!"

"Are you certain they were on the *Chase* and not some other ship?" Lily asked from where she sat in one of the side sofas, a deck of cards limp in her lap. No one had the motivation or interest to play games.

"Yes," Winnie said, telling the other passengers about her correspondences with Samuel. "And I didn't even write back!"

"Oh, dear. You mustn't feel guilty about that," Jessie said. "Had you thought he'd perish, you would have certainly written to him post haste!"

Charles Mortimer put down the book he was pretending to read at the table, stared at Jessie indignantly, and cleared his throat. "We don't have an official list of names yet," he said, ever the journalist. "Without seeing it in print, you can't be certain he's gone."

"See, darling? We can't lose hope," Nell said, thanking Charles silently with her eyes.

That brought Winnie some comfort. What did that passing ship know for sure? For Samuel Allen couldn't be gone. He was witty and kind, real and true, her friend since childhood.

"Those poor men," Lily said.

Men? But Samuel Allen was just a boy. An overgrown boy, who still had cherubic ruddy cheeks and couldn't grow more than peach fuzz on his face. Samuel had joked about it in his last letter, saying that the other whalemen made fun of him mercilessly. What good was a crew member who didn't even need to shave?

"I shave," Samuel told them. To which the other sailors had scoffed.

"I didn't tell you how often, though," Sam had said. "I like to just go after one whisker a week."

And of course, they loved him after that.

How could one die who had so much life in him? It was impossible.

"But—if they were in a whaleboat, what were they doing sailing in the San Francisco Bay?" Lily wondered aloud. No one had an answer to that.

"Maybe we'll pass another ship that can provide more specific news," Charles said encouragingly. "And, if not, I'll make it my first order of business in San Francisco to find out."

"Before even mailing out your articles, Mr. Mortimer?" Winnie asked, blinking back newly sprung tears.

"Before even that, yes. You have my word."

He said it for the benefit of the captain's daughter, with a confidence he did not truly have. For, although Charles had been feeling better about their travels just last week, he was now plagued by fears he hadn't even conceived of previously—of their ship going down not out at sea, but in the San Francisco Bay! Imagine making it almost all the way to your destination only to perish within sight of land?

As much as they'd already accomplished, the journey had really only just begun.

CHAPTER 15

June 20

The rain lasted for several days, casting a maudlin mood over the *Stargazer*. The news of the whaleship *Chase* going down in San Francisco Bay might have been lessened by sunny skies, but with torrential downpours and whipping winds rolling them, the crew soaked through on deck and the passengers damp and chilly below, the only thing anyone could feel was despair settling around them like a wet blanket.

But today, after four straight days and nights of gray skies and lashing precipitation, the skies cleared. A watery blue peeked out from the clouds, and, by the time breakfast concluded, clear skies greeted them, and a strange calm fell over the ship.

The *Stargazer* was entering the tropics. They would be sailing through summer as they passed Brazil and then into the wintry chill of Argentina and Chile. Crossing the equator would mark entrance into the most treacherous part of the trip, through the notorious—and aptly named—doldrums, and then encountering the horse latitudes before passing Tierra del Fuego—the land of fire—and rounding Cape Horn.

Winnie's life, mirroring that of the *Stargazer*, felt strangely calm, too. After receiving what she now thought of as her Death by Disembarkment sentence, Winnie had slowly tried to accept this as her fate.

She had many hours to mull it over, feeling angry one day, pensive the next, then sad the following day, and, at last, resigned. She didn't want to give up, but she was out of ideas. Stowing away had been such a stroke of genius. And, yet, it hadn't worked.

As they sailed on toward Cape Horn, Winnie's parents had assigned her regular duties in the galley. And although she liked working alongside Chin and Red and Cook and even her own mother, today she found herself looking longingly out the galley window to the bright sunshine, wishing she was on deck with the rest of the crew. That's where the *real* sailors toiled! She may be getting off in California, but she was on the ship for the next two and a half months. Plenty of time to be a sailor! She could swab the deck while whistling a shanty. She could tie all kinds of knots. With the help of other sailors, she could pull the lines taut to raise or lower the jib. She could even use a caulking tool to fill gaps in the planks of decking with oakum, and then seal the joins with pitch. She'd been watching the second mate, Jonathan, do that now for the better part of an hour and it looked rather easy—and fun. Her forearms would turn brown in the sun and her fingernails would get black with grime.

But, after helping stitch sails damaged during the dismasting, her father forbade her—as a young woman of good upbringing—to work on deck. Instead, Winnie was stuck in the stuffy, hot kitchen, her hands reeking of onions and her apron covered in grease. Beside her was Winnie's mother, using the side of a spoon to peel carrots that she piled next to Winnie for chopping.

Cook peered over his shoulder, inspecting Winnie's handiwork like a general with his troops. "Dice 'em into cubes. Nice and neat like. Orderly."

Winnie nodded and held her tongue as her mother continued to work quietly, too. She didn't need a *man* of all people to instruct her in the art of dicing carrots. A man might rightly order her around on deck. But in the kitchen? That felt all wrong.

On land, men hardly ever took employment in a kitchen—or in any part of a home, come to think of it. All of the maids and servants and cooks in East Brick had always been female. And in Macy House as well. Why, even at the Cambridge School for Girls, the entire kitchen staff had been female. So Winnie was not used to taking orders from a man in a sphere that had always belonged to women.

She didn't want to be stuck in the galley doing women's work, but, if she had to be, then a *woman* should be the one overseeing the work and bossing her around.

Which she knew was a silly idea, filled with faulty logic about traditionally male versus female roles. Women could do *anything*, she reminded herself. This philosophy was one of the basic tenets of the Cambridge School. She was taught that women just needed an opportunity to prove that fact to the men who currently ran everything. Her mother knew this, and yet her mother worked beside her here in the kitchen. This notion calmed Winnie's annoyance a bit. For maybe both things were true: a woman could work in the kitchen when needed *and* be the chief merchant on a voyage to China.

So Winnie continued to chop. Her body remained in the galley, but her mind was elsewhere. During the days of rain, she and Lily Bird and Jessie Lindquist had decided to put on a play, rehearsing scenes from their favorite Shakespeare comedies. The performance was set for next Saturday night. Winnie had been cast (by unanimous decision) as Miranda in *The Tempest*, and was running through her lines in her mind.

Standing next to her daughter, Nell continued to peel carrots. She was hoping that the physical sensation of the metal spoon scraping the side of each root vegetable in her grasp would help lessen her frustrations. She wasn't annoyed with the work; the work was to be expected. Nell was still irritated instead with her husband, who had decided on Winnie's punishment without consulting her—and then had told Winnie!

As a mother, she also felt the loss of something she had just found: her seafaring daughter, once again journeying with her and Peter. Nell hadn't dared dream of such a miraculous occurrence, for ever since that night aboard the *Shooting Star* in 1838, she had been resigned to the fact that their two worlds would have to be separate. As business partners, Nell and Peter had chosen to live a life of risk at sea. But as parents, they couldn't risk the safety of their child every time they set off on a new business trip. She and Winnie had survived that night in the Java Sea, yes, but the dream of Nell teaching her daughter the ambitious existence of sea merchanting had died.

So, upon seeing Winnie emerge from the hold, it was as if Nell's aspirations were reborn. Here was her grown daughter, a young woman with a powerful presence and seemingly unflappable inner strength, fighting for her birthright.

Aboard the *Stargazer* was where Winnie belonged. Nell fiercely believed this. And yet Peter had taken that belief away from Winnie and Nell both, without so much as one minute of consultation with Nell.

And thus, Nell's daughter would not get to witness her mother's greatest moments as a businesswoman in a world dominated by men. Winnie could not acquire firsthand knowledge of the China trade without being in China. Even more importantly, how could Winnie learn about being powerful when Peter made rules that kept his daughter from enacting her own strength?

With Nell rebuffing him this week, refusing to be intimate, Peter was growing increasingly frustrated. He believed the two events were not entwined, when Nell could hardly separate them: marital happiness was based as much on honesty and shared dialogue as it was on the conjugal act. In her mind, and in her body, if one part was in disharmony, the other could not exist. Lovemaking was a form of communication. Peter would have to apologize if he wished to touch her.

Winnie hardly even noticed her mother's frantic work beside her, lost as she was in the scene playing on the deck outside the galley window. Sully did not like the way a lowly sailor had spoken to him, and was threatening to use the cat-o-nines to teach him a lesson, but good. A line of Miranda's from *The Tempest* sprung to mind and Winnie said it aloud, spoken softly through the open window to Sully. "'Good wombs have borne bad sons.'"

"Watch what you're doing there!" Cook shouted at Winnie.

Winnie snapped out of her reverie and looked down to where

she had been chopping a pile of carrots over and over . . . into a pile of mush.

"What am I supposed to do with thah?" Cook snapped, his Cockney accent as fiery as his eyes. "Ya made baby food!"

"I'm sorry! Maybe I can . . . mix it with flour and sugar and make muffins?" Winnie suggested.

"Or maybe you can get outta my kitchen!" he bellowed, pointing toward the door.

Winnie dropped the small knife onto the cutting board. "My pleasure!" she huffed, her cheeks hot as the others in the galley looked on. Chin's eyes were wide in surprise while Red studied the ceiling. Winnie's mother only raised an eyebrow and shrugged, as if telling Winnie she was on her own for this one.

Winnie stood frozen in place until Cook picked up a wooden spoon and motioned again toward the exit. Winnie stomped out.

Although Cook probably could go easy on the captain's daughter, he felt like the best thing to do—for both his sake and her own—was to treat Winifred Starbuck just like he treated everyone else. If Chin had made carrot mush, he, too, would have been expelled from the galley for the rest of the working day. No special treatment for Miss Winifred, no siree. It was for her own good. The more she was viewed like any other member of the crew, the likelier she would become just that.

Winnie was so focused on storming out of the galley that she didn't even notice Lily Bird strolling the deck until she smacked right into her.

"Sorry!" Winnie said.

"So nice to bump into you like this!" Lily joked.

She didn't seem nearly as flustered as Winnie felt; she was smiling politely, seeming without a care in the world. Winnie's heart was already beating fast from her explosion in the galley, and now she felt newly angered thinking about how easy this voyage must be for Lily. It didn't seem fair. How nice to have time to amble and admire the sea.

Winnie tried to make her way past Lily without seeming rude. "I didn't mean to bother you."

"Actually, your timing is *perfect*," Lily added. "Jessie and I met a bit ago and were discussing which other scenes we might select for our Shakespearean extravaganza! I'd love your perspective!"

Playacting! Lily was creating dramas because she didn't have to face any such thing in her real life. Winnie was about to say no, and then quickly reconsidered. "Well, it seems as though I've just been relieved of my duties in the galley for the day, so perhaps we can rehearse later this afternoon, before dinner?"

"Splendid!" Lily cheered in her lovely British accent. "But why have you been let go from the galley?"

"Overzealous chopping," Winnie explained.

"Hardly a crime!" Lily scoffed. "Here, come sit with me." She guided them toward the cushioned chaise longues and waited for Winnie to sit before doing so herself.

But Winnie hesitated. Those were provided for passengers wanting to take in some sun and get respite on the deck. Should Winnie be spotted by any of the crew sitting with her feet up, she'd never be taken seriously as a sailor.

"I need to be with them," she said, gesturing to the crew working the day shift.

"Funny you should say that," Lily said, bumping her arm playfully against Winnie's. "Because *I* need to be with one of them, too!"

It took Winnie a moment to grasp the implications of her new friend's words. Once she did, she felt herself blush from head to toe. "That's not what I mean!"

"Oh, it's very much what I mean," Lily said again, her voice low and naughty sounding, like she was reprimanding an errant child. She even raised one eyebrow suggestively.

"I can't even lift one eyebrow at a time. You think I can—I would—with a sailor!" Winnie whispered. "No. I want to be *part* of the crew, Lily. I want to prove my worth on this ship."

"So that your father will let you stay on?"

Winnie's heart skipped a beat. Of course. Toiling on board wasn't just about using the time she had left on this clipper well, but using it to *extend* her time here. "Yes," she said, looking at the sails, the sky, the sailors as if making a pact with them all. Then she turned to Lily. "I need to work so hard and so well over these next months that I'll become invaluable to the crew—and to my father."

"Yes! He will then *beg* you to stay on past San Francisco!" Lily added.

Winnie laughed, giddy from the powerful idea. Then she imitated her father's deck voice. "Oh, Fred, I couldn't possibly make it to China without your expertise!"

Lily clapped.

But like a gust of wind that seems promising but suddenly dies out, Winnie's enthusiasm waned. "The problem is that I have no idea how to do that. I'm a greenhand."

But Lily waved her hands between them, clearing away any doubt. "All you have to do is pretend," she said.

"Pretend?" Winnie asked. "I cannot just pretend to be a sailor," she said, chastising herself in retrospect for having thought this very thing. But reading about sailors for all these years had not actually helped Winnie to become one. Not until she was on a moving, rolling ship with the fierce wind in her face and her fingers freezing did she realize that nothing could replace the actual experience of sailing. "I thought I could. But turns out, there's a lot of learning that goes into it! And my father forbids it!"

"Yes, but," Lily said, "your father forbade you from coming aboard this vessel, and did you let that stop you?"

Winnie tried very hard not to smile, sucking in her lips and shaking her head no.

"So. If you are confident, and act as if you believe in yourself, those around you will believe in you, too."

"It's that simple, hmmm?" Winnie asked skeptically.

Lily shrugged, a glint of something dark and teasing in her dark eyes. She took Winnie's hands in hers and motioned for them to both sit in the lounge chairs, facing one another. "You believe I'm British," she said in her upper-crust accent. And then her expression changed, and she said in a strong Boston accent, "But maybe I'm actually from Charlestown."

"Lily!" Winnie cried out. People on deck turned toward them, so she lowered her voice and drew her face closer to her friend's. "I cannot believe you would lie like that!"

"And whyever not?" Lily said, still in her very American tone. "You may see it as lying, while I merely see it as pretending. Playing a role. Being a British actress on this journey, so that, when I get to San Francisco, I can truly become a British actress."

"I suppose I can truly work on board, then," Winnie said.

"And I'll find a sailor to call my beau," Lily said, her gaze fixed on one man in particular, a tall, muscular fellow with a mop of strawberry blond curls.

"A noble pastime as well." Winnie smiled. The two young women shook on it.

CHAPTER 16

June 21

After weeks of sailing with the force of wind to drive them, the *Stargazer* was entering the doldrums. This belt of calm winds threatened the ship almost more than gale force winds and whitecaps. It was a ship's job to sail through rough weather, her hull engineered specifically for that very purpose, her sails made to harness and capture the ocean wind and use it to propel forward. But without wind, the sails were useless, canvas limp and lame, hull nothing but a giant carved bassinet. Without wind, a ship could drift for days. Weeks. Even months. There were tales of sailors going mad in the stagnant heat, the crew listless and bored as they drifted.

Peter was determined to make it through these calms quickly. He and Leo had been consulting daily about the best course through this belt of waters near the equator, and Leo consulted Maury's notes again and again, taking great pains to circumvent the worst of the calms. In the past twenty-four hours, Leo had taken six different observations, using sun sights and star sights, calculating both for necessity and for fun as he prepared to advise the captain and Zander about how to best navigate through this difficult terrain.

Leo was on deck that morning, as always, fifteen minutes before sunrise in order to find a fixed object in the sky—namely a star, a planet, or the moon—capture it in the mirrors of the sextant, and bring the image down to the horizon in order to determine the altitude of the celestial body, the first step in a long chain of calculations needed to figure out the ship's location on a nautical chart. He saw the captain emerge from his staterooms and waved him over. The day had just begun and the heat was already stifling.

"As you know, the weather has been acting oddly this year for this region. It's not typical to have as much rain as we did, plus that southerly wind in June."

"And now these strange northeasterlies, just as we are entering the doldrums," Peter said. "What do you recommend?"

"I had been planning to cross the calms at their thinnest point, right here," Leo said, pointing it out on a chart spread open on a barrel. "But it's possible that the entire weather system has moved farther north than Maury's predicted latitudes, so that may not work. Alternatively," Leo said, looking at the sky, "perhaps there's a large low-pressure system coming across from Africa—and we're caught in it."

They faced more questions than answers. Besides the seasonal weather pattern shifts, there was the location and size of the calms to consider, which altered on a daily basis. In some places, the doldrums were a hundred miles across, and, at other places and times, as wide as four hundred miles. Plus, once the *Stargazer* lost the weak southeasterly headwind they were currently using, not only might they have trouble catching a new wind, but they might instead get caught in a current that pulled them farther out to sea—and farther off course.

"I'm recommending a significant change of course," Leo exhaled. "Steer south-southwest."

From his place at the helm, Zander whistled, a loud and low exclamation of disbelief.

"That's a huge shift," Peter declared.

"I believe this is the only way. It will help us to use the southeasterlies more efficiently and account for the current."

Peter felt the weight of this decision acutely. If Leo was right, then they would make it through the calms and be on their way to Cape Horn in just a matter of days. And if Leo was wrong? Faulty navigation could cost Peter everything.

Although he'd sailed the oceans for years, Peter had never traversed the globe from this direction, usually heading straight to China from America by going east toward Africa and then around the Cape of Good Hope. So he couldn't rely on past experience, having no prior knowledge about what this particular journey's trajectory could be like. He'd have to trust Leo. And Maury, who wasn't even with them except as notes on paper, whispering to them through time and space like a ghost navigator.

"Well, then. I order you to change course," Peter said to Leo, hoping he'd not regret the decision. "And Zander?"

"Yessir."

"Do whatever Leo tells you to."

The two men nodded and began to consult with one another.

"Captain!" Sully called from the main deck. He had his hands on his hips and was staring up at the mainmast along with five or so other sailors. "We've got a situation."

Of course they did. Would Peter's worries never end?

Peter took the poop deck steps down two at a time. "Coming," he sighed.

THE HEAT WAS relentless and unforgiving. Lily and Jessie were lying on chaise longues under a canopy erected on deck to help shade the passengers from the sun.

"Where's Beatrice this morning?" Lily asked.

Jessie shrugged. "She wasn't feeling well, so I let her return to her room once she dressed me for the day. Remind me to procure some of those ginger candies for her from Mrs. Starbuck when we go to luncheon."

"Odd to be seasick now, after weeks of travel," Lily added.

Jessie seemed nonplussed as she adjusted the position of a large diamond brooch over her breast. "I gave up trying to understand Beatrice long ago. I just cannot even pretend to understand the ways of the working class." Jessie lay back and shut her eyes under her giant silk-and-taffeta hat.

Lily stayed upright, watching *her* sailor, the one with the strawberry blond curls and the muscular torso, as he gathered around Sully and the captain, all of the men gazing up at the mainmast.

"That can't be good, can it?" Lily said, although Jessie still had her eyes shut.

"What are they talking about?" Winnie asked, walking by her friends with a bucket full of hay and grains to feed the animals. After her fight with Cook, she had been allowed back into the kitchen the next day and had since resumed her regular duties in the galley, which included tending to the livestock. Much to Winnie's frustrations, she still hadn't figured out a way to make herself indispensable to the crew—and to her father.

"Something's wrong with the mainmast, I think," Lily said. This comment made Jessie sit up rather quickly. "I better go ask a sailor." Lily tossed a knowing smile back at Jessie and Winnie as she fixed her hair and ran her hands over her skirts, approaching the handsome young man whose name, they had discovered, was Nathan.

Jessie and Winnie watched as Lily tried to flirt with Nathan, but the subject about which they spoke seemed quite serious, and Lily returned moments later with her face drawn. "He says the mainmast has a crack in it. Probably from when the other masts broke weeks ago. Only no one noticed until now."

Winnie dropped the bucket she was holding and ran quickly to the center of the deck. Her father was removing his navy jacket and, seeing Winnie, handed it to her as he rolled up his shirtsleeves. "Father, is it true? About the mainmast?"

"I'm about to find out," he said, grabbing ahold of the standing rigging and climbing up.

Nell, seeing the commotion through the galley window, came out just as Peter began climbing. Winnie explained the situation to her, and both women shielded their eyes with their palms and looked up.

"Yes!" Peter called down a minute later. "It's cracked." He paused there, eighty feet above the deck and slightly out of breath. He couldn't believe what he was seeing, but there it was: a large crack in the mainmast, located a foot or so below the hounds, the large wooden shoulders that supported the topmast and topgallant mast above. It was incredibly dangerous for the mainmast to be damaged below the hounds in this way, for this compromised the integrity of the entire rigging, which could topple in bad weather.

Built in sections, the two-hundred-foot mainmast was huge; with the lower mast rising eighty-nine feet from the keelson, it was three feet in diameter and weighed close to thirteen tons. Also, unlike the upper masts, which were created from one piece of timber, the fore and main lower masts' girth was enhanced to be thicker and stronger with pine staves held together with iron hoops, heated to a red glow and then cooled with buckets of water until they shrunk, forming tight metal belts around them.

The *Stargazer* could survive without a topgallant or topmast, should one of those spars collapse in a storm. But she could not weather the loss of her mainmast, which served as the foundation for the others. Without a mainmast, all would be lost.

Peter climbed down to talk to his crew.

"WE'LL START REPAIRS right away, sir," the second mate, Jonathan, said. He and Sully organized the crew into groups, giving orders about who would man the deck as usual and who would go down below to get supplies and begin repairs with Doc.

"How do you fix this, Father?" Winnie asked.

"The mast can be mended like a broken leg with a splint attached," Peter explained. "Doc knows how to stabilize her."

"That I do, sir," Doc said. "But, if I may, that's just a surface fix." He cleared his throat and looked around nervously before continuing, all eyes on him. "I can make a contraption to hold the mast in place, certainly, but I cannot guarantee that it will hold against fierce winds and squalls."

"We'll stop at Cape Sao Rogue for more significant repairs, once we cross the equator and get to Brazil," Nell said.

Peter stared at his wife. Blinked. "We'll do no such thing," he declared icily, grabbing his jacket from Winnie's hand and walking away. "Doc! Sully! Get to work!"

"Well. Um, I better go have a look," Doc said as he began to climb the ratlines. The sailors grumbled quietly and dispersed to do their duties.

What is my father thinking? As she turned away from the crowd, Winnie caught the surprised look on Sully's face and realized this was probably the first—and only—time she was in agreement with the first mate, but neither would dare to disagree with the captain's orders.

Winnie returned to the spot where she had left the bucket of grain, smiled tightly at Jessie and Lily, who stood wide-eyed and dumbfounded, and shrugged. Then she went to feed the chickens.

"WHAT COULD YOU possibly be thinking?" Nell snapped at Peter that evening as the couple prepared for bed. Nell had already begun her nightly ritual of rubbing French skin cream on her face and hands when Peter entered the room, and so she spoke as she worked, massaging the mixture of beeswax, almond oil, and rosewater over her cheeks and then onto her elbows, gesturing wildly from her seat at Peter's shaving desk. "The health and safety of the mainmast are paramount to the health and safety of this voyage!"

"What is paramount is arriving in record-breaking time to San Francisco," Peter said. "Which absolutely will not happen if we stop in Brazil for repairs. That could set us back *weeks*."

Nell pivoted in her chair to face Peter, placing the glass jar down on the table. "And if the ship goes down?" She didn't want to state the consequences any more directly, afraid always of cursing the ship should she utter such a thing aloud, but Nell thought it, the phrase alive between them. *If the mainmast breaks, we could all die.*

Nell stood. She reached out to take Peter's hand in hers, to feel the warmth between them and remind him of their shared goals. But he slapped her hand away.

Peter looked at his wife with a hardness Nell had never seen. "On deck, you made a statement in front of the whole crew—*my* men—that we would stop in Rio as if this were your decision."

"I said something that seemed obvious," Nell said. "Because I thought you would agree."

"I do not tell you how to run your business as chief merchant. Do not *ever* tell me how to run my ship."

Then he pushed past her, roughly, the sudden motion causing Nell to step back into the small table and knock the cut-glass jar from France to the floor, where it shattered into pieces.

THE MOON WAS a swollen orb hanging above the skylight. Nell had been staring at it for hours, as stars winked back at her around it. Peter still had not come to bed. In the balmy night air, she supposed he might stay up on deck all night, catching a few hours of rest on a lounge chair, smoking a cigar with the skeleton crew, their faces blue-black in the moonlight.

Nell gave up on trying to sleep. She wrapped a dressing gown over her nightdress, went into the living room area, and lit a lamp above the piano. Something was amiss with Peter. He had always had a stubborn nature, a forceful will that tended to get exacerbated at sea, but, even so, he had always, *always* placed the safety of the ship and crew ahead of his ambition. Until now.

This lack of concern for the well-being of others was out of character. Something else was driving Peter forward, something that Nell couldn't see, and couldn't name.

What had Nell overlooked about this voyage? She reached for the huge folder of receipts from the many freight companies who had sent items on the *Stargazer* for sale in California, and began to read through them. When they failed to reveal anything new, Nell glanced around the space, her eyes falling on Peter's captain's log, which had been hidden underneath the giant folder of receipts. What was it doing there instead of out on Peter's desk?

Under the glow of the lamplight, Nell opened the leather logbook and began to read.

CHAPTER 17

June 22

Winnie awoke the next morning to the rhythmic sound of a mallet banging against wood and knew that the mainmast was being repaired as they sailed. Good. She had heard her parents arguing during the night and hoped that more than just the ship was being mended in the light of day.

Winnie's parents' marriage was a bit of a mystery to her. Having not grown up in a conventional household, Winnie had no way of knowing how other parents behaved, but her sense was that the relationship between her mother and father was atypical. Not only did Peter and Nell live together for years at a time in a floating nomadic home, but they worked side by side. She knew arguments were very much a part of a marriage; she wasn't so naive as to think two people could agree on everything all the time for the better part of twenty or more years. No.

But, when Winnie had fought with her closest friends at school, they could each retreat to their own rooms for privacy. Winnie had once even gone for a long hike in the hills behind the school to stomp off her anger and complain to the trees after being left out of a small gathering to discuss the works of Jane Austen. It had felt good to be alone with her thoughts and physically distanced from the source of her pain. She was able then to return to campus with her heart thumping from the miles walked and her mind clear of melodrama.

Winnie liked to think that she had handled it in exactly the way an Austen sister might have.

However, while at sea, an individual could not stomp off very far from one's problems.

Winnie had heard her parents argue loudly like that only one other time, when she was a little girl. The details were lost to her now, but the feeling it stirred in her was the same, of deep foreboding.

The heat in her room this morning was stifling. Winnie wondered if perhaps the South American heat was something half the world was just used to in a way that she was not. She used the head, dressed quickly in her lightest cotton dress, and went on deck to see if she could be of any help to the crew.

The sun was fierce, the dense heat surrounding her as if she was a loaf of bread baking in an oven. It wasn't any cooler out here than it had been in her room, and something felt odd. She heard a cow moo, and then the chickens cluck, and realized what it was that was so jarring and otherworldly: the wind had stopped. The boat was still. The water was calm. The air around her silent.

They had entered the doldrums.

Winnie sniffed the air—and heard herself sniff! She could hear each of her footfalls as she walked across the deck. For the first time on board, she recognized the bleating of each distinct sheep in the livestock pen, mellow and low, a cacophony she had hardly noticed before. She could hear men coughing and breathing and slurping tea, each sound magnified by the silent surround of the sea. The sails hung limply and quietly above them, waiting, waiting.

The stillness was disconcerting.

Without wind, the men still worked around her, repairing the mast and tending to their regular chores, but the ship itself lacked ambition, floating lazily on the unruffled sea.

Her parents were nowhere to be found. Perhaps, lacking anything else to do, they were enjoying a leisurely breakfast with the passengers.

Winnie watched as several crew members unlatched the chicken coop from the side of the deck house and, positioning themselves on either side of it, picked it up. They carried it toward the ship's railing, the chickens, turkeys, and roosters protesting loudly.

"What are you doing?" Winnie asked, somewhat alarmed and somewhat territorial. "You aren't . . . slaughtering them, are you?"

"Nah, miss," one large man huffed as he walked backward, trying to balance the unwieldy and heavy wooden pen.

"But feeding them is *my* job!"

"We ain't feeding 'em, either, miss," one greenhand said. This boy was so young that his voice hadn't dropped yet, his face round and pudgy and his hair matted with sweat and grime.

The large man whistled and the team dropped the pen on cue, eliciting more squawks from inside the pen's bars.

"We're givin' 'em a bath!" the young boy said, smiling wide and showing gaps where several baby teeth had recently been.

"A bath!" Winnie marveled. "Even I haven't had one of those yet on this ship."

"And you're not gonna. Unless you want us to put you in a coop and do this to ya!" the large man joked. "There are certain jobs we can only do during the calms, and this is one of 'em."

Four men, two on each side, stuck long poles through the pen and hoisted it up and over the railing, running the coop out well past the sides of the ship. Then several boys—including the one who had spoken to Winnie—raced up the ratlines with buckets of seawater and hurled it into the pens, dousing the poultry, who responded in angry surprise with caws and cries and screeches. They flapped their wings in agitation as their collected droppings and other muck from the floor of the large crate poured out of the pen and into the Atlantic.

"Fun, ain't it?" the large sailor said. "I'm Bart," he added. "And the little guy up there is my boy, Billy." He nodded toward the greenhand. "He's eight, and it's his first time sailin', so I'm tryin' to make this into an adventure."

"It's my first time at sea with my parents, too," Winnie said, waving up at the boy, who waved his now-empty bucket back at her.

"Hmmm. That so," Bart said.

Billy and a few other sailors grabbed more buckets of seawater from the block and tackles that hung over the side of the ship and then ran with them up the ratlines and hurled the water once more.

"Thatta boy!" Bart shouted into the still air. Then he turned to Winnie and said, in a lower voice, "His ma died last winter. Lucky your da let me bring 'im with me."

"Well, the life of a sailor seems to agree with him," Winnie said. "And I'm terribly sorry for your loss."

The coop now sufficiently cleaned, the four tall men who had been holding it out over the water brought it back to the deck and did the same thing all over again with the second coop. In the meantime, Winnie set about feeding the poor saturated poultry, shushing and cooing.

It had been kind of her father to let Bart bring his son along on the trip. This was the sort of important detail she would never have known had she not interacted with the crew, and she vowed to meet and get to know all the men a little bit over the next two months at sea.

"What's next, Pap?" Billy asked, his blue eyes sparkling. His face was so dirty, Winnie was tempted to wet her handkerchief and wipe him clean, but it wasn't her place. Plus, her motherly instincts might embarrass the little guy, who was clearly trying so hard to belong to the world of tough men—and succeeding, much more than Winnie had been able to, thus far.

Simply being born male went a long way in doing the work of acceptance from sailors. Perhaps instead of stowing away as herself, Winnie should have hid her identity—binding her chest tightly, donning men's pants, and placing her long blond locks under a cap—and stepped aboard proudly as a greenhand named . . . Walter.

It had worked for Anne Bonny and Mary Read, who had become not just sailors in the 1700s, but pirates!

Although how long could Winnie have pretended to be an anonymous greenhand in front of her father before he or her mother discovered the truth? Five minutes? Ten?

"Next, we're gonna clean out the pharmacies," Bart said to his son. Turning to Winnie with a mischievous glint in eyes that matched his son's, he asked, "Wanna help?"

"If it's as fun as cleaning out the coops, then maybe I will." Her mother hadn't called her in yet to the galley, and Winnie was desperate to find any way to prove her worth to her father.

Bart and Billy started laughing, and others around them joined in. "What's so funny?" Winnie asked. She wiped at her sleeves and her face. Had she gotten chicken poop on her?

"The pharmacies are what we call the latrines," Bart explained through the tears that were now rolling down his cheeks. "We clean 'em out, too, when we have calms. Makes it much easier to deal with all that crap when the ship's not really moving."

"As my pap says, it's a shitty job, but someone's gotta do it!" Billy exclaimed, clearly delighted to share the joke with a greenhand like herself.

"Why, thank you for the offer, but I'll have to pass." Winnie smiled and waved goodbye.

As the men's laughter died down in the still air, Winnie walked up the poop deck stairs and greeted Zander, whose hands barely touched the giant wooden wheel before him. "Not much need to steer at the moment," he said.

"I had not realized how loud and ever present the wind was until it was gone," Winnie said, a bit too loudly. In a softer tone, she joked, "I've grown accustomed to shouting." And to holding down her skirts, and keeping her hair out of her mouth, and constantly squinting her eyes, watery from the sting of the wind.

"Hopefully we'll get some puff of air back quickly," Zander said. "And then you can return to raising your voice."

The pair watched as the crew threw buckets of water onto the slack sails, wetting them down as best as possible.

Unlike the work done to clean the coops, this seemed completely unnecessary. "Why don't we just drop the sails? Since there's no wind." Winnie had read about boats drifting for days, but had never imagined the way the ship would look, her sails in a woebegone state, slack and sad.

"The sails need to be ready to catch even the smallest hint of air," Zander explained, sipping from a mug of cool tea that he kept balanced on a nearby barrel. He could only enjoy a drink on deck in the calms, when the ship remained steady and the helm hardly needed handling. "That's why they're wetting them, to keep the canvas as tight as possible, ready for any air to come by. Even just a tiny bit of wind can help. If we harness it, that puff can propel us out of the doldrums."

Winnie nodded, hanging on Zander's every word. This was the first time he had gone out of his way to teach her something about sailing, and she stood up straighter as she listened. Perhaps, without her father or Sully there to witness it, he felt he could talk freely. Perhaps, without much to do today, he felt more generous with his time.

Zander stuck out his unoccupied left hand and laid the palm down flat as if touching the water beyond the ship. "You see how calm the water is right now?"

Winnie nodded. The stillness, especially after weeks of constant motion and tumult, whitecaps, and wind, was eerie.

"Well, what we are looking for is called cat's-paws. Any little ruffle on the surface of the ocean can indicate that there's a hint of a breeze we can use."

Winnie had read about cat's-paws once; the surface of the water turning slightly darker in a patch that often resembled the marking of a cat's foot on something soft like sand or mud.

"This is when we really put our moonraker to work," Zander added, motioning toward the mainmast. "That's the smallest sail atop the skysail. The higher we go, the greater the wind. If there's any out there, the moonraker will catch it."

Winnie squinted into the sun. She found it hard to believe that the square sail up there, which was the size and shape of a dinner napkin, could be anything more than decorative, but she wanted to believe fervently in all Zander said.

"Hello, there!" Chin called from the middle deck, getting Zander and Winnie's attention. Chin held a sharpened stick in his hand, his signature red neckerchief wrapped around his head like a scarf. "Who wants to come fishing?"

JONATHAN AND NATE rigged some lines and dropped a lifeboat down to the water, as Lucky played the fiddle and the crew sang a ballad, the little dog barking along. News had spread about the fishing expedition and most everyone had come up on deck to either witness the excursion or be a part of it. Even those sailors who were off watch were on deck, for it was too hot to sleep in their cabin. They found shade in the corners of the deck and curled up there, their bodies tired from a month of work at sea, lulled to sleep by the repetitive nature of the song.

When first I landed in Liverpool, I went upon a spree
Me money alas I spent it fast, got drunk as drunk could be
And when that me money was all gone, 'twas then I wanted more
But a man must be blind to make up his mind to go to sea once more.
Once more, boys, once more
Go to sea once more
But a man must be blind to make up his mind to go to sea once more.
I spent the night with Angeline, too drunk to roll in bed
Me watch was new and me money too, in the morning with them, she fled
And as I walked the streets about, the whores they all did roar
There goes Jack Sprat, the poor sailor lad, he must go to sea once more.
Once more, boys, once more
Go to sea once more
There goes Jack Sprat, the poor sailor lad, he must go to sea once more.

Winnie had never heard this ballad, but as she watched the boat drop into the bathwater of the Atlantic and the men shimmy down the rope and land safely in the hull, she began to hum the verses and sing along with the chorus. *Once more, boys, once more. Go to sea once more.* Her mother stood fretting beside her.

"Are you certain you want to go fishing, darling?" Nell asked, her green eyes concerned. "Might you not just want to watch from here?

With me and your father?" Peter stood off to one side, brooding over the lack of wind, as if he could will it to return.

"Oh, Mrs. Starbuck, by now you should know that your daughter is like the very wind we are searching for! She has an adventurous spirit that cannot be tamed!" Lily declared dramatically, her fake British accent as perfectly sincere as ever.

"You should come with me!" Winnie suggested.

"Into the ocean in a tiny wooden boat? I'm no dolt," Lily said, shivering from the thought. "There are whales in there!"

"But Nate's going," Winnie said.

"And I shall enjoy watching his muscles work as he rows, and wave to him gracefully from the safety of the *Stargazer*."

Chin had climbed down to join the five other men in the boat—Sully, Jonathan, Nate, and a couple others that Winnie recognized but didn't know. Chin called up for Winnie, the last to join the party. "We're ready!"

"I must go to sea once more!" Winnie declared, making sure her sunbonnet was secured tightly on her head before taking the rope in her hands and using the side of the ship to help her find her footing as she inched down, down, down. Nate steadied her torso and, once Winnie's boot touched the boat, Chin told her to let go of the rope.

"You did it! Just like last time," Chin whispered.

"What do you mean, *last time*?" Sully asked, practically pouncing on Chin from the other side of the small skiff. As he stood, he rocked the boat and almost tipped it over.

"Steady there, Sully!" Nate said, putting out his arm to hold the first mate back as Chin held up his fishing spear in defense.

"I asked the boy a question!" Sully roared, now securely seated between Jonathan and Nate.

Winnie's heart hammered in her chest. She was thinking of an excuse for Chin when he spoke for himself. "I sometimes make mistakes with my words," Chin said, his accent heavier than usual, Winnie thought. "I meant that Miss Fred did good for her *first* time."

Sully's mouth was set in a tight line, his eyes shifting between Chin and Winnie. "Hmmm," Sully said. "So you're both very smart *and* very stupid, depending on the day. I see."

They hadn't drifted far from the *Stargazer*, but the distance still felt vast between the safety and security of the large clipper and this small boat, where Winnie was the sole woman.

Jonathan cleared his throat and began to pass out fishing poles and spears to those who didn't already have one. The sun had burned his pale skin, which seemed to exacerbate the angry acne on his cheeks. "We're looking for anything that moves, boys. And lady," he added quickly, nodding to Winnie. "Anything at all."

Winnie dragged her fingers through the warm water as Nate rowed the small skiff, the ocean stretching out in every direction like a giant, still pond. As the cleaning of the coops had reminded her, Winnie hadn't taken a single bath since setting sail three weeks prior. No one had. Her hair was oily. Sometimes her scalp itched. Winnie's mother combed a special scented powder through both of their locks each Sunday to try to keep the hair fresh, but they wouldn't bathe until they reached San Francisco. How great it would be to submerge herself in the water right now, her hair fanning around her like a mermaid's, her face and feet washed clean, her body's natural odors replaced with the scent of salt water.

"A shark!" Chin called, pointing to a small fin about ten feet from them.

A ripple of excitement ran through the boat, the men pivoting slightly in their seats to see it. Winnie pulled her fingers from the water, her fantasy of bathing and swimming in the Atlantic gone as quickly as it had appeared, just like the shark's fin.

"Drop a line, boy," Sully said. "Next time he comes by, we'll be ready." Three of the sailors had fishing poles and the others held spears. Winnie had been handed a pole, fastened with a line of twine and a hook attached at the end, which she dropped into the depths.

They stayed silent for several minutes, until a movement off the starboard startled them. A fish jumped out of the water and—flew through the air! And then a second followed, and a third. Suddenly a whole school of silver-gray fish with wings emerged from the water, floating along in the still air for several feet before diving back down into the ocean.

"Flying fish!" Jonathan exclaimed. "Hard to catch 'em, but fun to watch."

From behind her, Winnie could hear the crew and passengers cheering at nature's spectacle from the deck of the *Stargazer*.

"Amazing!" Winnie said. She almost put down her fishing pole to applaud, too. But then she felt a tug on her own line. She tensed her grip and tugged back.

Chin, seated next to her, dropped his fishing pole into the boat and grabbed on tight with Winnie. "Steady!" he said. "Hold on!"

There was definitely something caught on that hook. Together, they wrestled to keep the fish moving toward them, pulling until the flexible wooden pole was taut.

And then, a flash of fin. "By Jesus, you've caught a shark," Sully muttered in disbelief, picking up a spear. He crouched next to Winnie's other side. "Pull 'er closer," he said, quietly. "Just like that, there." And then, once the shark was a few feet away from them, he stood with feet planted firmly, gripped the end of the harpoon, and released it, sending the sharp metal point of the spear flying like a dart right into its target, hitting the side of the shark. Blood began to pour from the wound as the shark fought for its freedom, moving erratically from side to side. Winnie's whole body shook from the force of it: hands cramping, knees quaking, mind thumping. *Alive, alive, alive. Dead, dead, dead.*

"Doan let go now!" Sully yelled at Winnie and Chin, who had both, in the drama of the moment, let the pole slacken in their surprised hands. They snapped to attention and pulled the fishing pole tight.

Chin smiled, his teeth flashing bright white against his suntanned skin. "Look at us!"

"I see!" Winnie laughed.

Nate expertly took the line from them both and, together with Sully and Jonathan, hauled the small shark's body closer and then over the rim of the skiff and into the bottom of their boat.

"A pup?" Sully asked, breathing hard, his white sailor's shirt drenched and bloody.

"No, full-grown, but small. A blue shark," Nate said.

Blue, yes, Winnie thought. A deep, dark blue, just like the natural habitat he—or she—had been taken from. Sleek and blue and beautiful. And dying. One ghostly eye stared back at her. The shark lay there, open-mouthed and bleeding, its shiny white belly grown still and gills as slack as the dead air of the doldrums, as Jonathan rowed them back to the *Stargazer* to hoots and hollers and cheers from above, Winnie's hands bloody and numb.

"NOTHING LIKE WATCHING your fearless daughter win a fight against a shark to lift one's mood from the doldrums!" Nell said in her toast at dinner that night, a glass goblet raised in her hand. Her soft smile in the warm lamplight was filled with pride.

"To Fred and Chin!" Peter added. "For providing us with this bounty from the Atlantic."

"To Fred and Chin!" everyone echoed, raising their glasses in response.

All of the ship's officers had been invited to join the passengers for the celebratory meal, which Cook had prepared with the fresh catch of the day.

Chin chewed loudly from his honorary seat next to Winnie, excited to be waited on during the meal for once instead of being the one serving it. But Winnie couldn't eat.

"What is wrong?" Chin whispered. He didn't understand Winnie at all. The shark meat was delicious, her parents were finally proud of her, and even Sully seemed content for the moment. Or maybe the first mate was just drunk on brandy. Either way, the man was laughing by the unlit brazier, telling tales of other exciting fishing expeditions and having a jolly old time. His mind was not occupied with thoughts about who had helped Winnie sneak onto the ship, and for that, Chin especially was grateful.

"We killed a living, breathing, beautiful creature!" Winnie said through tears.

"Yes. And it's delicious," Chin said. Having grown up hungry, fishing for his family's food, he felt no sympathy for the shark.

"You really were brave out there today, Fred," Winnie's father said, coming up behind her chair and putting his hand on her shoulder. "You, too, Chin. You make quite a team. I'm proud of you both."

"Thank you, sir," Chin said through bites.

"Thank you, Father." As Peter walked away to join the officers telling tales, Winnie looked at her palms, which had sprouted calluses and throbbed with a dull ache. She had worked hard all of her life, earning top grades in school and now working in the galley on the ship. And she knew that, as Peter Starbuck's only child, she brought a certain sense of satisfaction and joy to his life. But her father had never expressed aloud and publicly his pride in her until today, when she had killed a living thing.

CHAPTER 18

June 23

Winnie had tossed and turned all night in the stale, fetid air of her cabin, the scent of the shark's blood ripe in her nostrils and its vacant stare haunting her dreams. She still had no appetite. So at the first light of dawn, she dressed and headed above deck, hoping to clear her head.

Several sailors from the skeleton crew on the overnight watch were now asleep, curled up in shaded corners. The rest had gone belowdecks for breakfast, leaving the usually busy deck feeling abandoned.

Winnie walked to the very back of the ship and looked out to the horizon, the soft blue sky meeting the slate-blue water in an endless expanse of nothingness. Winnie had thought the day of the dismasting was bad, and then days of sideways rain even worse. But this, helplessly drifting along in the doldrums, was the worst of all, because there was nothing they could do to change their current predicament. Sixty sailors and a handful of passengers with knowhow and brains and ambition and money were no match for Mother Nature.

A panicked fluttering filled Winnie's chest in the stifling, silent heat. A person could go mad in a listless state like this.

Lines from Coleridge's poem *The Rime of the Ancient Mariner* came to mind. As a student in a classroom in Cambridge, Massachusetts, Winnie had always loved the haunting nature of the lyrical ballad, titillated by the gothic horror of the sailor who had lost his mind at sea and now, as penance, was doomed to repeat the cautionary tale to anyone who would listen back on land. Winnie loved the clever storytelling frame of the story within a story, how the ancient mariner frightens a wedding guest with the gruesome, ghostly, ghastly tale of how he miraculously survived this terrible journey.

In the comfortable, beautiful library at the Cambridge School, Winnie had marked up her copy of the poem, underlining repetition and marking the rhyme scheme with pencil, dreaming of the day she, too, might go to sea. But now, looking over the railing into the vast expanse of the watery globe, Winnie truly understood the epic allegory, appreciating for the very first time what made it powerful. The poem wasn't merely made special by Coleridge's fanciful language and vivid imagination.

It was that Coleridge had been so very accurate and truthful.

She said the lines aloud, from memory, like a prayer.

"Day after day, day after day,
We stuck, nor breath nor motion;
As idle as a painted ship
Upon a painted ocean.
Water, water, every where,
And all the boards did shrink;
Water, water, every where,
Nor any drop to drink."

As soon as Winnie uttered the refrain, she saw and felt a change upon the sea and squinted into the brightness from under the wide brim of her hat. Was the glare off the water playing tricks on her? Had she gone as mad as the ancient mariner? Or was there a tiny ripple on the water off to the port side of the ship—in the shape of a cat's paw?

No, yes: there it was!

"Hello!" Winnie called, trying to get the attention of the only other person on the poop deck with her, a temporary helmsman. "Hey!" What was his name again? And then she remembered.

"Jimmy!" she called, to which the man lazily turned his head. "Jimmy! I see a cat's-paw!"

She was jumping up and down now, miming the motion of a cat's paw scratching the air. Jimmy joined her at the rail to see. "Where?" he asked.

"Port side, about nine o'clock," Winnie said. She pointed.

Two men who had been dozing in the shade or working on other parts of the deck heard the commotion and came to see what the fuss was about. "Cat's-paw!" Winnie kept saying. And then, glancing up at the moonraker, she saw a tiny flap and flutter of sail. "Up there!" she added.

Jimmy returned to his position at the helm with much more vigor in his movements, and turned the wheel slightly left, into the space where they believed the wind was. "Hold her there!" Winnie said, directing the giant man at the helm. He nodded. She saw the wind ruffle the spanker, the large sail at the stern. "Yes!" she cheered. Some of the sailors sleeping around her on the deck stirred. Recognizing Billy, the little boy who had helped clean out the chicken coops, she kicked his small feet, and then the larger pair next to him. "Billy! Bart! Wind!"

There was a hint of wind, yes, only there was no Sully to order the crew about, no Captain Starbuck to direct them in managing the sails or steering.

What would her father say if he were here? He would tell her to face the wind.

Men opened their eyes and blinked into the morning light, and, as they stood, Winnie ordered them about. "Bart, trim the main-royal, skysail, and moonraker! Jimmy, hold where you are! Billy, are you strong enough to trim the flying jib?"

Eight-year-old Billy nodded, but looked concerned. "He'll need some help, miss," Bart said, huffing as he pulled the lines as per Winnie's directions. There were no other hands on deck.

"I'll help him," Winnie said, rushing to the front of the ship. Billy untied the line from the belaying pin holding the flying jib in place and handed a length of the line to Winnie, who positioned herself a few feet behind Billy, her legs slightly apart and knees soft as she'd seen the sailors do, both of them holding on tight. "On the count of three, ready?" Winnie said, too frantic to think of a shanty they might use to keep them moving as one. Billy nodded, his dirty blond hair in his eyes. She counted down, and then said, "Heave!" and then a moment later, "Haul!" and then once more, "Haul!"

There was no response for a minute, but then, Winnie could feel the line tighten under her grasp as the canvas snapped to attention, filling the sail with wind and her heart with jubilation. The pair made off the line securely on the belaying pin and then did the same with the outer and inner jibs, Winnie complimenting Billy as they worked. From her position at the bow, Winnie labored, unaware of her likeness to the painted figurehead of the girl holding a gilded star positioned just underneath her.

"Jimmy! Steer to windward!" Winnie called over her shoulder as loudly as she could yell, for the wind was roaring back into its rightful place on deck, muffling her words.

"Aye, aye!" Jimmy called, adjusting the angle of the ship slightly, turning into the wind, the days of silence turning into a whoosh of nature's cacophony. Wind, after three long days without it, was glorious. It blew back Winnie's hair and brought tears to her eyes. But the wind wasn't agitating her. Instead, this time, she was crying real tears of joy and pride and accomplishment coming from the depths of her soul. Who thought wind could be so joyful and fill one with such a sense of relief?

"Keep her right there, boys!" Winnie yelled, and the small crew aye-ayed her back in acknowledgment.

Zander, Leo, Sully, and Winnie's father emerged onto the main deck from the captain's stateroom, watching as Winnie captained the *Stargazer* out of the doldrums and maneuvered the fifteen-hundred-ton vessel straight into the wind.

"*Semper porro*, Father!" Winnie shouted. "*Semper! Porro!*"

CHAPTER 19

June 24

The *Stargazer* crossed the line just after ten o'clock in the evening on June 24, entering the Southern Hemisphere to much celebration and fanfare. They had left Nantucket only three weeks prior, and had already traveled an amazing 3,780 nautical miles, now perched off the coast of Brazil. The ship had only spent three days in the doldrums, which might have set a new world record in itself—if anyone was counting.

Peter Starbuck was counting. As he and the crew and passengers, all sixty-seven of them, reveled first in the great cabin and now out on the deck in the soft evening breeze, he let himself feel the tiniest bit of hope. He could do this. He and his crew and his McKay clipper could beat the *Surprise*'s time and win.

It was completely dark on deck, but with the glow of lanterns spread about, he could make out distinct figures. On the port side, his daughter stood with her friend Lily, the actress, dressed in their finest gowns and holding champagne flutes as they laughed together in the moonlight. How elegant Fred seemed tonight. He couldn't quite reconcile this version of his daughter—this "Winnie," as everyone referred to her—with his Fred, the child he had seen captaining his ship yesterday in his absence, capturing that hint of wind with the canvas of the *Stargazer* and yelling orders at the few hands on deck around her. An eighteen-year-old girl turned captain, as if she were playing make-believe in a tree in their backyard. Only this was real.

Fred at the prow of the ship with the jib lines in her hands, shouting commands like a man. He chuckled with pride.

Of course, he always had to keep his emotions in check around the other officers, especially Sully, who had been standing next to him when they discovered the scene. Peter had immediately taken over command and encouraged Sully to bark like a bulldog to get his men to work, lest they lose the puff of air as quickly as Fred had found the fickle beast. "Let go of that line, now, Fred, and let the real sailors take over," he had said, thanking her only with a pat on the back as she walked past him, looking angry. She didn't like being rebuffed. Peter supposed no one did.

"Did you feel that?" Bart asked his son, Billy, as Peter looked on, sipping his champagne and remembering when Fred was that age.

"Feel what, Pap?" Billy asked his father, wide-eyed in the dark, his body tense.

"When we crossed the equator just now, we went over a bump," Bart said. "The ship dipped down and up! Don't tell me you missed it, child!" Then he raised his voice dramatically and called out, "Hey, everyone! Billy didn't feel when we crossed the line!"

"No?" Zander's voice called from the darkness. "Well, I sure felt it." Others grumbled their agreement.

"And me, too," Leo said.

"And me." Doc nodded.

"Mayhaps you have to be lucky like me to feel it." Lucky chuckled.

Billy's eyes filled with tears. "Maybe I felt it? I think I did!"

"Enough, men," Peter chided. He crouched down and looked the little boy in the eyes. "They're teasing you," he said.

The boy's expression changed from worry to understanding, and his shoulders lowered in defeat. "Because I'm a greenie," he said.

"Yes. But only on *this* voyage," Peter said. "Soon enough, you'll be an experienced sailor just like one of them. One of *us*," he added, amending his thought.

Billy nodded solemnly. "I wanna be one of us."

Bart apologized to Billy. "Now that we've crossed the line, we can see the Southern Cross," he explained. "And I'm being serious here, no more jokes. It's a steady presence, like the Big Dipper for the other half of the world."

"Does it really look like a cross, Pap?"

"It does," he said, taking Billy by the hand. "We've got to play hide-and-seek in the sky. Find the Pointers first, and then on to the Southern Cross. It's a good clear night for stargazing."

As they walked to the stern, Peter's thoughts returned to Fred. Just look at her now, enjoying her life as a passenger in her fine gray dress and matching silver silk hat with feathers, chatting without a care in the world. Around her neck, she wore the small diamond star pendant that he and Nell had given Fred for her eighteenth birthday, which glinted in the light reflected from the moon and the lanterns placed on deck. Bejeweled, happy, calm. After everything terrible that had occurred on the *Shooting Star* back in '38, hadn't that sense of ease been his and Nell's goal for their only child? After all they'd sacrificed to give her everything, Fred deserved to live her life in an uncomplicated, trouble-free manner.

Fred had a natural gift for leadership, a trait that could serve her well in a more traditional role than the one Nell had lived at sea. Fred could be an exceptional educator, and a mother, of course, too, a woman in charge of a large, prosperous household back home on Nantucket.

"Your daughter thinks she knows how to sail better'n me and Jonathan, now," Sully said, appearing at Peter's side. "I heard her boastin' about it to that actress, the one what pretends to be a high-falutin English lady."

"Lily Bird?" Peter said. "But she *is* British."

"No, she ain't, not any more'n you," Sully said. "That girl thinks she's a Brit and your daughter thinks she's a sailor. I doan like it. Particularly the sailor bit."

Peter sighed. He knew what it meant when Sully didn't like something: that he'd complain to others and get everyone riled up until Peter had a proper situation on his hands. And the last thing Peter needed on board the *Stargazer* was another situation. He drank the rest of his champagne in one gulp. "I'll handle it," he said.

Sully raised a full bottle of champagne he had stolen from the supply in the captain's stateroom and held it out in front of his captain, sabering the cork off with a small sword. Sully figured this would be a dramatic—and effective—way to show that he had access to all of the Starbucks' secrets and belongings. And to a saber. "You better," he said, walking away without refilling the captain's glass.

Sully did pause a moment later to refill Mrs. Starbuck's glass, however, bowing to her reverentially. "Here ya go, Mrs. Starbuck, a nice treat to celebrate crossing the line!"

"Thank you," Nell said, studying the first mate closely. Sully had never gone out of his way to do any nicety for Nell, so why now? The other night, when reading through Peter's logbook, she found one noticeably strange account: a tally of weekly payments made directly from her husband to Sully. As far as Nell could surmise, these installments were separate from—and *additional to*—the crew's salary, which was earned monthly. To get paid in full, they had to stay on in full.

But not so with Sully. Perhaps the first mate received a bonus for extra work? But what extra work was there to do? And then, wouldn't all the officers get such an arrangement?

The drink's bubbles tickled her nose when she held the glass close to her face, as if jumping with joy. Perhaps this was why champagne was considered festive; first there was the dramatic opening of the bottle, and then the aah of the sparkling wine as it applauded its release.

It was like discovering a secret.

You just had to get really close to the source.

Nell sauntered across the deck, stopping for a few minutes to converse with Charles Mortimer on her way to the source: her husband.

PETER ENJOYED STANDING apart from the crowd.

He watched as Fred laughed so hard at something Lily said that champagne spewed from her lips like a whale spouting water. She put her hand to her mouth in embarrassment and looked around. Peter caught her eye and smiled, raising his own glass across the deck to her in a pantomime of a toast, but she scowled at him and looked away.

She was very good at holding grudges, his daughter. A trait that had been passed down directly from Nell. These Starbuck women were formidable. Sometimes, the only way around their moods and resentment was through it. Much like facing a storm or the calms, perhaps he should just face Fred's anger head-on.

Yes.

He had been thinking about this all wrong, trying to protect Fred and shield her from true sailor's work, when in fact, he should be willingly *exposing* her to it. If she saw just how hard a life it was, then maybe she'd be happy to disembark in San Francisco. Yes, make it *her* idea. It would bolster their father–daughter relationship to let Fred feel in charge, to let her be the captain of her own destiny.

Instead of giving Fred *less* to do on deck, Peter would give his daughter more work as a sailor, just to test her mettle. To prove to Fred once and for all that this life was not the one she wanted.

His wife approached, a soft smile on her face. "Looks like you're deep in thought, Peter. I hope I'm not intruding."

"Perfect timing, my dear. I've made a decision."

Nell cocked her head sideways, listening.

"Fred wants to be a sailor? Well, fine. I'll let her be a sailor. As of tomorrow, she'll be on deck with the rest of the crew doing regular four-hour shifts, working under Sully's command."

"Peter, are you certain—" Nell began, but Peter shook his head and spoke over her.

"I am certain, Nell. Just trust me on this. Tomorrow, our daughter becomes a sailor on the *Stargazer*. And I cannot wait to see how she likes it."

CHAPTER 20

June 25–July 7

Winnie was ecstatic. She had found the cat's-paw and harnessed the wind and proved to her father that she was a capable sailor, and now, finally, she was being rewarded for all of her effort.

After her first shift as a crew member on the main deck, she was bone tired and her hands were callused and her shoulders ached—and she couldn't wait to do it all again in four hours' time.

The next week passed quickly, a combination of monotony as she toiled for hours filling cracks in the deck planking with oakum and then a flurry of activity as the wind shifted and all hands were called to alter the sail configuration.

In the evenings after inhaling her supper, Winnie rehearsed the play with Jessie and Lily, with Mr. Mortimer and Beatrice as audience members.

Winnie was reviewing Shakespeare lines in her head one night at the end of the meal when Beatrice laughed loudly and uncharacteristically at something Captain Starbuck said, her body rocking with merriment.

"I'm glad you're feeling well enough to laugh so heartily, Beatrice!" Nell said. "It seems that your motion sickness has passed."

Turning toward her maid, Jessie paused. "You would think seasickness would make you lose weight, Beatrice, but you seem to keep growing larger despite your illness!"

"Oh, I'm all better now, ma'am. I was only sick for a few weeks, and only in the mornings. Mrs. Starbuck's ginger candies really worked! Now I'm hungry as an ox!" Beatrice smiled, scooping mashed turnips onto her fork and filling her cheeks as she chewed.

At Beatrice's proclamation, the men around the table kept eating, while the women—Jessie, Lily, Nell, and Winnie—all dropped their forks and stared at one another in knowing disbelief.

"Beatrice," Nell said slowly. "When I was treating you for seasickness . . . were you really only sick in the mornings?"

"Oh, yes, ma'am. Sick and tired. So tired that I couldn't even lift my arms sometimes to button Mrs. Lindquist's dresses! And my head was filled with fog."

"I thought you were just being your regular old lazy self!" Jessie Lindquist exclaimed. "Lazy and stupid! Not that you were preg—"

"Ladies!" Nell said, stopping Jessie short of saying aloud in front of the male passengers and officers dining with them what they all now guessed about Beatrice's condition, which she herself seemed not to know. Nell quickly calculated the timeline in her head and realized that, if Beatrice was feeling better, she was probably entering her second trimester. Which meant she had gotten pregnant well before leaving port.

"Special dress rehearsal tonight, for the women only?" Nell then asked. "In the captain's staterooms, perhaps?"

Everyone nodded, including Beatrice, who slid a hand onto her stomach and widened her eyes in sudden dread. The true cause of her passing illness seemed to be dawning on her.

"And, Beatrice, bring your sewing kit and your blue dress," Jessie added. "We're going to need to alter some of the . . . *costumes* . . . for the *performance*."

LATER THAT NIGHT, alone together in the after cabin, the women interviewed Beatrice and pieced together that yes, Beatrice had "kept company" with "a very nice man" who owned a tavern in Dorchester for a few nights in April, when Jessie had given Beatrice some time off while Jessie traveled to her sister's country house. Jessie paced back and forth in the middle of the room while the others sat.

Lily let out the side seams in Beatrice's blue dress as Winnie held a lamp close over the work, the two keeping their eyes focused downward as they listened, giving Beatrice a certain kind of privacy as the conversation gained force like a small storm.

"Exactly when did you go to your sister's in Marblehead?" Nell asked Jessie.

"In early April. About two months before we boarded the *Stargazer*."

Everyone did the mental calculations at the same time.

"So, she's about twelve weeks along," Nell said.

"I suppose so," Jessie said, more concerned about whether or not Beatrice could still do her work than with the socially unacceptable predicament her maid had found herself in. "Why don't you ask *her*!" Jessie said.

Nell tried to bring the level of emotion in the room down by stepping fully into her role as nurse instead of the captain's wife. As a nurse, she was not going to judge the poor woman but rather help her as best she could.

On the couch on the other side of the room, both Lily and Winnie sat very quietly as they concentrated on altering the dress. Nell realized she'd never discussed the intimacy of the marriage bed at all with Winnie, choosing to wait until the girl was betrothed. For better or worse, her daughter would be getting some sort of an education about it now.

For better, Nell decided.

"Beatrice, do you remember being . . . naked . . . with this *very nice man*?" Nell probed quietly.

"Of course I remember! Because after we drank in the tavern each night, I would wake up the next morning in bed without my clothes on."

"My goodness!" Jessie exclaimed. Short-tempered to begin with, Jessie had quickly lost any and all patience for euphemisms in this discussion. She slapped the top of the piano with her palm, working out some of her frustration by pretending it was her maid's behind. "But do you recall having sexual intercourse with him?"

Nell had never seen the outspoken, brazen passenger this angry. Jessie's cheeks turned pink through her rouge, which was quite a feat.

Beatrice nodded.

"And . . . have you had your monthly courses since?" Nell asked, stepping in for Jessie.

The maid looked to the ceiling of the parlor as if the answer were hidden among the beams. "Not that I can recall," Beatrice stated.

"My dear, then you are with child!" Jessie exclaimed. "You'll give birth in San Francisco, early next year."

"Yes, January, I'm thinking." Nell nodded.

Beatrice cried. It wasn't clear whether this emotion came from shock, joy, or confusion, but in any case, Nell fully understood the young woman's reaction to the news.

Nell had some practice in midwifery—as all women of a certain age who had gone through their own childbirths did—but, as the nurse on a ship with an all-male crew, birthing babies had not been something she'd ever considered needing to know how to do. And she wouldn't have to now, thank goodness.

January was a ways off from where they were in July. By then, the *Stargazer* would be long gone from California, long gone from China, too, and well on her way back to Nantucket. Beatrice's pregnancy, therefore, was only a temporary problem for Nell. It was a much greater problem for Jessie . . . and certainly for Beatrice.

Since pregnancy and childbearing were squarely part of the woman's sphere, Nell decided not to share this news with Peter. Although as captain, one of Peter's rules was to know everything that was happening on his ship, this felt altogether more personal than ship-related business.

Not to mention, Nell knew Peter was keeping at least one secret of his own from her. She still hadn't figured out what the nature of it was, exactly, but she knew Sully was involved.

"Women," Nell said, standing and stretching the knots out of her tense back, "we will not talk about Beatrice's condition with anyone outside of this room. Promise?"

"Promise," they all said.

Winnie said good night to the group and went into her bedroom, shutting the door behind her. As Lily, Jessie, and Beatrice left the captain's staterooms and returned to their own cabins, Nell noticed that Jessie helped her maid stand gently, guiding her out with a hand on Beatrice's back.

The women had at least eight weeks before reaching California, which gave them plenty of time to come up with some sort of plan for poor pregnant Beatrice. Nell added that to the mental list of responsibilities that kept growing.

Nell could hear the group of women exchange pleasantries with Peter as they passed each other in the hall and he came into the cabin for the night.

"What was that all about?" he asked.

"Oh, nothing," Nell said as breezily as she could. "Just making costumes for the play." She found a small metal pin glinting on the floor and picked it up, holding it out to him as evidence.

THE WEATHER OFF the coast of Brazil was still mild and warm, an endless summer. On July 3, Chin came on deck to help slaughter a pig with Cook. The kitchen staff was preparing for a large Fourth of July celebration and a roasted pig on a spit was to be the main source of both food and entertainment.

"Hey, no fair!" Chin called, looking above him. Winnie had climbed the mizzenmast and was now hanging her torso over the lowest yard, balancing with her gut and a prayer. From the deck, they had just brailed up the sails of the crossjack and were now going to furl the sail above it, the lower mizzen topsail. This had to be done by hand, with men—and Winnie—folding their bodies over the wooden beam of the yard and gathering up canvas with their one free hand, securing it with sail ties called gaskets.

"Remember, one hand on the yard at all times!" Jonathan said from his position next to Winnie. "Otherwise, off you go." He looked straight ahead and out to sea. "We can't save you."

"Only I can save me," Winnie said through clenched teeth, focusing very hard on not falling off or throwing up, or both.

"I can catch you if you fall, Winnie!" Chin said, arms outstretched dramatically.

"No, you cannot," Cook said.

"Thank you, Chin!" Winnie panted.

Several minutes later, Winnie climbed down the mast and sat with her back against a barrel, dizzy with a sense of accomplishment. From somewhere behind the galley's deck house, the pig screamed in fear as it was slaughtered, a rod stuck through its body, ready for the spit.

THE FOLLOWING DAY, that same pig had become the shiny, crispy-skinned centerpiece of a feast celebrating the seventy-fifth anniversary of the founding of America. Nell inhaled the smoky, salty scent coming from the outdoor firepit erected on the poop deck as she, Chin, and Lily decorated the main deck for the occasion.

The flames under the pig were doused and Cook began to carve up the delicious-smelling beast. The best pieces would go to the officers and passengers dining in the great cabin, and the rest would be placed in a giant tub where it would be mixed with potatoes and given to the crew as a special way to celebrate during their regular eleven-thirty meal. Men were already lining up with their pewter plates, which they brought with them from home. They didn't use silverware to dine with each day, instead digging in with their hands and wiping their fingers on their clothes.

Nell had fashioned red, white, and blue bunting out of a bolt of new muslin and bits of rags that she'd dyed with cherry and blackberry juice. It was useful to have on hand extra cloth, to sell to anyone on board who might wish to make themselves a new shirt. Sailors had lots of practice stitching canvas and became quite deft tailors at sea.

"That decoration looks rather lovely, now, doesn't it?" Lily said, stepping back from the mainmast and admiring the group's handiwork.

Winnie agreed as she had helped hang the bunting from the yards. Now she sat hunched over the decking and filling any cracks or gaps with thin pieces of twine. Nell saw her daughter concentrating like she had as a child, the tip of her tongue sticking out slightly from between her lips, her gaze steady. Nell wanted to wrap her arms around Winnie and squeeze, hugging her the way she had when the girl was small, but she knew that now that action would cause embarrassment instead of comfort. Off to the galley to whisk cream for the apple pies, then.

THE BELL RANG out over the soft wind and blue skies, denoting the end of the afternoon shift. Winnie dropped the anvil from her hands and sighed, stretching out her hands where cramps had formed in her thumb and forefingers. She was part of the crew, yes, but Sully kept giving her the same boring job over and over again, crouching low over the planks and filling holes in the deck with oakum.

"All good over here?" Sully asked. He was always watching her, checking her moods, looking for any sign of weakness. When Sully was off duty, Jonathan let Winnie do whatever the other crew members were doing, no matter how dangerous or physically challenging. But as soon as Sully came back on deck, Winnie was given a litany of simple, dull tasks meant for the youngest and greenest sailors.

"Wonderful, thanks!" Winnie said, forcing a tight smile. And then she remembered that today was the Fourth of July, and that she had the next two shifts off to enjoy the party. Her grin grew exponentially and her posture straightened. She stretched the tightness out of her back muscles and stood straight. Winnie loved being taller than Sully. No matter that he outranked her; try as he might, physically at least he would never match her in stature. "Happy Independence Day!" She waved, walking away from the short, stout first mate.

Lily was finishing tying some extra bunting around a few of the barrels on deck when Winnie came up from behind her and jabbed her friend in the ribs. "Boo!"

"Nice try, Winnie. I can smell you coming from a mile off," Lily said.

"Is it that bad?" Winnie said, making a face. "I can't smell myself."

"Trust me," Lily said, putting the final touches on her last bow. "You're as ripe as a sailor."

Winnie beamed.

"That was not a compliment." Turning her gaze to a group of crew members lining up for their separate feast, Lily waved and smiled. "Happy Fourth, all!" she said in an entirely different tone, replete with the perfect British accent.

"May you have a happy Fourth, fifth, and sixth, luvly!" one of the men said, toasting them with a mug of ale that he then drank down in one gulp. America's independence was one of those special occasions when the crew was allowed to drink alcohol. Winnie noticed that the sailors took this task seriously and did a fair amount of imbibing.

Nate motioned Lily over to where he stood in line, and offered a sip from his mug. She took several, her upper lip frothy. Nate wiped her face with his thumb, a gesture that seemed both tender and rough to Winnie and stirred something strange in her lower abdomen.

"Cheers!" Lily said. Then she sauntered back over toward Winnie and whispered, her breath sour from the warm beer. "The only sailor who smells good to me is Nate."

Winnie had seen the pair canoodling in a dark corner more than once as she worked the evening or overnight shifts. Winnie would hear Lily's distinctive laughter carry on the wind, Nate's deep baritone mingling with the waves, and find their shape as if one silhouette under the moon. She wanted to warn Lily not to end up with child like Beatrice, only she didn't actually know what a woman and man did to end up with child. There was the matter of nakedness in a bed, as had come up during Beatrice's interrogation, yes, but also it seemed like one could perhaps also do it with one's clothes on? Perhaps not just while lying down, but also—standing up?

Winnie hadn't meant to see Nate's hand reaching up and under Lily's skirts, but one night the moon had been full and Winnie had been asked to keep watch from the stern, which was exactly where the couple happened to be.

So Winnie did what she had been ordered to do and kept watch.

But she still had so many questions.

To add to her confusion about the relations between men and women, Winnie had heard her parents again making noises together through the wall the other night, when she was off duty and desperate for a good night's sleep. She lay in the dark for at least an hour before finally drifting off.

As if conjuring them, here came Winnie's parents, her father in his navy captain's jacket and cap, freshly shaven, and her mother in an ice-blue dress. They were holding hands.

"You look ill," Lily said.

Winnie and Lily were upwind of the others and far enough from the crowd for Winnie to whisper without being heard by anyone else. "I think my parents have *sex* with one another."

Lily burst into laughter so fierce that she had to cover her mouth with her hands.

"Why is that funny?" Winnie asked.

Lily doubled over, hands on knees. She just couldn't believe Winifred Starbuck. Well educated, wealthy, and incredibly brave—and perhaps the most naive person Lily had ever met.

Lily wiped the tears from her eyes and took a breath. Then she dragged her friend by the arm up the stairs and to the very end of the poop deck, where she told her everything an eighteen-year-old woman should know about sex. "Now, you can also do it this way . . ." Lily said, using her hands to pantomime positions. "And, also, there's *this*."

Winnie's eyes grew wide ten times over. "Seeing your reaction is almost as much fun as doing these things with Nate!" Lily said. *"Almost."*

"But how do you avoid getting, you know, *like Beatrice*?" Winnie couldn't bring herself to say the word *pregnant* aloud, lest it be catching.

"Nothing is foolproof," Lily explained. "But there are ways to minimize the chance. Also, there are other things you can do together besides the full act."

How did Lily know so much and Winnie know so little? She felt like a fool to have to ask, and she also felt angry with her mother for not explaining at least the basics to her.

As Lucky played the fiddle and Chin pretended to know how

to play the lute, the crew ate their shredded pork, and Winnie got schooled in a certain kind of independence.

"Do you mean that a woman can get as much pleasure as a—" Winnie began, trying to formulate her question without sounding either crass or dumb.

"Thar she blows!" Jonathan called out, pointing into the Atlantic. "Whales off the starboard side!" The ship had passed Rio de Janeiro and was coasting toward Buenos Aires.

They halted their conversation and Winnie and Lily joined a crowd of people moving toward the railing to spy the whales with their own eyes.

"A pod!" Mr. Mortimer cheered.

The black whales propelled themselves fully out of the water and then splashed back in, breaching and playing and frolicking in the water, their enormous bodies graceful and slick. They seemed to be celebrating America's independence along with the ship, firecrackers coming up from the sea and exploding with excitement. They dived and resurfaced, their tails sticking out dramatically from the deep. At one point, they swam along with the *Stargazer*, with one whale coming quite close to the ship.

After a few minutes, the whales disappeared as quickly as they had arrived. The crew went back to their meal on deck as the passengers went below for their own feast, enjoying not only pork and potatoes, but also roast chicken, some vegetables, and warm bread with butter.

Winnie wanted to continue her educational conversation with Lily, but knew her unanswered questions would have to wait. She instead sat beside her mother as Chin served them a full Fourth of July feast.

"Enjoy that butter," Nell said, leaning toward Winnie as they ate. "It's the last of it from the icehouse."

Sometimes, Winnie forgot that they were being sustained only by what they had brought with them and nothing more. The drinking water, the butter, the potatoes—eventually, they would all run out. The goal was to make land before that happened.

Nell was vigilant about watching over the food stores on the ship. But, after a month at sea, the produce and other products were beginning to run out. Butter would only last so long anyway before rotting, so it was perfectly reasonable to use it up within the first half of the journey. But, with other foodstuffs, Nell would have to make sure that she and Cook grew even more strict in rationing what was left for the remaining two months of the journey.

After dinner, entertainment was provided by Winnie, Jessie, and Lily, who put on their play, dressing in silly costumes and acting out scenes from several of Shakespeare's plays. While Jessie and Winnie had fun participating in the scenes, Lily stole the show. She was a fine actress indeed, and all eyes followed her as she walked with a limp or manipulated her deep, gravelly voice into that of Shylock and Hamlet and King Lear. Winnie had never seen a person transform and blossom into who they were meant to be before, but that night, she felt certain that her friend Lily Bird would become a star of the stage in San Francisco.

CHAPTER 21

July 8–11

They'd had a great run down the coast of South America. With the winds coming across the deck and filling the sails, the *Stargazer* had traveled over seven hundred miles since the Fourth. Peter had been driving his crew hard to keep up this pace, having Sully use the whip when necessary, but look at how much they'd accomplished.

Peter met with his officers on deck in the chilly morning air. Gray clouds hung low, making it hard for Leo to get a good reading of the sky, although he had been able to catch a quick sun sight with the sextant when the sun peeked out for a few minutes just after breakfast. He confirmed that they were still on course, moving at a steady clip of about ten knots an hour.

At Leo's proclamation that all was well, everyone glanced up and around them, acknowledging the proud puffs of canvas sails, as if the *Stargazer* was a giant winged bird flying along the tops of the waves. It was hard to find fault with a magnificent clipper ship when she was showing off for Buenos Aires.

"Leo, tell us your plans," Peter said.

Leo nodded and rubbed his hands together, perhaps as a sign of his excitement at moving along, or perhaps to warm them. The crew had started to wear their wool sweaters and peacoats, especially in these early hours of the day. The afternoon might warm up a bit, but, as they headed toward higher latitudes, daylight was fleeting as the sun was setting earlier each day. Yesterday, it had set at five twenty. Tonight it would set at five. Winter was upon them.

IT HAD BEEN drizzling all day, chilly needles against Sully's face. They sailed through the night just ahead of a squall, staying in front of it as a northerly wind helped propel them three hundred miles in a twenty-four-hour period. They couldn't beat the storm that chased them, however, and by the morning of July 10, heavy dark clouds gathered ominously and then they were caught directly in the gale.

One minute, Sully was filling the scuttlebutt with fresh drinking water from an extra cask in the hold, and the next, the sky opened up with heavy sheets of rain and Sully fought off a wave that climbed over the port side railing and doused him with salt water. The empty wooden barrel was swept from his hands and nearly hit Jonathan in the face before flying off to sea. The second mate stood stunned, and then blinked himself back to life.

"Reef the topsails!" Sully called as the sky turned black.

The deck was chaotic as the crew sprang into action. Men climbed the masts and moved out onto the yards, gathering canvas as the driving wind and sideways rain blinded them. Another wave came at them, cresting above the ship as it dipped into the surf, the tower of water breaking onto the main deck and pounding it forcefully. Sully ordered Lucky to tie down anything that wasn't already lashed. The old man nodded as he tucked his yipping five-pound dog into a pouch he had made years ago in a vest he wore between his shirt and jacket.

The livestock made a racket and Sully feared the animals might be lost soon to the sea, just like that barrel. And if the water and wind could sweep away a barrel, it could sweep away a man just as easily.

"Grab lifelines!" Sully cried, noticing that several crew members had already started to do just that. "Tether yourselves!" Those that weren't hanging on the yards in direct line of danger picked up lines on deck and tied themselves to the masts and the deck railing, continuing to work as soon as they were certain that they would not be swept out to sea.

"You!" Sully roared. That pig-headed girl Winifred Starbuck had lashed herself to the mizzen and was trying to help the sailors with the lines. "Get below deck at once!"

"But I'm on duty!" Winnie yelled back. And then she experienced a flash of memory like lightning: being out on the sea with her father, pulling a line in tight as the boat heeled in a storm, salt spray in her face as she laughed.

Impossible.

"Listen to me when I give an order!" Sully yelled. The captain's daughter was going to get herself killed. Drowned. Beheaded by a flying object. Flattened by a mast that had already broken once and was now only being held on by Doc's carpentry skills and Sully's fervent prayers. And who would be blamed for the girl's demise in this freak storm? Sully would. For he was currently the commander on deck.

Winifred Starbuck was the bane of his existence, true, and his life might be a tad easier were she to be swept out to sea, but Sully wasn't going to allow the girl to perish on his watch.

Holding on to a line, he trekked upwind and untied Winnie from the line lashed to the mizzenmast, grabbed her around the waist, and pulled her back toward the steps to the staterooms, all the while holding on to that rope with his one free hand. He pushed the stupid girl toward the entrance of the cabin tucked under the poop deck and she lurched toward it, grasping the metal handle and pushing the door open. "There! You're off duty now!" Sully yelled over the roaring surf as the captain's daughter slammed the door shut behind her and disappeared from view.

"WINNIE!" NELL EXCLAIMED a minute later, looking up from the couch where she read in the captain's private living area, a shawl around her shoulders to help keep the constant chill at bay. Her daughter was gasping for breath and resembled a drowned rat.

Peter buttoned his oilskin jacket and pulled his cap low, preparing to go out on deck. "What in God's name were you doing out in that storm?"

Winnie's body was numb with cold. Her arms and legs shook from fear and just-realized trauma. Everything could—and did—change in an instant at sea. Life and death were just a moment apart. It was a truth she had always known, newly reawakened in her, exciting and terrifying in equal measure.

"Sailing," Winnie said. "I was sailing."

ON DECK, PETER joined Sully in shouting commands over the lashing rain as the crew tried to furl the sails. "Thah daughter of yours has always been trouble!" Sully yelled as he worked.

"Indeed," Peter said, because it was true. Sully seemed surprised that there wasn't anything to argue about, so he went back to barking orders at the crew. "Jonathan! Up you go!"

Second mate Jonathan followed the men who climbed aloft and out onto the yards, as was his job, and ordered them to furl as quickly as they could despite the ferocious sea and wind. The prow of the ship dipped down, down, down into what felt like a chasm beneath the waves, her nose disappearing under the water until a white crest broke over the bow, flooding the deck and drenching chickens and livestock locked in their pens, sending water into the forecastle, where most of the crew lived, their clothing, bedding, and belongings now certain to be soaking wet.

Rats scampered from the hold and made their way into public spaces they usually did not inhabit. Cook found himself flattening several in the galley with a cast-iron pan. He caught one by the tail and watched the bulbous cretin writhe under his foot for a few seconds before dropping the pan with satisfaction bordering on joy. He added that one to a bucket. He'd make Red throw the contents overboard.

IN THE GREAT cabin, Charles Mortimer wondered again—was this for the fourth, fifth, or sixth time? He'd lost track—why on earth had he volunteered for this assignment? He was completely at nature's mercy! Winifred Starbuck had just walked past him drenched and panting, leaving puddles in her wake as she headed to her stateroom! Heaven help him. Heaven help them all.

A pile of books, including the one he had been reading until the rolling of the ship made reading impossible, slid off the table despite the fiddles placed there to keep them from doing just that. He had sudden flashbacks to the dismasting, the way lunch had slid right off the dining table, the boat listing sideways in the same dramatic way again now as he fought to stay seated. Only five weeks at sea behind him, with two more months to go.

"I don't know how much longer I can do this," Charles mumbled. He needed to find his bed and lie down. He needed to find his Bible and pray. He might need to weep, just a tiny bit.

"MRS. STARBUCK?" LILY asked, entering the captain's staterooms through the door that separated it from the great cabin. The boat was rolling sideways so forcefully that Lily had crawled across the floor like an infant. Now she pulled herself to full height, using the back of a chair for support. Winnie was there, too, drying her wet hair with a cloth. "Something's wrong with Beatrice. Come quickly!" she panted.

Moving as fast as she could under the circumstances, Nell grabbed her traveling apothecary bag as Winnie dropped her towel and the two followed Lily, each woman holding on to the railing on each side wall and toward the two passenger staterooms at the front of the great cabin, where Beatrice lodged across from Jessie.

They found the door to Beatrice's cabin ajar, the sight of the maid lying prostrate in her bed worrying. The three women entered unsteadily as if by the force of a wave, and Nell shut the door behind them for privacy.

Jessie was sitting on Beatrice's bed, holding her maid's limp right hand. Jessie was still in her dressing gown, having not left her cabin all day in the storm, and her hair was a messy halo around her head. Nell had never seen Jessie Lindquist without her full face of makeup and didn't know what was more shocking: the pregnant maid in the bed or the rich socialite looking like a peasant. Nell pulled up a chair that sat in the corner of the room while Lily and Winnie sat gingerly on the end of the bed, trying not to disturb Beatrice.

"I called for Beatrice *several* times to come do my hair, but when she didn't respond, I used my own key to enter, and I found her lying here in a stupor, with this discarded bottle on her coverlet."

Jessie handed Nell the brown glass bottle.

"Rat poison?" Nell whispered.

"It's not hers," Jessie said, looking ashamed and frightened. "My husband asked me to bring it to San Francisco. The rat problem there is apparently fierce. Much like the influx of rushers, gray and black rats arrived on ships and quickly started to take over the harbor."

"How *horrid*." Lily shuddered.

Winnie nudged her friend. The rat infestation in California was not the point of this discussion, as disgusting as this new information was.

"Beatrice had been complaining of back pain. Do you think she took it mistakenly? Or do you think she—" Jessie said, unable to voice the rest of her concerns.

"Tried to kill the baby?" Lily whispered.

"Or herself?" Winnie added.

"No." Nell shook her head as if trying to free her mind of these awful postulations and began to examine the patient. "I'm sure it was a mistake."

"Yes," Jessie said, although her voice lacked conviction.

"Beatrice? Can you hear me?" Nell asked. The woman murmured something incoherent and moved her head side to side. "Good, she's conscious. Her pulse is weak but steady," she said, letting go of the woman's limp wrist.

Nell turned to the other women in the room. "However this occurred, it's my job to keep Beatrice and her baby alive, to the best of my ability. So . . ." she said, rummaging through her apothecary and locating ipecac. "I'm going to induce vomiting and go from there." She slid an empty chamber pot out from under the bed and placed it next to Beatrice. Then she asked Jessie to help her turn Beatrice onto her side and keep her propped that way despite the natural rolling from the squall outside.

Winnie and Lily exchanged a look and left the room together

silently. Having done a fair amount of throwing up that first week at sea, Winnie didn't even want to be reminded of the sensation in someone else.

ON DECK, PETER Starbuck gave commands to close-reef the topsails, making them as small as possible. Several of the other sky-sails had already been ripped from the yards and torn to shreds. Peter feared that in this gale, the sails could get caught aback, with the wind pushing at the front of the sails rather than coming from behind, and possibly ripping the masts from the spars. Canvas was meant to puff out, away from the masts. The weight of wet canvas coupled with the force of wind pushing the wrong way could severely damage or perhaps even knock down a mast.

The key was to sail as close to the wind as possible without actually going aback. To maintain that course, two helmsmen were required to hold the giant wheel steady in the storm. Zander and Jimmy put their full girth and mental fortitude to the task.

"That's it, men! Hold her right there!" Captain Starbuck yelled over the howling wind as the *Stargazer* heeled sideways, lying almost flat on her side at a forty-five-degree angle, until the weight of her cargo below and her 208-foot keel helped right her.

***SON OF A** bitch.* This gale was an unrelenting bastard, making it hard for Sully to do his job and convince these useless dunces under his watch to go aloft. Bart had sent his boy, Billy, under to the relative safety of the mostly drowned forecastle, and was climbing the rigging as high as he was able, but others weren't too keen on following, and Sully knew Bart couldn't bring in sail without a coordinated effort from others working beside him on the yard.

"Stay steady, Bartholomew!" Sully said. "I'm sending help!" Jonathan was still up there. On the quarterdeck, Sully grabbed a man they called Papa, a young Italian who spoke no English and had come on board in Boston without shoes. Shoeless he remained. "Up you go!" he told the man, gesturing skyward.

The masts above them rocked back and forth as the boat leaned and lurched, the few men at the highest points perched two hundred feet above the deck. As bad as the back-and-forth movement was on deck, it was nothing compared to the extreme shifting aloft, magnified by the height of the masts. The higher up you went, the more exaggerated—and worse—that swinging pendulum felt. Not to mention, the shrouds were slick with ice, making them hard to hold. Frostbite would quickly sting their hands and feet into numbness.

Suddenly, a sailor lost his grasp on the mizzen topsail yard and called out in fright, his voice echoing into the gloom. The man dangled above Sully and Papa. His fingers grazed a line he couldn't catch, and before anyone either on deck or aloft could react, he plunged deep into the waves.

That greenhand imbecile named Wallace, Sully thought. Well, good riddance, Wallace. Sully had seen it happen before, and worse: once a man he knew—and liked quite a bit—had fallen to his death on the poop deck, right by Sully's feet, the man's head cracking open like a ripe watermelon striking a rock.

"Climb! *Now!*" Sully yelled at Papa.

"No," the man said. Sully grabbed the wooden belaying pin he kept tucked into his buckle for swift discipline and began to swing it, hitting Papa across the arm once, and then, when the man turned away, hands raised to protect his face, Sully hit him again, this time across the torso, probably cracking some of Papa's ribs.

There was only one way to avoid being beaten to death. And so Papa began to climb.

LEO STAYED BELOW, rubbing his temples as he sat at the officers' table outside his cabin. It was too dangerous to go above deck and speak to Captain Starbuck. He stared at the chart spread out before him. There was an easier path the *Stargazer* could take, with the wind behind her instead of coming across the bow.

To sail in this other, more east, direction would put much less stress on the vessel and on the crew, but it would also send them far off course, drifting closer toward Africa than to South America. Leo knew that, for his captain, time was of the essence. And he, too, was keen to see if using Maury's notes and his own navigational skills could get them to San Francisco faster than the *Surprise* did. But wasn't part of his job as navigator also to preserve the integrity of the ship and her passengers and crew? And wasn't staying too close to the Falkland Current—and land—another kind of worry in itself?

To further complicate Leo's dilemma, Captain Starbuck had just yesterday offered the navigator a bonus of five hundred dollars should they take the world record.

Five hundred dollars! It was like striking gold without having to head to the mines outside Monterey. Imagine what he could do with that money, should he survive.

As the squall above showed no signs of lessening, Leo weighed several factors, all without the benefit of any astronomical calculations, all without science to help advise him. Using only his mental and moral compasses—and several sheets of paper—he got to work.

Leo took his midday calculation from right where he sat, relying upon intuition and deader-than-dead reckoning, since he wasn't even sure how far they had traveled in the past day, certainly being pushed off their course due to the wind and waves. He concluded that, to stay on the fastest course to possibly win the world record, the *Stargazer* should hold firm and remain on the trajectory they were on, staying in the Falkland Current and hugging the coast of Rio de la Plata, or "The Platte" for short.

Thinking about every step lest he accidentally fall and knock himself unconscious, Leo found Red cleaning the captain's quarters and asked him to send a message to the captain to stay the course.

"Yessir," Red said. Red returned to the galley to tell Cook and Chin what Leo had asked him to do. The steward knew this was an important task, but he also feared flying off the deck like he had just seen a barrel do, and so he took his time buttoning his oilskin. Was his own life worth less than the ship navigator's life? Considering the impact of each of their jobs, he supposed so.

"You only need to go about ten steps out," Chin said. "And then yell like your life depends on it. Here. Hold on to this." Chin extended a coil of chain that lay in the corner, used only when Cook suspended several pots at one time above the stove. He held one end, and Red, nodding, held the other. Then Red walked out into the storm, sloshed through several feet of water on the decking, shouted his message at the captain, who nodded his acknowledgment of it, and returned to the galley, grateful to have done his duty without incident, and soaked through to his underwear.

Then Cook handed Red a bucket of dead rats and ordered him out again.

ZANDER'S CAP HAD been blown off his head in the first moments of the intense squall, hours before. Or was it days before? How long had he been out here, manning the helm? Several lifetimes, maybe. Squinting and blinking into the distance, he tried to keep his eyes clear enough to see where they were going, although in this weather, direction was more of a sensation than anything one could see. It was like knowing you were on the right path in life, despite God continuously blanketing that very path in thick white fog.

Zander blinked again and saw it: off to the lee side. He nudged Jimmy, who held tight to the wheel with him and followed Zander's gaze. "That real?" Zander shouted, even though the other man was shoulder to shoulder with him. "You seeing what I'm seeing?"

"Yes!" Jimmy called back over the howling wind.

A dot on the horizon, bobbing up and down. It was a small ship in certain distress. No sails, and clearly dismasted, she floated helplessly a few hundred yards past them like a cautionary tale, until a white wave a quarter of a mile high swallowed her whole and she was lost to the sea.

CHAPTER 22

July 12–19

The *Stargazer* had survived her first major storm at sea, although just barely. In the gale, the mainmast had been sprung below the hounds, with an oblique crack running through the mast, thus further damaging it. There was no denying that the ship was compromised and badly in need of repairs.

And there was no doubt that Peter Starbuck would sail on regardless.

Oh, he'd have Doc do what he could to mend the mast, but they were so close to Patagonia that there was no stopping Peter now. And, at this point in the journey, the exhausted crew and strained passengers knew well the stubborn fortitude and competitive nature they were dealing with in their captain, and thus no one even tried to stop him.

Papa lay in the small infirmary between the galley and the deck house, shivering with fever and alternating between cursing the ship captain in Italian and thanking God in Latin. Papa had pneumonia, but at least he hadn't died out there. He was having trouble feeling his toes, in particular the two smallest ones on his right foot.

"We'll watch that little one the most," Mrs. Starbuck said, pointing to the blackish-purple swollen nub at the end of his right foot. Papa didn't speak the language, but he knew what she meant: that toe might be dying. He tried not to look at it, even though the foot was elevated and easy to see from where he lay in the single berth.

Mrs. Starbuck wrapped the foot gently in a strip of linen cloth and instructed Papa to drink the meadow-bark tea to reduce his fever. His body felt like fire. No, ice. No, both. He thanked her as she covered him with a blanket and left.

THE SEA WAS still a rolling, roiling monster, but the clouds were thinning out, providing pockets where the sun was visible in the leaden sky. Peter called Leo onto the deck to take a sun sight with the sextant for the first time in three days.

"Mark!" Leo called, reading the measurement from his sextant for Peter to write down. After making his calculations, Leo sighed. "We've only covered forty miles in the last day."

"That puts us here," Peter said, placing his pointer finger on the chart. They had left Nantucket only forty-three days prior, and now they were well on their way to Tierra del Fuego, the land at the end of South America, made up of a large archipelago of islands formed by the submerged tips of the Andes mountains.

The captain and his trusted navigator discussed the advantages of each possible route south, and agreed on taking the more dangerous but direct path, a shortcut through the Le Maire Strait, the notorious narrow passageway between Tierra del Fuego and the Isla de los Estados. Sailing in the wide-open ocean proved challenging in many ways, but drifting within striking distance of rocky shoals was a different worry indeed.

Leo reminded his captain of all that was at stake: going aground in an unusually shallow tidal region, hitting an iceberg, crashing into one of the many rocky crags dotting the waterway, getting caught in the force of wind that funnels down the strait, being hit broadside by a colossal wave and, although unlikely but not impossible, perhaps capsizing. "And dismasting again, of course," Leo concluded.

"Of course," Peter said. "Let's not forget that one." He tried to find the humor in the situation, but they were approaching the deadliest place in the world for a sailor, a ship's veritable graveyard. Navigating through the Drake Passage and around Cape Horn was a trip that Peter, even with all his years of sailing experience, had never done before. Nor had his ship. Until gold was discovered in California, the Horn was primarily a path used only for whalers hunting in the Pacific.

"I've been round the Horn three times, sir, but I've never gone through the strait," Leo said, wanting to make his prior experience known so that, should anything go awry, he couldn't be blamed for it. Not entirely, at least.

Neither man knew quite what they were doing, then. But what a victory if they managed it well. Once they navigated through the strait, they would be less than a day from the Horn.

THE MORNING OF the nineteenth was very cold, the sky a pale icy white against a blue-black sea. In the past few days, the *Stargazer* had made tremendous progress, sailing over 750 miles at an average of twelve knots an hour. During the late day and overnight hours, the crew on deck had successfully maneuvered the ship toward the strait, and now, with the wind blowing strong and steadily, the *Stargazer* was at the tip of Patagonia. Rocky inlets jutted out from the coastline, the rugged, desolate landscape barren of trees or life of any kind, except that which could swim between the icebergs or fly over the rough promontories. Condors soared above and around the *Stargazer*, their black wings spanning ten feet across, while other strange and unfamiliar birds perched on craggy islands, watching with predatory mendacity.

The crew paused in their work to watch penguins waddle awkwardly across the rocks and then dive into the water, swimming with speed and grace.

It rained constantly, except when it misted or drizzled. There were not enough words in the English language to describe all the types of precipitation that had kept Winnie wet the past week.

"We call this an Irishmen's hurricane," Bart whispered to Winnie and Billy as he squinted at the sky.

"Why d'you call it that, Pap?" Billy asked.

"Because the Irish make a big deal outta *nuthin*, son," he explained once Sully had walked past and was out of earshot. Sully had no sense of humor, and he certainly didn't like it when sailors made fun of his country of origin. It wasn't personal, Winnie now knew. Sailors picked on just about everyone. Joking was a good way to pass the time, and laughing reminded the crew that they were human.

Once that squall off Buenos Aires had abated and Winnie had been allowed back on deck, she had all but lost herself in the mind-numbing, grueling work of being a sailor.

Something had changed in her that day when she had been out in the madness, facing the arbitrary mood of Mother Nature, something essential about herself suddenly clear. Because despite everything that told her she should be afraid, she wasn't. That day, she had been surrounded by danger—a man had died, for goodness' sake! Another, that Italian named Papa, had pneumonia and still lay in bed with frostbite threatening to take a toe or two—and yet, instead of feeling cowed, she had felt invigorated.

Perhaps there was something wrong with her for not being more demure, more ladylike, more fearful. Certainly, Jessie Lindquist thought Winnie had gone mad, wanting to sail when she could be in front of the fire playing whist with Jessie and the other women—including the now-recovered, although still weak, Beatrice. Lily had been more understanding, or at least had used her acting skills to pretend so, encouraging Winnie to sail if she must, but within reason. Lily had made Winnie promise to leave her post voluntarily should she ever be in harm's way again, which Winnie dutifully did, swearing on a copy of *The Taming of the Shrew* because neither woman had a Bible handy.

It turned out, swearing thusly to Lily was unnecessary, for her parents had expressly forbidden her from being on deck in a storm ever again. "Use common sense, Fred," her father had said, his face lined from exhaustion and worry after the squall had passed, his beard dripping wet as the icicles melted from the matted hair.

The three of them had gathered in their living room after their first hot meal in days. They had changed into dry clothes, and Winnie's heart stopped galloping. "You fought your way on board this ship like a scrappy sailor, yes, but now you can't just act like any old sailor, because you're not. Their lives, while important, are also—how can I say this without sounding callous?—dispensable. But you, Fred—you are my child, our only child, and are thus irreplaceable."

"If I'm not a scrappy sailor, then start treating me like what I am, a *Starbuck*. The daughter of a successful ship captain and sea merchant. Give me something real to do, something important."

And so, the three agreed that Winnie could be on deck as long as conditions were mild. "But as soon as we get to the Le Maire Strait, you're inside until I say so." One thing that made this approach to the Horn particularly difficult was that they were sailing west against a strong east-moving current and into the wind, the wrong way, so to speak, all the way around. Ships that made it through were rewarded on the back side with the calmer, more favorable winds and tides of the Pacific.

Today was probably going to be Winnie's last day on deck for a while, she knew, feeling the drastic change in temperature as she said hello to Lucky and Yip.

Yip stayed tucked inside Lucky's vest, safe against the arctic chill, one tiny pointed ear sometimes poking out. The waves were like nothing Lucky had ever seen before, even in a half century at sea. They gathered strength from thousands of miles of open ocean and appeared before the *Stargazer* as tall as the white spire atop Old North Church in Boston. "Don't let these honkers scare ya," Lucky whispered into his vest, but the dog trembled nonetheless.

Winnie could see her breath as she worked beside Bart and Billy, changing the sail configuration once more as the crew navigated the unpredictable and choppy push-and-pull currents where the Atlantic met the Pacific at the bottom of the world.

THEY HAD TO attempt the strait during daytime, for trying to sail through the channel without being able to see the craggy shoreline on either side was certain death, according to both Maury's navigational advice and years of tales of doomed ships that learned the hard way. And at this time of year, as close as any intrepid sailor or explorer had been to the South Pole, there were only seven hours of daylight. A ship and her captain had to time it just right so they didn't get caught in the middle of the channel in a sheet of darkness.

Peter met with his officers, Zander staying mostly quiet as the others blew almost as hard as the winds, sharing opinions about when might be the best time to get through the strait.

Wearing their heaviest, warmest gear, the group huddled together on the poop deck and shouted to one another over the increasing storm. "We should go now, while we still have plenty of daylight!" Peter said.

Leo said, "Or we could wait an hour to see if the wind shifts in a more favorable direction."

"That's a lost hour!" Peter roared back. "We need all the daylight we can get, weak as it is."

Sully nodded, agreeing with the captain. Sully almost always agreed with his captain, and Zander wondered, not for the first time, if there was something else behind this man's blind loyalty than actual blind loyalty. Was Captain Starbuck paying Sully a bonus for keeping his men in line and doing whatever the captain ordered? Or was it the other way? Did the captain have something on Sully that kept the first mate afraid and on his best behavior?

I feel like I'm looking at an iceberg with those two, Zander thought, *only seeing what's visible above the surface*. But there was something large—and potentially dangerous—hidden beneath. So, like the helmsman that he was, Zander decided to give their personal glacier a wide berth and steer clear.

Within minutes, the rain turned to heavy, wet snow, and Peter dismissed Jonathan and Sully to reef more sails with the crew, lest the canvas grow too heavy with ice already forming upon it. Then the captain looked around him, calling, "Fred! Where is she? Someone better make sure my daughter gets inside safely! *Now!*"

"Yessir!" a male voice called from somewhere on the quarter-deck, and Zander saw Winifred Starbuck stomp off, her boots leaving angry little prints in the dusting of snow on the planks. He knew sailors in the forecastle enjoyed gossiping about that girl bringing not only bad luck to the ship, but perhaps having a death wish, too. Zander thought that was all hogwash. He admired her for her spunk.

"Visibility is dropping by the second, sir," Zander said, and Captain Starbuck nodded and sent him to his post. The horizon line had completely vanished, and all was white around them as Zander returned to the helm to help Jimmy steer. Although Zander couldn't see much, he could see the captain and Leo gesturing wildly to one another, clearly not in agreement about what to do.

Enormous whitecaps towered above the ship, cresting and breaking around them. The *Stargazer* kept her ballast but rocked and rolled and moved perpetually as part of the sea's dance.

MAKING HER WAY back into the staterooms, Winnie bumped into the corner of the dining table with one hip and then her father's desk with the other thigh. By the time she reached her own cabin, she was bruised and beaten—and incredibly thankful not to be outside anymore. She sank to her berth and peeled the wet, woolen gloves from her numb hands, rolling her ankles to bring feeling back into her feet.

Although she'd read sailors' accounts of the brutal conditions from Tierra del Fuego down and all the way through the Drake Passage, Winnie had never imagined waves that high, with hurricane-force winds as part of the everyday weather pattern, the sky dark even when it was daylight.

This place was truly a nightmare. For the first time since those days locked in the hold, Winnie was properly scared. Maybe she should have been all along.

"Winnie? Are you here?" her mother called.

"Yes, Mother!" she called back over the roaring of the wind and the creaking of the ship. "Safe in my berth."

Her mother wrenched the door to Winnie's cabin open, eyes panicked. "Oh, good. I need you in the sick bay. Now."

"What? Why?" Winnie said, fastening the wet boots she had just been removing.

"Papa, the Italian man," her mother said, pulling up the hood on her wool cape. "Two of his toes have turned black. An infection is going to set in tonight if we don't remove them."

"Now?" Winnie asked. They had no daylight to work by, and the ship was pitching and rolling. How would they keep their hands steady? How could they see without lighting a lamp that might fall over and catch fire? Not to mention—how exactly did one remove toes from another person? Had her mother ever performed an amputation before?

"Now," Winnie's mother said.

Inside the sick bay at the rear of the deckhouse, Cook stood with a sharp, serrated bread knife in one hand and a bottle of brandy and a lit lamp in the other. Red held Papa's shoulders down while Chin took charge of the man's legs. "He drank half the bottle to dull the pain and now he's good and sleepy. I cleaned the knife with some of the bourbon. So. He's as ready as he'll ever be," Cook said to Mrs. Starbuck as she and Winnie shrugged off their wet coats.

"I suppose we all are," Nell said, taking the knife from Cook and moving toward the bed.

"Wait!" Chin said. "You have to take a swig of the drink. We all did." *Swig* was one of Chin's new favorite words: more than a sip and less than a gulp.

Nell took the bottle from Cook and winced as she swallowed the fiery alcohol. Then she passed it to Winnie, who did the same.

Cook held the lamp close to Papa's right foot, which smelled of rotting meat. The pinky toe and the one next to it had to go, that was clear.

Papa moaned softly as Nell uttered a prayer. This was followed by a loud *crack* as Nell cut cleanly through the small bones in Papa's two blackened toes.

The man's fierce screams were swallowed by the sea.

"WE'VE GONE AS far south as we can go without turning!" Leo shouted to Captain Starbuck on deck. He had to explain to this stubborn, singularly focused man how much in jeopardy they truly were. "If we go any further in this direction, battling the east-northeast winds and the churning current, we risk being pushed onto a lee shore." The two watched the water running out behind the ship, which instead of running straight, pulled off to the east, confirming everything Leo was saying. Since a square-rigged ship like theirs had a hard time sailing to windward, they could very well end up on the rocks around the curve of Tierra del Fuego known as Cape San Diego.

"We *cannot* get through the strait today!" Leo added. "We must turn back and wait out this storm and try again tomorrow."

Peter Starbuck barked at Leo, a harsh sound that was part laugh and part growl. "Wait out *this* storm? Welcome to Cape Horn, my friend, where every day presents a new storm! We cannot decide based on weather alone or we'll never get through the strait!"

"It's a whiteout, sir. Right now, our man on watch wouldn't even see rocks ahead—or an iceberg below—should we be right upon it."

"But we're at the mouth of the strait, Leo! I hate to give up now."

The captain's dark eyes appeared black against the white ice clinging to his lashes and eyebrows, like the man himself had grown numb from the inside out, his heart hardened against anything but winning. Leo didn't know if Peter Starbuck cared at all about the safety of the ship or his men at this moment, so focused was he on speed. So Leo used the only argument left that he could think of that might remind the captain of his humanity. "If you want to win the world record, we have to make it past this alive. Think of Winifred," he said. "And Nell. Think of your legacy—and of what kind of story you want people to tell about you someday."

Leo saw something shift in Captain Starbuck's face, a softening in his eyes as he blinked. It may have been a vision of his wife and child, sure, but Leo would bet it was the last bit that truly won him over, for he knew Captain Starbuck cared greatly about his reputation and legacy.

"Very well," he said. He removed the speaking trumpet from where it was lashed to the deck inside a wooden box and turned to address Sully and the crew.

"Mr. Sullivan, all hands! All hands on deck! We're turning her north!"

Leo felt relieved as the crew around him prepared the clipper to turn, although his relief was fleeting. He knew they weren't completely done with danger yet. Turning a ship was a difficult and precarious maneuver amid these giant waves, and they had to time their turn just right. Should a huge wave hit them astern as they were in the middle of changing course, they could end up pooping the ship. A tidal-sized wave breaking at a speed of twenty knots on the poop deck would shatter skylights, wash sailors overboard, and flood the ship, the force of water traveling across the deck and smashing the forecastle to bits.

Deciding that advising the bullheaded captain was no longer his concern, he excused himself to the galley to stand by the roaring fire, only to remember upon entering the chilly room that the warm stoves couldn't be lit. To add to his frustration, the cook, the steward, and the cabin boy were all absent! And the bourbon was missing from the hiding spot where Cook kept it. Damn. Leo imagined these men drunk and warm and merry in their officers' cabins and he hated them for it, the cowardly bastards.

IN THE SICK bay, Cook gathered the two dismembered, fleshy nubs in a piece of cloth and stuck them deep into his pocket to discard overboard. He handed more clean cloth to Mrs. Starbuck, who bandaged the wound as Papa writhed in pain.

"Thatta boy, Papa," Cook said. "You're doing just great. The worst is over."

Winnie found the bottle of bourbon on the bed and passed it around the small room. Red, trying to hold Papa's torso down without passing out himself, looked like he needed it the most.

CHAPTER 23

July 22–23

The *Stargazer* managed to come about without pooping the ship, and then made two more failed attempts at approaching the Le Maire Strait over the following two days before finally being graced with more favorable conditions on the morning of July 22. With a strong easterly wind and clearer skies, and Peter Starbuck in a much better mood, the ship sailed through the seven-mile strait.

Although the waves were still mammoth and the temperatures frigid, the passengers joined the crew on deck for the first time in more than a week, dressed in their warmest clothing, stretching their legs and turning their faces toward the dim but present sunlight. The scenery was majestic, with snowcapped cliffs rising on both sides of the ship. The caw of pigeons, giant albatross, and other birds filled the air with a living cacophony that they had all missed hearing out at sea, the ship so far offshore at points that no birds had flown above them.

Charles Mortimer squinted into the sunlight, feeling like a bear coming out of hibernation as he walked along the main deck. Overnight, they would enter the Drake Passage and tomorrow they would round Cape Horn. These desolate sea swells were mesmerizing and terrifying and somehow made Charles Mortimer feel more alive.

Nell and Winnie also came up on deck, joining Peter and congratulating him for taking such good care of the ship—and of her crew and passengers. Peter had bags under his eyes and gray stubble growing amid his dark whiskers. He looked pale and thin.

"I'm exhausted," Peter said. Had he slept at all in the past week? Who could remember? "I had a waking dream in which you amputated a sailor's toes!"

Nell smiled sadly. "Oh, that was no dream. It was truly a nightmare."

"Did you really?" He looked around for confirmation.

Winnie nodded. "And I assisted, Father."

"My God!" he said. "And the man . . . survived this?"

"He did." Nell nodded. "We avoided infection and he's looking much better overall. Now, leave Sully in charge and get some rest. Doctor's orders!"

Peter promised to lie down after lunch.

Lily sat in a deck chair, her sketchbook open before her as she tried to capture the magnificent landscape in sharp lines of charcoal pencil. Next to her were Jessie and Beatrice, now fully recovered, both women also enjoying the view.

"Only a few people in the world will ever get the opportunity to see what we are, to experience this," Jessie said. "We are lucky to be alive. Aren't we, Beatrice?"

"Yes, ma'am," Beatrice said, her smile small but sincere.

Jessie took Beatrice's hand in her own and held on. Beatrice seemed much better since that whole fiasco with the rat poison. Beatrice never said whether the act was accidental or not, and Jessie, pushy as she usually was, had decided to let the matter drop. As long as the woman was healthy, which she seemed to be. And just yesterday, Nell had put her ear to Beatrice's belly using some contraption called a stethoscope, similar in shape to the captain's trumpet, through which she could apparently hear the baby's little heartbeat! So, that meant both mother and baby were well. Tears stung Jessie's eyes. What a scare. For as brave as Jessie Lindquist appeared to the world, she didn't know how she'd truly navigate without Beatrice by her side.

"I must say, it *is* much nicer to be at sea without the constant fear of death," Lily joked as she shaded in a bit of sky on the parchment.

She wanted to remember this day forever, so she was drawing an image to keep in her journal, to capture it all.

THE NEXT MORNING, Chin climbed down from his berth atop the triple wooden bunk in the deckhouse—as the smallest, he slept on the top, nose inches from the ceiling, while Red took the middle and Cook the bottom. He was about to relieve himself in a chamber pot, when he looked out the small window and saw . . . sun! For the first time in weeks, the sun was a glowing bright orb glistening on the water. And the water! Chin couldn't believe it. Gone were the ferocious whitebeards, replaced with smaller, gentler blue waves. Normal waves. Regular waves.

A lovely day to relieve oneself outside, then. Chin stepped into the deceptively warm morning air and went to urinate in the head.

"It's fifty degrees out!" Chin announced, stepping into the galley minutes later. He had just checked the barometer nailed to the side of the mizzenmast and confirmed what his body had told him: despite being close to the tip of South America, it was warm out there.

"And calm like a lake," Cook added. "I fired up the stoves."

Cook gave Chin a list of chores for the day and started humming "Roll the Old Chariot Along," for despite everything they'd encountered—the ship's masts breaking, the stowaway girl reveal, days of nothingness drifting through the dreary doldrums followed by nights of violent storms in the frigid Tierra del Fuego, an act of poisoning, and an amputation—today the *Stargazer* was rounding Cape Horn.

NELL, PETER, AND Winnie stood together on the poop deck, the soft breeze moving gently against Nell's dress skirt while the sails around them billowed. Peter had called for all hands on deck, not due to calamity, but rather to witness as one the moment the *Stargazer* rounded Cape Horn. As the passengers and crew gathered below them on the main deck, Nell felt sentimental for an earlier time. Just seven weeks prior, they had launched the *Stargazer* from

Nantucket Harbor, Peter wearing a starched white shirt under his navy captain's jacket, freshly shaven and just pressed. Although her husband had been pompous from the moment he donned his captain's gear and assumed command, Nell never could have predicted the ways in which he would have grown so altered, so singularly focused over this journey.

Peter looked at her as he scratched his thick beard. This had become a nervous habit of late, Peter incessantly scratching his facial hair, although perhaps it had nothing to do with being anxious and everything to do with fleas.

Nell would get a lemon from Cook and, tonight before bed, make sure Peter lathered up his beard and gave it a good scrub, using half of the juice for an aftershave tonic that worked as a natural flea-killer and repellent. The other half she'd save to drink in her tea, part of everyone's weekly dose of citrus to avoid scurvy.

It had been a wondrous and difficult time at sea. Perhaps neither one of them had been taking enough notice—and care—of one another, so busy had they been with more pressing, daily concerns. But nothing was more important than their union, Starbuck & Starbuck, husband and wife, mother and father, sea captain and merchant. None of this was possible without their partnership. Success relied on speed, certainly, but also on their shared vision for the future.

The passengers stood in the front row. Lily, Jessie, and Beatrice held hands with Mr. Mortimer close beside them. At the last moment, Winnie left her parents standing on the poop deck and took the steps down to join her friends—and her crew—on the main deck. She linked Beatrice's free hand with her own and looked up at her parents. They made a striking couple, with the majestic snowcapped Andes now shrunken behind them while towering icebergs glowed turquoise in the distance ahead, looking otherworldly. But Winnie didn't belong with them. She belonged on deck with the crew.

Together, they had traveled over 8,200 miles, sailing approximately 160 miles a day. *Semper porro.* Ever forward.

Standing with Chin and Red just behind Winnie, Cook began to sing, the tune he had been humming all morning rising up from his throat like a prayer, the words of the song bursting forth: "Oh, we'd be all right if the wind was in our sails, We'd be all right if the wind was in our sails, We'd be all right if the wind was in our sails." By the time he had finished the first line, other voices joined in to finish the stanza, "And we'll all hang on behind," until all on deck sang the chorus together.

Oh, we'd be all right if we make it round the Horn
We'd be all right if we make it round the Horn
We'd be all right if we make it round the Horn
And we'll all hang on behind.

On July 23, 1851, fifty days and eighteen hours after leaving Nantucket Harbor, the *Stargazer* rounded Cape Horn and entered the Pacific Ocean, well on her way to breaking the world record.

PART II

San Francisco

The Golden Gate

CHAPTER 24

November 26, 1850
Aboard the Nantucket whaleship Chase
San Francisco Bay

The fog came out of nowhere.

First the balmy blue sky darkened, purple pink over the Pacific, day softening into evening. Then a heavy blanket enveloped the Nantucket whaleship *Chase*. Quicker than you could say Cal-if-or-nay-ae, everything in front of them—and behind—disappeared. And above and below, too: the sky that had just been was no more, the headlands evaporated, the waters gone. Even sound vanished.

She's like the Gray Lady, the crew thought, troubled by this sudden change in atmospheric events. Wary even. But wary not because fog was new to them. Rather, the inverse: their worries came precisely due to fog's familiarity.

Because if anyone knows fog, it's a Nantucketer. Born and raised on an island shrouded in mist helps one learn to respect fog—and to fear it. Located thirty miles out to sea, Nantucket was both master of and mistress to the fickle weather. When fog rolled in quick and thick over the island, navigation by boat was nearly impossible.

"Clew up the sails! Prepare to drop anchor!" the captain ordered.

"Aye-aye, sir!" they called back.

The whaleship *Chase* had not planned on docking in San Francisco Bay, but the nearer it came to the jagged coastline of California, the stronger the lure of the lore. Gold. Shimmering in the rivers of the mind, tributaries of possibility, wealth the likes of which the crew of the *Chase* had never seen. Years of relentless hard work hunting whales in the Pacific had brought each man on board—what? A percentage of a percentage of nothing? All the profits going to the captain and ship owners! After two years of this foolishness, the crew was tired of sharing food with rats and maggots, tired of stinking like blubber that made their eyes water. Tired, in fact, of living a life at sea. What they wanted now was to dig their hands into soil, to feel the earth beneath their feet, to stand on solid ground and mine for riches. Riches of their own making and for their own taking.

And no more close quarters. In the great new state of California, there was room aplenty and it was every man for himself. Each individual entitled to the entirety of what he mined. Finders keepers.

Thus, called by a potent mix of curiosity and greed, the *Chase* found itself inexorably pulled toward the green-and-gold hills of San Francisco, her bow passing through the narrow Golden Gate Strait, excitement turning into a fervor over gold fever.

Imagine striking a rock and finding gold.

Imagine striking a rock.

As fast as it arrived, the fog lifted, giving the crew a moment to see the craggy reef before the *Chase*'s port side smashed into it, ripping a gash in the hull.

"All hands on deck!" the captain cried through a sudden fierce wind. "Drop the rowboats!"

The mainmast snapped in half and the ship took on water and began listing, the rowboats inaccessible.

This place is far worse than the Gray Lady, they thought. *Far, far worse.* Nantucket's notoriously dangerous shoals had claimed many a vessel's—and a man's—life, earning that region the nickname "the graveyard of the Atlantic."

These intrepid whalers were quickly learning the secrets of this equally treacherous waterway fed by the Pacific, where twice a day with the tides, tremendous volumes of water rushed in and out of the immensely deep bay, pushing and pulling salt water at speeds of up to seven knots an hour, creating vortexes of eddies, treacherous riptides, and perilous whirlpools.

Their only hope now was to swim to shore.

On the eve of Thanksgiving, 1850, as the *Chase* sank into the chilly depths a quarter mile off the harbor, thirty-two men from Nantucket prayed to God.

And an eighteen-year-old navigator named Joseph Allen was among them.

CHAPTER 25

August 31, 1851

The sun rose pale and perfect on the last morning of August, the crew of the *Stargazer* having worked through the night to navigate her up the rocky California coastline. At 6:00 a.m., the ship was in sight of the Farallon Islands, the "Devil's Teeth" of sea stacks that announced the entry to San Francisco, thirty miles from the Golden Gate Strait. Peter Starbuck stared out at the sea from the ship's prow, spyglass in hand, as if picturing an invisible finish line, a dotted demarcation in the Pacific Ocean.

The *Stargazer* had sailed to San Francisco in eighty-nine days and twenty-one hours, compared to *Surprise*'s ninety-six days and fifteen hours, completed the year prior.

"He's done it," Leo said to Zander, the two watching the sun rise behind their captain and the approaching islands, where they would meet a pilot boat in about an hour that would guide them safely into the notoriously treacherous bay.

"He has." Zander turned the helm ever so slightly to starboard. "Thanks to you, in large part."

Leo shrugged, his face unreadable and his jaw set. Now that they had reached California, he might as well confide in the thoughtful, strong helmsman who had been like a ballast on this journey. "He can thank me with the bonus he's promised if we win."

Zander kept his expression neutral. A bonus for the navigator. Interesting. Meanwhile, Zander had nearly been blown off the poop deck, trying to keep the ship on course in those storms off Tierra del Fuego, while Leo sat warm and dry belowdecks, leaning over a paper chart, and yet no bonus had been offered to *him*. Just the twelve dollars a month of a regular salary for an officer on a merchant vessel, plus profit sharing from the cargo. "Money is a powerful way to express gratitude," Zander said.

"And a powerful way to suddenly chart your own course," Leo said.

Now Zander showed his surprise. "You're not continuing on with us to China?"

"After the hell Captain Starbuck put us through, not stopping in port for repairs, not using common sense in the deadliest spot in the world? I understand having a competitive drive, but this man cares more about profits than people. Playing with not just us sailors, but the lives of his wife and daughter! He got lucky on this trip, but his hubris and greed will lead to his downfall eventually. I've seen it on the seas a thousand times, and I've got better ways to spend *my* time—and to use my knowledge—than to argue with an avaricious captain like him."

"But—without you, who will navigate us?"

Leo shook his head. "All I can tell you is it's not going to be me, not even for all the tea in China."

THE PAST THIRTY-NINE days at sea had been smooth sailing by everyone's estimation, with mild weather and limited stress on the ship and her crew. Winnie had been allowed to work on deck for much of the time in the Pacific, and could now tie knots in her sleep.

Her hair had grown long, the sun bleaching the tips from gold to flaxen, her skin a light bronze, making her green eyes glow even more than they did before. Where she had at first felt soreness in her arms and shoulders, she now felt muscular and strong, and she knew she had rightfully earned her place on board the *Stargazer*. Her father said nothing against her, which was almost as good as being praised, and Sully had stopped making her clean out the latrines.

After all she'd done to help on this leg of the journey, Winnie felt certain that she had more than made up for her surprise appearance on the ship three months ago, and further, that her father would allow—no, *invite*!—her to continue on to China with them. How could he not?

As the ship came closer to the Farallons, Winnie made a mental list of plans once they docked inside the harbor: explore this frontier city, learn about buying and selling goods with her mother, and see a show at the Jenny Lind Theatre.

But as much as she looked forward to exploring San Francisco, a nagging and persistent worry kept bubbling up: was it true about the fate of the *Chase*? Had thirty-two men really died in the bay that her own parents' ship was about to enter—including her friend Samuel Allen and his brother Joseph?

Nell came up from behind her daughter, grabbed her around the waist, and pulled her close. "How do you feel?"

Winnie turned to her mother and realized they no longer saw eye to eye as they had for the past year. "Taller," Winnie said.

"Inside and out, I'd say. Let's go congratulate your father," Nell said, leading Winnie by the elbow to the bow.

As they walked across the deck, Winnie stopped to greet Lucky, scooping up his little dog by his feet. Yip licked Winnie's chin and cheek as she rubbed his fur. "I know you barked a lot when we first met, but now we've become friends," she cooed.

"Nah, miss. He always liked ya," Lucky said. "Even when you were a little thing—"

Winnie cocked her head sideways and stopped petting the dog. "When I was little? Did I meet you and Yip then?"

Nell cleared her throat as Lucky realized his mistake.

"No, miss. Pardon me. I'm old and I sometimes confuse even myself. I mean, because *Yip* is such a little thing, sometimes he gets overly excited, but he's always been fond of you, since finding you in the hold."

Lucky had corrected his mistake and also spoken the truth; Yip had always felt protective of Winnie, ever since finding her in the hold when she was five . . . and again when she was eighteen.

"Now, if you'll excuse me, Yip and I need to round up some boys to help us man the capstan and lower the anchor at a mooring." Winnie handed over the dog to Lucky, who shuffled away as quickly as his old body and bum leg would allow.

Winnie stared after the pair. "I feel like I did meet them when I was a child," she said, turning to her mother. "Is that possible?"

Nell shook her head. "No, my dear, it's not. I'm afraid the old man is losing his grasp on reality."

Winnie's face fell. She had been certain she'd met him before. "And what about Sully?" she asked. "And Red and Cook, too? I could swear on a Bible that—"

"You've spent every day these past months with this crew, so of course they feel familiar to you," Nell said, walking quickly up the three steps to the raised bow, her back to Winnie.

"But I feel like I've known them *forever*," Winnie added.

"You've always had a marvelous imagination, Winnie. But now that you're older, it doesn't serve you to seem so fanciful."

At the sound of his wife and daughter squabbling, Peter dropped his spyglass and turned. He had just made history, for goodness' sake! Couldn't a man have a moment to relish in his glory? Nell flashed him a tight smile and Winnie looked perturbed.

"Darling!" Nell said, putting her arm around Peter's shoulder. "We've made it to San Francisco in record-breaking time!"

"Congratulations, Father," Winnie added.

Something was amiss. "What are you two bickering about?"

"The more time I spend with the crew, Father, the more I feel certain that I've known some of them since childhood. And Lucky said—"

Peter held up his hand. "Enough. It will be good for you to get off this ship, Fred. You've spent too much time at sea."

Peter and Nell exchanged a quick, knowing glance.

Winnie sighed. "I suppose. I am looking forward to a hot bath," she said.

"As am I!" Peter laughed.

"Me, too!" Nell added.

Winnie examined her hands. "Although, I hope my calluses won't heal too quickly."

"How lovely that you want to keep your rough hands as a memento from your sailing adventures," Nell said.

"Yes, but also because when we sail to China in a week or so, it's best if my palms are still toughened like they are now."

Peter furrowed his brow. "Fred, you're not going to China. We made that clear months ago."

Winnie looked back and forth between her parents. "But—that was before I became a sailor! I got us out of the doldrums! I helped on deck in storms—I even climbed the yards! And I cleaned out the latrines, and polished the brass fittings, and worked dawn 'til dusk to prove my worth!"

"And yet none of that makes up for the fact that you lied to us and snuck on board as a stowaway," Peter said.

"You cannot be in earnest," Winnie said, her heart beating furiously. Tears sprang to her eyes as she pleaded silently for them to change their minds.

"Oh, we are," her father said.

But her mother said nothing. Nell glanced down at her feet, not able to meet Winnie's gaze.

Winnie took a deep breath and dried her tears. "Well, then. I hope to learn a great deal from you, Mother, in the coming days about how to be a successful merchant."

"Now, there's the Starbuck spirit I like to see," her father said, patting his daughter on the back. No matter what he achieved, would his family never be satisfied?

"Captain! We're in sight of the pilot boat," Sully said.

Peter nodded.

"Crew! Heave to!" Sully called.

"Heave to!" the crew echoed, as the sailors worked together to slow the ship by pulling the sails on the foremast to leeward and those on the mainmast to windward.

Anxious to show her continued dedication to her work as a sailor despite her parents' supposed plans for her, Winnie echoed the order as well, and moved into position to help Jonathan at the mizzen. "Why are we slowing here, at this outcropping of rocks? Why not just sail into port?" she asked.

"It's a new system, miss. They started it recently to avoid the catastrophe greeting so many ships heading into the bay in search of gold. If you don't know these waters, they can be treacherous. Guide boats now wait all day and night on shifts to lead vessels safely through the Golden Gate Strait."

Something dawned on her as she undid a line along a belaying pin and got behind Jonathan to pull. "Do you think the *Chase* entered the bay without a pilot boat?"

Jonathan's face clouded. "If it's true they were here and went down? Most certainly so."

"Haul!" Sully called to the crew, and they pulled as one.

A MAN WORKING atop the stone tower on Telegraph Hill received the signal from points south and kept watch through his telescope until he himself spied the tall ship entering the harbor. Then he, too, set a signal via movable arms attached to a tall pole that relayed the information, which, thanks to a pamphlet that had been printed and passed around town, everyone in San Francisco could decipher: "Clipper ship, not in distress."

With the sun now glowing brightly, illuminating the gold-and-green hills along either side of the Golden Gate Strait, the crew of a small sailboat waved to the *Stargazer* and guided them past rocky shoals and into the wide harbor.

Nell and Peter Starbuck stayed on deck for the whole of it, not wanting to miss even a second of their arrival. They did not speak about Winnie. Peter believed the matter was decided. And Nell, who still harbored hopes for bringing her daughter to China with them, knew that this was not the right time to push him on the matter.

"If you'll excuse me, I have a lot of work to do," Nell said, kissing Peter on the cheek. While everyone else on staff was looking forward to a rest on land after all of their hard work at sea, Nell's main duties were just getting started. It was helpful to be arriving in the morning, for that gave Nell a full day to oversee the unloading of the cargo in the hold. Those many tons of goods would be carted to an empty warehouse along the wharf that she had rented for a week, and companies would come there to pay for their orders and take their merchandise. Nell also kept the books for sailors' pay. While sailors could not get fully paid out until they reached the end of the trip back in Nantucket, they could ask for some spending money, which Nell would deduct from their salaries. In fact, she spied several of the crew lining up right now outside the door to the captain's staterooms, so anxious were they for a bit of cash in hand and a saloon to spend it in.

NEWS TRAVELED FAST in the frontier city of San Francisco, from the taverns and dance halls to the fancy homes of the newly rich to the whorehouses and flophouses by the wharf. From the palatial hotels to the many shops selling imported goods—since almost everything but the gold was imported—word of each new ship entering the harbor came quickly and frequently. "Clipper comin' in!" swept through the city faster than the fires that had swept the city six times already, leaving whole neighborhoods flattened in the morning as thieves picked among the ashes at night . . . and the young, gritty city was once again rebuilt by light of day.

And the ships kept coming.

And coming.

The news traveled from person to person, and shop to shop, wending its way through the gritty streets of San Francisco, eventually reaching the post office at the corner of Pike and Clay Streets.

The first post office this side of the Mississippi, a small barnlike structure that was both a general store and a place to gather and send out mail, had been built in 1848 at Stockton and Clay Streets. But, after the gold rush of 1849, as the town grew into a city seemingly overnight, a larger structure was built a block away, this one equipped to handle and sort the ever-increasing bagfuls of mail that arrived each week.

Every day, prospectors lined up here before sunrise to collect their mail and perhaps buy a newspaper—or read through a discarded one from the day before for free. Men came down from the mountains after months spent digging through silt and mining for gold along the rivulets, streams, and rivers north of the city, mostly without success. They arrived at the post office tired and dirty, longing for a break from the wilderness before heading back out with their pick and pans. Longing for civilization and connection, a long letter from home or the warm arms of a girl. Usually both.

Sometimes these men waited all day to discover that no mail from home awaited them. Standing in line for ten hours outside in the oppressive heat—or the sideways rain—at the second-ever post office this side of the Mississippi was a lot like prospecting for gold: putting in the time with no results. It was hard to remain hopeful in a state of mind like that, even in the newest American state of California.

At least this morning's weather was mild as men lined up on the dirt street leading to one of the three post office windows, waiting to speak to a clerk. The lines inched forward and the men moved slowly, one step closer to the post office windows. The building had a wooden overhang like a front porch, shielding those closest in line from the weather, and each window slid open to reveal a clerk at his post on the other side, stationed behind a long wooden counter.

Talk helped break up the monotony of standing still. Plus, chit-chat quelled the gold miners' fears that they'd been all but forgotten at home, and that the hope that had brought them across the nation was for naught.

"Didja hear?" one rusher asked, pulling at the suspenders of the man in front of him to get his attention.

"Hear whah?" the second asked from under his wide-brimmed hat. A mangy dog panted beside him.

"A ship just came in!"

"So what? Ships come in all the time," the man with the dog said.

"Well, this one just took the world record!"

"Well, that is something," the other agreed.

After a few minutes, as the conversation waned, the man with the dog asked a question. "Since you know so much, d'you know what the ship is called then?"

"*Star*-something. I can't remember 'zactly, but I know it had the word *star* in it." He had reached the front of the line. Before turning to the clerk, he added, "And the clipper hails from Nantucket."

The clerk behind the window snapped his head up, the cowlick in his sandy hair moving from the force of his surprise. "Did you say Nantucket?" he asked through the open window. The clerk had been listening with one ear, sorting some of the never-ending mail while waiting for the next man in line to approach.

"Yeah." The man nodded. "*Star*-something. A clipper."

The clerk's eyes grew wide. "The Starbucks," he said.

"Nah, that ain't it," the man said, frustrated. "You gonna get me my mail, or what?"

The clerk blinked and nodded, then wrote down the man's name and went off to search through the cubbies and slats where the organized letters and packages lived.

The clerk walked through the post office in a daze, passing the rows of wooden cubbies and the giant wooden table where he sat in the evenings eating with one hand and sorting mail with the other.

He couldn't believe it. The Starbucks from Nantucket were here. In San Francisco.

He walked right past Lucas and then Paolo, the other clerks manning the lines.

"Hey, Joseph! You okay?" his friend Paolo asked, his accent thick. Paolo was from the Sonoran Desert and handled mail for the Spanish-speaking line of miners. "You look lost."

"I'm fine," Joseph said, glad he had written down the prospector's name.

A minute later, he handed over a small stack of envelopes to the man in line. Joseph's face had grown pale and a line of sweat was gathered on his top lip.

"Well, lookie here, it's my lucky day!" the man said, waving the mail over his head as he walked away whistling. "It's almost like I struck it rich. Bye, fellas! See ya in Coloma!" He untied his gray mare from a post and took off for the hills.

The men grumbled their farewells and moved on up in line.

Oh yes, news traveled fast in the frontier city of San Francisco.

Almost as fast as it did in Joseph Allen's home port of Nantucket.

CHAPTER 26

His life was supposed to be glorious.

Joseph Allen had spent his entire childhood training for the day he would eventually go to sea, journeying to the Pacific to hunt whales and their precious oil, just as his older brothers did, just as his father and grandfather had done before settling down to farm what they could in the sandy Nantucket soil. Joseph would grow tall and broad; he would be gritty and smart. He could navigate a ship using only the night sky. He would lead with confidence, being approachable most of the time, but rough when needed with the men in his charge, somehow both respected and liked by all.

He would quickly rise through the ranks on every whaleship, showing bravery beyond what the men of Nantucket had ever displayed. He would single-handedly slay great beasts at sea and win the hearts of great beauties in port. At saloons, other sailors would jump at the chance to pay for his beer. Sea shanties would be sung in his name, his glory immortalized for all time.

He came of age in a time when the whaling industry was dying, but did he let this stop him? No, sir. In the spring of 1849, when Captain Tristram Chase Gardener placed an advertisement in *The Nantucket Inquirer* looking for knowledgeable and skilled young men to join him on his whaleship *Chase*, Joseph Allen knew it was the call he'd been waiting for. He ripped the corner advertisement right out of the paper and hoped his ma wouldn't notice. And when Captain Tristram Chase Gardner not only shook Joseph's hand and told him he was welcome on board the *Chase* as cabin boy and apprentice to the navigator—and a harpooner during whaling missions—he felt like he was meeting his true destiny head-on. And when that same captain asked if Joseph knew of any other fine young men interested and willing to go to sea, Joseph said, "Yes, sir, I can think of one."

And then he also hoped his pa wouldn't care that Joseph signed on his little brother Samuel with him.

But the son of a sailor-turned-sheep-farmer should have known how quickly life could turn to shit.

All you had to do was step in it.

CHAPTER 27

By the time the giant clipper ship dropped anchor at Yerba Buena Cove, word had spread, and all of San Francisco knew that the *Stargazer* from Nantucket had arrived safely and speedily, besting the *Surprise* by a week.

Local children who spotted her from the hillocks ran down to the docks to see the instantly famous clipper ship up close, but she was easier to see from afar. Down at North Beach, it was hard to make out the *Stargazer* amid the eight hundred other boats crowding the harbor. Some were still actively working, but most had been abandoned, their crew jumping ship to try to strike out for gold, the wooden ships left to rot in the bay. Thousands of spindly masts stripped of their canvas sails pointed skyward, creating a jagged, skeleton-like skyline. "A forest of masts," it had been called.

On deck of the *Stargazer*, Lily Bird watched closely as the ship dropped anchor and was tethered to an offshore mooring until they could bring it closer to unload cargo at the docks. Unlike the other passengers, who had their gaze out toward the horseshoe-shaped harbor and the city hills rising beyond it, Lily looked upon her beau. Nate was working the capstan with other sailors, singing a shanty as they pushed the bars of the device, which looked to Lily like the wheel of a helm on its side. She hadn't seen them drop anchor before because, well, they never had stopped the ship before. It seemed like a big job. Nate walked slowly with the others around in circles as they rotated the capstan, his biceps bulging against his stained and threadbare linen shirt, his beautiful face hidden under the brim of his sailor's cap. He looked up and, his gaze meeting hers, winked and smiled.

She loved him.

Oh, how she loved him!

How could she leave this wonderful man? Tears stung her eyes and she looked away, wiping them with a handkerchief and finally seeing the port city of San Francisco, which provided a powerful distraction to her heartache.

Winnie stood next to Lily and Jessie at the railing. She had never seen so many ships at once. Vessels were everywhere, clogging the harbor and beached on the muddy flats. Why, there was even a ship or two pulled up right into the town, standing between other, more conventional buildings of brick and stone and wood, although those were set up higher, on stilts or pilings, all along a pier that acted like a street.

"What are those ships doing there, wedged between other structures on dry land?" Winnie asked Jessie. Lily sniffed beside them and pocketed her damp handkerchief.

"They've been dragged up from the beach and converted into buildings," Jessie explained. She squinted, trying to make out the signage. "That one there says Store Ship and the one further down on the right is a saloon. You see the ladders? The buildings are raised on wooden pilings to keep them from washing away in the changing tides, and the wharves and piers act like streets. And when the water rises around them on the mud flats, the ships just float!"

"Remarkable," Winnie said. It was the oddest town she'd ever seen. Her work on deck was done, and Sully had dismissed them all for the day. There would be repairs to do—lots of repairs—but the crew was given time off first, which they were more than due after months of relentless hard work. Time to explore this unique maritime frontier.

"Miss Lily Bird of London, England," Nate said, approaching the group with the knowing swagger of a sailor who'd been around the Horn.

"Mr. Nathan Barnes of Newburyport, Massachusetts," Lily said, pulling back her shoulders and jutting out her chest, her fake accent drawing out the *ah* and *ow* sounds in the words.

Nate removed his sailor's cap and got down on bended knee before her. "I cannot live a single moment without you, Lily. Marry me."

"Oh, Nate!" Lily said, taking Nate's outstretched hand and sinking to the deck with him, smothering him with kisses.

"Is that a yes?" he asked from underneath her.

"Yes! Only . . . where will we live? Could you possibly ever give up sailing to live in San Francisco?" she asked, pulling back from him, her accent all but forgotten.

"Oh, Lily, I can't wait to get off this ship. I only took this job as a way to travel to California!"

As the couple embraced, Winnie and Jessie clapped and cheered. The sailors around them made lewd gestures in lieu of hearty congratulations.

"Did you hear that, Beatrice?" Jessie said, turning to her now obviously pregnant maid. "It's a yes!"

"How exciting, ma'am."

Only Beatrice didn't look excited for the happy couple at all. She cradled her growing belly and looked out at the landscape with what Jessie could only describe as dread.

"What will become of me, ma'am?" Beatrice asked softly.

"Become of you? Why, you'll live with me and be my maid, same as always."

"And the baby?"

Could babies be maids? No, Jessie supposed not. But a baby could be raised by a maid who was her mother, and tended to by the other female staff in the home when her mother was occupied, growing up in the warmth of a big kitchen, a bassinet in the corner of the room, the baby smelling like a bundle of fresh-baked bread. Yes, Jessie could absolutely picture it. And she and Bernard had no children of their own, nor any family at all out here in California, and their home was large enough to house many, many people—including a baby. Maybe Jessie would even hold the little thing from time to time, and sing to it. Any baby would be lucky to hear a lullaby sung in Jessie's lovely voice.

Jessie explained this arrangement to Beatrice, who smiled shyly. "Have you been worried about this the whole trip?" Jessie asked.

"That—and the fact of not having a husband. What will people say?"

"Beatrice! You of all people should know that I don't care what people say!" Jessie barked indignantly.

"But I'm not like you, ma'am."

Jessie stationed herself in front of her pregnant maid and took both of the woman's hands into her own. She stared into her eyes. "Repeat after me, Beatrice. *How tragic that my beloved husband died at sea, on this long and treacherous journey*."

Beatrice blinked once, twice. Then she repeated the sentence. "How tragic that my beloved husband died at sea, on this long and treacherous journey."

"Did you hear that, everyone?" Jessie said, raising her voice and calling those on deck to attention. People turned away from the newly betrothed and toward Jessie and her maid. "Beatrice, please repeat what you just said. Louder this time."

"Yes, ma'am." Beatrice cleared her throat and spoke haltingly but clearly.

"Sure sounds tragic," one sailor said, bowing his head.

"Sorry for your loss, miss," another added.

"Bollocks," Sully said, shaking his head as he coiled a last bit of rope around a cleat.

Look at these wonderful folks supporting each other and forging new bonds, Charles thought, smiling at his fellow passengers. He had grown fond of them over these past months, and he was even more fond of them now that they were about to say their farewells, that bittersweet moment of departure. To think of what they had endured together, a bond forged like that among a troop of soldiers after wartime. A connection like theirs might stretch over time and distance, but it would never truly sever.

He reached into his jacket pocket for his notebook and pencil.

Yes. He'd write that.

The words came fast. His right hand could hardly keep up as he scribbled in uneven cursive. Charles had been more inspired since embarking on this trip than he'd ever been before in his life. He had so much to say that an article—even a series of them—couldn't possibly capture it all. How could a journalist adequately paint a picture of Tierra del Fuego in one thousand words or less? Impossible.

A small rowboat approached to take the passengers off the ship first, before the crew disembarked to gallivant and carouse. Their luggage would follow.

Nate told Lily he'd find her in town once he gave the news to the Starbucks that he was leaving, and collected his pay for the portion of the trip he'd completed. He helped unfurl the rope ladder attached to the port side of the ship as the ladies prepared to go.

Speaking of the Starbucks, Winnie wondered where her father was. She was certain he would want to see the passengers off. There. On the poop deck, in what seemed to be a heated conversation with Leo. Their voices were hushed, but her father had his arms crossed angrily while Leo pointed a finger in his direction, wagging it back and forth.

As Winnie drew closer, she could make out the words *irresponsible* and *dangerous* from Leo and *imbecile* and *renege* and *contract* from her father.

"Sorry to interrupt," Winnie said.

"What now?" Her father turned his cold gaze to her, and she flinched.

"It's just—the passengers are setting off. I thought you'd want to—"

He nodded curtly. "I'll be there in a minute. As soon as I finish with Leo."

"Oh, we're *finished*," Leo said, shaking his head and walking off.

Her father coughed, but said nothing about the unpleasant exchange with the navigator.

Winnie decided to change the subject. "Did you hear? Lily and Nate are getting married! He's leaving the ship!"

Her father responded with a wrinkled brow. "Not you, too," he said to Nate, his disappointment clear.

"Me, too, sir?" Nate asked. "Is someone else getting married?"

"No, but someone else is leaving the ship," Captain Starbuck said, looking back toward the poop deck.

Winnie instantly understood the exchange between her father and Leo.

They could sail to China without Nate. But without Leo, who would navigate the *Stargazer*? Winnie wondered.

Peter Starbuck, reminding himself that he was now the captain of the fastest ship in the world, decided to rise above his distress. He was only losing *two* crew members, after all. If he could rebound from his ship's masts cracking and from blinding storms in the southern Atlantic Ocean, he could certainly rebound from this. He shook the sailor's hand and wished him well.

"Thank you, sir," Nate said.

"Here's my address," Jessie Lindquist said, handing over a small calling card to Nate. "I'd already invited Lily to stay with me until she rented a room in a woman's hotel, but now I suppose she can just stay until the two of you get married and find proper housing together."

"How kind of you, ma'am," Nate said to Jessie.

"I invited Winnie into my home, too, although she said she'd rather stay with her parents until they depart for China without her," Jessie said, cutting a sideways glance at Captain Starbuck. "And then she'll come to my estate atop Rincon Hill, where we'll stand on my grand porch and watch the *Stargazer* depart together."

"Maybe she'll never visit your home, Jessie. Maybe she'll stow away again and make it all the way to Canton!" Lily teased, jabbing a finger into her friend's side.

Nate laughed, too. "Now that I'm leaving, Captain, you'll need all capable hands, and your daughter more than proved her worthiness as a sailor."

"Thank you for your unsolicited opinions," Peter said, trying to maintain his composure, especially in front of the journalist, who still had the power to publish, saying anything he wished about the captain of the *Stargazer*.

Then Peter heard cheers and music. A huge crowd had gathered on the pier, some waving the American flag. This celebration reminded him of the one on Nantucket back in June, the fanfare and grand send-off on the Eastern Seaboard now mirrored on the other coast of America. This helped buoy his mood, and he addressed the small group with good humor. "I'd just like to say that it has been an honor and a privilege to make you a part of world history. And now, I'd like to invite you all to kindly get off my ship!"

They laughed good-naturedly, and Nate gave a rousing "aye-aye."

"And, before the *Stargazer* departs for China," Jessie said, "I'd like to throw a huge send-off party for the Starbucks at my home, and all of the passengers—and Nate—are invited."

"Aye-aye!" Nate said again.

"I'll see you then, on Sunday evening at the top of Rincon Hill. You can't miss it, or so my husband tells me. Isn't that right, Beatrice?"

"Yes, ma'am."

With the aid of a step stool and holding hands with Winnie for support, the women carefully made their way over the ship's raised railing and onto the top rung of the ladder, descending one by one into the small skiff in the bay. Beatrice went first, then Lily. Finally, Jessie went up and over.

"Charles? Aren't you coming?" Jessie asked, the top of her feathered bonnet still visible.

"Be right there!" he said. He closed his notebook and looked out at the sloping hill that had been a pioneer town and now was an intrepid city that was expanding every day. Change, reinvention, discovery. And he was here. He had made it here.

San Francisco had first piqued Charles's interest five years earlier, in 1846, when the US won the San Francisco Bay in the Mexican–American War. His editor asked him to write about the victory for the readers of *The Boston Pilot*, which culminated in the Battle of Yerba Buena. Today, everyone *thought* that gold brought American settlers to the region, when really, gold merely accelerated what had already been put into motion: the US had claimed an important port city, their first on the West Coast of North America. It was a territory that would connect them easily and readily to Asia, bringing a strategic economic link for US trade with the East.

Charles wrote about the city again in 1848, with the discovery of gold at Sutter's Mill and the subsequent rush across the Great Plains, across the Isthmus of Panama, or around the Horn, individuals hoping to get pans in their hands and riches in their pockets. And what followed, of course, was everyone else heading to the port city and surrounding areas, trying to reinvent themselves and make a buck by selling goods and services to those prospectors, creating an economy and building a city by the bay.

In San Francisco, you could forget your past and be born anew.

Charles had just witnessed this very transformation occur, right before his eyes, to both Lily and Beatrice: a single woman becoming a wife, and one pregnant with an illegitimate child becoming a widower.

Charles Mortimer would remake himself, too, here, in this city beyond the Golden Gate Strait. He would write a series of glowing articles for *The Boston Pilot* as he had been hired to do, making enough money from both Peter Starbuck and the newspaper to live off for the next six months. And with that time, he would pen a full account of his journey aboard the *Stargazer*, a true story disguised as a novel. Charles could see the characters now: the hard-driving captain and his astute, hard-working wife, their stowaway daughter, and the malicious first mate, among others. He'd of course have to include several brave passengers on this record-breaking, dangerous passage around Cape Horn, like perhaps a witty and wise journalist.

He'd call it *Sailing for Gold*.

"Charles! We're going to leave without you!" Jessie called up to the deck.

"Coming!" he said, going up the stool steps and over the rail, his foot making contact with the top wooden rung as his fists clenched the rope handles.

And with one last look at the main deck of the *Stargazer*, Charles Mortimer backed inch by inch toward his future, overcome with a swelling sense of happiness at his great good fortune to be alive and well and full of ideas. He couldn't wait to see this city by the bay, certain that San Francisco was destined to become his new home.

Several men on shore pulled the rowboat out of the harbor and onto the mud flats of North Beach. Charles's leather shoes sunk into the soft, dark sand and he vowed never to get on another ship again.

CHAPTER 28

Nell sat at the dining table in the captain's staterooms, the door open to let in the fresh balmy air, as well as to accommodate the long line of sailors waiting to meet with her and collect spending money for their shore leave. Some, she knew, would be careful with their cash, making it last the full week spent in port, while others would gamble it all away the first night, hungover and penniless by dawn.

A medium-sized bound leather logbook was open before her, revealing an alphabetical list of the crew with columns to fill across the page for items they had bought on board the ship and an accounting of what salary they borrowed now against their future payout.

"I leave," Papa said, standing before Nell with the aid of a cane. He had come a long way in the past six weeks at sea, regaining use of his foot and finding his balance on three instead of five toes.

"What do you mean, you're leaving?" Nell asked the injured sailor.

Papa's English had improved a little over the course of the last few months, but verb tenses were still a challenge. "I go," Papa said, using his pointer and middle fingers to pantomime a person walking away. "Off ship."

"He'd like to collect his full pay now, Mrs. Starbuck," a man behind him in line clarified. "For the portion of the trip completed." He was bearded and tattooed and had bunked near Papa before the man was moved to the infirmary. "As would I. We're getting off here and not coming back on for the trip to China."

"But—" Nell was stymied. On their past trips, no one had ever left mid-trip before. Perhaps that was because they previously had only sailed to China and not to the newest booming port city in America where gold ran in the rivers. She looked around her for answers.

Chin sat next to Nell with a wooden box of cash on his lap, while Sully stood sentry behind him, his back against the wall and a pistol from storage in his hand, just in case anyone thought about stealing the money. Chin explained, "I heard a few of the crew talking about jumping ship, ma'am. I tried to tell them about the wonders of China. But no one seemed that interested in trying my mother's delicious chicken feet or duck's tongue. They don't know what they're missing, I said, but—" Here he shrugged, as there was only so much he could do to convince dumb Americans that the world was bigger—and tasted better—than they could possibly imagine. Delicacies that well surpassed the disgustingly doughy and sickly sweet duff pudding, that was for certain!

Nell thought for a moment. These sailors knew that, to get paid in full, they had to stay on in full. But she couldn't keep a man prisoner on the *Stargazer*. If his full pay for nine months at sea was to be ninety dollars, technically, she *could* give him a third now, for these first three months. But there had to be a penalty for leaving the Starbucks without a full crew. In addition to everything else she and Peter needed to do as merchants in port, they'd now have to find new recruits and train them at sea.

"I believe we're each owed thirty dollars, Mrs. Starbuck," said the man speaking for himself and Papa.

"Chin," Nell said, "give them fifteen."

Chin narrowed his eyes. Sometimes he had trouble translating, although hardly ever when it came to money. Had Mrs. Starbuck really just cut their pay in half?

"You heard me," Nell added.

As Chin counted out the bills and Nell wrote notes in the ledger, Peter entered the cabin. Nell explained what had just transpired, a troubling turn of events given that Leo and Nate were also disembarking and abandoning their posts.

Peter turned to the line of sailors. "How many of you plan on jumping ship?" he asked, his voice raised.

Every single man raised his right hand.

WINNIE LET A tear fall as she watched the passengers make their way to shore. Even though she would visit with them in Jessie's home atop Rincon Hill, nothing would be the same after this moment. They all seemed to be sure of where they were headed, while Winnie felt rudderless.

After the group landed on the beach, Winnie headed to the captain's staterooms. She knew her mother would need help processing all of the paperwork for each item of cargo in the hold and checking pieces for damage from the journey as they were taken off the ship.

Complete pandemonium greeted her. A throng of crew members had pushed their way inside the captain's cabin and were yelling at one another about something—or, no, they were yelling at her father! And her father was screaming back at them! She was jostled to and fro in a sea of bodies. Was this a mutiny? But they were moored.

Sully aimed the pistol toward the ceiling and shouted, "Shut up or I'll shoot!"

Everyone promptly shut up.

Winnie put her hands over her head and ducked, as if that would save her should the first mate fire. Chin had slid under the table, where he sat on the money box. Winnie locked eyes with him, his panic mirroring her own.

"That's better," Sully said. "Now listen to yur captain, because until your legs and arms and arse are off this ship, he's still yur commander."

Peter was speechless. He did not want the sailors to get even more agitated and turn to physical violence. So he used the most persuasive method he knew, a tool more powerful than a weapon or a fist or the law. "I'll double the salaries of anyone that stays on," Peter said. "And give a bonus of five dollars to anyone who recruits a new man to join him."

"How does that sound to ya ungrateful babies?" Sully asked, pistol still raised.

"Good, sir," one man said. The others around him relaxed.

Peter nodded confidently while Nell shook her head in disbelief.

ALL TOLD, TWENTY sailors still chose to abandon the ship for California, even though they were only paid fifteen dollars for their months of service at sea. One third of the crew was lost.

Even with the incentive of extra pay, it would be hard for their remaining crew members to recruit fellow sailors in a city where they knew no one. Especially if they were drunk the whole time, as Nell suspected they would be.

Peter pulled Sully aside and offered him ten dollars per head as personal motivation. From the interested look on Sully's face, he thought the idea might work.

"We can't rely solely on our crew to recruit for us. We're also going to have to get the word out ourselves," Nell said once she and Peter had paid the sailors and everyone had left. They went quickly to their cabin to get dressed to disembark and greet awaiting journalists.

"Those that quit are foolish," Peter said. "Gold is not just waiting in the hills. You and I know that it takes incredibly hard work to make a fortune, and even then, there's no guarantees, no such thing as blind luck. I worked so hard that eventually I got lucky. Like with this trip."

Nell said nothing in response. She powdered her nose while looking in the mirror. Her silence was deafening.

"What?" her husband asked.

"Peter, have you considered that perhaps your crew chose to leave because they thought *anything*—even a life in an unknown city far from home with an unknown future—was better than serving under you and Sully?"

"Not that again. Sully and I drove this ship hard, yes—but that was the only way to achieve what I did!" Seeing his wife's face, he quickly amended his sentence. "What *we* did!"

Nell fixed her hair in the mirror. "Was it worth losing a well-trained crew in the process?"

"Yes, absolutely! I cannot believe you don't see that, Nell. And no matter how I treated them, they were going to leave. Apparently, many of them had planned to desert all along. They used the *Stargazer* as a means to an end. They don't even seem to take *pride* in the fact that they sailed the fastest ship in the world! Say what you will about me, but in the end, *they* made a mockery of *me and my ship*!"

Ah, so this was about Peter's ego. Like pushing against the wind, Nell would have to try a different tack. "Today, the *Stargazer* became the fastest ship in the world, and nothing can mar that honor. And by doubling the sailors' salaries and offering a bonus to recruit, you convinced many of them to stay on."

"Luckily, everyone has a price," Peter said. He put his navy coat over his white-ish shirt, shining the brass buttons with a cloth. He needed to look his best for the reporters waiting at Long Wharf.

"So you use money to obtain loyalty?" Nell asked, newly angry. And then a flash of memory: Sully's name written in Peter's logbook, with extra expenses paid for no apparent reason. Perhaps that explained why the first mate did whatever his captain asked without hesitation. "Peter, is that what you are doing with Sully?"

The look on her husband's face—the surprise of her pronouncement coupled with the correctness of Nell's guess—said it all.

Peter explained. How Sully threatened to report to a maritime court that Nell had murdered a sailor aboard the *Shooting Star*. How he demanded not only to be well-compensated for his silence, but also promoted on every subsequent Starbuck voyage.

"But that was thirteen years ago," Nell said.

"Yes," Peter said.

"So—he's been blackmailing you ever since?"

Peter's nod was almost imperceptible. A twitch of the head.

"And *that's* why he's our first mate? That awful, awful man?"

"An awful man often makes a talented first mate," Peter said. Peter did not add what he thought was obvious, that the real job of the first mate was to bear the brunt of the crew's hatred so that no one tried to kill the captain.

"So we have to keep Sully so he will keep my—our—long-held secret a secret?" Nell said.

"Yes. And now we couldn't let him go, anyway. Not on the same day that we've lost twenty sailors *and* our navigator."

"Our navigator?" Nell paused. "What happened to Leo?"

Peter sighed. "We parted ways."

"I see," Nell said. "Don't tell me *he's* a gold digger."

"No," Peter said, honesty softening his brown eyes. "He left because of me, that much was clear."

"I see," Nell said.

Peter cleared his throat. "Also, you should know—"

"Know what?" Nell asked, worry creeping up her spine.

"When Fred was discovered stowing away, Sully promised me he'd stop asking for Fred's removal and instead treat her fairly—for a price."

Nell closed her eyes and pressed her fingers against her brows, covering her face with her hands, and groaned. Sully was making a fortune off her family's actions.

"So, you see—the sooner Fred gets off this ship, the better it will be for all of us."

"That's one way of looking at it," Nell said from under her hands. She sank into the chair at Peter's shaving desk, head in hands.

"I had no choice. I did it for you and for our daughter."

"Be that as it may, the fact is, you kept these secrets from *me*. Your *wife*. Your *business partner*. The money you are paying Sully comes from *our* bank account, and *our* profits are going toward *your* corruption."

Her rage was visceral. It pumped from her heart and through her veins like blood. It blinded her until all she could see before her was the whiteness of her fury.

"Nell, darling—" Peter said, reaching out to touch her arm.

Now he wanted to touch her? She pulled away.

Peter sat on the bed across from where Nell sat. "I am so very sorry."

Was he sorry for lying to her? Or for being caught?

Today was supposed to be the greatest day of Peter Starbuck's life. Making the journalists at the pier wait for him wasn't terrible, as it probably heightened anticipation, but there was only so long a crowd would wait with enthusiasm.

"Can we please move past this? I've apologized," Peter said, pulling the white cuffs of his shirt out of his dress jacket sleeves, making sure just a bit of his gold star-shaped cufflinks showed.

It was just like a man to assume that once he apologized, everything was settled, Nell thought. As if feelings could be mended as easily as darning a hole in the toe of a sock, the rip hardly noticeable. *See? It's gone!*

But every time Nell wore that sock, she would feel that extra stitching rub against her tender skin. "You have to promise me one thing," Nell said.

"Anything," Peter said, desperate for this conversation to be over with.

"That you'll never lie to me again," Nell said, standing and facing her husband.

"Never," Peter said. "I promise, Nell. Honesty from here on out." He held his palm up like he was taking an oath.

Nell appraised Peter with cautious acceptance and pressed her palm against his.

Oh, how she wanted to believe him.

"MOTHER?" WINNIE KNOCKED on the door. "I'm ready to help you with the cargo," she said.

"One moment, dear," Nell said.

"Actually . . . Fred, come in," her father answered.

Winnie stood in the doorway, looking back and forth between her parents. "Yes, Father?"

"I need you to do an errand for me," Peter said.

Winnie raised her eyebrows. "An errand? In . . . San Francisco?"

"Yes. Your mother and I were just talking about the need to advertise for new sailors. Although I believe any man would be lucky to sail on the *Stargazer* to China, your mother disagrees. Find a printing press and take out an ad in their next paper. And while you are there, have some signs made, too, for us to distribute and post around the city."

Winnie followed him into the parlor, where her father scratched out a few lines of text on his stationery and handed it to her, along with a thick stack of letters. "And mail these while you're at it, and collect whatever is waiting for us at the post office." He provided a small leather satchel with a strap that she could put over her shoulder to carry the mail. "This morning, I wrote to Robert Forbes telling him of our winning time, and to Grinnell & Minturn to let them know that their freight has arrived safely in San Francisco. Important letters that must go out today. And I don't want you walking the streets alone, so take someone with you."

"Yes, Father. But don't you need me here? I wanted to help Mother and learn how to—"

"Fred, your mother and I have been off-loading and selling cargo in ports without your assistance for the past twenty years. We'll be just fine."

Winnie tried not to flinch from the sting of his words.

"You can help me tomorrow, darling," her mother added, entering the room in a beautiful new bonnet. "We have a whole week's worth of work to do. I promise. Go explore! Tell us all about it at dinner tonight."

Winnie bit her tongue and tried to look grateful.

"Hide that cash somewhere a pickpocket can't get it," her mother advised. "Here." Winnie was wearing the same Italian jacket that she had taken from her mother's wardrobe before they left from Nantucket, and her mother showed her a secret pocket she had had sewn into the lining just for that purpose. "And have fun with the Argonauts!"

"Thank you," she said, exiting the captain's staterooms, disappointment now quickly replaced with excitement. San Francisco!

She passed Lucky on the deck giving Yip a bath in a wooden bucket, the dog's face soapy. "Are you going ashore?" she asked.

Lucky shook his head no. "Not today, at least. I need a day or two docked before I feel steady enough on my feet to be on land," Lucky explained. "I've got the opposite problem, you see. Some people need to get their sea legs, but I need to get my shore legs." He looked down and clarified. "Leg."

She laughed and wished him well and headed to the galley. Maybe Red could be her escort.

But Red had his hands full, literally. He was holding the giant metal cauldron that Cook used for stews and soups while Cook crawled on all fours in the stove's alcove cleaning out the ashes with a handheld bristle brush and pan, his backside raised to them. Winnie told them what her parents had asked her to do and invited Red along.

"Not possible," Cook said, standing and wiping the soot from his hands and knees. "First day in port, I give this place a proper cleaning, for which I need Red's help. He could go with you tomorrow, though," Cook added.

"I have to do this today," she said, wondering who else she could ask. Most of the crew had either defected or disembarked already. "Hey, do you know who the Argonauts are?"

"Yes!" Red nodded. "I read about that in one of Mr. Mortimer's old newspapers—most of the crew just crumpled 'em up and stuffed 'em in their shoes to keep their feet warm, but I read 'em. It comes from *Jason and the Argonauts*. That Greek tale of the ship *Argo* looking for the Golden Fleece. It's a nickname for the men who come here in search of gold."

"Well, look who's smart!" Cook said, and Red's face instantly flushed red.

"Finished!" Chin said, popping his head into the galley. "The chicken coop is clear of chicken poop. Well, until the next time they poop, that is."

"A Sisyphean task," Winnie said.

"And never ending," Chin added.

Cook put his hands on his hips and sighed. "Take Chin with you," he said. "I could use a day off."

CHIN COULDN'T BELIEVE his luck. He and Winnie were taken to shore in a small skiff along with Mr. and Mrs. Starbuck, where they disembarked at Long Wharf to crowds of people cheering.

"Chin is not who I meant by a chaperone," Winnie's father said, looking unhappily at the twelve-year-old boy by his daughter's side.

"We'll be fine," Winnie assured him as a swarm of people gathered around them.

"Captain Starbuck! Mrs. Starbuck!" reporters called, vying for Peter's and Nell's attention.

"We'd be happy to answer your questions one at a time," Peter called, raising his hand, and a hush spread through the crowd.

One journalist asked about the journey, and how it was possible to have beaten the past record by one full week, while another inquired about the ship's seaworthiness and rumors about the mast cracking the first week out at sea.

Winnie listened as her father spoke animatedly about the use of Maury's navigational charts and notes—without once mentioning the skills of Leo, the navigator, Winnie noticed—and explained the dramatic tale of the dismasting, fixing the vessel while actively sailing her in the Atlantic. He was asked about storms and the perilous journey around Cape Horn.

"Did any sailors lose their lives?" one reporter called out from the crowd.

"Yes, sadly, we lost one brave man named Wallace Smith. His family lives in Portsmouth, New Hampshire, and I'm sending a letter today to let them know and to share condolences with them."

"And give them his pay?" someone in the crowd asked.

"Yes, and that," Peter said, although he had completely forgotten to enclose a check. "Now, if you'll excuse us—" He put his hand on Nell's back, hoping to steer her away from the crowd. But along a wharf, there was nowhere else to go but up and toward the city, and the crowd blocked them. "We hired a journalist to come with us who will be reporting on all our adventures," he said, hoping that would quell their interest for now. "Mrs. Starbuck and I have much to do while we're in port."

Winnie and Chin tried to push past her parents and disappear into the crowd, but they couldn't move, either.

"Just one more question, sir!" someone called. "For the world-record holder!"

"Very well," Peter said. He liked being reminded of that new title.

"Is it true that your daughter stowed away on the ship?" The crowd began murmuring to one another about this interesting bit of news.

"I do not know who told you that—" Peter began, although he pictured the entire crew of the *Stargazer* pouring into the local taverns an hour prior, talking up a storm and tipping off the local gossipmongers.

"And is it true that she's here? The blonde girl standing right beside you? Winifred, is it?"

"Damned sailors," Peter muttered through his clenched smile.

"The cat is no longer in the bag," Chin said.

"Well?" the man asked.

With all eyes upon her, Winnie smiled and waved to the crowd, and all of San Francisco burst into applause.

"NOW THEY'LL HAVE to let you sail on with us to China!" Chin said, practically running to keep up with Winnie. On the ship, they'd never had to walk very far together and, in a city, it turned out she was fast on her feet.

If only it was that easy! Winnie wished. She paused at the top of Long Wharf, looking right and then left. The wooden planking stretched on and on, a city beginning right at the beach and extending onto protective wharves and piers that kept people and businesses safe from the rising and waning tides along the mudflats. Where regular brick, dirt, or stone streets would have flooded, piers worked just fine.

"Let's try that way," Winnie said, pointing right, and they were off again.

They came upon a huge section of town that seemed to no longer exist. It looked like there had once been businesses there, with an eerie, ghostlike feeling of abandon. In a few spots, new buildings were going up, but it felt like the city just stopped for several blocks and then continued on again. Fire.

A man in a black suit walked by in a hurry, newspaper under his arm.

"Excuse me?" Winnie asked. "When did this happen?"

"Keeps on happening," the man said. "Sixth fire in three years. This last one, in May, was the worst. We keep rebuilding each time, though. Faster than the last."

Nantucket had survived three Great Fires, so Winnie knew how devastating such a catastrophe could be. "We rebuilt my hometown in brick and now we feel much safer."

The man shook his head. "All of San Francisco *was* built of brick. Didn't matter. It burned anyway. Sixty structures, about." He started counting on his fingers, listing the buildings. "And the new idea was to build with iron, but . . ." He trailed off, looking pained.

"But . . . what?" Chin asked.

"The iron doors were supposed to keep fire from spreading, but instead, the metal expanded in the heat, trapping people inside the buildings."

"Oh," Chin said, sorry he had asked.

"How terrible," Winnie added, viewing the empty lots quite differently.

The man began to walk away.

"Sir! Your newspaper!" Winnie called out.

"What about it?"

"Where is the closest printer? We'd like to take an ad out in one of the local papers."

"There were five or six newspaper offices before the fires, but now we're down to one. Two blocks that way." He pointed. Then, tipping his hat, he was off.

"I can't believe it," Chin said.

"I know—the fires sound awful," Winnie said.

"But—the man didn't notice that I am Chinese!" Chin had grown accustomed to receiving stares of blatant shock from Americans and Europeans, whether he met them on a ship or in a port. But this man hadn't even flinched.

"Perhaps he was so caught up in his memories of the fire that he didn't notice."

They arrived at the printer's and Chin held the door open for

Winnie. "We'll tell your father we found the best newspaper in town!" The pair giggled and entered the shop of the only surviving printing press in San Francisco.

THE PRINTER TOLD Winnie that the ad would go out in tomorrow's newspaper. He handed her change, his fingers stained with ink, and said to come back in two days' time for the pamphlets.

They asked him for directions to the post office next.

"Take a right out of the shop here on Front Street. Follow the burnt district out to the other side of Portsmouth Square, where a large new hotel has just gone up. Can't miss it. You'll find the post office on Clay, past Kearny." He paused, then added, "Just be prepared to wait all day for your mail."

"All day?" Chin asked. Waiting was the worst!

The man looked at him and nodded. He, too, didn't seem to notice—or care—that Chin was Chinese. Something weird was going on here.

"This city has grown in the past three years from about nine hundred people to a population of over ten thousand—with boatloads more arriving every day. And all of them want news from home. And news from my paper, too, thank goodness."

News. Winnie swallowed her nerves and asked, "Sir, did you happen to hear about, or report on, the whaleship *Chase* from Nantucket? Around Thanksgiving of last year, maybe?" Her heart was in her throat.

The printer's face fell. "Yes. I remember that story. A real tragedy, all hands lost."

"All of them?" Chin asked. "Even Samuel and Joseph—what was their last name?"

But Winnie just pushed Chin out into this most strange city, without even saying a thank-you or goodbye to the clerk.

"I'm sorry about your friends," Chin said, taking Winnie's hand in his. They walked in silence this way for a few blocks.

"Hey!" Chin pointed at a man walking toward them along the opposite side of the wide street. It was crowded with people and horses and carts, so perhaps the man didn't notice Chin's wave. Chin approached him and began talking loudly and fast in a language that Winnie didn't understand. The words sounded almost melodic, full of emotion.

The man's brows knitted together in curiosity, but he shook his head and kept walking past them. Chin stopped right where he was in the street. "Did you see that man? He was Chinese!" Chin blinked back the tears in his eyes.

"I saw him. But why didn't he talk back to you?"

"Maybe he speaks another dialect. We have so many!"

Winnie laughed, until she realized that Chin wasn't joking.

"It's been so long since I've spoken Cantonese. I didn't realize how much I missed it." Chin sighed.

"You can talk to me in Cantonese," Winnie said. "Even if I don't understand it. Maybe you can teach me some words and phrases."

"Hou hou!" Chin exclaimed. "That means *very good*."

Winnie repeated the phrase. Chin corrected her a little bit and then, the third time she said it, he seemed satisfied with her pronunciation. When she returned to the ship, she'd write it down, and then keep a running log of new vocabulary.

For all of these months, Winnie had been wanting to learn from her mother and father about the China trade, thinking she had been living with experts. But now she realized how foolish she had been to miss what was right before her: an actual expert. If Winnie truly hoped to travel to China as a merchant who understood the customs of the place and its people, in order to trade with them respectfully and well, she should have been studying with Chin all along.

"Oooo, look! A giant rat!" Chin said, shooing away the rodent who sat in the street like a kid at a fair, a crabapple in his mouth. "Go away, you!"

Perhaps Winnie should forgive herself for not thinking of Chin as an expert sooner, at least not in any vocation other than having a rollicking good time being himself.

CHAPTER 29

After three hours in line at the post office, Winnie and Chin were both growing tired and hungry. Since they were used to three meals a day at scheduled hours, they hadn't thought about where to eat—or what to eat—in San Francisco.

The lack of food was making Chin cross. He watched as the men around him took hunks of bread from their horse's satchels or passed a can of beans among them. Someone was heating a pot of coffee on an open flame and selling it, but you had to bring your own cup. Who walked around with their own cup *off* a ship? Miners, he supposed. Winnie and Chin were not like these others, who camped out and seemed to have brought everything on their backs—or the backs of their horses. They were down from the goldfields, these men, dirty and stinky, looking much worse than the crew of sailors from the *Stargazer*. Chin got the sense that prospecting for gold wasn't nearly as glamorous as owning it.

But working at the post office seemed like kind of a fun job, if you could read English, which Chin could not. As the line inched slowly forward, Chin watched as the men behind the counter were each told a name and then went in search of mail: Jackson, Rodriguez, Marshall, Jones, Thomas, Smith, Suarez. One man asked for mail for ten different people, explaining that he was an expressman, paid by miners who wanted the mail delivered to them at the camps.

"Now, that's a smart business, right there," Winnie said. She couldn't wait to tell her parents about this, the way a problem was identified—men not wanting to leave the gold fields for days on end just to collect mail that may or may not be waiting for them in San Francisco or Sacramento—and then solved profitably.

The expressman walked by and tipped his hat, having heard her comment to Chin. "Why thank you, ma'am. I work for the Western Express. Adams & Company at your service. You look like a lady with some wealth about you, so you should know who we are. In addition to being mail couriers, we also handle banking services for miners, bringing their gold dust down from the hills, getting it weighed, and sending the value to an express office somewhere on the other side of the country to a gold dust widow. All services for a fee, of course."

"Of course!" Winnie said, delighted. "And I'm Winifred Starbuck from Nantucket, a merchant-in-training aboard the fastest clipper ship to ever sail the seas. We're heading to China next."

"Well, count me impressed, miss." The man mounted a dappled gray horse and kicked her side. "Seems we're both going places." The mare turned around and was off.

Winnie watched the spot where the expressman had just been, an idea settling around her along with the kicked-up dust. To win her parents' favor and be welcomed on the trip to China, she needed to provide them with an invaluable, *irreplaceable* service. She had tried being a sailor, but that hadn't worked because it wasn't specific enough. She needed to come up with something no one else could give them. Whether that was a service or a product, she didn't yet know. But she had a week to figure it out.

Whether her parents liked it or not, she had inherited from them the soul of an American capitalist.

"Only six more people to go!" Chin told Winnie, fidgeting so much he was practically dancing. The boy just could not keep still, which Winnie hadn't noticed on a ship that was always moving.

Chin had studied the whole post office system in the past few hours, but he still had some questions about it. There were two lines for English speakers and one for Spanish speakers, and one line to pick up newspapers, but no lines for Chinese speakers. Were he and the man he'd seen today the only two people here from his country? There *had* to be more.

China wasn't that far from here, after all. Maybe, in the year since he'd been gone, his countrymen had heard about the rush for gold and come on ships across the Pacific to try their hand at panning and mining for riches. And, if there were more Chinese people here, where did their mail go? Chin would ask the clerk, a young-looking man with sandy hair that stood up a bit in the front, when it was their turn.

A woman with long black hair tied back in a braid approached them. She wore a colorful skirt and held a basket of some kind of hand pies. "*Tres* dollars," she said, in a mixture of two languages. She held up three fingers.

"Three dollars! For a single snack?" Winnie asked. Hand pies on Nantucket cost two cents apiece!

"What are they?" Chin asked.

The woman said "Empanadas" and started to explain the ingredients in Spanish. Chin heard "queso" for *cheese*, a word he knew from some sailors on the ship, and that was good enough for him.

"Two, please," he said, holding up his fingers and nodding.

"But we don't know—" Winnie started.

"We know those men are eating them over there and not dying from poisoning, so our decision is made!" Chin had been eating bland American ship food for a year now and was certain anything would be better than that. No offense to Cook.

"My father will kill me for spending so much money on these," Winnie said, sighing and handing over six bills.

"Which is why we won't tell him!"

The woman thanked them and then, moving on to solicit more customers, said something in Spanish to the man behind them. He laughed and translated it for Winnie and Chin. "She says she makes more in one day selling food at the post office than her husband does all week at the gold mines."

"Interesting," Winnie said. "That could mean something good for merchants here."

But Chin didn't really care about adding to the Starbuck fortune, at least not on an empty stomach. "On the count of three," Chin said, and they each took a bite. It was warm and crispy, with gooey white cheese that stretched with each bite.

"Delicious," Winnie said, her mouth full.

Chin nodded. As they turned back to their spot in line, he noticed that the clerk with the sandy hair was gone.

JOSEPH ALLEN CROUCHED on the floor of the post office, hands over his head.

"What is the matter with you?" Lucas asked, looking over from his spot at the window next to Joseph's. He scanned the crowd outside. "You hiding from someone?"

"He's *definitely* hiding from someone," Paolo said from across the room, where he manned the Spanish line. "He's been acting weird all day. Must've lost a bet last night at the Old Ship Saloon."

"Or kissed a girl he wasn't supposed to," Lucas said. "Like that pretty blonde over there. Eating empanadas with the Chinese kid."

The two of them made oooooo-ing sounds followed by moans and grunts. This being a pioneer town full of men, they hardly ever saw fancily dressed American girls about their age, so when they did, they acted ridiculously.

"Enough!" a deep voice called from the large wooden sorting table behind them. Their boss, a tall thin man with a thick cloud of white hair and a beard and mustache to match, dropped the pile of mail in his hands, rose to his feet, and peered at the first window, behind which Joseph was indeed squatting uncomfortably.

Leland Banks, postmaster, put his hands on his hips and sighed. This kid sure was an odd duck. Joseph was smart, and even funny sometimes, with a kind manner, but, just when Leland and the rest of the team warmed to him, he'd pull a stunt like this without any explanation. Screaming out in the middle of the night, crying when he thought no one was looking, taking a day off work saying he was "sick" when he looked just fine to Leland. Staying on his sleeping mat once for three days straight, not talking or eating.

Leland knew these boys arrived in San Francisco with some sort of past, but every other one of them unburdened themselves, sharing stories and moving on. But not this kid.

"Looks like you need a break there, Joseph."

"Yessir, I do," Joseph said.

"Can you get yourself back together in twenty minutes?"

Joseph stared at his boss's dusty brown cowboy boots and nodded before shuffling across the room on his hands and knees.

"Next!" Leland called, taking Joseph's place behind the first window counter.

JOSEPH CRAWLED TO the back of the post office and turned right, around the corner to where newspapers were stacked up for distribution at the lone window on the side of the building. There he put his back against a cool, dark wall and straightened his legs on the wood floorboards. He was shaking all over.

Close call.

That was Winifred Starbuck out there. He had thought so, with that blond hair and those green eyes, her parents' ship newly docked in the harbor. And then he heard her say her name, and any question of doubt was suddenly replaced by a stabbing, paralyzing fear.

Joseph couldn't let her see him. He couldn't let *anyone* from Nantucket see him. Then they would know he was alive.

Because the thing was, Joseph Allen wasn't alive, not really. His body was here, somehow, going through the motions of life, chewing food, saying words, walking with one foot in front of the other. But the rest of him had died that day, sinking with the *Chase* in the bay with every other sailor, including his own brother Samuel.

Three letters had arrived from Joseph's mother over the nine months he'd been here in San Francisco, working in the post office. "My dear Joseph and Samuel," the letters began. He couldn't read past their names. Not one more word. He tore them up and burned the scraps in the campfires prospectors set up to warm themselves and their food as they waited overnight so as to be the first in line for the day.

Some men broke down into sobs when they didn't get a letter—or when they did. Meanwhile, Joseph was destroying his mail, a terrible new loss that filled him with even more self-loathing than he'd thought possible. But he didn't deserve to hear his mother's voice in his head, to imagine her sitting in the sunny front window of their farmstead on the Madaket Road, looking out past wildflowers and sheep in the meadow as she thought of her two youngest sons and sent them news from home.

After what happened on the *Chase*, Joseph deserved to be dead. And so he would pretend to be dead until the day he actually died.

JOSEPH HAD A harder time than usual falling asleep that night. The post office windows closed at 7:00 p.m., and he, Paolo, Lucas, and Kit—the kid who worked the newspaper line around the side of the building—swept the floors and moved packages into corners.

Then they gathered at the giant farm table they used for sorting mail and ate a simple meal of cold pork and sliced apples with their boss, Mr. Banks. Although the weather was mild, the post office clerks had found it dangerous to spend too much time outside amid the gold rushers. They got ornery waiting for mail and were known to blame the clerks, once even mobbing the post office until a riot broke out.

If Joseph and the others wanted fresh air, they'd head downtown to the marina to gamble and drink and flirt with women who got paid to flirt back—and to do much more.

Not that Joseph had ever done that, either by paying for it or getting it for free. He had met a gal at a saloon on his nineteenth birthday last month who was willing, but he chickened out at the last minute.

A smaller one of his life's failures. A nineteen-year-old virgin, for goodness' sake. He had been a pathetic sailor and a terrible brother, and now he was turning out to be a pitiful man.

"Who's dealing?" Paolo asked, shuffling a deck of cards in his hand. Poker was Joseph's favorite, a game he had learned aboard the *Chase* from a French sailor from New Orleans.

Joseph's fellow clerks were smart and quick, and made worthy opponents. In this way, for an hour or two each night, Joseph lost himself to the strategy, a competition with no real risk involved. They made poker chips from tree bark and invented some of their own rules.

It felt almost like a life.

But tonight, after they had put away the cards and rolled out their sleeping mats and Lucas had blown out the lantern, Joseph stared at the wooden beams in the ceiling and imagined he was on Nantucket, lying in the grass and staring at the stars in the sky with his brother Samuel beside him, instead of a snoring Lucas.

In his teen years, Joseph learned as much as he could about astronomy, including how to read, track, and use the movement of the stars for navigation from Miss Mitchell, who ran the Nantucket Atheneum and, in exchange for work in the library, trained boys who wanted to go to sea. And late at night, Joseph would wake Sam from the narrow bed beside his and the two would sneak out of the house to study the sky, careful not to let the door creak on its hinges and wake their parents. Joseph taught Sam everything Miss Mitchell had taught him, so they could go to sea together, navigators both.

August had been their favorite month to observe the purple blackness, when Mars and Jupiter were both visible in the Nantucket sky, sitting close to one another in the constellation of Taurus. Jupiter glowed more brightly than Mars, and, around the middle of the month, they swapped places.

August was also the month of the Perseid meteor shower, when the sky showed off its brilliance, hundreds of meteors shooting through the sky leaving long tails of light. The Perseids occurred in California, too, peaking in mid-August through all of North America, but Joseph hadn't gone outside to see them this year.

"You asleep there, Joseph?" Mr. Banks asked, his voice low and gruff. He slept in the doorway of the post office with his gun under his mattress. Mail was a serious business, and Mr. Banks protected it—and the clerks—with fierce loyalty. *The first line of defense*, he called it.

"Yes, I'm asleep," Joseph joked back.

The man chuckled. "I guess I should've asked the opposite."

They settled into a companionable stillness. Joseph listened to the crickets outside, mating in the hills. Only the male crickets chirped, running their wings together to attract the females. Stridulation, the process was called.

That's the kind of useless knowledge Joseph Allen had stocked away in his brain, dumb scientific tidbits that helped no one, and certainly hadn't been able to save his brother. Hot tears rolled from his eyes, down the sides of his face, and into his ears. He choked back a sob.

"Wanna tell me about it?" Mr. Banks asked.

"No, sir." Joseph sniffed.

"Keeping it to yourself doesn't make it go away." When Joseph didn't reply, Leland Banks told stories about his time growing up in St. Louis, his voice soothing and soft. It carried across the room like a lullaby, rocking Joseph to bed like the waves under the *Chase* used to.

By the time Leland reached the part in the story in which his wife died giving birth to their first child, a girl he named June for the month in which she took her only breath, Joseph Allen was fast asleep.

CHAPTER 30

September 1–2

Winnie woke before the sun. Along with everything else in storage, her mother had gotten their metal bathtub hauled out of the hold yesterday. It now sat in the middle of the main deck with a curtain hung around it, available for anyone to use after Winnie bathed in the hot water Chin had dumped into it.

What a luxury! Winnie scrubbed at her body and hair with a bar of her mother's French lavender soap, leaving only when the water grew tepid and filthy around her.

"Next up!" she called, alerting Chin when she vacated the area wrapped in her mother's silk robe. Besides bathing themselves, all the sailors were washing their things and hanging them out to dry on the lines, socks and shirts and pants waving in the gentle breeze, making the ship look like a hastily dressed ghost.

Breakfast in the great cabin with Winnie's parents felt lonely without all of the passengers. Sully and Jonathan and Zander were talking to Doc, who was in charge of overseeing all repairs being made to the ship while she was docked. A shipbuilder had come aboard yesterday and assessed the damage, and now the crew was reinforcing the masts, but not replacing any of them.

"Good news," Winnie's father said, sipping from a cup of tea. "That will save me both money and time."

Doc nodded. "And Rip's gone into town today to see if we can buy extra canvas."

"Shouldn't be too hard," Zander said, "seeing as there are hundreds of ships just sitting around us, not needing their sails." Unlike the others, Zander had not disembarked yesterday, uncertain about how a Black man might be treated in the new state of California. It had been founded as a free state, true, but Zander had heard that slave-owning folks who settled here with their slaves—or anywhere out west, really—faced very little trouble from the authorities. Why, he could just imagine the way white men would conspire to have captive Blacks and Natives mine their gold for them, much like they had been enslaved to pick their corn, cotton, and tobacco back east. California could become just another plantation in time. This country's soil wouldn't be safe for him until the entire country abolished slavery, and who knew when—or if—that would ever happen.

Instead, Zander had used his spyglass to peer onshore and around the harbor.

Curious about a ship that seemed to have movement on it by Central Wharf when every other ship around it was abandoned, he watched for a while. The *Euphemia*, it was called. A chill went through him once he figured out that it was a prison.

No thank you: Zander wasn't leaving the *Stargazer* until he reached China. No thank you very much.

AT THE LARGE warehouse Nell had rented, fog hung low around them and blocked the view of the expansive bay. The warehouse was filled with items carried out of the hold once the ship was properly docked at Long Wharf: iron stoves and crates of liquor, bolts of fabric, furniture and carpets and on and on. Each crate was labeled, and many of the goods had been unpacked yesterday and sorted and checked for damage. Winnie put her hand to one of the crates reading Wright's Leather Goods, Boston, with the word Shoes underneath, and thought about who would purchase them and where they would walk in their lives.

"Nostalgic for your days in the hold?" Sully asked, dropping a large wooden box near her feet, his brow sweaty and his face red from exertion.

Winnie bristled but said nothing. Everyone in the world now knew that she had stowed away, which meant his words held little power over her. Secrets worked like a candle given air. They had a way of burning out quickly once breath was on them.

Throughout the warehouse, a few other sailors detached the nailed-down tops of crates, removed the hay stuffing, and checked the contents, while Winnie's mother roamed the makeshift aisles in the barnlike space with her log open, counting dishes and building materials, iron bed frames and horsehair mattresses, sacks of onions and grain and flour, coal, cotton, silk, candles, spices, and barrels of oil.

Nell was overjoyed to see that most of the cargo had survived the trip with little damage. Some of the cut-glass goblets that she had originally imported from England had chipped, but they could still be used as decoration in one's home. She made a note to reduce the price by half.

Having heard about the historic arrival of the *Stargazer* without need for the Starbucks to advertise, the mercantile and saloon owners, builders, and manufacturers lined up outside the giant open doors with their carts and horses at the ready.

"Winnie!" Nell called.

"Coming, Mother," Winnie called from somewhere on the other side of an upright piano. They had brought three pianos with them, although only one had been purchased beforehand. It was like this with much of the freight on the ship; some of it had been preordered or shipped and paid for by large companies, while other items were purchased by Nell for resale in the open market. A merchant had to study the market in order to invest in products and goods that they felt confident would sell in certain ports. Items like gin and wool imported from Europe sold very well in New England but less well in the South, because Southerners preferred to wear their own cotton and drink their own whiskey. But everyone drank tea from China. And in San Francisco, Nell had taken a gamble and felt that people needed just about everything here, including upright pianos.

The bay smelled like low tide. The morning's fog lifted and the sun peeked through clouds, illuminating the warehouse's high windows with a golden glow. San Francisco weather certainly was finicky.

Nell and Winnie settled behind a wooden farm table with a large box of alphabetized receipts while Peter introduced himself, shaking hands and clapping men on the back like old friends. "Yes, we had quite a journey!" and "You are correct; that is our daughter, the stowaway."

Winnie's job was to find the original sales slip from Boston, where the freight had been loaded onto the ship months before. Nell then collected the sum due and wrote up a final bill of sale, giving one copy to the person before her and making a second copy for their own files. Then someone from the crew located their specific items in the warehouse and loaded the cargo for the purchaser to transport.

Peter invited the men to peruse the left side of the warehouse, where items Nell had brought specifically for this market were available for purchase. "We even have carpets from India and silks and furniture from China," he boasted, using a line that had often worked in the past when trying to off-load goods. Peter did not mention that these items were left over from their last trip to Asia in 1846. Even the best merchants weren't right 100 percent of the time, as trends changed and people—and their neighbors—decided they'd rather have a Louis XIV–style wardrobe from France instead of Chinoiserie from Canton.

Several men nodded and took a walk up and down the aisles. One shrugged and said he had plenty of Asian goods already, noting that China was close by, relatively speaking. "Ships come pretty regularly from that side of the Pacific to here," he said. "Bringing tea—and Chinese workers and prospectors by the boatload. Items from Europe, though—those are special indeed."

Peter steered him toward Nell's slightly damaged red cut-crystal goblets from England.

Chinese workers and prospectors by the boatload! That explained it. Winnie couldn't wait to tell Chin.

The next man in line announced himself as the owner of the Verandah Resort, which had been destroyed in the last Great Fire in May. "I placed this order for bed frames and mattresses a year ago, when my business was thriving, but I don't have insurance and can't rebuild," he said to Winnie and Nell, his hat in his hands and worry creasing his brow. Hearing the man, Peter came over.

"But I came here in good faith," the man continued, "to ask for your kindness in letting me out of this contract."

"What are you going to do next?" Peter asked. Perhaps the man could get another job and pay off the cargo in time?

"I plan on trying my luck in Sacramento, away from this city's corruption and the hooligans who keep starting these fires."

"I see," Peter said, thinking. The onions and spices could be taken with him for use on his own ship. But what could he do with a dozen beds?

"Father," Winnie said. "I think I can help."

"Oh, yes?" Peter asked with cynicism. "Do tell."

"Chin and I passed a new hotel yesterday by the post office on Portsmouth Square. They were just painting the signage . . . the Colona? No, the Colonnade!" Winnie said. "I can go there tomorrow after I pick up our flyers from the printer. It's a large hotel. I'm sure they will need beds."

Peter raised his eyebrows. "Fine. Inquire." He turned to the man. "Return here in two days. If I sell these to another hotel at the same price, I'll void your contract. If I take a loss, I'll have to pass that on to you."

"Thank you, sir," the man said, putting on his hat and leaving.

Winnie bit her tongue and kept herself from boasting about what she already knew would be true, for, based on the inflated price of an empanada outside the post office, she'd sell those beds at a great profit.

THE NEXT DAY, with Red this time as an escort, Winnie picked up the printed flyers and headed to the Colonnade Hotel. As Winnie expected, the hotel manager was delighted to hear about the brand-new beds. Winnie asked for double what had been on the original sales slip from Boston. The man didn't even flinch at the price, although Red's eyebrows shot up to the lobby's chandeliers.

"Thank you very much, Mr. Simmons," Winnie said. "You can collect the items anytime before Sunday at our warehouse off Long Wharf." Winnie glanced around the large lobby space, which had sofas and tables and a bar along the right wall. "Such a lovely reception area," she sighed. "It's a shame you don't have a piano for entertainment. Think of the crowds you'd draw to your bar with that."

And, from the dreamy look on his face, Winnie knew she had just sold a piano. She'd triple the asking price and see what he said. If he balked, she could always back down and offer him "a great deal" and still double her profits.

"WOW!" RED SAID, a spring in his step. His hair, eyebrows, eyes, and ears all seemed especially excited. "You are really good at selling stuff!"

"I know!" Winnie laughed. "And you of all people should already know that I'm good at convincing people to take things they don't know they need or want."

Red stopped in the middle of the square, next to a wooden pole where the American flag had been erected. "You mean like me helping you aboard the *Stargazer*!" He smiled, understanding dawning.

"And you would be terrible at cards. You must learn to keep your face neutral and hide your true emotions!"

They handed out flyers in Portsmouth Square to any man with interest. Children poured out of the doors of a public school across the street, running to the square for recess. With a stick, a girl drew a series of boxes in the dirt while several others lined up behind her for hopscotch. A boy playing tag with some others touched the flagpole where Red and Winnie were standing and called, "Safe!"

Moving aside to avoid bumping into the boy, Winnie had a sudden flash of memory. At the start of fourth grade, Winnie's parents sent her to the Cambridge School. The day before she left, she visited the Allen family and played tag with Samuel for old times' sake. They had grown too old for such games, really, but as soon as Sam's older brother Joseph whistled a start, Winnie's natural competitive spirit kicked in. The next thing they knew, Joseph had gotten in on the chase, all three of them screaming and running through the field, avoiding the chickens and sheep as best they could as they aimed for tagging one another with "you're *it*" or being the first to reach the safety of the pine grove that bordered their property.

Samuel declared Winnie the reigning champion of tag, even though his older brother Joseph had actually beaten them both.

Did they know that day would be the last time they ever played tag? Maybe. Maybe not. They probably hadn't given it much thought one way or the other. More often than not, you only recognized *the last time I*... in retrospect.

RED SPOTTED A bustling saloon across the square and suddenly grew very, very thirsty. He hadn't had much alcohol at all on the trip, as Captain Starbuck forbade it except on holidays and special occasions. And he hadn't disembarked and gone exploring with the rest of the crew on that first—or even second—day in port because Cook had needed him to scrub and clean the galley. He was behind schedule in getting properly sauced in California.

But what to do with Winifred Starbuck? Only certain kinds of women went into saloons, and although they dressed expensively like Winnie, they were nothing like her. Red watched as two such women entered the saloon now, dressed finely in silk gowns with full hoop skirts and fanciful feather-plumed hats. Their hair was nicely coiffed and jewelry sparkled on their wrists and necks. They seemed well-mannered, thanking the gentleman who held the wooden door open for them, but Red knew looks could be deceiving. In fact, he was counting on it.

"How about we divide and conquer, eh?" Red said. "Like, I can talk people up in the saloon while you enter some stores and such. What are men doing drinking in the middle of the day over there? They must need jobs, right?"

Winnie found his playacting almost comical, but she went along with the ruse. Hadn't they just established that he was terrible at masking his true feelings?

"That's a good idea, Red," she said, stifling a smile. "Meet you back here in an hour?"

Red looked longingly at the saloon. He wondered if there were rooms upstairs where he might take one of the ladies. Spend a little time and some of his hard-earned money. "Give me two," he said.

WINNIE MEANDERED AROUND Portsmouth Square, asking to hang up flyers in both a barbershop and at a mercantile and then inquiring about other places to distribute the ad. She was told to try Washington Square and Union Square, as well as the ship saloon and some other places down by the wharf where sailors-turned-prospectors-turned-maybe-sailors-again might congregate.

"And the post office, of course," the barber said, wiping a dirty razor on his apron before shaving the other side of a man's face.

"Of course. I was heading there next," Winnie said. She felt certain that she could tap into the potential of that waiting crowd, exploit it even. Last time, she had learned what was what. And this time, she had come prepared to do business.

But first, there were the eggs to sell. She had taken them from one of the coops on the deck this morning—with both her mother's and Cook's blessing—and nestled a dozen in straw at the bottom of her father's leather mailbag. She first approached several men off to the side around a makeshift campground of sorts, sitting in a circle made of logs and cooking coffee over a flame. She extended a metal cup, handing out a dollar in exchange for the steaming hot black liquid. "You know what would make for a nice breakfast?" she said, not pausing for an answer. "Fresh eggs." And with her free hand, she dug two out and held them in her palm, as solid as golden nuggets. She was betting that at least one of them had a cast-iron skillet in the canvas or leather knapsacks by their sides.

"Ten dollars," she said.

"Each? You're crazy," the man who had served her coffee said, his voice thick with a Southern drawl, a blue bandana around his neck.

A man to his left tipped his cowboy hat back to get a better look at Winnie. He looked her up and down as if she were the hen who had produced those very eggs. "Must be ten for the pair," he decided. "Nice-looking pair, indeed. Almost worth it."

His pals snickered at the not-too-subtle meaning of his words. Winnie rolled her eyes. These men sounded *just* like sailors. She'd spent three months working alongside men who said snide remarks to her—and one another—almost as much as they breathed. Teasing didn't bother her anymore.

She put the eggs away quickly. "Nothing to be ashamed about, if you didn't make money in the hills," she said. "That group over there looks richer." She signaled toward some men on horses nearby and pretended to walk away.

"Now, wait right there, missy," the man with the bandana said, standing. He reached for something in his leather satchel, and for a moment, Winnie feared it was a pistol. She flinched. But instead, he held out a small leather pouch and shook it. The pouch glimmered in the sunlight, as if it were made of gold. "I got plenty of gold in my poke. And I'd like to buy those eggs off you. I just don't have what you'd call strictly *money*."

"Your . . . poke?" Winnie asked, wondering if his meaning was again innuendo.

"That's where we keep the dust we find," the man with the cowboy hat explained, as if she were slow. "You new here or something?"

Winnie was relieved to know that a *gold poke* was not a dirty suggestion. "Just passing through on my way to China. I'm looking to make money in port."

"Story of my life," a third man said in a deep voice, nodding over his coffee.

"How long have you been out here, doing this?" Winnie asked.

The answers ranged from six months to a year and a half.

"This prospecting. Is it everything you thought it would be?" Winnie asked, looking from man to man, their eyes tired, their clothing caked with dirt. Men who worked their bodies hard every day and talked just like sailors.

"Why do you ask?" the cowboy said, tilting his head sideways and crossing his arms on his chest.

She reached into her bag, withdrew a flyer, and handed it to him.

Forget eggs. Winnie suddenly had another, much bigger idea of what to sell to these men. "Have you ever considered a life at sea?"

SHE HAD DONE *it!* Single-handedly, she had recruited four new crew members, just like that. And they weren't all greenhands, either. Two of the men had been sailors on merchant vessels from New York to California, and they promised to help train up the others. Harry, Merle, Don, and JJ the Cowboy.

Harry, Merle, Don, and JJ the Cowboy.

Winnie hummed their names as she reached into her bag and took out a few eggs, still determined to sell them. With enthusiasm, Winnie rounded the street corner too quickly and bumped right into a post office clerk.

"Sorry!" the clerk said.

"Oh no!" Winnie said, yoke coating her fingers and the front of her dress, broken eggshells lying on the ground between them. "Look at the mess you made!"

"Yeah, well. That's nothing new." The man sighed, looking away. "Now, if you'll excuse me—" He tried to walk around her, his face still turned to the side, as if not wanting to be seen.

His profile revealed a pug nose and sandy hair, lifted in the front by a cowlick. He looked familiar.

It couldn't be. Except, this man was the right height, the same build as her long-lost friend. "*Samuel?*" she whispered, her body numb. *"Samuel Allen?"*

"I wish," the man said, turning to face her.

"It is you," Winnie said.

"No, Winnie. It's not Samuel. It's me, Joseph."

CHAPTER 31

Joseph Allen. Here. *Alive.*

Winnie almost fainted.

Joseph held Winnie steadily by the crook of her arm and led her into the back of the post office, toward a small, cool room with a bench. The postmaster's office. "Sit," he said, handing her a rag to clean off the sticky yoke.

Winnie's shocked green eyes were so, so wide.

She sat. She wiped her hands and dress.

"Where's Samuel, then? What happened to the *Chase*? I heard it—We heard—"

"You heard right." He sank beside her onto the wooden bench.

"All hands lost?"

"All hands. Except mine," he said. Unable to meet her gaze, Joseph looked at his palms, which, after nine months on shore, were no longer rough like a sailor's.

All hands.

Winnie reached out and grabbed ahold of Joseph Allen.

NO MATTER HOW she tried, Winnie could not get Joseph Allen to join her and her parents for dinner aboard the *Stargazer*. Nor could she get him to say anything at all about what happened to the *Chase* beyond the obvious. Instead, he begged Winnie for her silence. "I don't want anyone to know I'm here," he said, his soft brown eyes sad and searching. They were flecked with copper and hints of gold. "Promise me."

"But, Joseph! That's madness. What about your parents? Haven't you written to tell them you survived the shipwreck?" Winnie asked, still clutching his hand in hers. She told him how the *Stargazer* had first heard of the *Chase*'s demise from a passing ship headed back east. "And that was months ago now. I'm sure news of the *Chase* has spread."

"I don't want anyone—even my mother—to know I'm alive."

"But—" Winnie protested. She imagined Mr. and Mrs. Allen learning that not just one, but two of their beloved sons had perished in one terrible moment at sea. How could Joseph let them believe it?

For the first time maybe in her entire life, Winnie couldn't come up with a way to sell someone on something, no compelling rationale to make Joseph act. Winnie had a will unlike any other. But, how could you *will* someone alive if they wished to be dead?

"You have to come with us, Joseph!" Winnie said, the answer clear as day. Sailing was the way to both revive Joseph's spirit *and* aid the ship, by handing her father a well-trained—a *Nantucket-trained!*—navigator. "I mean, you have to go with my parents. To China on the *Stargazer*."

"Not with you, too?" Joseph asked.

Winnie shrugged, like it didn't matter. "I won't be joining my parents on this part of the journey, apparently." She explained—very briefly—how she had stowed away on the ship and, although she had made quite a fine sailor indeed, as punishment, her parents were making her return straight home on a steamer.

"You cannot be serious," Joseph said.

"I am! Look at these calluses!"

Joseph shook his head sadly. "I believe *that* part. Samuel always said you were fearless. Or . . . did he say *reckless*? *Stupid?*"

She bumped Joseph's shoulder with hers.

"What I mean is, you cannot seriously think I'll get on that clipper. After what happened in the bay? Trust me: I'm never getting on a ship again."

"Joseph!" a deep, slow voice called. "You getting back to work or are you moving to China?"

Joseph stood quickly. "That's my boss. I gotta go."

"But—" Winnie said. "We just found each other! I can't say goodbye yet."

Joseph was surprised to find that, after going out of his way to avoid Winnie, he now wanted to see her again. "Come back tomorrow night? We close at seven."

"Perfect!" Winnie said.

"Perfect," he echoed, one corner of his mouth smiling.

Winnie walked briskly to meet Red at the flagpole in the center of the square, her heart buoyed. Although still mourning Samuel, Winnie was thrilled to find that Joseph had survived such a terrible tragedy, and that he was smart and funny to boot.

Joseph could be exactly what—or who—Winnie had been searching for, her own Western Express. Delivering Joseph to the *Stargazer* was an irreplaceable service that only Winnie could provide. If she was successful, her father would be so delighted and impressed that he'd have to let Winnie sail with them, both as payment and in appreciation.

Fearless, reckless, stupid: Joseph could call Winnie whatever he wanted. He had no idea who he was dealing with. The formidable determination of Winifred Starbuck was stronger than any harsh wind or rough waters. Winnie was a force of nature, and she was going to push this sailor back out to sea.

Never say never, Joseph, she thought, just before greeting a very-drunk Red.

Red smelled rancid, like strong booze and stronger rose perfume, and his hair was even more askew than usual. Winnie wrinkled her nose in disgust, giving the ship's steward a withering look just like Red's mother used to when he had spent all night out with his friends at the pub. "What?" he asked, genuinely surprised. He was certain he was hiding his inebriation with mastery, putting one foot in front of the other just like—*that.* Completely nonchalant and not swaying at all.

"The top button of your shirt is undone," she said, shaking her head at him. She also saw a purple bruise blooming on his pale neck but did not point it out.

Red quickly buttoned his shirt. Next, he felt for the fistful of dollars in his pocket and, realizing he had none left, smiled. Now *that* was money well spent.

AS RED AND Chin served supper, the Starbucks caught each other up on their day. Victorious for all the shrewd business she had accomplished, Winnie reported about having sold off the bed frames and mattresses, one of the pianos, and all of the eggs—except for the broken ones, which she didn't mention, because she didn't want to reveal anything yet about Joseph Allen.

From opposite sides of the long, empty dining table in the great cabin, both of her parents stared at her in disbelief.

"And the manager from the Colonnade is sending a horse and cart to the warehouse to pick up the bed frames and mattresses tomorrow. And the piano. I told him that he might have to make several trips, but that didn't seem to bother him."

"Incredible, Fred," her father said, clearly impressed, and not even able to hide it behind a stern facade. "I'll gladly have two of our men bring the piano over on a dolly for no additional charge, considering what you've gotten him to pay for everything. Unless. The hotel isn't located up a steep hill, is it? Those sandy slopes seem nearly impossible to navigate." Peter had walked around town and found that, while the main streets like Stockton and Mission were flattened earth, several of the hills rising up and out of the harbor were basically sand piles in which his feet sunk into the softness. Like climbing a beach!

Winnie stabbed three peas on the tines of her fork and ate them one by one. "No. It's not up a hill. And one other thing—" Winnie beamed "—I recruited four sailors, two of whom have already worked on merchant vessels. They'll be coming by in the next day or so to sign with you, Father."

Her father pushed back from the table, his arms open wide.

“That’s tremendous!” He went to Winnie’s chair, and she stood for an embrace. “Look at our daughter, Nell, saving the best news for last.”

Only it wasn’t the best news, and it hopefully wouldn’t be the last. Based on the work being done to repair the ship before leaving port, Winnie had six more days to persuade Joseph Allen to sign on. And when she did, she couldn’t wait to see the look on her parents’ faces.

“At the rate she’s going, our daughter may turn out to be a better merchant than both of us combined, Peter,” Nell said.

Red placed a second helping at Peter’s setting.

“Ah, Red!” Peter said. “Winnie was just telling us about her incredible conquests in San Francisco today! Please tell us that you accomplished greatness today, too.”

“Greatness! Yessir.” Red bowed—and then burped quite loudly.

That made Chin laugh all the way back to the galley. There, he told Cook, who chortled all the way through the next morning’s breakfast, letting Red sleep in—and sleep it off.

CHAPTER 32

September 3–6

The next few days were busy beyond comparison, a mixture of selling off goods to make room for purchases from China and restocking foodstuffs for the voyage. Everywhere Nell and Winnie went, they handed out recruitment flyers, inviting any and every man they passed an opportunity to sail to China aboard the fastest clipper ship the world had ever known.

Nell had traveled the entire world and yet had never seen a city quite like San Francisco, which was simultaneously gritty and well-to-do, destitute and charming, depending on which way you turned your head.

Although the physical landscape was unfamiliar, Nell's brokering work was well-traveled territory. Nothing made Nell feel more comfortable than heading to Market Street, aptly named in just about every city around the globe, and negotiating with suppliers for salt pork and dried beans and rice and barley and flour and wheat—*and butter! Don't forget the butter!*

At the end of the long shopping day, as she argued with a butcher over the price of cured ham, Nell grew practically apoplectic with joy.

Winnie enjoyed observing how her mother made deals with both ruthless calm and eternal optimism, employing a practiced distance that belied how much she actually cared about the outcome of the deal. But Winnie's arms were heavy with packages and they hadn't taken a break all day. "Can we return to the ship now?"

Exiting the butcher's, Nell turned her head and peered through the glass window of the next shop. "Oooo! An apothecary! One last stop, I promise. Let's see if they want to purchase French lavender soaps!" Nell reached into the basket on her arm and pulled out a new sample. A bell over the door rang as Nell entered the shop, looking as fresh as she had that morning.

The more Nell worked, the more energetic she became. She would push and drive a hard bargain and love every minute of it. Barter, sell, trade, negotiate, exchange—whatever she was up to, Nell Starbuck had to exit a shop victorious.

Back on the street, Nell smiled contentedly. "Sold!"

"I have learned so much from you today," Winnie said. "Gleaning several different ways to bargain: underpricing an item to get rid of it quickly, overpricing it because of its rarity and scarcity, and also appealing to something in the middle, namely fair market value. All of these techniques can be used to sell the very same item, depending on the circumstance in which you are holding your negotiations. It's about perception, more than anything."

"Exactly! And if you speak with confidence, people have a tendency to believe you. Even a woman."

"Well, then, believe me when I say that, when it comes to driving a ship hard, you and father are exactly alike: confident, competitive, and completely stubborn."

Nell raised her eyebrows in surprise. "Well. That is quite a tutorial."

"Yes. So I'm calling eight bells. This shift is officially over."

PETER STARBUCK FINISHED one pint of ale and gestured to the bartender for another. He had been waiting for over twenty minutes at the end of the long bar inside the Old Ship Saloon for a Mr. Mulholland to show.

Peter had arranged the meeting so that he could cancel his plans for involvement in the opium deal in China. Thanks to his wife and daughter, Peter had secured enough profit to pay back his business partner, Robert Forbes, with interest. And that meant Peter didn't need to get involved in the illegal smuggling of exceptionally profitable opium anymore. His business had always been a legitimate one and would remain so.

Peter had just sent word—and payment—to Forbes's offices in Milton, Massachusetts, via Adams & Company, an ingenious express system that prospectors used to send money home from the gold mines. Instead of having to risk mailing the funds directly to Robert Forbes, Peter had written a check to Adams & Company for the full amount owed to Forbes—forty thousand dollars for the ship and another eight thousand in profits from its cargo—and paid a small fee to make the transaction.

Peter no longer owed Robert Forbes anything. He had paid back the loan for his half of the ship and was back on solid financial ground again after leveraging his house as collateral. East Brick was no longer in jeopardy and the *Stargazer* belonged solely to the Starbucks. The ship was his.

Gone was the financial pressure that had sat on Peter's chest like a brick for almost a year. Gone was the sense that he had acted impulsively and gotten in over his head, replaced with relief so great that it felt like a celebration. He had come to the surface, no longer trying to breathe underwater. And so he drank like a fish.

Where was this man?

Peter ordered a third beer, putting a five-dollar bill down on the wood-planked counter of this ship-turned-saloon, another ingenuity born in San Francisco. The bartender hustled over with a refill and pocketed the cash quickly. Money always spoke louder than words.

"Ah, Starbuck," a man said, slapping Peter on the back. He was short and was cloaked in a brown capelet. "There you are."

"Mulholland, finally," Peter said. The two men shook hands. "Come, sit."

"Afraid I haven't got the time to stay," Mulholland said, distracted.

"Oh. Well, I'll get right to it, then. I'm pulling out of the China deal."

"A prankster! Drinking has gone to your head."

"I'm not joking," Peter said.

Mr. Mulholland's countenance shifted from indifference to irritation, his small beady eyes hardening. "And neither am I, my friend. This isn't a thing you can just change your mind about. The deal has been a year in the making, the steps already put into motion. There's no reneging on it now."

"But I don't like it," Peter said.

"What's not to like about making a quick buck?"

Peter lowered his voice to an angry whisper as he looked around for possible interlopers. "I refuse to take part in smuggling opium into China."

"And yet, you wanted to a year ago, when you signed the contract with my bosses at Jardine Matheson."

"I sent them word yesterday," Peter said. "I've called it off."

"And that letter will take two months to reach them in Scotland, by which time your *Stargazer* will be in China."

Peter's heart galloped like the Pony Express. "That's why I asked to meet directly with you, as their representative in California. You must be in a position to make decisions on behalf of your employer."

"Oh, I am very much in that position," Mulholland said. "And, on behalf of Jardine, Matheson, and Company, we flat out refuse your proposition. Be prepared to enjoy your riches."

Mulholland and his cape turned and walked out of the Old Ship Saloon.

ALL DAY, WINNIE had been thinking of Joseph Allen. Part of her mind was present in her body, grounded with her mother as they traipsed through the city. But another piece of her mind floated away, above the noise and crowds of the markets and shops and food carts and gambling dens like a homing pigeon aimed toward Joseph. She imagined him standing at his post office window, handing out letters and packages, his neck stiff and legs growing tired as people blurred by.

Winnie thought of Joseph again as she slipped away from the ship after dinner, asking Chin to cover for her—a request for which he merely rolled his eyes and stuck out his hand so she could place a dollar bill into it. Winnie knew she wouldn't be missed for an hour or so.

Walking down Long Wharf and through the city as dusk fell, Winnie pictured Joseph. His face was both like Samuel's and also not. Samuel's eyes were dark brown, while Joseph's were lightened with flecks of copper. Samuel's face had always remained baby round and freckled like a boy's, with that signature Allen pug nose, while Joseph's face had grown more angular as he matured, his jawline square, his nose straighter and more prominent. Even his hair had grown up, no longer hanging straight into his eyes but gaining texture and movement. He looked both familiar to Winnie and like an entirely new person.

FROM THE BACK room of the post office, Joseph heard the knock on the window and knew without looking that Winnie Starbuck had returned.

"I'm looking for Joseph Starbuck!" Winnie said through the glass.

"Hey, isn't she that pretty one in the fancy dress that we saw here the other day? Waiting with the Chinese kid?" Paolo asked.

"Yes, that was me!" Winnie yelled, her face practically pressed to the glass. "The pretty one! Now, somebody, let me in!"

"A woman who knows what she wants," their boss said, striding across the room and unlocking the side door before Joseph could get there himself. "I don't know about you boys, but I feel compelled to do as she says before she breaks the pane."

"Nothing says trouble like a good-looking woman who knows what she wants," Lucas said, making a crude gesture with his pelvis.

Joseph introduced Winnie, his cheeks aflame with embarrassment. He had spent two years aboard a ship and thus should have anticipated how men would react to a woman's presence. "This is Winifred. Winnie," he said, quickly ushering her out of the main room and into the alcove where Kit sorted and handed out newspapers.

"All we get is two versions of a first name?" Kit asked.

"Nice to meet you all!" Winnie said, waving over her shoulder as the men chuckled.

"Your friends are charming," she said once they were alone.

A corner of Joseph's mouth smiled a fraction of an inch.

He sat on a stack of newspapers that acted like a stool and rubbed his face with his hands to hide his flushed cheeks. Winnie dragged over a similar-sized stack and sat facing him, knees almost touching. To get past any awkwardness, she told him about her day of shopping with her mother, and realizing how alike her parents were, both consumed with being the best, the fastest, the most profitable.

"You say that as if it's a bad thing, wanting to win," Joseph said. "When it's probably exactly what you want, too. I mean, why else would you sneak aboard their ship? To *lose*?"

"You wouldn't understand. I *need* to see China."

Joseph raised his eyebrows and sat back. "Oh, I think I would. Because I thought I needed to see San Francisco."

They let that sit between them with the growing darkness. Joseph lit a lamp and placed it by their feet.

"I've been thinking," Winnie said.

"A dangerous thing for a girl to do," Joseph said. His brown eyes were teasing. Copper flecks, yes. And also, a hint of gold. His hair was medium length and slightly tousled, and the front swooped up from his forehead like a cresting wave.

"I think—" Winnie continued.

"Too much, obviously," Joseph concluded. Winnie kicked him lightly in the shin.

"I believe—" she started again. And when he didn't interrupt her, she continued, "I wonder—"

"Ladies and gentlemen, Winifred Starbuck thinks, wonders, *and* believes! Samuel not only mentioned your fearlessness, but also often spoke of your intelligence, and now I get to witness it for myself."

She could have kicked him again, made sure he felt some pain. Instead, she sensed that this comedic deflection was a way to cover up all he was really feeling, including immense pain. "I cannot imagine how much you miss him."

Joseph frowned. No one could imagine what he missed and how much. Home. Samuel. His mother's cooking. His mother. Nantucket. The sea. The list was endless.

He had tried to let all the things he missed—along with all he felt about it—sink with the ship in the bay. Otherwise, it would pull him under, too. The feeling was too much. Too sad. Too sickening. Too permanent. And here came Winnie, a tsunami bringing everything back up to the surface. "It's getting late. You should probably go," Joseph said.

"But—" Winnie chided herself for having pushed too far. She wanted to use one of her mother's tactics for continuing negotiations when a shopkeeper was being difficult, but Joseph's face had already closed for business for the day.

She would have to try again tomorrow.

HAVING RETURNED TO the ship with a throbbing headache, Peter sat forlornly on the couch in the captain's staterooms. His mind kept returning to the dreadful conversation with Mulholland at the saloon. How could the man have delivered such a decisive no, and such a quick one at that? Was there really no room for negotiations? Would Peter and his *Stargazer* truly have to smuggle opium into Canton?

"Peter," Nell said, finding her husband with his head in his hands in the dark. "Are you unwell?"

Peter made a noise somewhere between a grunt and a sigh.

Nell lit the oil lamp hanging above them, casting the wallpaper scene of the Cantonese harbor in a soft glow. She placed the back of her hand to Peter's forehead. Cool. Clammy. "No fever, at least." She sat next to him on the sofa. She had been married to Peter for over twenty years and knew when something was wrong. "How can I help?"

Peter couldn't tell Nell about the opium deal now, not after having promised just days ago to tell his wife the truth—and then promptly refusing to do so. Had he disclosed the specifics right then when taking that oath, he'd now be able to share openly with Nell the fact that he'd tried to do the right thing tonight. And that, because of Mulholland's refusal, he now felt like Odysseus sailing home and encountering Scylla and Charybdis, stuck between a rock and a hard place. "I'm not sure you can help me," he mumbled through his hands.

What he needed was a skilled negotiator, a person with guile and cunning who didn't accept *no* as an answer.

What he needed—he realized—was actually his wife.

His head snapped up and he turned to Nell. "When serving as a broker between two others, is it possible to get out of a deal once a contract has been signed?" Peter asked Nell. He wanted to explain his role without exposing the true story, so he substituted one product for another. "For instance, if I tell Forbes that I'll accept one thousand dollars from him and use that money to buy tea that I'll then bring back to Forbes. As a middleman, for a fee. Can I get out of buying the tea?"

"It *is* possible," Nell said slowly, trying to be diplomatic in giving solid advice as a businessperson and not accusatory as Peter's wife, wondering what in the world he'd gotten himself into. "But it depends."

"Depends on what?" Peter asked, hope fluttering in his chest like a small caged bird.

"Whether or not money has exchanged hands," Nell said.

"Go on," Peter asked.

"Let's just say for argument's sake that you signed this paper committing yourself to accepting one thousand dollars from Forbes to purchase five tons of tea. Well, if you don't accept the cash, then the deal hasn't yet begun."

Peter's mood instantly brightened. "So, without money from Mulho—Forbes with which to do the deal, I couldn't possibly buy the tea and thus wouldn't play any role as a broker."

"Exactly," Nell said.

Peter hugged Nell so tightly that the small brooch at her neck nearly stabbed her in the throat. She loosened herself a bit, arms still around one another, until Nell felt Peter's heartbeat settle.

Peter smiled over Nell's shoulder. Without money to do the deal, the deal could not be done. He'd visit Mulholland in his office tomorrow and relay this in no uncertain terms.

"Everything all right now?" Nell asked, pulling out of the embrace.

Nell's eyes sparkled like emeralds in the lamplight. She was gorgeous, his wife, and brilliant, too. How lucky he was to have married her. "It will be, darling. Thanks to your sage advice, it will be all right soon."

PERSISTENT TO A fault, Winnie showed up again at the post office the next night, and the one after that. Both times, she was met at the door by Joseph's boss, Mr. Banks, who shook his head sadly, his large mustache hiding his frowning top lip. "Sorry, Winnie Winifred. Joseph says he doesn't wish to receive guests tonight."

"But, sir, if I could just talk to him for *five* minutes . . ." Winnie said when she was about to be turned away the second time. The post office wasn't that large, and so she knew that wherever Joseph was hiding out, he could probably hear her. She peered around Mr. Banks and saw the others sorting mail very slowly, clearly listening in as they pretended to work. "It's of utmost importance. Please tell Joseph that the *Stargazer* needs a navigator. My father hasn't been able to find one willing to join us. Them."

"Oh, really? A navigator?" Mr. Banks asked, his interest piqued. "What makes you think our clerk here—who tells us nothing about himself or where he came from—would be good for that particular job?"

"Because Joseph Allen is a sailor from Nantucket, sir. And I've known him my whole life."

Leland Banks's bushy eyebrows shot straight to the sky. "Really?" he whisper-asked, leaning in closer to Winnie.

She nodded.

"Huh." Mr. Banks stepped outside and closed the door lightly behind him. He crossed his arms over his chest. "Tell me more."

"Yessir. Joseph was taught about astronomy by Miss Maria Mitchell at the Atheneum, so I know he's well trained. And he sailed on the *Chase* for two years before it . . . well, you must know that part. And we—I mean, my parents—really need someone with Joseph's skills for the trip to China. My father knows a good deal about navigation, and together with our helmsman, they can kind of do the job, but a trained navigator would be preferable. So, we need to take Joseph with us to China and then we'll bring him back home."

Home. Home was a powerful word, especially to a man like Leland Banks, who didn't have one anymore. He had assumed Joseph Allen didn't have one, either, because if he did, why was he remaining in this godforsaken nowhere? Leland Banks smelled a campfire and heard the clinking of tin as men settled in for an evening meal by the fire, their home a tent, their bed the hard-packed earth.

"He got family back there? On Nantucket?" Mr. Banks asked.

"Yessir," Winnie said.

A look of understanding crossed his brow and then a heavy determination settled into the lines in his face. Mr. Banks opened the door again to the post office and raised his voice, almost in a theatrical way, like when Lily Bird and Winnie had rehearsed their Shakespearean scenes back on the ship. "Do me a favor, miss, and listen to what I'm saying. Please honor Joseph's request and leave him be!"

"Fine!" Winnie shouted back in exasperation. She had thought she was making progress, but clearly not. And now she only had two days left before the boat sailed for China. She was running out of time.

Just as the postmaster was about to close the door in Winnie's face, he leaned down and whispered in her ear, "I think we might be able to get somewhere with him, missy. Thank you very kindly, and do come again tomorrow."

He slammed the door shut and winked at Winnie through the glass.

THE NEXT EVENING, while the rest of the crew was at dinner in the city, Sully skulked past the galley and wended his way down into the hold. He loosened the nails and opened the cache of weapons Captain Starbuck kept just in case the ship was attacked, and removed all of the guns, putting them into a cloth sack. Without nailing it shut, he placed the top on the wooden box as if nothing had happened.

Back in the officers' quarters, Sully hid the sack under his bed. Tomorrow he would sell the pistols for a mighty fine fee, a real West Coast profit. In twenty years at sea, the captain had never needed those guns the way Sully did. Someone else would now put them to good use and the crew and captain would be none the wiser.

"What have you got there?" Zander asked, a pistol in his hand. He held it loosely, in an almost nonthreatening manner.

Sully stood slowly and faced the helmsman. "What do you think you're gonna do, heh? Shoot the first mate? Imagine what people would say when they come back from dinner: an empty ship and a white man shot to death by a Black one." He shrugged. "A runaway slave, no less."

"I'm not a slave," Zander said, raising the gun a few inches.

"Sure you are. I saw you hide that day we spoke to that other ship in the Atlantic. And I suppose that's why you didn't join the group for dinner tonight. Too dangerous to step foot on land. You do understand that, while we're still in port, I can go to the post office, compose a letter to the catchers back east, describing you and tipping them off to your whereabouts?"

Zander said nothing. The hand holding the gun went numb. Was there no way to outsmart a scoundrel like Sully? Would the first mate always be one step ahead?

Zander didn't have a plan. He had come upon Sully accidentally, following the sound of noise on the ship. Since everyone was leaving tonight, Zander had decided to keep his gun on him for protection, should thugs try to board the ship and rob it while it was seemingly deserted.

"But I'm not going to do that yet. I'll just hold it over ya for a bit. More fun that way. And we'll pretend we didn't see each other here tonight," Sully said, pushing past Zander and leaving his stateroom, guessing correctly that Zander wouldn't search it.

Zander almost shot Sully in the back, but instead, he waited until the man left. Then he punched the wall, wrapped his throbbing knuckles in cloth, and drank a big pull from Cook's hidden bottle of whiskey up in the galley.

TONIGHT WAS WINNIE'S last chance to convince Joseph Allen to join the crew of the *Stargazer*, because tomorrow night, she would be attending Jessie Lindquist's send-off party and wouldn't be able to slip out. The morning after the party, the ship would depart for China.

She knocked on the side door to the post office. It was now or never.

"And looky who's here," the postmaster said, opening the door for Winnie. "What a surprise!" His bushy eyebrows rose and lowered dramatically as his voice grew louder. "I thought we told you to go away and not come back!" Stepping aside to let Winnie in, he whispered, "Your timing is impeccable."

"What did you want me to do with this package, sir?" Joseph called from the back. He entered the room cradling a large wooden box in his arms and saw Winnie across the room. "Oh, you." He dropped the box by his feet.

"Lovely to see you, too, Joseph." Winnie smiled.

Mr. Banks addressed Joseph. "This package needs to get delivered to the wharf tonight."

"Tonight?" Joseph asked, incredulous. "Can't they just come pick it up here tomorrow, whoever they are?"

"It must get to the Coffee Stand now," Mr. Banks said, looking around the room as if searching for something. "The one you've got there with the new receipt slips in it . . . and this one here, too." He picked up a package from under the farm table. It seemed lightweight, but was larger even than the other one. "Cloth napkins," he explained. "And since you can't carry both, and I need my other clerks here to help me sort tomorrow's mail, why—I think we're going to have to ask this Winnie Winifred if she can help you deliver them."

"I'd be happy to take that from you, sir," Winnie said, extending her arms. She sensed that she was following along with some sort of script, but she didn't know quite what the play was about.

"Really?" Joseph whined, sounding like a petulant child. "We have to do this now? Together?"

"Yup," Mr. Banks said, shrugging as if it were perfectly reasonable for a ramshackle restaurant on the pier to need napkins and receipts immediately. Winnie already had a lantern dangling from her right hand, so Mr. Banks handed one to Joseph for the walk back. Then he held the door open. "Take your time, Joseph. And, since you'll be missing supper here, why don't you grab some food down there at the wharf." He shoved a ten-dollar bill into Joseph's back pocket.

"That's not necessary," Joseph protested. "I can feed myself, thanks."

Winnie was catching on. "I'm pretty hungry, though." The more time she spent with Joseph, the more time she'd have to convince him to join the crew of the *Stargazer*.

"Yeah, Joe, feed the lady!" Kit called out from the back room. The others snickered along, all unseen.

Joseph groaned. "I feel like you're in on something, and I don't like it."

"And I don't like you accusing me of being calculating, Joseph. If you want a good job tomorrow, and every day after that, then you'll do what I say," Mr. Banks said with finality.

Joseph pursed his lips and said nothing. He picked up the wooden box and marched past Winnie with angry steps. Winnie would have to be quick to keep up. She hesitated for one second before leaving, looking at the postmaster with confusion.

"I've done all I can, missy. The rest is up to you. Now, go show him that incredible record-breaking ship of yours and pray that she wins his heart," Mr. Banks said, slamming the door in her face, a sly smile appearing under that giant mustache.

"JOSEPH!" WINNIE CALLED across Portsmouth Square. "Wait up!" The package she held was made of linen strips tied together and bound with twine. The thing was solid but kept slipping as she walked, especially at a brisk pace. "This is harder to carry than I thought it would be! Please," she called out. Some people in the green turned their heads as she complained, and one man in a top hat even offered to assist her, which she declined as Joseph marched on ahead. "I feel like I'm carrying a very chubby and unwieldy toddler!"

At that, Joseph paused, and Winnie imagined him smiling despite his urge not to while she caught up with him. "You're panting, too," she said. "Let's walk at a slower pace. I don't really believe there's a rush to get the items there, do you?"

He shook his head no. They walked side by side down Clay and toward Front Street, carrying a heavy silence along with their packages. As evening fell, Long Wharf was crowded with people coming and going from the taverns and gambling dens that lined the pier. Winnie could see the *Stargazer* docked in the deep water at the end of the half-mile long wharf, but she felt fairly comfortable with her anonymity in the crowds.

They delivered the goods to one of the owners of the food stand, who balked at the timing. "I'm busy serving dinner! Come back tomorrow!" he said, sweating over a charcoal stove where he was cooking fresh fish.

"Nope, here you go," Winnie said, leaving her parcel by the back of the tent that served as the restaurant.

Joseph copied her. He next reached into his back pocket and withdrew the ten-dollar bill from Mr. Banks. "And we'll take some of that herring," he said to the man.

"Now you're talking!" the man said, letting them jump to the front of the line amid protests from the other customers. "For ten bucks, you can even keep the plates!"

They carried their tin plates away from the crowds, looking for a good place to rest and eat. Winnie sat on the edge of the pier between two storefronts, her feet dangling over the edge. She looked out over the bay in the growing darkness, the sky deep pink and the hills in the distance a jammy plum.

Joseph sat down next to her. He gazed out over the water and shivered slightly, although the air was mild. "I don't like to come down here," he explained.

"Do you just—stay at the post office all the time?" Winnie wondered aloud. From the plate in her lap, she picked up one of the small skinless fillets, which had been charred nicely and were glossy with butter and sprinkled with sea salt. The cook had removed the heads, which she greatly appreciated.

"Mostly. There's so much work to do there." The excuse sounded feeble even to him. He looked at his food but didn't eat it.

"You must go out sometimes? With the others?" Winnie asked between bites, butter dripping down her chin. Joseph passed her a handkerchief from his pocket. The food stall really did need those cloth napkins.

Joseph looked sheepish. "Drinking sometimes. The one time I went out gambling, I lost all my money in the first game of dice."

"No!"

"Yes," Joseph laughed. "Luckily, I had only brought three dollars with me. Otherwise, I probably would have kept betting to try and make back my losses, and lost even more money. This way, I only lost my pride. Trust me, it's much safer for me to stay put."

"Speaking of which . . ." Winnie began.

Joseph scoffed. "Are you really going to try and sell me again on getting on your father's ship?"

Winnie bit her lip and nodded.

"You are incorrigible."

"And you work in a place that sends and receives mail from around the world . . . and yet you won't travel *at all*? Not even, it seems, within your newly adopted city? And you could easily write a letter to your parents *from your place of work* to let them know you are safe, yet you refuse to?"

"The irony of that is not lost on me."

"It's like you're purposefully punishing yourself, working there."

"Maybe I am," Joseph said.

Winnie could see Joseph's expression darken as it had the other night. She knew he felt bereft; she did, too, when thinking of Samuel and the fate of the *Chase*. But being with Joseph helped lessen her own sadness over the tremendous loss, and she hoped their new-found connection was helping him, too. "You really should try the herring. It's delicious."

"Yeah, I can see the enjoyment all over your face." He smirked.

"Did I ever tell you about the time I worked on deck in freezing temperatures off Tierra del Fuego?"

"Um, since I just met you again four days ago? You haven't told me much of anything," he said, finally biting into the herring and nodding appreciatively.

And so, as Joseph ate, Winnie relayed her story from the beginning. About how she stowed away but eventually became quite a decent sailor, and about the mast breaking on their sixth day at sea, and the way her father acted cooly, with such a single-minded goal as captain, and about Sully the bastard first mate, and about her strong mother, who seemed confident in most areas except when dealing with her father, and about Lily and Jessie and Beatrice and Charles and Chin and the doldrums and poisoning and frostbite.

"Somewhere in there . . . did you say that you helped your mother amputate two of a man's toes?" Joseph asked, taking back his handkerchief to wipe his own face and hands clean.

"Yes," Winnie said. "And I'm certain I'm still forgetting *something*."

Joseph snorted. "You mean there's *more*?"

"Much more." Winnie stood and put her hand out to help Joseph up.

"Time for dessert?" he asked. They set their plates aside, leaving them for someone who might really need them.

"In a way," she said, leading him down the pier. They wove between food stalls and drunken sailors, the night air tinged with sharp ale and low tide. Inside a saloon, someone played a pipe while several men slurred the lyrics to a song off-key. "But first, I want to introduce you to her." Winnie gestured to the prow of the *Stargazer*, where the figurehead was lit by the glow of the rising moon.

"She looks just like you," Joseph said, pointing his chin out and up. "Those blond curls, that confident gaze."

"Well, she's fashioned after my mother, and the two of us look alike."

"It's more than just that, though." Joseph stepped forward a few paces to admire the full scope and scale of the McKay clipper. "She's a glorious ship. Just look at her lines." A bit of wind picked up around them, and for a moment, Joseph imagined being at full sail in the open ocean on such a fine vessel.

"I can see why you don't want to leave her," Joseph added, looking at Winnie.

"It's going to be the hardest thing I ever do, walking away from the *Stargazer*," she declared.

"Harder even than getting aboard her?" Joseph smiled half a smile and shook his head. "After all you've done to prove your worth on this tremendous ship, your parents still won't allow you to stay on for the remainder of the journey?"

"Yeah, well . . ." Winnie looked sheepishly at Joseph. "I had a scheme all planned out to remedy that, but I fear I won't be able to go through with it now."

"You, with a *scheme*? Impossible!"

Winnie's expression turned even more shameful as she looked at Joseph. She felt a pang of guilt in her gut. It was one thing to try to convince Joseph to join the ship so that her parents could have a practiced navigator sailing with them. It was another matter entirely to try to profit herself by making that arrangement happen.

"Why are you looking at me like that?" Joseph said, holding her gaze as if reading her mind. "Oh, I *see*. *I* was a part of your scheme. Is that why you kept returning to the post office?"

"Yes and no."

"So, yes. And here I thought you liked me," he said, his voice teasing but his eyes sad.

"I do like you, Joseph, which is exactly the problem with my plan." Winnie sighed. She couldn't lie to this smart, cute, boy-turned-man, the older brother to her long-lost friend. Just look at him! With his sad puppy face and sweet lopsided smile, his sparks of wit shone through even in his pain. "I felt desperate to bring my parents—and my father in particular—something of value so he would let me sail with them to China. And then I met you, a skilled navigator from Nantucket."

"So, I'm the something of value. And you thought you could use me to improve your own chances with your father."

"Something like that, yes," Winnie said. "But tonight, witnessing your ill ease at the waterfront, I felt like I was trying to trick you into something that you might not be ready for, mainly because it's something I need."

Joseph studied the ship and said nothing. Winnie continued on.

"But now, I truly believe in my heart that boarding this ship and heading to China with my parents is the right thing for *you* to do, Joseph. Because I've seen how you live here, and I know that living isn't merely about being alive. And I am certain you understand that, because you have the soul of a Nantucketer, with adventures at sea in your blood. You didn't die on the *Chase* with Samuel, which makes me think—"

Joseph put up his palm. "That's enough."

"But—" Winnie said.

"No." Joseph's eyes were wild in the moonlight. "You don't understand. The *Chase* went down because of me. I can never go to sea again. It's not safe. *I'm* not safe."

Winnie had sailed in this treacherous bay, where an escort boat had to guide them in for their own welfare. Add thick fog to the unknowable, tempestuous currents, and one could be in big trouble. Whatever calamity greeted the *Chase* couldn't have been Joseph's fault. "I don't believe you," Winnie said, crossing her hands in front of her chest.

"Well, you weren't there, and there's no one else left to ask, so you have to believe me." Mimicking Winnie, Joseph crossed his arms, too. A flop of wavy hair fell over one eye.

Stubborn, foolish boy. "So, you think staying in San Francisco and never sailing again is your penance?"

Joseph shrugged. "What I do with the rest of my life is none of your concern."

"Fine. You can stay here and wallow and feel sorry for yourself and just grow old until you die, wrinkled and sad and alone in the San Francisco post office." Winnie knew she was laying it on thick and didn't care. Maybe for the first time in her life, someone else's fulfillment mattered more than her own. "Or you can help the Starbucks—and all of Nantucket—by being the navigator they so desperately need."

Joseph cut his eyes sideways to look at her and then looked away again. The first star of the evening had appeared in the sky.

"Imagine it, Joseph, visiting China! And at the very end of the entire journey, when the *Stargazer* approaches Nantucket, you'll see the three lighthouses appear, first Great Point, then Sankaty, then Brant Point. Disembarking, you'll embrace your mother and father and siblings, and you will become victorious, a hero overcoming the losses of the *Chase* by ensuring the legacy of the *Stargazer*! The best thing you can do for your family and Nantucket is to move ever forward. That's what Nantucketers do in the face of tragedy. We sail on."

"*Semper porro*?" Joseph asked. Seeing Winnie's surprise, he added, "What? Everyone knows your father's motto."

"Everyone from Nantucket, you mean," Winnie said, feeling even more sure that Joseph belonged on the *Stargazer*. "You want redemption? Navigate the *Stargazer* safely to Asia and then bring her home. She leaves on Monday morning at sunrise."

All of this time, Winnie thought her destiny had been to sail to China, when maybe her life's mission was to get Joseph there instead.

"Incorrigible beyond belief," Joseph said, shaking his head. He waved goodbye and left Winnie standing on the pier without an answer.

JOSEPH COULDN'T SLEEP. He often couldn't sleep, haunted by the past as he was. But tonight, his mind wouldn't let him rest because he was haunted by something else: his future.

The old him, the Joseph from Before, would have jumped at the chance to get aboard a ship like that. And not just sail her, but navigate her all the way to China, and then back home the *other* way, heading west past India and going around the Cape of Good Hope. Exotic and wondrous.

But the new him, the Joseph from Now, knew tragedy and loss. He knew that charting one's own path could be treacherous and filled with unknowns.

Should he stay in San Francisco? He turned his body to the right, staring out the windows at the front of the post office.

Or should he set sail to places he never thought he'd see, along a course he never imagined he'd chart? He flipped over, now staring at the blackness of the back wall.

Back and forth, back and forth, he tossed and turned.

"Joseph!" the postmaster whisper-hissed. "Pick a side already. You're making me seasick."

So he fell asleep with his eyes to the ceiling, and above that, the sky.

CHAPTER 33

September 7

It was hard to believe this was their last night in port. Nell sat at Peter's desk in the living quarters of their staterooms, mostly dressed for tonight's party at the Lindquists', poring over the final accounting, a single lantern burning overhead. In a city teeming with thirsty sailors and miners, Nell had easily sold off all six thousand bottles of ale imported to Boston from Edinburgh, making a nice profit along the way, but it had been harder to sell off the Chinese tea. She hadn't considered the fact that so many other merchants were now profiting by bringing tea directly from China to San Francisco in an expedited and relatively easy two-month journey.

Thus, the tea Nell had carried on the *Stargazer* was considered old, having started in China last year, gone around the Cape of Good Hope to arrive on the Eastern Seaboard of America, and now brought all the way back to the West Coast. Those bricks of tea had traversed the globe to no avail. Ah, well. Most of it had been sold for a hefty profit in Boston months ago. Nell supposed she would just absorb the small financial loss by drinking the rest of the cargo and replenishing her stock with fresh tea in China.

Unlike this quick stop in San Francisco, the *Stargazer* would be docked in China for several months to make the most of the trading season. Nell looked forward to the visit for the commercial aspects of the trip, when she would get to negotiate for gorgeous products made by Chinese artisans, as well as the chance to meet up with other merchants and their wives. Of course, Nell was the only wife who worked. The others lived in beautiful homes in Macao and Hong Kong, where, for the entirety of the trade season, they raised their children and ran their households much as they did back in the English countryside, London, Massachusetts, or New York.

When she and Peter were invited to a gathering of merchants in China, she would certainly wear the outfit she was wearing tonight, since it featured the Starbuck colors. A navy blue silk skirt fanned out around her, thanks to the four petticoats underneath it, worn with a matching bodice in navy trimmed in gold thread that came to a V below her waist. The sleeves were her favorite part of the dressmaker's design, tight to the elbow and fastened closed with a long row of seed pearl buttons, the sleeves then ballooning out in a dramatic puff of fabric around the upper arms. The dressmaker had also fashioned a less-formal top for day with looser, fuller sleeves to wear with the skirt, making the outfit both alluring and quite practical.

"Always working," Peter said, entering the living room from their bedchamber. "Let me help you with the back of your dress."

Nell stood, and Peter stepped behind her and carefully buttoned the gown. She had not yet put up her hair, so he moved her long blond waves aside to fasten the top pearl buttons. Then he delicately kissed a spot behind her ear. "You look lovely," he said.

Nell turned and kissed him on the lips.

"Here," he said, pulling a velvet box out of his pocket.

"Peter!" Nell said. "What could you possibly get me from San Francisco? A gold nugget, perhaps?"

He laughed. "I had it made in New York, by Tiffany, Young, and Ellis. I was going to present you the gift in China, to thank you for all your hard work. But, thinking how much you've already accomplished as chief merchant on this voyage, I decided now was the perfect time."

Nell kissed Peter again. After so many years in business together,

Peter hardly ever complimented Nell for her labor, the expectation being that she would do her job well, as always. So this special surprise felt a bit out of character for her husband. Not that Nell was complaining.

Nestled in satin inside the box sat an extravagant diamond brooch in the shape of an eight-pointed star. The center of the star was composed of one large round diamond surrounded by eight smaller marquise-shaped diamonds for the points of the star. Tiny diamonds set in gold elongated and tapered to the tip of each point, a spray of sparkle in the lamplight.

"Oh, Peter," Nell sighed. "It's exquisite."

"It's just right for the start of a new era, for the chief merchant on the fastest clipper ship in the world. Do you recognize the center stone?"

Nell studied the jewelry, inspecting the large diamond in the middle. "Is that—the diamond your father gave to your mother when they married?"

"It is. The four-carat Starbuck diamond is now yours. And, since I gifted it to you on this journey, I think we should call the brooch Stargazer."

"Stargazer," Nell echoed.

"Who can help but gaze at you, my dear, the brightest star in the sky?" Peter helped fasten the pin to Nell's collar, where it sat perfectly at the top of her navy dress, just below her throat. The jewel represented more than just his devotion to his wife; it represented the legacy of their wealth and prosperity. "Our fate is in your capable hands, my dear."

"Thank you," she added, touching the piece, overwhelmed by the magnitude of the present. "I'll just do my hair and be ready in ten minutes." She hastily closed the accounting log on the desk, revealing the stack of letters underneath. Most had been final confirmations of orders to place in Canton from the East Coast, and one had been a letter filled with Nantucket gossip from her friend Eliza Macy.

"I almost forgot—this came for you today. A local correspondence. Someone delivered it right to the ship," she said, handing

Peter a letter. She didn't recognize the name Mulholland or the return address on Grant Avenue, but it seemed like Peter did, because his face immediately darkened. "What's wrong?" Nell asked.

"Nothing." Peter tucked the letter into a breast pocket inside his jacket. "Just a business colleague, asking for help with a deal in China. I keep telling him no, but it seems he doesn't want to hear it."

"Is this the contract you were referring to the other night?"

"Yes," Peter admitted.

"Interesting. Could it be profitable to us? Do we have room for the freight?" Nell asked, immediately thinking like a sea merchant. These fast clipper ships had been built with less cargo space than the older, slower models, but Nell still felt certain she could make room for a bit more cargo in the hold, especially if that cargo was commercially successful. "Perhaps you can share the details with me as we walk to the Lindquists', to decide if we can reconsider. Winnie can send a letter out to them for us tomorrow, when we set sail."

"I don't want to think about business tonight," Peter said. "I want to think about *you*, my dear, and our beautiful *Stargazer*. I want to enjoy our last night with our daughter and celebrate our triumphs thus far and toast to the journey yet to come."

"Of course." Nell's heart broke every time she thought of leaving their daughter behind, but after having months to get used to the idea, she was now resigned to the fact. There were consequences for one's actions, and that included Winnie's. No exceptions. Otherwise, how would the girl ever learn? "Has Winnie packed?" Nell asked.

"She has. But she wants to sleep here tonight and thus wouldn't let the crew off-load it all until tomorrow morning."

"Stubborn to a fault, God love her," Nell said wistfully.

"The spitting image of her mother," Peter chided.

"Says her stubborn father," Nell added, giving Peter a peck on the cheek on her way to the bedroom to do her hair.

Once Nell had gone, Peter took the letter from his pocket and read it through. Mulholland had sent back another decisive no, firm in his commitment to the deal. He also explained how small Peter's role would be in this simple money-making arrangement, with guaranteed profits. But, like most—if not all—quick paths to wealth, this one was illegal. The ship's hold would be used as a place to store the opium, with men smuggling it on and off in the middle of the night as needed. No one employed by the *Stargazer* had to get their hands dirty. No one on board even had to know.

"Stop acting like a fool," Mulholland had written.

But Peter's ship would leave in the early-morning hours, before Mulholland could get payment to Starbuck. *So who's the fool now?* Peter thought, shoving the letter into a black lacquer box in his desk drawer and going on deck for some air.

SEATED AT PETER'S shaving table in front of the small mirror, Nell admired the new diamond brooch at her neck. It certainly was lavish, the nicest single piece of jewelry she had ever seen, much less owned. She touched the star, outlining the points with her fingers and feeling her collarbone underneath.

Nell should have felt delighted. And yet. Would this new era of theirs prove to be both lucrative and lucky? Or would something get in the way, as it had on the *Shooting Star* all of those years ago? Nell wanted to be cautiously optimistic, but she knew how quickly life could change. All she could do was work hard, accept this generous gift with a generous heart, and hope for the best.

Then, much like one does when seeing the first star appear in the night sky, Nell Starbuck closed her eyes and made a wish.

CHAPTER 34

Jessie Lindquist's home atop Rincon Hill was as impressive as Jessie had promised. She and her husband, Bernard, stood on the wide, colonnaded porch of the Greek Revival home overlooking the bay and greeted guests as they arrived, some by horse and carriage, and others, like the Starbucks, out of breath from walking up such a steep incline on foot.

Upon seeing them, Jessie shrieked and ran down the porch steps and into the street in a voluminous burgundy gown, hugging Winnie and Nell like long-lost sisters. "Oh, how I've missed you both!" Jessie said.

"It's only been a week!" Nell laughed.

"Yes! And we have so much to catch up on!" Jessie gasped. "For instance, tell me *everything* about that glorious brooch!"

Lily Bird came out from the house to see what the fuss was, and then promptly joined in, the four women happily reunited on the Lindquists' front lawn. "Jessie, you certainly have a flair for the dramatic. When the theater rebuilds, you should join me in auditioning for a stage role."

"Lily," Winnie said, slowly and with caution, "you don't seem to have your British accent anymore."

"Oh, that," Lily said, flopping her hand in the air. "Now that Nate and I are engaged, I felt compelled to tell him the truth. Lying isn't good for a marriage."

"How smart of you to know that," Nell said, cutting a sideways glance at Peter, who smiled tightly back at his wife.

"Everyone!" Bernard Lindquist bellowed from the porch. He was as short and wide—and as loud—as Jessie, the pair like a pot with its matching cover. "Thank you for providing my wife with such excellent company on her journey round the Horn, as they say, and for delivering her safely to me here in San Francisco. Jessie is my everything, and now that we are together, my life is complete." Bernard kissed Jessie's cheek and the small crowd on the lawn aahed appreciatively. Then Bernard held the large, ornately carved wooden front door open. "Now, I'd like to invite you all inside for a toast, celebrating the Starbuck family and the *Stargazer*!"

"Oh, Beatrice!" Jessie called, racing up the steps and inside the front hall as rapidly as her heavy skirt would allow. "Beatrice! Open all the champagne at once!"

THE PARTY WAS in full swing as the sun set, a glorious show of pink and red fire over the bay, the Lindquists' home overlooking it all. The living and dining rooms were crowded with influential and important guests. A formal seated dinner for thirty was followed by a dessert reception on the back lawn, with lanterns on poles glowing in the balmy night.

"How momentous to have all of the passengers from the *Stargazer* in one place!" Charles Mortimer said, shaking hands with Winnie. He looked well, with color in his cheeks from either the California sun or the champagne, or both. He had found a decent room to rent in the city and told Winnie how relieved he was every morning to wake up on solid ground.

Charles was writing for the local paper, and told Winnie about plans he had for a book based on their trip. "I shall make you the brightest star on my fictional *Stargazer*, Winifred," he said, to Winnie's delight. Someone in the crowd called out to Charles, and he smiled broadly upon recognizing the figure. "Now, if you'll excuse me, I have been summoned by none other than my hero, Sam Brannen from *The California Star*. Here's my card. Please come visit me one afternoon for tea!" Winnie said she would and put Mr. Mortimer's card in her skirt pocket.

Then Jessie introduced Winnie to so many people that she could hardly keep them straight. While her father talked politics with the recently replaced former mayor, John Geary, her mother discussed confections with an Italian man with a heavy accent who kept handing out pieces of chocolate.

"I see you've met my Mr. Ghirardelli," Jessie said, placing a protective hand on the man's arm as she joined the group. Everyone tonight was personally owned by Jessie; she paraded them all as "my so-and-so," such as "my mayor" and "my architect." And now the candymaker belonged to her, too!

Jessie was quite the character, and Winnie was reminded of how much she enjoyed the bold woman's company. Perhaps it wouldn't be all that terrible to spend a few weeks living in the Lindquists' beautiful home, being a woman of leisure, playing card games with Jessie and Lily and meeting Mr. Mortimer for tea service and not having to work or scheme or plan or think—or sail.

"Well, well. And who is *that* handsome fellow?" Jessie said, looking from the garden toward the house. A young man stood on the back porch, cap in hand, searching the crowd, his back toward Winnie. "I made up the guest list and yet I have no idea who this gentleman is. Please, excuse me." Jessie sashayed her way through the sea of people and up to the back porch, tapping the man on the shoulder.

The man turned and smiled. In the lamplight, Winnie could make out his sandy-brown hair cresting like a wave above his forehead. It was Joseph Allen.

"Oh! He's here!" Winnie said with truly surprised delight. She quickly abandoned her mother, who felt certain that Winnie was up to something.

"Joseph!" Winnie said, interrupting something Jessie Lindquist was saying. "You're here!"

Joseph smiled warmly back. "You're a difficult woman to track down. I inquired at the docks and an old man with a yippy dog told me to climb Rincon Hill, with no specific address except *you'll know it when ya see it*!"

"Why am I not surprised that you came here tonight for Winnie?" Jessie asked Joseph.

"Oh, he's not here for me, Mrs. Lindquist," Winnie began. "He's here to see my father."

Nell reached the group looking like she had seen a ghost. "Joseph Allen?" she asked.

He nodded.

"Oh, Joseph!" Nell said, grabbing the man-boy by his jacket collar and pulling him into a tight embrace, tears springing to her eyes. "I'd recognize you anywhere, even on the other side of America. We all thought you had departed this world."

"So did I, Mrs. Starbuck," he mumbled into her dress. "So did I."

NELL LOCATED PETER on the edge of the expansive back lawn, engaged in a heated conversation with a man Nell didn't know. Not wanting to interrupt, she waved for his attention.

Peter mentally grabbed onto Nell's waving hand like a lifeboat in rough seas. He would have the last word with this Mulholland character now and dash away before Mulholland could get in any retorts. "My wife needs me. Plans with you and Jardine Matheson are *not* finalized," Peter said before walking away. "I didn't accept payment, so this conversation is over!"

Mulholland wore a top hat along with the same cape from the other day and stood partially in darkness, the smoke from his pipe clouding his face. "Oh, but you have accepted the payment, Starbuck. This very minute, as you stand here drinking your champagne, a chest filled with gold is being loaded into the hold of the *Stargazer* by your crew, with orders you signed, so the deal is as good as done. All you have to do now is let the rest play out as planned."

"You forged my signature?" Peter asked, incredulous.

"Did you think opium dealers were honest?" Mulholland smiled. "It's a petty crime considering the rest of it."

"But—" Peter flailed, extending his palms out. Mulholland used this as an opportunity to place an iron key into Peter's hand, presumably to unlock the chest.

"What is it you Starbucks say? That pompous Latin phrase which translates to—*ever forward*?" Mulholland shrugged. "They'll see you in China."

"What was that about?" Nell asked, coming upon her husband as the man he'd been arguing with walked away.

"Nothing," Peter said, but his face was hardened in anger. "This interruption of yours better be important."

"YOU'RE SURE ABOUT this?" Winnie whispered, sitting quite close to Joseph on a beautiful red velvet sofa.

"Yes," he said, eyes filled with yearning. "You were right. I feel stuck here. I haven't really been living."

"But—are you scared? To get on the ship?" Winnie asked.

"No," Joseph said. He'd been thinking about it all night. What did he have left to lose, after losing so much? "I mean, we're all going to die someday, right?"

"Hopefully not *soon*, though." Winnie smirked.

"You've helped me feel better—and bolder. I don't think you know how brave you are. It seems to be contagious."

Winnie fought the urge to take Joseph's hand in hers.

Peter entered the room with Nell, and Joseph stood and introduced himself. Peter's eyes grew wide as Joseph relayed an abridged version of his story. He omitted the details of what happened to the *Chase*, and ended the tale with Winnie imploring him to join the crew of the *Stargazer* as navigator.

"Amazing," Peter said, his hand to his mouth. His mood lightened in an instant, and he began to pace with newfound vigor. To think that he had just left one disastrous conversation to enter into this one, filled with hope! Life was as changeable as the San Francisco weather. "And you're saying that you were trained by Miss Maria Mitchell to navigate—and that you then served that role on the *Chase*?"

"I was in training," Joseph said. "But, for the last month of the trip, I handled all of the daily calculations and charting."

Peter took a moment to study the boy, who stood with his chin out and his hands clasped behind his back as if he was already a sailor under Peter's command. Joseph was tall, at least six feet, and broad shouldered. Physically strong, then. His eyes were a warm, soft brown. A sensitive kid, hiding under a brave facade. Joseph had the sandy hair and pale complexion of his father, and the kind, rounded face of his mother, both of whom Peter had grown up with on Nantucket. Handsome—not that that mattered, although it never hurt. Maybe Peter could mentor the boy. Maybe Joseph could become a captain someday.

"You certainly have the pedigree," Peter said.

"Yes," Joseph acknowledged. He didn't state the obvious error, in that the last ship he had been navigating had sunk, drowning everyone on board but himself. He shifted uncomfortably under Captain Starbuck's gaze. He could feel Winnie standing close beside him, everyone in the room waiting for Captain Starbuck's decision. If this didn't work out, Joseph would convince himself it was for the best. He'd return to the post office and pretend that Winnie and the *Stargazer* had only been a ghost ship in the bay's fog.

"You're hired," Peter said. The benefits of employing the Allen boy greatly outweighed any doubts. There was an edge of sadness to him, sure, which was understandable given the circumstances he had lived through, but Peter also saw honesty and grit in his eyes. This kid was a survivor. The two shook hands. Strong grip, too. "How lucky I am to have found you in the nick of time," Peter added.

"Winnie found me, sir. And, if I may say so, you're lucky to have her as your daughter."

"Yes, yes," Peter said. "Fred is terrific." But his mind was lost at sea already, eyes glowing with excitement. To think: a full-time navigator to replace Leo, freeing up Zander and himself to harness the best wind and sea currents and manage the partially green crew to attain maximum speed to China.

"Winnie told me a lot about the trip here, sir. Like how she got you out of the doldrums after only three days," Joseph said.

"Indeed, she did! Now, if I can get a piece of paper from Mrs. Lindquist, we can draw up a quick contract—with a nice salary for you—and we'll both sign it, and we'll see you at the harbor at morning light." He pushed down thoughts about another contract he had signed and what awaited him in the ship's hold—and in China.

"That's fine, sir," Joseph said. Peter gathered paper and quill and ink from Jessie Lindquist and sat at Bernard's desk in the corner of the room. Jessie lit a candle as Peter wrote, the tip scratching loudly, then signed and dated it. Peter waved a hand over the ink and let it dry. He passed it to Joseph, who paused. "I just have one condition," Joseph said, straightening to his full six feet.

"Absolutely!" Peter said, standing up from the desk chair to meet Joseph eye to eye. "I should have mentioned a bonus. We can work out the details of that once we're at sea."

"I'd certainly like a bonus, thank you. But that's not the condition, sir." He glanced from the captain to the captain's daughter.

Winnie became suddenly and extremely alert.

Joseph nodded at Winnie, his light brown eyes filled with serious intent.

"My one condition, sir, is that we bring Winnie along on the *Stargazer*. Because I'm not sailing to China without her."

PART III

To China

Semper Porro

CHAPTER 35

Monday, September 22, 1851

They had been at sea for two glorious weeks, and Nell Starbuck had never been happier.

Once Joseph Allen had made his declaration clear that evening in the Lindquist home, forcing Peter's hand by insisting Winnie come with them to China, Peter had no choice but to relent. And, suddenly, Nell's lost dream of what her life could have been was returned to her whole. She was sailing on an incredible merchant vessel with her husband and daughter by her side, just as she had been on the *Shooting Star* before disaster struck. It was everything she'd ever wanted.

And now that Winnie was headed to China, there was so much Nell had to teach her! Oh, Winnie came by the art of negotiations naturally; that much was clear. She had convinced four prospectors to join the crew, as well as swayed a top navigator who was loath to return to sea. Nell's daughter was cunning and wise, traits that could help her travel quite far in most of the world.

But most of the world wasn't like Canton.

In Canton, Winnie needed more than just sales savvy; she needed to be able to discern the difference between a high-quality piece of porcelain and a shoddily made one, between a lacquer varnish on wooden furniture that would retain its gloss for a hundred years and a cheap one that would stain one's hands. She needed to understand the underglazing process by which an object became more than just a vase to place next to a fireplace or a punch bowl centerpiece, elevated to an heirloom-quality work of art.

Winnie needed to become a merchant.

And Nell couldn't wait to teach her everything she knew.

WINNIE PINCHED HERSELF every morning, a physical reminder that this wasn't a dream. She was to see the wallpaper come to life in the harbor at Canton! All thanks to Joseph Allen.

Winnie had persuaded her mother that, while thrilled to be learning the art of merchanting, she still wanted to help crew the ship part-time. Thus, her mornings were devoted to swabbing the deck and tying knots and setting the sail configurations, while afternoons were set aside for tutoring from her mother. In this way, Winnie balanced strenuous physical demands that toughened her body with a fine-art education that sharpened her mind. Both activities delighted her soul.

Overall, the crew on this China-bound trip seemed more content and slightly easier to work with than those who had come around the Horn. In the first two weeks, most of the new recruits had even caught on to the basics of how to sail a three-masted, square-rigged clipper. And, if they bungled their work in any way, maybe stepping into a coil of rope on the deck or not gripping and pulling the lines correctly—*right hand over, left hand under*—Sully was ready with a harsh word and his trusty belaying pin to remind them. They caught on rather quickly after that.

"Everything in order, Sully?" Captain Starbuck asked, walking the deck.

"Yessir."

"The new sailors are behaving?"

"Yessir," Sully said, not even needing to lie.

"Good, good." The captain walked away with his hands clasped behind his back, eyes skyward.

That was it? No further interrogation, and no questioning of the green sailors one by one as to their background and knowledge? Sully was relieved, but also flummoxed. This wasn't the same captain he had known for twenty years, the harsh driver of the world's fastest clipper ship. This Captain Starbuck was distracted. It was as if the man had so much on his mind that he couldn't care to think about the present time and place. The captain must be anticipating a particularly complicated deal with the hong merchants in China, Sully decided. At the rate they were sailing, they'd be there in no time.

They had journeyed roughly sixteen thousand nautical miles from Nantucket to San Francisco. In comparison, this leg of the trip was practically easy, sailing six thousand nautical miles in a fairly straight shot across the Pacific Ocean to reach Canton, where the *Stargazer* would dock in just about six weeks. The ship would remain in Canton's harbor for the entirety of the season while the Starbucks lived in one of the large furnished apartments created for American merchants as they purchased cargo to bring back to the States.

While the captain was on shore, Sully would be in charge of the ship. He couldn't wait. Being at the top of the chain of command was his life's goal, and he was close to attaining it. The potent anticipation of having absolute power in the near future contributed substantially to Sully's bright mood.

JOSEPH ALLEN ALSO seemed to be enjoying his time on the ship, despite all of his earlier protestations to Winnie during their time together in San Francisco. He enjoyed watching whales breach the Pacific, knowing he didn't have to chase them down and kill them.

In fact, the more distance that grew between the ship and California, the more Joseph's spirits seemed to buoy. Perhaps all he had needed was to get away from the place where tragedy had occurred. He was happiest sleeping with the current shifting under him and waking to the snapping of wind-filled sails. He felt better by being made useful again at sea, focusing his sharp mathematical mind and skillful training on charting a path ahead. And perhaps Winifred Starbuck's piercing green eyes had a little something to do with it. Perhaps, after ten months of deep, unrelenting grief, it was time to move on. Perhaps *semper porro*.

EACH MORNING, WINNIE worked on deck with the other crew members or made small repairs with Rip, the sailmaker. When the sun was high in the sky, Joseph had gotten into the habit of calling Winnie over to help him take the midday observation. He waved to her now, and she waved back.

Joseph had moved into Leo's cabin that first day on board, and had found, much to his pleasant surprise, that the talented navigator had left Maury's notes behind. Even though Maury's work—and Leo's handwritten notes in the margins—concerned the trip around Cape Horn, the principles and lessons about wind charts and tidal movements were still incredibly useful to Joseph, and he learned much from the charts and anecdotes in the handbook.

"Mark!" Joseph said, squinting into the bright sunlight and reading aloud the measurement from his sextant. His sandy hair had grown lighter in the sun, and the small freckles sprayed across his cheeks and nose had become more visible. Winnie tried not to be distracted by Joseph's appearance as she noted the exact time of day and wrote the measurement in a log. Next, the pair traded objects, Winnie folding the brass navigational tool and tucking it back inside its box and handing the log to Joseph so he could work out the noontime calculations. When he was done, he'd meet Winnie and her mother and the other officers in the great cabin for lunch.

Zander stood nearby at the ship's wheel, noticing everything from Sully's good mood to the captain's distracted one. The new navigator seemed to be getting on quite well.

"It looks like smooth sailing ahead, Zander," Joseph called to the helmsman.

Zander nodded. Smooth sailing indeed. Winnie and Joseph would make a good match, both at sea and at home on Nantucket.

Zander appreciated the fine weather and calmer seas in the Pacific Ocean, where the fear of drowning in a storm was greatly lessened. There had been the occasional squall, but they were fast-moving and easy enough to get through without much panic, not like the days upon days of constant bad weather off South America.

Sully rang eight bells, signaling the end of the four-hour watch period. *Eight bells and all is well*, Zander thought, stretching. JJ the Cowboy, whom Winnie had recruited at the post office, came to relieve him and take the next watch. The guy was nice, and a quick learner. Even with the wind whipping around them, he wore that darned cowboy hat at sea, and the nickname had stuck, with everyone forgetting about the JJ part.

"Hey, Cowboy," Zander said. The man tipped his hat in greeting, making Zander laugh. With Winnie's help, he'd fashioned a small leather strap that attached under his chin and kept the hat from blowing away with the wind.

"What's so funny?" Sully barked.

"Nothin'." Cowboy shrugged.

"Nothing, *sir*, you mean," Sully said. "You're talking to an officer, remember."

"How could I forget?" Cowboy said under his breath, and Zander had to stifle another laugh. Cowboy leaned in close and added, "You know what I'd love to see? Sully's fat ass trying to ride a horse across the Great Plains."

"Giddyap," Zander said, coughing into his hand to cover an even bigger hoot. He went to lunch thinking about how good it felt to have some allies.

NELL AND WINNIE finished lunch in the great cabin just as Zander, Doc, Sully, and Peter were coming in to dine.

"We can only stay for a few minutes," Nell said. "We have a full schedule of lessons."

Peter had to admit, as much as he had fought it, having Fred on board was doing much to lift Nell's spirits, keeping both women busy and productive. After struggling to remove his daughter from the ship, Peter had lost the battle and decided not to cause further friction. Anyway, he had enough to fret over because of the impending opium deal. As soon as he had gotten back on the ship after the Lindquists' party on their last night in San Francisco, Peter had taken the key from the galley and rushed to the hold. Aside from some food stores, it was mostly empty of goods. To weigh down the ship until new merchandise could fill the hold in China, large bags of sand had been brought in as ballast. The hold was dark and dusty, with rats scurrying about. In one corner, there was a box of munitions. And at the other end of the large space, Peter found a wooden chest wrapped with iron chains, making it too heavy for anyone to lift.

Peter almost laughed once he'd unlocked the chest and looked inside. He had been imagining gold bars, but this was the raw material from the banks of California's rivers: pure gold nuggets like jagged pebbles of every size and shape. Thousands of pebbles of pure gold.

It was real. It was here.

And there was not much he could do about it now.

So, he tried to be present as a captain and as a father, although his mind often drifted. Peter smiled politely, ignoring the nagging worry that something might go wrong, and sat down at the head of the table, motioning for Chin to serve him and his two officers. "Ah, and what is the lesson today?" he asked, pushing himself to make pleasant conversation.

"Today we are discussing small, decorative objects for the home," Nell said, "including tea caddies and jewelry boxes. Some clients purchase these ahead of time, but more often than not, we buy them with our own money and sell them to stores back on the East Coast. So, Winnie must understand quality issues and craftsmanship before we arrive. There are many to choose from, and I can't explain what's wrong with the piece in front of the hong merchants. They will find it insulting. Instead, we praise what we like and move on until we find superior products."

Winnie grew excited thinking about hand selecting items that she thought were beautiful, hoping that some young bride in Newburyport or New Bedford, looking for a special object for her new home with her new husband, would agree with her tastes.

"Your mother is well respected. The hong merchants know to show her only the best," Peter added.

"Let's start the lesson right now," Nell said. "Chin, can you please bring me the tea caddy from the sideboard?"

Chin brought the box over, placing it in front of Mrs. Starbuck. He knew the design well, for it was very much like the art that his father and grandfather had made before they had both gotten sick.

The square box was decorated in intricately patterned gold-and-silver filigree. On top was a circular cap where a tiny gold star perched. This small opening limited tea's exposure to air, ensuring the leaves stayed fresh for as long as possible.

This box was atypical, Nell explained. "Most of the expensive Chinese tea caddies we see in the US are made of black lacquer, or traditional blue-and-white porcelain or colorful hand-painted enamel designs with gold edging. Those are all lovely, and we sell many of them. We also offer something more affordable for our customers, like ones made of beautiful rosewood without ornamentation of any kind. But this," Nell said, turning the tea caddy so that the metalwork adorning it caught the light, "*this* is something special. It's similar to items made for the emperor rather than for export. Finding such rarities to introduce to American consumers is what sets Starbuck & Starbuck apart."

"The artistry is exquisite," Winnie said. "To think, we've been using this tea caddy for this entire trip, and I hadn't truly appreciated its beauty."

"As a merchant, I always try to think of the people behind the work I sell. And whoever made this was a highly trained craftsman with the finest skills."

"For a hundred years, my family has made metal boxes like that," Chin said, not caring that he was interrupting Mrs. Starbuck. "Or they used to," he backtracked. "Before."

"We have the descendant of a Cantonese artist among us," Captain Starbuck said.

"But, Chin, as their son . . . wouldn't they teach the craft to you?" Nell asked.

Zander stopped chewing. He knew the reasons why the son of the son of a once-great family might find himself adrift at sea.

"Yes," Chin said. "Every father taught his son our family's trade.

But my grandfather got ill, and then my father followed. Now they are both gone, and so is their knowledge."

"How terrible," Winnie said. "I'm so sorry, Chin."

"But what befell them?" Captain Starbuck asked. "Typhoid? Cholera? Smallpox?"

"Opium," Chin said.

CHAPTER 36

The great cabin was eerily silent when Joseph entered. "What did I miss?" Joseph asked as he pulled out a chair and sat. His calculations had taken longer today, and he was positively starving after finally plotting the *Stargazer*'s latitude and longitude on the chart.

Sully broke the silence. "We learned that Chin's family is typically Chinese. A bunch of lazy, no-good failures."

"Shut up!" Chin cried, anger coursing through his veins. Chin's father and grandfather had been respected for their talent and hard work, artists making imperial artwork for the Qing Dynasty. Their pieces were still treasured in the palace today.

"That's enough, both of you," Nell said.

Peter cleared his throat, where a stone felt like it had lodged itself, making it hard to breathe. "Chin told us about his family's proud legacy as artisans."

"Legacy?" Chin asked. It wasn't a word he knew. It felt heavy in his mouth.

"It means what's left behind, what you inherited from your family," Winnie explained.

Chin nodded. What he'd inherited from his family was the fear that opium would ruin him like it had them.

Joseph hadn't spent much time with the cabin boy, but he did know that Chin had helped Winnie sneak on board, and then further risked his own safety by helping her get through her sick and lonely days in the hold. Sure, she had paid Chin for his efforts, but

Winnie still considered him a dear friend. That was all Joseph needed to know. "Are you okay?" he asked.

"I'm fine," Chin said, although the kid looked distraught.

"Do you want to play chess later?" Joseph asked. Winnie said that Chin was skilled at the game. "After dinner, maybe?"

Chin blinked away some tears. "That would be nice."

Zander passed by on his way out, squeezing Chin's shoulder as he went. "Don't ever let anyone else tell you who you are," he said.

"Yessir, Zander," Chin said, blinking away a few more tears.

"If you'll excuse us, Winnie and I must be off," Nell said.

IN THE COMMON area of their private quarters, Winnie opened her notebook to a fresh page and titled it "Small Decorative Objects." But she couldn't concentrate. "What does it mean that Chin's father and grandfather died from opium?"

"It means that they were addicted to the drug and couldn't stop taking it even once it made them ill. Unfortunately, opium addiction is a widespread problem in China," Nell said.

"Why?"

"Why what?" Nell asked, looking for an example of an ivory-inlaid box in Peter's desk drawer. She knew it was here somewhere; Peter kept important correspondences inside it. Ah, there.

"Why is opium so common there?"

Nell sighed. Her daughter's natural curiosity was draining. "Smoking opium is a disgusting habit and it is none of our business. We Starbucks don't trade in it and we don't use it, and that's all you need to know. Unless you plan to wander into an opium den in Canton, that is?" She raised her eyebrows questioningly.

"No, Mother," Winnie said.

"Good. Those terrible places are only open to men, anyway. Now," Nell said, presenting the beautiful ivory letter box inlaid with mother-of-pearl flowers to her daughter. "Tell me what you see."

CHIN'S MOOD IMPROVED substantially when he beat Joseph quickly and brutally that evening at chess.

"Nooooo!" Joseph cried, raising his arms to the ceiling of the great cabin in an overly dramatic display of defeat.

Winnie, seated on the settee opposite them, looked up from her book and smiled. Everyone else had retired to their cabins for the night. "I told you he was good."

"Good? I'm the best," Chin said, resetting the board for another round at the dining table. "Let me beat you again, Joseph."

Winnie folded a corner to mark her place in the book—Maria Mitchell from the Nantucket Atheneum would have to forgive her—and closed it. She couldn't really concentrate on the story.

"How do you say *win* and *lose* in Cantonese, Chin?" Winnie asked. Her vocabulary was expanding every day, and Joseph had decided to learn along with her. They both knew *hello* and *goodbye*, and could shout "Help!" if they were in trouble, and could ask someone for directions to the port, were they to get lost. The first word Chin had taught them was *tea*.

Chin explained the pronunciation in Cantonese for *winning* and *losing*, *jeng* and *syu*. He then rattled off an indecipherable sentence.

"Slow down," Winnie said. Chin repeated it slowly, but still the two Americans shook their heads in ignorance.

"I just said, 'I beat the dumb American sailor.'" Chin beamed.

Winnie lightly smacked Chin's head with her book. "Your humility is awe-inspiring."

"Thank you," Chin said, taking the compliment without caring what *humility* meant. "Now, who wants to learn some curses?"

After about thirty minutes of playing around with Chinese swear words, it had grown dark. Joseph stood and stretched. Time to take the evening calculation.

"Want company?" Winnie asked.

Joseph picked up the chronometer and chart that he'd brought with him to dinner. "Sure." He shrugged, aiming for nonchalance.

"Ooooooo," Chin teased.

"It's not like that," Joseph said, blushing.

"Don't be ridiculous," Winnie said simultaneously.

"I'm young, but I'm not stupid," Chin said, setting up the chessboard for another game. Chin watched the pair exit through the forward cabin and climb the companionway to the portico. He'd play against himself this time, ensuring once again he'd be the victor, not that he ever had any doubt.

UNDER AN INKY sky freckled with a million stars, Joseph and Winnie made quick work of finding Polaris and the Big Dipper and obtaining a reading. Joseph placed the sextant and chart inside a secure empty barrel. He'd do the mathematical calculations soon, but first he chose to savor time alone with Winnie.

They walked the length of the ship, saying hello to the helmsman on evening watch as well as the few sailors making up the overnight skeleton crew. A soft warm breeze blew around them.

"Is it true what you said? About not being good at learning languages?" Winnie asked. Joseph seemed so capable at just about everything.

"It's true! I was the *worst* student in the entire class, by far. I'm glad you weren't there to witness my humiliation when Miss Stockton asked me to orate all seven declensions of the noun *girl*. And *girl* is one of my favorite words in the English language!"

"Oh, really?" Winnie asked.

"Really," Joseph said, pausing on the deck and kicking his shoe against some uncoiled rope, pushing it back into place. "Although some girls are definitely better than others." He looked up and smiled. They stared at each other for a moment.

"I think that's part of the nominative case," Winnie said, breaking the tension. *"Puella, puellae, puellae . . ."*

"Show-off," Joseph joked, bumping his shoulder with hers. "I was always happiest learning math and science. That's why I became a volunteer at the library." He looked at the stars and pointed out a few constellations and stars of interest.

Winnie loved the Milky Way, the blur of hazy stars that smeared a band of snowy light across the sky.

Joseph agreed. "Stunning," he said, looking at Winnie.

"I bet you say that to all the girls on this ship." She smiled, her heart quickening.

"Just the one," he said. They didn't speak for a while as they looked out over the railing from the stern, the moon casting a path of light onto the ocean.

Eventually, Joseph spoke. "My favorite is the Summer Triangle. It's made up of Vega, Altair, and Deneb." He pointed out each star and the triangle they created in the sky. "I like it because it's not a constellation on its own. The Summer Triangle is made up of three bright stars from different constellations that come together to form their own pattern."

"Like you, me, and Chin! From three separate worlds, brought together here." Winnie's hand accidentally brushed against Joseph's, and she felt a small spark of excitement. She tried to concentrate on what to say next. "Chin must feel left out when we go off by ourselves."

Joseph nodded. "I used to hate it when my older brother Charlie started courting Emily Folger. He stopped paying any attention to me."

"Courting?" Winnie asked, her eyes searching for Joseph's.

He gazed at her quickly and then away, out to the dark horizon. "I didn't mean us, doing that. Just that—" He trailed off, feeling stupid for letting his mouth reveal what his mind was thinking. Winifred Starbuck was the captain's daughter, for goodness' sake! And Joseph was under contract as an officer, not a swarthy sailor trying to make untoward advances on the only single woman on the ship. "I'm sorry. I overstepped. We're friends. You and me—and Chin."

"Right," Winnie said, her heart deflating like a cake removed too quickly from the oven. "Well, I'm on first watch tomorrow, so I better be off to bed."

"Wait!" Joseph called out, but she walked briskly to the captain's staterooms and was gone.

How could he possibly convey the swirling eddy of emotions that he felt for this girl and this ship and this life? Lovesick and foolish and grieving and wanting and regretting and hoping. He felt too much and had explained too little.

Alone in the dark with Winnie Starbuck: aside from navigating this ship safely, that was what he wanted most in the world.

CHAPTER 37

September 30

Joseph finally beat Chin at chess a week later, making tactical opening moves and thinking strategically about controlling the center of the board. "Yes!" he cheered while Chin pouted. Winnie looked on from one of the great cabin's settees, where she read *The Tempest* for the third time.

Joseph was getting sharper. As he lifted a pawn to move it, he could feel his mind strengthening like the muscles in his arms did when working the capstan to raise and lower an anchor. Chess was teaching him how to think shrewdly. It was an important education, and one he hoped to translate into other victories, like perhaps in winning Winifred Starbuck's heart. He'd consider wooing her like a game of chess from now on. All he had to do was make the right moves.

"Joseph, they need you above," Red said, entering the great cabin with a plate of scouse, a delicious leftover mix of beef hash with potatoes that he and Cook were having for supper. They always ate after everyone else had dined.

"I was going to play another game of chess with Chin," Joseph said.

"It's your head." Red shrugged. "Sully and the captain were talking about tacking and then Sully called out 'Where in the hell is the fecking navigator!' so I thought I'd alert you."

"Thanks?" Joseph joked, getting to his feet.

Cook entered and settled next to Red to dine. "Chin, time to start washing up," Cook said.

"Yessir," Chin said.

"I'll help," Winnie said, and the pair headed up to the galley, where dirty plates were piled high next to a bucket of sudsy water.

In the galley, Winnie finally asked Chin about his family, which she had not been able to do privately for the past several weeks.

Chin lit up and talked nonstop for the next ten minutes, until they were almost done with the washing.

"And how did they get involved with opium?" Winnie asked, pretending it was an afterthought.

Chin shrugged. "The same way everyone in China does."

"I don't understand. How does everyone get it?"

Chin dropped the wet rag on the counter and turned to Winnie, confusion turning to anger. "You mean—you don't know?"

"Know what?"

"Know anything about everything, it sounds like." Chin looked at Winnie with resentment. "You are headed to China and you know nothing about us. About me."

"That's not true!" Winnie said. "I am trying to learn your dialect! And I know that the world gets its tea from China, and that we buy beautiful objects made from porcelain and carved wood and jade, and pearls and . . . so much tea . . . !"

"And what do the Chinese get in return? The global business your family is involved in is called the China trade, after all. So what is the trade?"

Winnie tried to think like a global merchant. The Americans traded in cotton and tobacco from the South and sugarcane and rum from the Caribbean, and, in return, got wool and whiskey from Ireland and Scotland and lace from France and Italy. The question was one of what resources each country had and what they lacked—and needed from elsewhere. She put down the plate in her hands, surely made in China. "I'm not certain, Chin. What do the Chinese need from us?"

"Nothing," Chin said.

"Nothing?" Winnie echoed.

"The Chinese people are . . . What's it called when you are able to do everything yourself?" Chin asked.

"Self-sufficient?" Winnie suggested.

"Yes. Self-sufficient. We do not import anything from the rest of the world because we make everything that we need, which is also everything that businesses and people around the world want. But the British who started the East India Company didn't like that, because suddenly all of their money was going out to pay for tea and other Chinese goods with no cash coming back to them."

"So . . . does China make opium, too?" Winnie asked, trying to follow Chin's economic history lesson.

"No," Chin said. "Opium comes from India. It was the *one* thing China didn't have. But we also didn't need it or want it."

"So, how did you get it?"

"The British—and later, the Americans—purchased opium in India and sailed it to China to sell. They introduced opium to my people as a way to trade goods. The drug made them rich. And the more they sold, the more the Chinese needed opium to feed their addiction."

"So they stopped selling it?"

"No," Chin said. "They went to war over it after China destroyed over one thousand tons of opium, trying to stop the British from bringing it in. And in the. . . ." He trailed off, thinking through his mental vocabulary list, while Winnie dried another plate. "Negotiations! In the negotiations, China gave Hong Kong Island to the British, to operate their own trading port in Asia. The emperor also opened up five other trading ports on mainland China for foreigners when the war ended in 1842. And then he was forced to pay for the lost opium!" Talk about unfair.

"So, for the past nine years, the British and Americans have stopped importing and selling opium," Winnie concluded, with a sense of relief.

"No," Chin said. "They continue to smuggle it in by the ton, making millions of dollars by destroying my people. My family. My father and my grandfather."

Cook entered the galley with Red, who was carrying the rest of the dirty dishes and the tea service on a giant tray.

"What did we miss?" Cook asked as Red put the tray down on the wood countertop. "Looks serious!"

"Nothing," Winnie said, coming back to herself.

"Yeah, nothing serious," Chin said, his eyes filled with disappointment as he left the galley. "As you Americans might say."

Winnie waited until Chin left before asking Cook and Red if they knew the origin—and extent—of opium addiction in China.

Cook nodded sadly. "Red and I were in Canton with your parents in both '38 and '41, during the Opium War. There were opium dens all over the harbor. I personally never touched the stuff, but I know a few sailors who did. Terrible." Cook tried very hard not to meet Red's gaze.

Red had been one of those sailors in '38. He had rowed from the Starbuck ship to a pleasure boat in the harbor, looking for a lady to spend some time with, and the next thing he knew, he was high as a kite and limp as a noodle. He woke up two days later, his mouth like cotton. He had no memory of having lain with a prostitute, but all of his cash was gone, so he had certainly gotten screwed.

Red picked up the story where Cook had left off. "Most people report being sleepy and happy on opium, but we know this one guy, who sailed with us on the *Shooting Star* in '38, who ended up mixing opium with whiskey and—"

"And the poor lad ended up very sick indeed," Cook said, cutting off Red in the nick of time, his eyebrows to the ceiling. Even sober, Red could sometimes be a complete idiot. "Let's not scare Miss Winifred here with any tales of the old days, Red. Hmm?"

"Oh, right. Sorry." Running off at the mouth, Red had momentarily forgotten exactly who he was talking to.

CHAPTER 38

October 6

After weeks of pleasant weather, the *Stargazer* hit a strong squall on the afternoon of October 6, a month into the journey, surprising the crew with gale-force winds and giant rolling waves.

Sully called all hands as sailors scrambled to keep their footing on the suddenly wet and jig-dancing deck, their vision blurred by a deluge of rain. "Lifelines, men! Hold on to the lifelines!" Sully yelled. The greenhands ran around in a soaked panic, looking very much like the rats a few decks down surely did, chasing their tails. It would be comical if it wasn't so dangerous. The new crew members hadn't yet seen a storm like this one, and Sully feared that one of the particularly stupid ones might just wash away.

The first mate was glad Winnie wasn't currently on deck, instead taking lessons from her mother in their stateroom about how to get richer and richer. Sully didn't need one more thing to worry about, like keeping the captain's daughter alive while she pretended to be a sailor. How deprived for attention the girl must be to keep trying to get her father to notice and praise her. *Look at me, Father! I'm so wonderful! I'm a girl but I can act brave like a boy!* A person shouldn't have to beg like a dog to prove their worth. They should just rise through the ranks on merit and then boss others around and earn their power. Winnie made Sully sick. He took out his anger on a slow-moving greenhand named Pierce, slapping him across the back with the belaying pin and calling him worthless for good measure.

"Let's furl her t'gallants and reef her topsails and courses!" Sully called, and the crew got to work, climbing the masts and inching out on the yards with bellies folded over them. Pierce coughed up some blood but otherwise seemed fine.

The *Stargazer* dipped down between a swell of the Pacific, and a giant wave crashed atop them, hitting the ship broadside. Zander held on to the helm for dear life and prayed this wouldn't be the end for him, while Sully wished the helmsman would just let go already, let go and disappear.

"We can do this without cha if we have ta!" Sully roared to Zander over the waves.

"Same to you!" Zander yelled back, refusing to let go.

THE DAYS WERE mercifully banal after that. The *Stargazer* sailed west-northwest across the Pacific, racing against time not for the glory of a world record, but rather to arrive in China in time to enjoy the full trade season and sail off before the monsoons began in earnest in April.

Peter thought about China as he took an afternoon walk around the deck, something he did every day after lunch to both aid in his digestion and keep an eye on his crew. But today it was as if his surroundings disappeared, for all he could see in his mind's eye was the hold, which contained ballast, dry food storage, and tea, and, in a dark corner, practically glowing with his guilt, a chest filled with nuggets of gold.

Driven by a compulsion that he could not explain, Peter then went down to the hold like he had done almost every day since the ship set sail and examined the gold. Yes, it was real. And yes, it was still there, weighing him down.

CHAPTER 39

October 17

The *Stargazer* had been averaging 175 nautical miles per day. Joseph studied the chart, adding another dot to his markings of progress across the Pacific. According to Joseph's latest projections, they were now only five days out from Canton. Once they reached Taiwan in the East China Sea and then passed Hong Kong, they'd turn into the South China Sea and then up the Pearl River when the tide was high enough to carry their large ship through the narrow, shallow channel.

He shared the data with the captain, Zander, and Sully during a morning meeting on the poop deck. Everyone seemed pleased with the ship's progress. Everyone except Captain Starbuck, who scowled at the news.

"Only five days? Are you certain?" the captain asked.

"Yessir," Joseph said, squinting into the sunlight, which blotted out the captain's face. "And I've been wondering if you have a particular route you'd like to travel. Based on another chart Leo left behind, there are two possible paths to sail into China from this direction."

"The wrong one and the right one, most likely," Sully grumbled. He had never liked that navigator Leo.

"The popular merchant waterway will be well-traveled, so we'll probably see a lot of ships coming and going. But there's another trajectory that takes us a bit farther west before we head south, which can be faster—or slower, depending on the winds."

"There's no need to go off the beaten path," Zander said. "We're a merchant ship, after all."

Sully agreed with Zander but didn't want to admit it, so he harrumphed instead.

"Captain?" Joseph asked.

Peter knew it would make sense to follow the path favored by other merchant vessels. But then there was a greater chance of being seen, and possibly even exchanging words across the bow. With the gold on board, Peter wanted to remain as anonymous as possible until docking at Whampoa Reach outside of Canton. "Let's try the second option, Joseph," he said.

"Up for an adventure, are you?" Zander asked. It was unlike the captain to choose a lesser-known approach.

"Something like that," the captain said before disappearing down the rearmost companionway steps and into the hold.

The other officers shared an uncomfortable moment in which each held back from asking the others if they believed their captain was of sound mind. Then they went back to work.

FOUR DAYS OUT from China. Then three.

On the morning of October 19, the *Stargazer* passed the island of Taiwan on their starboard side, signaling they were 446 nautical miles from Canton and thirty-six hours from China's coastline.

Peter exhaled for the first time since leaving San Francisco. Before supper, Peter shaved and let Nell trim his hair. He fastened a tie around the crisp collar on one of his new white shirts—replenished by his wife while in San Francisco—and donned his captain's jacket.

"You look quite dashing," Nell said, fastening gold clips on her earlobes. "Are we celebrating something special that I don't know about?" Perhaps she should fetch her diamond brooch from the safe, hidden behind a secret wooden panel next to Peter's desk.

Peter pulled Nell toward him and kissed her on the lips. She tasted like rose oil and black tea. "Every day on this ship is special with you, my dear," he said.

“These last two months of sailing have been a high point of my life. And I have you to thank for that, Peter.”

“It’s I who should be thanking you,” Peter said. If Nell only knew the extent to which that was true, for she and Fred had kept them profitable. To think, he could have lost his home if their business dealings had turned out differently in San Francisco. But they hadn’t.

Nell looked at Peter with concern. “There’s something you’re not telling me.”

Peter smiled tightly. “Just thinking ahead, my dear. Repairs and such will have to be made to the ship in China.” He ushered his wife to the great room for supper, where he offered everyone a drink. Even Chin.

EVERYONE GATHERED ON deck after dinner, for the night was warm and the wind was at their backs.

The mood was infectious. Cowboy and his pals lit some lanterns on the deck while Lucky played his flute and Yip sang along with energetic, off-key yowls.

Whiskey glass in hand, Peter looked around the main deck and smiled, his temper mellowed by the magic of warm and spicy single-malt Glenturret. Soon, they’d arrive in Canton upon the fastest ship that had ever sailed the seas. Global merchants would be gathered there for the trading season. Peter had known many of them for the past twenty years and couldn’t wait to see their faces as he showed off his record-breaking ship with a figurehead that resembled his gorgeous and industrious wife and daughter.

“Hold this,” Peter said, passing the goblet to Nell and heading back to their staterooms. For he had had an ingenious idea, if only he could locate what he needed. “I’ll be back in a few minutes.”

JOSEPH HAD NOT touched any alcohol during dinner, for he had the night watch ahead of him. But Winnie had taken a few sips of red wine and was swaying along with the music as tendrils of her hair came loose in the breeze. She was wholly unselfconscious.

They stood together at the bow, Joseph looking through a spyglass to try to spot oncoming ships. They had passed a few vessels early on, closer to San Francisco and then farther into the Pacific, but hadn't seen any since deciding to veer off on the new route a few days ago. Off to the north, Joseph thought he saw a flash of something moving on the water. A flag atop a mast from an approaching ship? A pod of whales breaking the surface? Who could tell? It was a moonless night and the ocean was shrouded in black.

"Dance with me," Winnie said, extending her hand.

"That's not a good idea," Joseph said, placing the spyglass into a wooden box by his feet and scanning the deck for the captain, not finding him. Mrs. Starbuck stood alone, tapping her feet along with Lucky's flute while sneaking sips from a glass in her hand. Some of the crew laughed and danced around Yip, while others sat with their faces glowing in the lamplight, drinking copious amounts of beer, wine, whiskey, and rum that the captain had allowed. No one was aware of Winnie and Joseph.

"Well, I think dancing is a fine idea," Winnie said.

"Because you're incorrigible," Joseph said, moving closer to Winnie and wrapping one arm around her slender waist. She instinctively leaned her body toward his. Winnie was tall and their torsos lined up perfectly. She put her arms around his neck. Joseph could feel her chest against his, the beating of her heart.

Winnie looked up at him, her eyes filled with a question of longing.

And oh, how he wanted to answer her. His whole body was flooded with sensation, both a sinking ship and a rising tide.

Before rational thought could stop him, Joseph led them in a dance, guiding Winnie with light pressure from his hands and feet.

"A waltz," Winnie said as they continued their box step, her body mirroring his in a small square on the deck.

"The only dance I know," Joseph admitted. "My brother Charlie taught it to me."

"The same Charlie who courted his sweetheart and left you all alone?" Winnie said, closing the gap between their bodies as they danced.

"The very same," Joseph added.

"He taught you well," Winnie said, her breath warm and close.

The music from the main deck grew louder as a fiddle began to play along with the flute. Clapping and cheering followed as someone called out, "Well done, Captain Starbuck!"

Was her father playing the fiddle? Did she care? Although the beat of the music gained momentum and speed, Joseph and Winnie waltzed on. After a while, they sat with their backs against the hull of the bow, legs out in front of them, and talked. And talked.

Minutes turned to hours. The music dropped away, followed by the chortling and conversation of the rowdy, drunk crew. Millions of stars appeared in the black sky. Joseph and Winnie talked on.

Midnight came and went and the men grew sleepy, drifting off to the forecastle in small, staggering groups, and then one by one. Cook, Chin, Red, and Sully sat under the few remaining lamps with Winnie's father. A skeleton crew of five men, including Zander at the helm, worked quietly as the *Stargazer* journeyed through the western Pacific Ocean and into the Philippine Sea toward the Asian continent.

"I cannot believe we'll be in China tomorrow," Winnie said.

"Tomorrow is today." Joseph smiled, one half of his mouth turned up. He knew he was being funny and was trying not to show it.

"I sort of love when you do that," Winnie said, gesturing to Joseph's lips.

"Do what?" Joseph whispered, leaning in close. "This?"

Joseph brushed his lips softly against Winnie's. A whisper of a kiss. Just enough to prove to them both that this was real. He'd do no more than that, to protect her honor—and his own hide.

Winnie's head was a hot-air balloon. The first touch of Joseph's lips on hers sent her flying, even though she was grounded by the deck of the ship beneath her. She leaned into Joseph for another, and then another, this time deeper, longer. Joseph made a soft noise that sent Winnie's body buzzing. She opened her mouth to him, dizzy with desire. If she could stay locked in this embrace forever, she would. Nothing mattered but this moment.

"We should stop," Joseph said, pulling back. His breath was ragged and his lips were swollen.

"We definitely shouldn't," Winnie said. Kissing Joseph Allen was even more fun than pulling sails tight on a keeling clipper ship racing through the wind.

"Sail, ho!" a voice called through the darkness. And then again, louder this time, "Sail, ho!"

"Zander?" Joseph asked, standing suddenly and looking out across the ship toward the poop deck where the helmsman was waving his arms.

"Sail, ho! Starboard side!" Zander called.

Joseph grabbed the forgotten spyglass from the box on the deck and put it to his eye, his hands trembling as he looked right. But he didn't need the lens to help him locate the other vessel, because there she was upon them: a two-masted brigantine with a black flag raised. "Oh no."

He turned to Winnie, now standing beside him. "You must hide! Now!"

She nodded, her face white.

Joseph raced down from the bow, along the main deck and up to the poop deck at the back of the ship. The captain and Sully were already there. Panting, Joseph asked, "What did I miss?"

Captain Starbuck glared at Joseph and grabbed the spyglass from the navigator's hand. "You're on night watch and you missed everything!" he said, whiskey on his breath.

"A ship's upon us," Zander said. "Not friendly."

"Not *friendly*?" Sully said. "She's fulla pirates! And she's *here* thanks to your fecking lovesick navigator!"

"We can tack and sail away," Joseph said, desperation growing by the minute. Had Sully seen his and Winnie's embrace? And, further—had he seen the pirate ship approaching and not sounded the alarm, hoping Joseph would get in trouble?

"It's too late to sail away," Zander said.

But it couldn't be too late, Joseph thought, willing his mind to reverse the hands on the clock by minutes. Just five. "We can outrun her. Just let her try to chase the *Stargazer*!"

Captain Starbuck turned to Joseph, his eyes black. "Don't *ever* tell me what to do with my ship, boy. Your carelessness led to this mess, just as I'm now certain it led to the demise of the *Chase*. So stay silent and get out of my way."

Shots were fired over the bow.

"Men, arm yourselves!" Captain Starbuck yelled. "Fred, seek cover!"

But Winnie didn't move.

Staying low, Joseph ran toward Winnie. More shots were fired, some blowing holes in the sails, others splintering chunks of wood along the masts and yards.

Finally, as if a spell was broken, Winnie dashed down the steps. Joseph lost sight of her. "Winnie!" he cried in a panic.

"Here," she called back, now crouching behind the chicken coop at the end of the middle deck. A bullet grazed the pen and flew past, striking the side of the hull. Joseph and Winnie clung to one another as the hens clucked nervously and more shots were fired.

Then, eerie silence. As suddenly as it had begun, the siege stopped.

"Why did they stop?" Winnie asked through tears.

"Reloading," Joseph guessed.

"But—why did they come in the first place?" Winnie asked, her eyes frantic.

"Must have seen our lanterns," Joseph said. How much more of a target could they be, glowing yellow in the middle of the vast ocean? Like the captain was asking to be spotted in unknown waters.

AT THE FIRST sound of gunfire, Red dashed down to the hold, the large iron key shaking in his hand as he opened the lock. Chin and Cook were close behind, the trio looking for weapons from a crate of munitions kept in storage.

Red cursed aloud, upset that they were not more prepared for an attack. The ship was in foreign territory, after all, on a route they'd never once traveled. An empty cargo ship was still a cargo ship, after all. Pirates wouldn't know they were not weighed down with loot.

Red opened the top of the crate easily, which wasn't sealed. "It's empty!"

"Impossible," Cook said, pushing Red out of the way so he could see for himself. "I loaded those rifles and bullets into this crate myself back in Boston."

"Did you nail it shut?" Chin asked, noticing bent and missing nails on the top of the wooden crate. Cook nodded yes. "Then someone else opened it."

"Here's something." Red pulled a small knife sheathed in leather from the chest, which Cook swiftly took for himself.

"Now, *that* I know how to use," Cook said, his face pale and sweaty.

"We should raid the kitchen!" Chin suggested. Agreeing, Cook raced quickly back up to the main deck to grab knives from the galley to distribute to the crew, a chef's tools being all the weaponry they had.

Red threw the key to Chin. "Lock it back up!" he shouted, more out of habit than any need to protect what was inside.

Chin was about to when he noticed a large wooden chest wrapped in iron chains in the other corner of the dark room. "What the heck is that?" he said to no one. Maybe more guns? His curiosity piqued, Chin decided to investigate.

SULLY RAN TO the forecastle to wake the crew and see what small weapons they might have hidden in their bunks, knowing the others would find nothing useful in the hold. But even with the lamps lit, the sailors were passed out cold, limbs hanging loose over the sides of swinging hammocks. Snores of well-sauced fools. Sully could rouse them, but sloshed sailors might do more harm than good in a situation like this, slicing off their own damned fingers and toes in a fight. He'd wait and see what the other ship wanted before rousing these good-for-nothings.

"What's wrong?" Cowboy asked. He was whittling a piece of wood with a sharp blade.

Sully jumped. "Dammit, you scared the bejesus outta me! What are ya doing up?"

"I'm more the thinking kind than the drinking kind." Cowboy shrugged.

"Musta been thinking real hard not to hear those shots fired," Sully said.

Cowboy looked confused. "I assumed someone was just playing out there, setting off firecrackers!"

"A pirate ship, and I shit you not," Sully said. "You got any weapons bigger than that knife?"

"You bet," Cowboy said, dropping his carving. He reached under his bed and pulled out a small revolver. "A Colt Paterson. She's got five bullets."

Sully had heard about these guns, which didn't need to be reloaded after every shot, but he'd never seen one himself. "Well, the nickname sure suits ya. Now, rouse your fellas and meet us out there."

THE GUNFIRE HAD been replaced by whistling sounds followed by dull clomps. "Grappling hooks," Joseph said, his face growing even more fearful. The pirates, approaching in a small boat, had sent metal hooks attached to long lines of rope across the water and were using them to pull the *Stargazer* close. Once they did that, they'd climb the rigging, making their way up the ratlines and into the shrouds. "They're going to board our ship."

"But—why? We've got no cargo," Winnie said.

"They'll want her," he said.

"Who is *her*?" Winnie asked as understanding dawned. "Not—the ship?"

Joseph nodded grimly. They both knew their captain would rather die than give up the *Stargazer*.

Within seconds, three pirates had climbed the rigging and dropped to the deck. Two were large, scruffy-looking redheaded men, one with a long beard and one with a jagged scar across his cheek, and the third was a small clean-shaven boy in a cap, with a fringe of red bangs. Two brothers and a son? They wore dark clothing that blended into the night, although the cutlasses in scabbards around their hips were easy to make out in the light from the ship's swaying lanterns.

Zander motioned for another member of the skeleton crew to man the helm so he could join the others on the main deck, standing next to Sully.

"Give me your pistol, Zander," Sully whispered. When Zander pulled back, Sully stepped closer. "I know you've got it on ya, and chain of command means you'll do what I say."

Zander reluctantly passed his gun to Sully.

"Any extra bullets?" Sully asked.

Zander shook his head. "Nah, just the one." A white lie that adjusted the balance of power just slightly. "So I hope you're a good shot."

"Idiot," Sully scoffed.

Zander may have been outranked and unarmed, but he was used to relying on brains and brawn for defense.

Cowboy came out of the forecastle with his gun raised. Merle, Don, and Harry were next to him, each with their own cutlass in hand. They approached from the bow, surrounding the pirates.

"Where is your captain?" the bearded pirate yelled.

The accented voice cut through the night. "Aussies!" the Cowboy said, aiming his pistol at the trio. "What are kangaroos doing in China?"

"Business, same as you," the pirate answered.

Awaiting orders from their captain, no one on the deck moved. Cowboy figured there were a dozen of their own men on the deck of the *Stargazer* against three pirates. And one of those pirates was a kid smaller than Chin, so Cowboy held steady.

"We said, *where is your captain*?" the short pirate called out, with that same Australian twang.

This second pirate's voice was indeed childish, but also something else. *Female*, Winnie realized from her hiding spot. Like Anne Bonny and Mary Read! Here was a girl pirate, hair hidden under a cap, raiding a ship with her—father and uncle? Winnie would be impressed if she weren't so afraid.

"I'm the captain," Peter Starbuck said, stepping forward. He had met Red in the galley and, learning of the theft of munitions, was armed with a jagged steak knife up his sleeve and a thick butcher's knife at the base of his spine. When this confrontation was over, Peter would personally and severely punish whoever took their weapons, but right now, he'd funnel his added anger toward the pirates. They didn't know the ship wasn't well armed and Captain Starbuck would not stand down. At least Cowboy had a revolver at the ready. "And, as the captain, I'm not giving up this ship."

"Oh, we don't want your ship, as we've got a fine vessel ourselves, taken just last month in a rather bloody battle. What we want are supplies." The pirate turned to the other two and began whispering rapidly. The leader pointed this way and that, toward the galley and the animal pens, giving the others orders.

"Give 'em the chickens, sir," Sully said, "and then maybe they'll leave us be."

"And if they don't?" Zander asked.

Sully shrugged. "Then I'll shoot 'em, unless you want to kill 'em with your bare hands."

"Stay right where you are," Captain Starbuck said. "And we'll bring you goods."

The pirates nodded. "We're agreeable to that, as long as you don't try anything funny. There's more of us in the boat below and a band of hungry pirates on our brig just waiting for my signal to attack."

Peter faced the tall Aussie while several sailors headed toward the chicken coop where Winnie and Joseph hid. Joseph grabbed Winnie by the hand and pulled her to her feet. "Quickly, go now."

"But what about you?" Winnie asked as she and Joseph headed around the back side of the galley and toward the door to the captain's staterooms. Seeing her approach through the small glass window, Winnie's mother opened the door and immediately pulled her inside.

"I'll be fine," Joseph said, nodding solemnly. "Don't worry."

Joseph heard a wooden bar slide into place to barricade the women inside.

DON'T WORRY! **HOW** could Winnie not worry? Everything she cared about in the entire world was on the deck of this ship, and suddenly all of it was threatened.

"Pirates!" Winnie wailed. Conjuring fantastical imaginings about a life at sea for years, how had she never before considered *pirates*?

"Shhh." Nell took Winnie's cold hands in hers. The girl was shivering from the inside out. Shock. Nell led her daughter through the officers' cabins and the quiet great cabin and into their own living room parlor. "We've been in terrible situations before," she said. "Your father knows what to do." Although, of course, in '38 aboard the *Shooting Star* it had been Nell who had known what to do—and was then the one who had done it. And Winnie at age five had not been nearly as frightened as she was now at eighteen, now that she was old enough to understand what was at stake.

"One of them is a girl," Winnie added.

"Really?" Nell said. "Hmmm. I suppose that once a girl leaves the confines of her conventional life and dares to do something else, she can be anything."

"Like a criminal," Winnie said bitterly.

"Or a merchant," Nell added.

"Will everything be okay?" Winnie asked.

"Your father knows not to engage with them in battle. Just give them what they want and get rid of them as quickly as possible. Pirates feel safest roaming the seas. As soon as they come into a port, they can be arrested and hanged for their crimes. So their goal is to stay afloat indefinitely, by fishing for their sustenance and raiding other ships for food and supplies."

"And riches, too, right?"

"Yes, but luckily, we don't currently have much to steal." Nell's mind flashed to her new diamond brooch, the Stargazer safely hidden in this very room. "If we were attacked coming back to America with tons of cargo, that would be much worse."

"So, what do we do now?" Winnie asked.

"Now we wait," Nell said, mentally reciting the sailor's prayer over and over.

THE PIRATES TOOK all sixteen of the ship's remaining chickens, which they sent down in a crate to the small skiff waiting below using a rope-and-pulley system. They took the two pigs as well.

Cook watched with one hand on his new knife and the other protectively over his hidden stash of liquor as the pirates next ransacked the pantry off the galley, taking all of the sugar, flour, and rice, as well as three sacks of potatoes.

"Now it's time for you to go," Peter said.

But the largest pirate stealthily maneuvered himself around the captain, opening the center hatch and climbing down the ladder toward the ship's hold before the captain and the crew had time to react.

The gold, Peter thought.

Not the gold.

"Steady there, Captain," the small pirate said, seeing Peter's attempt to move. She unsheathed her saber.

"I wouldn't go anywhere if I were you," the other pirate said, blocking the entrance to the hold. As if on cue, four more pirates climbed the ratlines and landed on the ship's deck. They stayed a few feet away, ready to pounce should their leader need them. Cowboy and his pals stood nearby.

"We'll fight 'em, Captain," Sully said. "To the death, if need be. Just give us the word."

It was a goddamned game of chess, Joseph thought, picturing Chin's rooks and pawns against his own. The captain must be thinking this out ten steps ahead, deciding what move of his would cause what kind of reaction—a loss or a gain—from the opposition. Chin was probably thinking the same. Joseph scanned the small crowd for his friend but couldn't find him.

Peter imagined his wife and daughter, just on the other side of that door: beaten, raped, tortured, and then, having endured every atrocity, mercilessly slain.

Nell and Winnie. And Joseph Allen from Nantucket, and men

he'd known for twenty years, and some he'd just met a few months ago—this crew who followed his orders and would again now, no matter what. They were all his family aboard the *Stargazer*, and he would protect them to the end.

The gold was worth a fortune, but their lives were worth more.

Peter had to let it go. This Aussie would either find the treasure in the hold or not, and Peter would have to face the consequences.

CHIN WAS ABOUT to exit the hold and climb the stairs to the rear companionway just as a large man came upon him like a bolt of lightning and knocked him to the ground. Chin looked up at the pirate, seeing past the unkempt beard and looking into his gray-blue eyes.

"There's nothing in here!" Chin exclaimed, inadvertently looking toward the chest in the corner.

"Oh, yeah? Then what're ya doing down here guarding it?" the pirate said in English with an accent Chin had never heard before.

"We took out all the weapons," Chin said, sitting up. "And there's no key to open that chest."

The pirate kicked Chin hard in the side with his boot, knocking the wind out of him. "Who needs a key when you've got *this*," the pirate said. He sauntered toward the lone wooden trunk, unsheathing his sword and using its metal handle to knock the lock right off of it.

"Don't!" Chin said, getting to his feet unsteadily. He had to protect that treasure chest. Whatever was in it must be valuable—otherwise, why was it wrapped in chains? Chin stepped in front of the chest and blocked it with his body.

AFTER A MINUTE or two of tense silence, Red said, "Um, Captain? Where's Chin? He was with us before and now he's not."

Peter tried not to panic. "Where did you see him last?" he asked.

"In the hold? Sir?" Cook swallowed, exchanging a worried look with Red.

"Captain, take this!" Sully said, handing Zander's gun to the captain.

Gun in hand, Peter Starbuck pushed the pirate aside and raced down the ladder. "On my command, crew, do not follow me! Everyone must stay above!"

The other pirates rushed forward to follow the captain into the hold. Cowboy took aim and shot one man in the back, the force sending the pirate across the deck and overboard. With no time to waste, Cowboy turned and shot the other four men on deck dead. Five shots. That's all the Colt Paterson had. He was out of ammunition.

Only the girl was alive now, her hands raised in surrender.

"Go!" Cowboy yelled, and the girl ran to the side rail, grabbed onto a rope, and slid out of sight.

Shots from the brig came heavy over the bow now, tearing sails and pockmarking the wood rails and masts and planks. While ducking for cover behind the gunwale, a few of the crew took hatchets and knives to the ropes holding the grappling hooks in place and severed them, rendering them useless.

PETER RACED DOWN the ladder and into the hold. Chin held his skinny little arms out in front of the gold-filled wooden chest, the lock broken.

"Chin! Move!" Captain Starbuck yelled, pistol raised. He fired his one shot at the pirate but missed. He dropped the gun, now useless, and reached for the knife up his sleeve.

The pirate slashed Chin's torso with his cutlass. As the pirate was about to stab Chin a second time, the captain pushed the boy out of the way.

Chin clutched his wound and fell to the ground, blood drenching his white shirt and covering his shaking hands. He rolled away and hid in the darkness, watching in horror as, with renewed anger and force, the pirate lashed out with his bloodied sword and stabbed Captain Starbuck across the stomach. Out and in the blade went. Out and in again.

Chin lay panting on the floor, eyes wide in fright. The pirate removed his bloody sword from the captain's limp body and held it high. "This is the key, kid. The key to life or death." Then he stepped over the captain. Weak and in shock, Chin closed his eyes. He could hear the man breaking the chains around the chest and then hooting in surprised delight. Treasure, just as Chin had suspected.

Clattering on the ladder was followed by a throng of voices from the stairs outside the hold.

"Help!" Chin cried before passing out.

EVERYTHING AFTER THAT was a blur. Cook scooped up Chin and carried him up the rear companionway and to the galley, assuring the boy when he came to that he and Red would bandage him up but good and not to worry. Wanting to watch over Chin every second, they did not take him to the sick bay.

"Just a scratch, really," Red said, trying to make light of the injury. The kid was a bloody mess, although the sword didn't seem to have pierced any organs.

"Sliced off your baby fat is all," Cook said, putting pressure on the wound, which spanned about nine inches across the right side of Chin's flank. Cook made Chin drink a sip of whiskey before using the same alcohol to clean out the gash.

"Owww," Chin cried.

Cook bandaged Chin's side with strips that Red had made from a clean apron. The bandage, however, did almost nothing to staunch the bleeding.

"He needs stitches but quick," Red said to Cook.

"Do you think Mrs. Starbuck could—" Cook asked.

"No," Red said. The captain's wife had enough to face tonight, both physically and emotionally. Maybe she could attend to Chin tomorrow.

"Can you survive the night?" Cook asked.

"Ask me again in the morning," Chin said.

If Chin could joke, then Chin might live. Red and Cook alternated turns where they kept their hands on the bandage, using pressure to slow the bleeding.

"How is the captain?" Chin asked.

"Fine," Red said.

But Chin had seen the attack. He knew what that pirate had done. "Liar," he said before blacking out again.

IN THE HOLD, Zander and Joseph rushed to the captain's aid. He was bleeding profusely. His breathing was shallow, eyes glassy and unfocused. They didn't have a lot of time.

"Someone fetch Mrs. Starbuck—and her medical kit!" Joseph cried.

Cowboy tucked his gun under his arm and dashed out to the hallway and up the steps. Zander and Joseph lifted the captain's body onto some small, discarded crates left outside the hold.

Sully found the small pistol Captain Starbuck had used in a pool of blood. He picked it up and cleaned it on his shirt, feeling the weight of it in his grasp. Power. He would take command of the *Stargazer* with this. No matter that the gun had no bullets.

"The fighting stops now!" Sully announced, brandishing the gun in the redbeard's face as if he could do real harm. The bearded pirate had a medium-sized crate by his feet. Old tea, probably. As far as Sully knew, there was nothing worth anything in the hold, so why not let the pirate have at it. "Take that if ya must, and get offa my ship!"

The man grabbed the metal handles on the crate and hoisted the box up the companionway steps. Sully kept his pistol at the man's back and followed him above deck, arriving just as Nell Starbuck, her green eyes wild, exited the staterooms with Winnie on her heels. Nell gripped a leather satchel of medicines and Winnie clutched a spare bedsheet.

"You bastard!" Nell said to the pirate's back, shaking in rage. She took a glass vial from her bag and hurled it across the deck, where it shattered ten feet away from the pirate's feet, spilling white powder by the bodies of the four slain pirates. "Somebody, shoot him!" Nell cried.

"It wouldn't do any good, missus," Sully said. "Go help Captain Starbuck. He needs you."

The pirate sent the crate down, and then the bodies of his slain men. Finally, the bearded man slid down the rope and was gone.

Twenty minutes of hell. Thirty at most, Zander thought, watching the pirates row back to their awaiting ship. If he hadn't given his pistol to Sully, he'd be shooting at them now. Now that it was too late, of course.

In the dinghy, the leader opened the top of the stolen chest, revealing what was inside. The girl and the two rowers whooped and hollered, their elation echoing across the Pacific.

What the hell was in that crate? Zander wondered.

"DARLING," NELL SAID, dropping to the floor by Peter's side and taking his hand in hers.

Winnie crouched next to her mother.

"Nell," Peter said. "Fred. Good. You're here."

Joseph had been left alone with Captain Starbuck in the intervening minutes, covering the captain's torso with discarded sailcloth to hide his grave injuries and to provide the man some dignity. Disembowelment. A torturous way to die.

While the captain had drifted in and out of consciousness, Joseph had apologized over and over, pleading for forgiveness he did not receive. He also gave the captain sips of rum from a flask Sully had tossed him.

"Thank you for sitting with my father," Winnie said to Joseph. She reached out to take his hand in hers, but Joseph flinched and pulled away.

"Excuse me," Joseph said, exiting the door to the hold and leaving the Starbuck family alone.

The quiet around them exaggerated Peter's labored breathing. "I love you both eternally. And. There's something I must explain," he said.

"Let me tend to your wounds first," Nell said. She peeked under the canvas and tried to hide a gasp. There would be no saving him.

Nell made Peter drink laudanum mixed into some rum so he would be more comfortable. Then she took a deep breath. "Tell me everything."

And while their daughter wept silently beside them, Peter did.

Nell could hardly believe it. "Darling, did you just say that you are—that *we* are—contracted to serve as intermediaries for an opium deal aboard the *Stargazer*?"

Her husband's face, already morphed by physical pain, grew even more grave. "I'm sorry."

How could you? Nell wanted to scream.

Why would you? she wanted to yell.

The fastest, the best, the richest. The secrets.

She tamped down her anger and clutched her husband's hand, which had grown cold and clammy. "Our lives were perfect. We already had everything. We didn't need more."

"I know that now," Peter said. Oh, how stupid he had been. Did everyone think that on their deathbed, regret bubbling to the surface like the blood pooling in his chest? Or was that a curse saved only for men blinded by their prideful needs? A life spent gaining, a life misspent.

"Winifred Starbuck. I always joked about wanting a boy, calling you Fred."

"It's okay, Father. It's just a silly thing—"

"You are brave, wise, and fearless. I'm so proud to call you my daughter."

Peter grew very pale and closed his eyes.

"Peter, don't leave us," Nell begged. "Please."

Peter began rambling about a garden and a man named Mathewson. "Jardin," he kept saying, as if the word were in French.

"A French garden?" Nell asked, trying to understand. "Are you talking about the Tuileries, darling, when we visited the Louvre?"

"Jardin," he repeated.

"Yes, Peter, the gardens there were very beautiful."

Nell and Winnie exchanged a concerned look. They sat in silence for a few minutes, and then Peter opened his eyes. Nell could see him pushing past the pain, and she leaned in close to hear him.

"Just hand over the gold and all will be well," Peter said, staring into Nell's eyes.

"Gold?" Nell asked.

"That chest with the chains," Peter wheezed. "The key is in our safe with your brooch."

Winnie took the lantern by her feet and walked around the cavernous room, her stomach filled with newfound dread. Hadn't that lone pirate left with a box?

Winnie found one box marked Munitions on its side and a few barrels of potatoes and crates of tea in one corner and, in the other, a pile of discarded chains with a broken lock.

The pirate had taken the gold.

Winnie faced her mother and shook her head no.

So. Nell would keep this fact a secret from her husband, the man who had kept so many secrets of his own.

Peter's eyes were closed and his breathing had become a death rattle. The agony was enormous.

"It's all right, darling," Nell assured Peter. "You can go. We love you."

"We love you, Father. And we'll miss you, Captain Starbuck," Winnie said, sinking to the floor by her father's feet.

Satisfied that he had left his wife and daughter without a care in the world, Peter gave in to the encroaching tide, letting it pull him out to sea.

CHAPTER 40

October 21

The *Stargazer* sailed into China at dawn with tattered sails and a broken heart.

The captain had died overnight. The hungover crew was roused from slumber and told the news in the predawn hours, working numbly in a pall of funereal silence, their faces displaying despair that none of them could yet express with words. Following the Starbuck motto, they sailed on.

Only one person's voice penetrated the fog of grief. "Speed the hell up, you fecking weasels!" Sully barked, lashing at crewmen's legs indiscriminately with a quickly made whipping knot. "A buncha sad-sack losers, drinking yourself blind and sleeping like babies while yur captain battles valiantly and dies by a pirate's sword!"

The men grumbled but didn't fight back. In fact, the more Sully terrorized them, the harder they worked, seeking absolution through every insult and lashing.

Zander shook his head from the helm. "Captain" Sully still hadn't returned his gun.

They had sailed all night through the Philippine Sea, on a southwest course, keeping the rocky coastal shoreline of mainland China on their starboard side. Now the morning light pierced the horizon in flecks of blue and gold.

"Land, ho!" Merle yelled from the crow's nest.

They were about twelve miles from Hong Kong, Joseph figured.

He added another dot to the chart and told Zander to stay on the current course. Although Canton was only about seventy-five nautical miles from Hong Kong, Joseph would have to navigate upriver through a heavily trafficked and narrow, shallow waterway. This last part of the journey had to be done slowly and would take another two days.

The last time he had approached a narrow channel was when sailing into San Francisco Bay on the *Chase*.

This wasn't the *Chase*, Joseph reminded himself. They weren't all going to die. But last night, Captain Starbuck had accused Joseph—rightly so—of not doing his job, neither here nor on the *Chase*. Every insecurity, every doubt Joseph held about himself as a worthwhile sailor and a worthwhile brother, son, and man had come rushing back in an instant.

"You okay there, Joseph?" Zander asked.

The navigator went pale and then sank to the poop deck floor before Zander could catch him.

IN THE GALLEY, Chin woke up disoriented, his side aching. Why was he lying on the kitchen floor? He tried to move, and then remembered. The pirates. The captain. The treasure chest. He felt dizzy and put his head back down. Closed his eyes.

He heard someone enter the galley. "Am I alive?" Chin asked.

"You are," Mrs. Starbuck said.

Mrs. Starbuck! Chin was so surprised that he tried to sit up.

"Don't move," she said softly. "You've been hurt badly."

Mrs. Starbuck searched Chin with those emerald eyes of hers, so he did his best to look brave. "You'll need a surgeon. We'll be docking in a few days. Can you hold on?" she asked.

"I think so." Chin felt cold and faint and then hot, searing pain. "And . . . the captain? Did he—*hold on*?" Chin asked.

Mrs. Starbuck shook her head.

Chin nodded grimly. "And the treasure chest?"

Mrs. Starbuck looked surprised. "You know about that?"

"I saw it in the hold last night and tried to protect it."

"Oh, Chin. That was very courageous."

"And how's the patient today?" Cook asked, aiming for good cheer he didn't feel. He crouched by Chin's side. "We only had shitty ingredients left, so I made ya some shitty broth."

Chin's smile was more like a grimace. He declined. "I think—" Chin said, tilting his head up a little bit. "I think—"

"What?" Cook asked. "Are you feeling worse?"

"Not a fever, I hope." Nell quickly felt the boy's head, which was cool to the touch, thank goodness.

Chin's face crumpled as tears sprang to his eyes. "I think Captain Starbuck saved my life."

WINNIE CHANGED OUT of her bloodied gown. She and her mother had spent the night stitching together a shroud for the captain's body. His navy jacket with the gold buttons had been ruined, and Winnie's mother refused to bury him in such a garment.

After ringing eight bells for their fallen master, several of the crew had cleaned the captain's body, brought him upstairs, and laid him on the table in the officers' quarters. Winnie's mother had then wrapped his body in the handmade shroud.

Winnie couldn't stay inside her cabin any longer, knowing that her father lay dead nearby. On deck, Winnie's mother was just coming out from the galley, and the two held one another up in a long embrace.

"How is Chin?" Winnie asked.

"Alive for now," her mother said, looking exhausted.

"Mrs. Starbuck, Miss Winifred!" Zander called out from the poop deck.

"What now?" Nell asked the air and the sky, heading up the steps to the raised back deck, where they found Joseph on the ground, back propped against a barrel.

"He passed out," Zander said. "Like he had seen a ghost, and then whoosh, gone."

"Are you all right?" Winnie asked.

"I'm fine," Joseph said, waving a hand and begging off help when Winnie came toward him. "It's nothing." As if to prove it, Joseph stood unaided, although he still leaned against that barrel.

"You!" Sully roared from the main deck, pointer finger extended in accusation. He bounded up the poop deck stairs toward his target.

Joseph steeled himself against Sully. He deserved whatever punishment the new captain deemed proper for his crimes: the cat-o'-nines, or being bound in chains, or having his neck placed in a stockade in front of the American factory in Canton. Leaving the night watch unmanned warranted nothing less than torture and public humiliation.

Sully's eyes blazed with hatred. He balled his fists as if ready to strike. But he stopped short of Joseph and faced Winnie, spitting at her feet. "This is all because a you!"

"Me?" Winnie asked, taken aback.

"Her?" Joseph wondered.

"Yes, *you*, missy. You cursed our ship once before and now you've done it again. Your father's death is your cross to bear."

Winnie didn't understand. She had distracted Joseph last night, true, but it was Joseph who failed to do his job. Why wouldn't Sully accuse them both equally, at very least?

"That was a long time ago, Sully," Nell said. "The *Shooting Star* has nothing to do with this. Your anger is misdirected."

"The *Shooting Star* has everything ta do with this, missus, and you know it."

"What are you two talking about?" Joseph asked, looking back and forth between Mrs. Starbuck and Sully. "I'm the one to blame. I'm to be held responsible."

"Oh, I'll get to you in a moment, Joseph. But first, Mrs. Starbuck, it's well past time to tell your daughter what you did, murdering that sailor in front of her when she was a girl," Sully said. "And Captain Starbuck made us keep it a secret all these years."

The ship's crew responded with a silence so powerful that it felt alive.

Nell clutched Winnie's hand with her own. "I did that in self-defense, to protect my daughter. And it was a secret that you've been blackmailing my husband with for thirteen years, Sully."

"Self-defense or not, you killed a man, which needs to be brought to the authorities. And when I told your husband such, he decided he'd rather me keep silent. Can't blame me for that."

"You're a real son of a bitch," Joseph added.

Sully pounced. "And you should know, being one yourself. Joseph Allen, the sole survivor of the *Chase*! Isn't that bit of news suspicious to anyone else, huh? And then Joseph just happens to be the night watchman who left his post unmanned so he could put his tongue inside Winifred Starbuck's mouth—everyone's beloved cursed daughter!—and that's what got us into this mess. Well, when we get off this ship, I'm gonna head straight to the United States consulate and finally report Mrs. Starbuck for murder. Maybe she'll be hanged for her crimes." He smiled. "Joseph and her both."

Cowboy and Zander were upon Sully so fast that he didn't have time to fight them off, bucking as Zander wrenched Sully's hands behind his back and threw him to the ground. Cowboy bound Sully's hands and then his feet in one long line of rope, leaving the man in a neat bundle. "Hog-tied, we call that," Cowboy said.

"This is mutiny!" Sully yelled, his face to the deck.

Yip started barking loudly and running in frantic circles. "I agree, Yip!" Lucky said. "Now, listen here, crew!" Lucky called over Sully's protestations, every man and woman's attention upon the scene unfolding on the poop deck. "Yip's got a question for ya. Whoever thinks Sully here should be our captain, say *aye-aye*."

Sully quieted, waiting for affirmations. The ship remained silent, except for the sails snapping in the wind.

Lucky spoke again. "Duly noted! And who here thinks Sully should be held in contempt while Zander becomes captain of the *Stargazer*?"

"Aye-aye!" fifty sailors called.

Several men came forward to help drag Sully into the pantry, where he'd remain until they docked and decided what to do with him.

Zander turned to Lucky. "You're sure about this?"

"Sure, I'm sure. And so is your crew."

Zander scanned the faces around him. Joseph nodded, as did Cowboy and Winnie and Mrs. Starbuck.

"Then, Jonathan, you'll be promoted to first mate," Zander said.

"Aye-aye, Captain!" Jonathan said, coming forward from the crowd and taking his place next to Zander.

"Just tell them what to do, Captain," Mrs. Starbuck said.

From his place at the helm, Zander cleared his throat. Dawn had broken. The ship was passing Nam Tong Island and a set of rocky, moss-covered cliffs, and would then pass the islands of Hong Kong, Lamma, and Lantau before turning northward into the Pearl River and then through the Bocca Tigris. Two more days before they docked.

Chin would never make it that long, Zander realized.

Unless.

Unless Zander decided to be a different type of captain entirely, leading not for his own glory but for the benefit of the ship and crew. In which case, the *Stargazer* could tack now around Tathong Point and dock in Hong Kong. It would be difficult, but not impossible. Clipper ships like theirs did it every day. Then they'd sail northward into Victoria Harbor, where they could find a surgeon to tend to Chin.

"Helms a lee!" Zander called, turning the wheel of the giant ship and aiming her toward Hong Kong.

"Aye-aye, sir!" the crew called back, adjusting the mostly intact sails accordingly, and doing the best they could to ignore the shredded canvas along the main and mizzenmasts, and the angry muted curses emanating from the pantry.

CHAPTER 41

"Did you truly kill a sailor to protect me when I was young?" Winnie asked, alone with her mother in the cool dark interior of their staterooms.

Winnie lay down on the blue velvet sofa and closed her eyes. She was bone-tired, a feeling that no amount of sleep would ever alleviate. Unlike the physical exertion of sailing, this ache both numbed her and gnawed at her.

Nell sighed and sank into Peter's desk chair. She didn't speak.

And in that quiet, Winnie remembered. She *knew*. A part of her had always known, but whenever the memory had surfaced, she had treated it like an annoying buzz in the air, shooing it away before it could land on her and sting.

"I did go to sea with you and Father," Winnie said. "When I was a girl."

Behind Winnie's eyelids, she could see and smell it all: the days and days of delight followed by the woodsy scent of the damp hold, the acrid sweat from the crazed sailor, the night breeze and the tune of a shanty and the barking of a dog, and the cool panic of hide-and-seek behind crates, the sense of being little in a big, scary world. And then, the face of her mother, shining down on her from above like a golden-haired fairy encircled in light.

"Something terrible happened," Winnie added. A pool of blood around the sailor's body, his eyes wide open as he stared at Winnie. "And that's why you forbade me from ever sailing again."

Winnie opened her eyes. The handmade wallpaper around the

room glowed softly, illuminating some of the sampans in the Canton harbor. Winnie turned to face her mother, who nodded, a solemn and simple affirmation of Winnie's guess.

And then Nell told her daughter the story of the *Shooting Star* in its entirety.

As Nell talked, she relived the horror of that night. But she also recalled so much that was special and poignant and perfect about those days at sea with her husband and child. One wrong decision had led to her life's biggest regret.

She would never regret murdering the sailor to protect her family. But that action led to the death of her life's dream of raising Winnie at sea, to learn to be a merchant like her.

When the Starbucks returned to East Brick after that fateful voyage, Nell and Peter had argued for days.

"The worst decision I ever made was allowing your father to convince me to leave you behind on future voyages," Nell said to her daughter. "And for that, I hope you can eventually forgive me."

"WE'RE GETTING A surgeon *today*, Chin," Red said, scrambling into the galley sideways and reaching for a wall to help stabilize him as the hull beneath them shifted as they tacked. "I'd say within the next hour or two."

Chin was sweaty and pale. "Good. Because I wasn't going to make it to Canton. I just didn't want to upset Mrs. Starbuck."

"What can I do to help?" Red asked, leaning down to give the boy some sips of water.

"I've missed China so much. Go see it for me. Then come back and tell me everything," Chin said, closing his eyes.

"Yessir, Chin."

In many ways, the entrance to the Port of Hong Kong reminded Red of San Francisco Bay: a wide-mouthed strait leading into a deep, protected harbor with mountainous hills on both sides. But there was one distinction, and it wasn't the landscape. It was the boats.

In San Francisco, the harbor had been crowded with abandoned ships. Hong Kong Port, in contrast, was alive, a vibrant, moving landscape teeming with vessels of every size and shape. Red had been to Canton twice before, but this was his first time in Hong Kong, a relatively new international port city ceded to the British nine years earlier. Hong Kong was thriving and bursting with life.

Large oceangoing ships known as Chinese junks floated past, painted with colorful designs along the hull and painted eyes on either side of the bow to help these ships "see." Junks were sturdy, speedy, and easy to handle, with curved bows and linen sails that looked like the fans women carried, reinforced with bamboo batting that bisected the sails like vertebrae along their spines.

Smaller, flat-bottomed river boats called sampans served as fishing boats, family shelter, or cargo transportation, ferrying goods up and down the Pearl River. Sampans provided shade and shelter with arched bamboo coverings and were rowed with long oars.

A crab boat rowed by. Oared by many men and low to the waterline, these fast vessels smuggled opium up and down the Chinese coastline.

Red followed the vista out and up, up, up to the tippy top of a towering hill called Victoria Point, where a few giant homes perched over the growing port city like birds in the treetops.

Red raced back into the galley to tell Chin all about it.

THEY ANCHORED AT a mooring in Victoria Harbor that was close to land. Instead of wasting time sending down their own skiff, Red called out to sampans already in the harbor. "Does anyone in this harbor speak English?"

"I do," one fisherman said, waving up at the *Stargazer*.

"Me, too!" another man said, reaching their ship quickly.

"Great!" Cook said as Red unrolled the ladder they had used to disembark in San Francisco. "Can you take us to shore? We will pay you, of course!" Just like with the extra whiskey, Cook kept a stash of cash hidden for use in emergencies, and this counted as such. The man in the sampan heartily agreed to being paid to row them to shore. The two had never been to Hong Kong before and thought it was best to travel in pairs, less likely to both get completely lost.

"Joseph!" Cook said, motioning to the poop deck where the navigator was watching them all, sulking. "Come keep Chin company while we're gone!"

Joseph walked toward the galley as the others rowed to shore. Getting a doctor for Chin was the right decision. With quick thinking and compassion like that, Zander would make a great captain.

He just wouldn't be Joseph's captain, because Joseph needed to get off this ship. Get off and never come back.

MEANWHILE, COWBOY AND some others packed up Sully's things and prepared to take him to shore. Sully's protestations had grown weaker, but he still occasionally banged on the pantry door with his feet, yelling obscenities. Getting him off the ship would require a few strong men. "The sooner the better," Zander said.

"Yessir," Cowboy said, tipping his hat.

"And, another thing while you're there," Zander said, looking pained. "Ask around and find a suitable place to bury Captain Starbuck."

"Of course." Cowboy bowed his head.

In the officers' quarters, the group huddled around and stared into Sully's sea chest, which was filled with cash. In the false bottom, they found an unloaded pistol and a promissory note from Captain Starbuck for the rest of the payment to be made in Canton.

"I'll be damned," Cowboy said. He picked up the gun, which was marked with the Starbuck crest on its ivory handle. There was supposed to be an entire crate of these in the hold, but Cook and Red had found it empty when the pirates attacked.

"Do you think Sully sold off the rest of the weapons?"

"Nothing would surprise me less," Merle said.

"Let's tell Mrs. Starbuck. Maybe Sully's been the real curse all along."

JOSEPH SAT ON a small crate by Chin's makeshift bed on the floor and tried to think of something—anything—to say to the cabin boy. His happy-go-lucky nature and optimism had always reminded

Joseph of Samuel in the best way possible. Now the same traits made Joseph feel wretched. One of them had been his brother, and the other he had grown to love like a brother. How could Joseph have let both of these boys down so tremendously?

And still, Chin was happy to see him. It was like a dagger through his heart.

"Let's play chess in our minds," Chin said, eyes closed. "I'll go first. I'm taking white, and I'm moving my king pawn two spaces."

"A fine first move," Joseph acknowledged, recognizing the King's Pawn opening. "You probably already beat me."

"Come on," Chin said, eyes still closed.

It was hard to argue with him. "Fine, then—d5."

"The French Defense!" Chin said. "Interesting. Let me think."

Chin's thoughts led to eventual shallower breathing until the boy was asleep. Joseph moved to the floor and kept his hand on Chin's wrist for the next hour, willing him to stay alive.

A commotion from the deck startled Joseph awake, voices piercing the silence. They were back with a surgeon. Joseph grabbed Chin's hand, still warm, and located the weak pulse in his wrist.

He roused Chin and told him that the doctor was here.

Dr. Loring arrived on the *Stargazer* with a medical bag and a British accent.

Chin greeted the doctor with relief. "Can you help me?" he asked.

The linen bandaging was stuck to the wound, helping the blood to clot. But Loring would have to remove that dressing to sew up the gash. "I'll stitch you up, but it won't be pretty," Loring said.

"Sounds *tremendous*," Chin said, using a vocabulary word he had picked up from Red, who had described the junks in the harbor as such just an hour or so earlier.

The doctor prepared for the surgery, removing items from his bag and asking for help from Cook and Red. "Just drink this and we'll get started," Dr. Loring said to Chin, removing the stopper from a small dark glass vial. He leaned over Chin, whose head was propped on a pillow. But the boy turned his head away.

"It's a simple combination of alcohol and opium," Dr. Loring said. "We give it to babies who are teething. I wish we had something stronger to offer you, but this is the best we've got."

"No opium," Chin said.

"But—" the doctor began, stymied. "We'll use it on the wound, at least," he said, taking the now-wet sponge from Cook.

"Don't touch me with that!" Chin cried.

"Here, use this," Cook said, handing over his secret bottle of whiskey. Chin gladly accepted a few sips of the alcohol.

"And now this," Cook said, placing the handle of a wooden spoon in Chin's open mouth and telling him to bite down hard. Then everyone left the room as Dr. Loring began the procedure.

AS CHIN WAS tended to by the surgeon, Nell and Winnie Starbuck sat together in their staterooms and began to grieve. The cloak of night and the panic of those hours had made the events as they unfurled feel preposterous, a play acted upon the stage of the deck. The bright light of day made the truth inescapable: their father, husband, business partner, and captain was gone.

And now, Nell also had to finish an illegal opium deal left incomplete by her deceased husband. This last confession of Peter's, told on his deathbed in a delirious spew that at first Nell thought must be a delusion, complicated Nell's grief even more. For it left her with a sense that she didn't truly know Peter at all.

A knock at the door interrupted Nell's circuitous thoughts. Cowboy had returned with information about a cemetery in Happy Valley, located across from the popular racecourse. "My apologies for being so frank, but Zander—Captain Washington—suggested I find a proper burial ground in Hong Kong."

"For merchants?" Nell asked, sitting up straighter. "Americans?" They'd have to have a service for Peter, something she hadn't yet considered in her immediate grief. They'd either bury his body in foreign soil or give him a sailor's burial at sea. The crew and captain were doing the thinking for her, which she appreciated.

"Yes, ma'am," Cowboy said. "It's a cemetery for civilians including merchants and bankers, traders, artisans, missionaries, and British and Chinese people, too, you name it."

"I must think for a bit and I will let you know," Nell said. The two women thanked Cowboy through their tears, then dismissed him.

Could Nell leave Peter behind, in a grave so far from home? Generations of Peter's namesake had been buried on Nantucket.

Nell knew of a family of merchants from New Bedford whose child had died at sea. The parents had somehow preserved the body in alcohol and brought her back from the Far East for burial in Massachusetts. Nell tried to imagine that for Peter, not alive but not properly blessed and sent off to heaven, traveling to Nantucket in the hold as if it were some sort of River Styx. No. Peter would never want that.

A burial at sea had a romanticism about it, Nell supposed, with one's beloved ship and the wind and the sky and the birds at send-off, until one considered the fate of the body once it sank. No.

There was only one choice.

Nell turned to her daughter. "Can you please tell Cowboy that we'd like to arrange a proper funeral for the day after tomorrow?" She didn't even know what day it was at this point, and had to check her log to figure it out.

Winnie stood and grabbed her bonnet. She would go with Cowboy to shore. After years of trying to get on board a merchant ship with her parents, suddenly all she wanted was to disembark and feel her feet on solid ground.

CHAPTER 42

October 22

Chin woke up in the bottom berth in the bunkroom off the galley. Cook's bed. He heard Red shift in the bunk above his and tapped on the wooden planks to get the man's attention. "I'm not dead!"

"Hooray!" In an instant, Red's head dropped over the side of the bunk, facing Chin upside down with his hair sticking up every which way. Chin laughed, but it hurt when he laughed, so he stopped.

"The surgeon said you'll need to rest for a few weeks, and that you shouldn't move more than necessary." Red jumped down from his bunk to face the boy. "Cook and I will bring you everything you need."

"So I still have to shit in a pot?"

"That you do," Red laughed.

"Can we at least make Sully dump it overboard?" Chin asked.

"Sully's gone."

"Dead and gone?"

"No, just the latter," Red explained. He told Chin about the forcible removal of the first mate. And then he explained what *latter* meant.

"I'm starving!" Chin said.

Red thought that was definitely another good sign.

"WE HAVE ARRIVED at the American consulate," Cowboy said. And considering the varied architecture of Hong Kong, the building looked quite *American* to Winnie. It reminded her of Hadwen House,

Winnie's aunt and uncle's home on Nantucket, with columns and a wide portico fronting a white clapboard building of two stories. An American flag waved proudly from a tall pole on the left side of the structure and a palm tree bowed over the right side. The only difference was the roofline, sloping in a four-cornered boxlike fashion instead of a triangle, and topped not by slate but with red clay tiles that curved atop one another like waves.

Inside, a center-hall staircase led to the second floor. With an Oriental rug over marble floors, it looked like a private home, except that the paintings lining the walls were of men in military dress instead of husbands and wives. They walked through a formal sitting area with a large marble fireplace and a portrait of President Fillmore above it. Winnie led the way toward closed mahogany double doors at the back of the room, on which was a small plaque with the name Frederick T. Bush, Consul.

Winnie knocked.

"One moment, please," a voice called.

Cowboy tipped his hat. "I'll wait for you in the sitting area," he said, walking away.

Winnie could hear men's laughter from the other side of the doors. How was it possible that some people were experiencing joy while she was numb with grief? The door opened and Winnie stood up straighter.

"I hope I'll be seeing you on Saturday evening, then," a man said in a Scottish accent as he exited the consul's office. He was an older gentleman in a dark suit, ginger hair swept back from his high forehead. He wore a white cravat tied over his perfectly starched high-collared white shirt.

"You throw the best party of the season, Mr. Blair. My wife and I wouldn't miss it for the world," another man said, his voice distinctly Bostonian.

As the Scot moved to leave, he studied Winnie with pointed interest.

"Hello, sir," Winnie said, then introduced herself.

"Miss Starbuck? Of the *Stargazer*?"

"Yes?" Winnie said. Did he know her?

"Loren Blair, of Jardine, Matheson, and Company," he said, kissing her hand. "You probably saw our East Point offices and godowns—our factories here—when your ship arrived."

Winnie nodded, agreeing without admitting that she hadn't seen his business's buildings. Winnie hadn't seen a single thing while coming into port, too busy mourning to leave her staterooms, but she didn't want to seem rude. She forced herself to smile politely, sensing she was being judged like a blueberry pie at a fair.

"What a nice surprise, if a bit unexpected. I didn't know you were joining your mother and father on the *Stargazer*!"

"You know my parents?" Winnie asked.

"Certainly! In fact, I'm supposed to be meeting your father in Canton in a week's time. He very kindly offered to do an important errand for me."

Winnie felt her stomach drop. Was this so-called errand the opium deal, or was it something else entirely? Opium was legal in Hong Kong, but smuggling it into Canton was strictly prohibited. Winnie needed to know more while being as benign as possible. "Regarding . . . *cargo* . . . from San Francisco?"

Mr. Blair looked pleasantly surprised. "Why, indeed! Precious cargo."

Winnie nodded. What her father had said before passing away became clear. He hadn't been rambling nonsensically about a garden in France or a man named Mathewson. He had been trying to tell Winnie and her mother about Jardine, Matheson, and Company, a global shipping business here in Hong Kong.

"Where *is* your father, anyway?" Blair asked, looking around as if Captain Peter Starbuck might appear from the dining room at any second.

But Winnie was spared from having to answer. The consul emerged from his office and invited her inside. "Mr. Blair, it has been a delight meeting you," Winnie said, her voice measured. She couldn't get away fast enough. She needed to tell the consul about her father's death, and then she needed to return at once to the ship to alert her mother about what she had just discovered.

"The delight has been all mine, Miss Starbuck," Mr. Blair said. "I'd love for you and your family to be my special guests on Saturday night, at a ball I'm throwing to celebrate the trading season." He reached inside his black waistcoat and withdrew a card from a breast pocket. "Here's my card with the address."

"Thank you," Winnie whispered.

Mr. Blair bowed slightly before departing. "And please tell your father I send my regards—and hearty congratulations about winning the world record!" he said, disappearing around the corner. "I cannot *wait* to climb aboard that magnificent ship!"

CHAPTER 43

October 23

On the wrong island entirely, a mahogany casket was lowered into the ground with Captain Peter Starbuck inside. Birds chirped and Victoria Harbor sparkled in the morning light. Hong Kong wasn't a planned part of their maritime journey and yet it had become Peter's ultimate destination, over ten thousand nautical miles from his Nantucket home.

How did we get here, Peter? Nell wondered, looking out from under her parasol at the gray stone markers dotting the sloping green hill. Even at eight in the morning, the air was stifling. Nell was sticky with sweat, an October heat wave that felt like the height of summer in this subtropical climate. The humidity wrapped itself around her face like a cloak and she had to remind herself to breathe.

The cemetery had been built away from town, on swampy marshland in a dip between the mountains where the mosquitoes were relentless. No wonder women in Hong Kong carried fans! And here Nell had always thought they were for fashion. Winnie had wisely brought one with her and was moving it back and forth so quickly that it lifted the wisps of white-blond hair escaping her bonnet.

Zander stood beside Winnie, with all fifty of the crew fanned out on the sloped hillside behind them. The sailors had shaved and cleaned themselves up. They wore their better clothes, a kind and respectful gesture that overwhelmed Winnie with poignancy. Even

Yip looked tidy, sniffing around the gravestones, his wiry gray hair combed down and parted between the ears.

Red and Cook had stayed behind to prepare a banquet and keep an eye on Chin. Perhaps Joseph had stayed back to help, too, as Winnie couldn't find him in the crowd at the cemetery. In fact, she hadn't seen him much at all since the incident, as she'd now begun to think of that night. The more abstract she was, the better.

"I'd now like to recite some words from the Gospel," the English pastor said. "If that's all right with you, Mrs. Starbuck?"

Nell thought that was fine, not that she was listening. Her mind kept wandering, as it had been doing so since the fateful night of Peter's death. Could she have changed the outcome of the events? Saved Peter? Or, if not Peter, then the chest of gold? Winnie had told Nell about Mr. Blair of Jardine Matheson, solving the riddle of what Peter had been saying on his deathbed. Nell supposed she'd have to speak to Mr. Blair about some sort of new arrangement, but what could she offer him in place of the gold?

Nell had to keep bringing herself back to attention by yanking the chain of her mind like a puppy on a leash.

From this angle, she could see Peter's casket in the ground and the entire ship's crew fanning out on the hillside amid gravestones and banyan trees. And, there, half hidden by a large red pine tree, stood Sully with his hands clasped behind his back. He looked down when their eyes met. Deferential, then. It was possible that the man was here to pay his respects and not to cause trouble, so she'd not disturb the service by calling attention to him.

Nell looked left instead, where the land sloped away and then became flat, the perfect spot for a racecourse. The long-limbed horses were out with their trainers, warming up as they walked the track. Mr. Bush had told her there would be a race later today, which was one of the reasons they had decided on a morning service. Heat was the other.

"You don't want to be paying your last respects while the horses are running, ma'am," he had said. "The noise and cheering are quite—distracting."

Although, maybe it would have been better to have the two events take place simultaneously, in this place where the British had erected a cemetery right across from a racetrack and named it Happy Valley. Perhaps the only thing that would drown out Nell's sorrow was the reminder that life was a vibrant and competitive horse race. Victory meant you were paraded around the track wearing a blue ribbon, and a false step could land you in an early grave.

COPYING THE OTHERS, Joseph had dressed his best, in a pair of dark britches with an (almost) white shirt tucked in nicely. He wet and combed his hair to try to tame the cowlick, but the front eventually arched up no matter what he did.

Once at the docks, Joseph lagged behind as the group of sailors with whom he had come to shore began following directions to walk the few miles to Happy Valley.

Joseph could not stand by the grave of a man whose death he had caused. No. The best way to pay his respects to Captain Starbuck was to steer clear of the funeral. So, eventually, when the crew of the *Stargazer* turned left, Joseph turned right and watched the men march on without him.

Joseph tried to focus on the sights, sounds, and smells of this fascinating island, but the tears in his eyes made it impossible to focus on anything other than putting one foot in front of the other. Because he knew who would love to explore this place with him, this lush, green, mountainous, eclectic city where the foreign met the familiar: his brother Samuel.

Samuel had never seen San Francisco, and now he would never see China. He would never fall in love with a woman and grow old by her side. And Captain Starbuck would never hear the cheers as his famous ship pulled into Nantucket Harbor, never see Winnie marry, never meet his grandchildren who would carry on his legacy. And all of it—from Sam's untimely death to Captain Starbuck's—was Joseph's fault.

And today was not only Captain Starbuck's funeral. It was October 23, which would have been Samuel's eighteenth birthday. The two brothers should have been prospecting for gold together, striking it rich or at least having a good time trying. They should have been drinking a dram of whiskey each night and sleeping under the stars.

How could Joseph face this day? Today—and forever after?

Joseph walked the city for hours, with no plan in mind except to drift like an unmoored rowboat. He walked to the eastern end of the harbor, where several large, white granite warehouses with red clay-tiled roofs stood clustered together, flanked by an enormous matching porticoed office building with signage on its side for something called Jardine, Matheson and Company. He turned around and walked back the way he had come, his explorations taking him away from the harbor.

Like most port cities, Hong Kong was densely packed with life down by the waterfront, but the farther out he walked, the less inhabited it became. He walked until the land grew steep and he couldn't traverse it on foot. At the base of Victoria Peak, two laborers holding a sedan chair on bamboo poles called out to him, asking if he needed a ride to one of the mansions perched on the hill. He declined.

Eventually, it grew dark and Joseph's stomach grumbled. The funeral must have been over by now, he realized, the officers and crew likely dining together with Winnie and her mother on the deck of the ship. He felt a pull toward them, but did not let himself go.

He wandered back into town as the sun sank, passing rows of small shops of similar size and shape, each two stories tall with a columned portico creating a first-floor shaded porch, with colorful awnings draped over the second floor and an open balcony to let in air and light. The dirty streets smelled ripe, a potent combination of horse manure, cooking food, and human sweat. As a sailor who hardly bathed, Joseph was used to foul odors, but Hong Kong was new to his American nose.

The businesses distinguished themselves from their neighbors with distinctive flair: an ornamental balustrade of carved wood here, a pretty red-and-yellow sign there. The china shops set some of their larger vases on their front landings, tempting passersby to stop, admire, enter the shop, inquire, and perhaps buy the object—plus three more just like it.

Joseph paused in front of a small restaurant made of wooden beams lacquered in red paint. The scent of garlic and ginger reminded him that he lived in a body and not just a mind.

An elderly Chinese woman leaned over a cane and, without uttering a word in any language, led Joseph to a cushioned bench under a paper lantern on the front porch. She fed him rice with red barbecued pork and brought a pot of tea.

His body was sated, but his mind was still jumbled. Captain Starbuck's death had unmoored him. He felt untethered. Uncomfortable in his own skin. Completely and utterly un-everything.

"Well, looky who's here," a familiar voice said, Irish accent and all.

Joseph groaned. Then he turned toward the street, where Sully stood with his hands folded across his broad chest.

Bald, mean, and large: in many ways, Sully looked the same as always. But something about him was different. It was the clothes, Joseph decided. A new uniform, in fact.

"Don't tell me somebody hired you," Joseph said, bypassing a greeting.

"Nah just *some*body," Sully said, leaning on the restaurant's ornate wooden railing as if gossiping with a friend, "but the biggest somebody of all."

Sully didn't elaborate. He wanted this little shit to ask him—beg him—for more information. And then he wanted Joseph to run back to the *Stargazer* and squeal, telling the crew all about Sully's transformation into Mr. Sullivan, the newest warehouse manager at Jardine Matheson.

The firm had hired him because he was big and bossy, and because he was familiar with the China trade, having had years of experience sailing on a merchant vessel similar to the fifteen ships in Jardine's own fleet. During Sully's interview, Mr. Blair had been impressed with what he called Sully's pedigree. Plus, how could he deny employment to a fellow intrepid British citizen here in Hong Kong?

But most of all, Sully was hired because he had told the manager, Mr. Blair, about his last position. "Captain of the *Stargazer*, sir," Sully had answered with pride. Blair didn't need to know that he had held the position for less than a day, and that his post had ended in a dramatic fashion, being hog-tied and thrown off the ship.

"Captain? Of the Starbuck vessel?" Mr. Blair had asked. "But how can that be, with Peter Starbuck as captain?"

"Peter Starbuck is dead, sir." Blair had practically fallen out of his leather wingback desk chair in surprise over that bit of news! "And I know everything about that ship."

Sully had been hired on the spot.

Joseph sat and sipped his tea, biding his time. Who would be stupid enough to hire Sully? Joseph wasn't going to ask.

Across the dusty road, a Chinese man at the door to another establishment called out to them in accented English. "I hope you left room for dessert! Come see me after you pay Mrs. Lo for your meal," he said, gesturing with a long thin pipe. "I can make all of your problems disappear."

"You can do that with dessert?" Joseph asked, incredulous.

"It's an opium den, you arse," Sully said.

"Oh."

"You think you're so *smart*," Sully laughed. "All that math and astronomy, navigatin'. But you are the kind of stupid that can't be learned, because it comes so natural. Missing what's right in front of you! I wouldn't be surprised if the *Chase* hit a rock in the bay and you didn't see it coming, just like with those fecking pirates."

Sully's greatest skill was wounding not with physical brawn but with cruelty. Sully pressed on Joseph's wounds, revealing his biggest failings. It was true; Joseph was a navigator who never saw what was coming.

Sully leaned in closer, his eyes gleaming. "I went to the funeral, you know."

Joseph's head snapped up.

"Yeah, to pay my last respects. And they say *I'm* the disgraced one! You weren't even brave enough to face him and his bereaved family."

Joseph had nothing to spar with. He took the blows.

"See? You agree with me!" Sully said. He tossed some British coins onto the table where Joseph sat. "Worthless. You probably don't even have the correct currency for yer dinner!"

Sully stepped back into the dark street, where paper lanterns glowed red and white and the traffic of commerce had been replaced by the traffic of evening revelry. "This man is not worth a single shilling and he knows it!" he called, pointing his face to the sky. His rough laughter echoed down the alleyway as he walked off.

Sully had even been correct in assuming that Joseph didn't have the right money on him. Joseph really was stupid. He thanked Mrs. Lo and walked across the street.

The Chinese man guarding the door to the opium den wore a simple black silk robe and a black cap over hair that was shorn on top with a long, thin braid down his back. He greeted several men in Western dress who called him Jerry. They pushed past Joseph and entered the dark parlor.

Jerry put the long, odd pipe to his lips and exhaled the smoke into Joseph's face. The smell was strong and unpleasantly sour.

Opium.

Jerry whispered to Joseph through half-closed eyes. "Dessert, like I said. Because the sweetest treat of all is *oblivion*."

The poison that had destroyed Chin's family was here for the taking.

With any luck, it would destroy Joseph, too.

"Do you accept American cash?" Joseph asked.

"Always." Jerry smiled. He opened the door, and Joseph stepped inside.

CHAPTER 44

October 24

Today was the first day of Nell Starbuck's life as a widow. She woke expecting to feel the now-familiar veil of sadness, but found that a different emotion had supplanted her grief now that the funeral was behind her. After days of mournful sorrow, Nell felt anger.

She was so mad at Peter.

Her husband was gone, truly. Vanished. And Nell was left alone to figure out what the hell to do to clean up his mess.

Was that the definition of widowhood? She thought perhaps it was.

There was no time to grieve in China. Not until the incomplete deal Peter had begun and left Nell with was done. Sadness was for another day, another time, another country.

Nell dressed quickly, reaching for the silk-covered buttons on the back of her dress and realizing that Peter would never again close them for her. Another definition of widowhood: to have to complete difficult tasks by yourself.

"Mother?" Winnie knocked, as if she knew her mother had been thinking of her. "Will you please eat some breakfast?"

Nell opened the door to her sleepy daughter and quickly turned around. "Can you do up the back of my dress?"

It was her mother's best dress, the navy taffeta with the gold trim. "It's a bit formal for daytime, don't you think?" Winnie said, pushing each tiny button through a coordinating rouleau loop.

"No, actually, I don't." Nell moved to sit at Peter's shaving desk, where the mirror was propped open and a velvet box sat waiting for her.

Winnie's mother removed the large diamond star brooch from its box and fastened it to the neckline of her dress, over the lace detail just between her collarbones.

"There." Nell turned to her flummoxed daughter. "I think it's the perfect attire for a meeting with Mr. Loren Blair of Jardine Matheson, don't you? Now, get dressed, because you're coming with me. It's time to start acting like a merchant in China."

COWBOY DIDN'T WANT to alarm the Starbucks, but Joseph Allen was missing. No one had seen him since before the funeral yesterday. He hadn't reported for duty last evening, nor had he been in his berth this morning.

He and Zander silently rowed the Starbuck women to shore. They didn't ask where the two were headed so early in the morning in their fancy clothing, and the women didn't ask about the men's plans, either. Good. They would use the time in town to search for Joseph.

"Shall we meet you back here in an hour?" Zander asked.

"That should be plenty of time, thank you," Nell said.

She and Winnie waited until the men ambled off before turning toward the eastern point of the cove, where the offices for Jardine Matheson stood on an elbow of land perched above the city like a Greek temple. Which was fitting, since all Nell could do was pray that her plan worked.

ZANDER HAD ONLY been captain of the *Stargazer* for three days and already he'd lost a sailor. And not just any sailor, but the navigator! And not just the navigator, but a Nantucket-born son beloved by all, most notably loved by the former captain's daughter.

"You're up the creek without a paddle," Cowboy said as if reading Zander's mind. "But don't worry, we'll find him. I once lost a heifer and her calf in a dust storm in the Plains."

"And?" Zander asked.

"Found 'em eventually." Cowboy shrugged. Unable to seek shelter, the heifer and her calf had been suffocated by the dust. Cowboy found them curled up together, the cow trying to protect her babe. Cowboy didn't mention that part of the story.

"This is an island, after all—how far can he go?" Zander asked.

"I admire your optimism," Cowboy said. They turned down an alley that was shady even in the light of day and came upon the first of what would turn out to be many opium dens, gentlemen's clubs, officers' clubs, and bars and saloons. An hour wouldn't get them very far, but they'd cover the area they could before meeting the women back at the harbor. "Now, as we say in ranching," Cowboy said, opening the black-lacquered door to an unmarked place that was clearly hiding something nefarious, "let's ride out."

NELL AND WINNIE Starbuck walked through an allée of palm trees and up the gravel walkway toward the white granite offices of Jardine Matheson. It was imposing, and despite herself, Nell felt anxious. Inside a two-story marble entry hall, they were greeted by a man who introduced himself as a manager at the firm. Nell explained who they were, and they were led through to the offices behind the grand front parlor to wait for Mr. Loren Blair.

"Is he expecting you?" the manager asked in his delightfully proper and pleasant British accent. "I don't recall you being on the schedule." He pronounced the word with a *sh* sound instead of a hard *k*, which Winnie would have found humorous if she wasn't so nervous. It was the kind of tidbit Chin would like, and she felt guilty for having left the ship this morning without saying hello to him and checking in on his recovery, although last night after the funeral he had been sitting up in bed and almost smiling. Progress.

"We're arriving unannounced, I'm afraid," Nell said. "But Mr. Blair will know what this is in regard to."

"Very well," the man said. He invited them to wait in a formal sitting area decorated with ice-blue silk couches, Oriental rugs, and Chinese lacquerware.

Nell and Winnie declined the clerk's offer of tea and were left alone to wait.

"I really hope you know what you're doing," Winnie said.

"So do I, darling," Nell agreed, nervously touching the Stargazer diamond at her collarbone. "So do I."

CHAPTER 45

The acrid odor of opium was so sharp that tears had sprung to Joseph's eyes as he entered the tightly sealed, very dark room last night.

"You'll get used to it," Jerry had said, waving his hand through the fog of smoke. Joseph paid him ten American dollars and was handed off to a beautiful young woman with glossy black hair pulled back into a tight knot. She had pale skin and wore a dark red robe and introduced herself as May.

"Like the month?" Joseph asked.

"Sure." May shrugged. She led Joseph to an empty spot at the back of the room. This wasn't like a regular bar or saloon. Besides being so dark inside—perhaps why it was called an opium "den"—everyone was lying down on furniture less like couches and more like beds. Some men even appeared to be asleep on these beds, with their eyes closed, heads on square pillows, limbs loose.

Oblivion.

They passed the group of men Joseph had just seen outside, who had been lively and animated just moments before. Now they were quiet, reclining while female attendants held long pipes to their lips. The patrons were a mixture of Chinese and Westerners, and all were male.

May and Joseph sat side by side on a secluded daybed with a lacquered table beside it. Joseph watched as May put a sticky ball into the clay pot atop a pipe and held the pipe over a decorative-glass-

and-metal lamp to heat the substance. "Once it becomes vapor, you breathe it in," she explained.

Joseph had a bad feeling about this. A really bad feeling. What was he doing? He didn't even particularly like the sensation of being drunk, that loss of control as the room spun around him. And this place, with its eerie silence, somehow felt more sinister than a room full of drunken sailors slurring shanties and sloshing beer on one another. "Maybe I should go," he said to May.

"And maybe you should stay," she answered, pushing him gently back on the bed and passing him the pipe.

Within minutes, Joseph was floating. Above the bed where his head lay on a satin pillow, above the clay-and-bamboo roofs of Hong Kong, above the blue-black waters of the protected cove where the *Stargazer* sat. Among the stars.

"This is nice," Joseph tried to say. He slept and smoked, slept and smoked. At some point, Jerry came over and Joseph paid him again. Then he smoked and slept some more, letting his feet splay on the daybed's mattress, letting his eyes and mind rest. Night turned to day and Joseph woke. Jerry led him outside, to a back alley where Joseph relieved himself and thought he heard chickens. Then he went inside and lay back once more.

NELL GREW IMPATIENT waiting for Mr. Blair of Jardine Matheson to call them into his office. "Do you think he's even in?" she asked Winnie, looking around the opulent sitting room. "You don't think he'd keep us waiting as some sort of tactic, do you?"

"I really don't know, Mother," Winnie said. "Why would he do that?"

"To have control. To make me feel unstable or lesser than," Nell said. "A French perfumer once made me wait alone for three hours in the vestibule of his factory, even though I had confirmed the appointment the day prior. Just to show off his importance!" Nell hadn't slept in days and the strain was getting to her.

Winnie put her kid-gloved hands on top of her mother's. "You're not in this alone," she said.

This statement brought tears to Nell's eyes: her precious, loyal daughter. Why had it taken a tragedy to see what was right in front of her?

"Ah, Mrs. Starbuck," Mr. Blair said, opening the double doors to his office. "It's wonderful to meet you. And, Miss Starbuck, how delightful to see you again. Please, ladies, do come in," he said, motioning them into his office.

The room was large and bright, with many windows facing out over the far side of Victoria Harbor. Winnie was impressed by the secluded beauty of this particular vantage point. Almost no one else on the island was privy to this exact vista, as the Jardine headquarters built on the ridge blocked it from public eyes. You had to be invited inside the building, and more specifically, into Mr. Blair's offices, to see it.

"Before we get to business, which I am certain is why you are here," Mr. Blair said, sitting down behind his grand desk, "I'd like to express my deepest condolences. Captain Starbuck was a pioneer in the China trade, and a revolutionary sea captain. He shall forever be remembered for his financial success, winning leadership, and for owning and captaining the ship that broke the world record to San Francisco, which no amount of misfortune can erase."

"We appreciate your condolences, Mr. Blair. Although I didn't know you were aware of Peter's passing," Nell said. "When you met Winnie at the American consulate—"

"I heard shortly thereafter. News travels fast through an island community such as ours. I'm sure it's similar on Nantucket."

He was wearing another cravat today, this one bloodred, tied over another perfectly white high-collared shirt. "It's quite unfortunate," he added, shaking his head. "Pirates populated the seas when I first arrived with Jardine Matheson in Hong Kong nine years ago. Now the British navy protects the waters more vigilantly than in '42 and the attacks have all but disappeared. But I heard you were farther out when the pirates appeared. Off the coast of Taiwan, was it? A band of Australians?"

It made sense for Mr. Blair to have heard about the funeral, as a procession of fifty sailors traipsing through the city streets and out to Happy Valley was hard to miss. But how had he heard about the pirates? Another secret that had slipped from Nell's control. She had hoped to keep Peter's dignity intact by not divulging the cause of his death. "In fact, that's why we are here."

"Because of the pirates?" Mr. Blair asked, a crease of skin gathering between his eyebrows.

"Yes. Unfortunately, in the events of that evening, the gold was taken," Nell said.

"Jardine Matheson's gold? Well. That *is* unfortunate," Mr. Blair said, sitting back in his chair. He turned and looked out the grand windows, thinking.

"We didn't know it was yours. In fact, we didn't know about its existence at all until Peter—" Nell said, picturing her husband bleeding out.

"Nobody knew, sir. Which is why our first mate, Sully, who briefly became the captain upon my father's passing, gave the gold freely to the pirates as they left the ship."

Mr. Blair's eyebrows rose at this. "He did, did he?"

"Yes," Nell said. "And we were unable to defend ourselves properly against the attack because our weapons were missing."

"We have reason to believe that the same first mate sold our guns in San Francisco for his own profit, leaving us unprepared," Winnie said. "He had been blackmailing my father for years and—"

Nell put out a hand to stop Winnie. "At any rate, the situation was—mishandled. And we'd like to ask to take out a loan against future profits in order to pay you back. Every penny, plus interest."

"That's impossible, I'm afraid," Mr. Blair said, quickly dismissing the idea. "As we are not a bank, and we don't give lines of credit."

"But your firm has the resources to cover the transaction. Peter and I have made similar arrangements like this several times," Nell said. "That's what merchants do."

"But you're not a merchant, Mrs. Starbuck. If your husband were here, I'd be happy to discuss the financial particulars with him," Mr. Blair said. "And I'm certain we could work something out."

"But—" Nell said, feeling as if she'd been slapped. "I *am* a merchant! I am one half of Starbuck & Starbuck, and I have been for twenty years."

"You are a *she* merchant, a title that reminds everyone—even you—that a woman in business is not the same as a man."

Nell felt like she had been slapped. She had sacrificed motherhood to travel the globe and prove that she was as good as, if not better than, any man. But in the world of men, she would never be good enough. Not without a man by her side to vouch for her. Nell's years of hard work were instantly rendered meaningless.

"You'll have to come up with the funds another way. Now, if that's all, I really must attend to other things," Mr. Blair said. "In fact, I have a shipment of opium arriving from India on Monday that must be transported up the Pearl River in a crab boat, and then onto *your* vessel for the exchange in Canton. So we both have much work to do. I expect that you will not renege on our deal. That would look very bad for both of us."

This was not at all the way the meeting was supposed to go. "I have another proposal for you, Mr. Blair." Before making her final offer, Nell wanted clarification on something else that had been troubling her. "But why is the *Stargazer* necessary? Why didn't Peter just plan to meet you here in Hong Kong and give you the gold, letting you handle the rest?"

"By *the rest*, Mrs. Starbuck, you mean the illegal part. Opium is legal here in British-run Hong Kong. It's in Canton where things get *indelicate*, which is why I was relying on your husband's ship. An American merchant vessel already planning to be in Canton for the trading season—a record-breaking one at that—makes for a great decoy. No one would suspect it housed opium in the hold."

"I cannot believe Father would agree to that," Winnie said, unable to control her anger. "He was an ethical, moral person."

"And he was also a businessman, who, after years of saying no to us, eventually was persuaded to prioritize principal over his principles. And rightly so, I'd say. Where do you think all of *this* came from?" Mr. Blair asked Winnie, gesturing around the room and out the windows to Jardine's many warehouses and ships. "Of course, Jardine Matheson deals in many other commodities besides opium." He smiled in satisfaction before turning his attention back to Nell. "Now, how do you *really* plan to pay for the lost gold, Mrs. Starbuck?"

Nell touched the brooch at her neck. "I am prepared to offer you diamonds instead."

"You can't!" Winnie gasped.

With unsteady hands, Nell unclasped the back of the pin and removed it, the tip of the pin pricking her thumb and drawing blood. She passed it across the desk to Mr. Blair, who, in his curiosity, leaned forward to take it. Nell pressed a handkerchief from her dress pocket against the cushion of her finger.

Mr. Blair studied the jewelry in the light, the facets of the large diamond sending rainbow shimmers of reflection around the room. "We call it the Stargazer," Nell said. "With the four-carat Starbuck diamond in the center. My husband had it custom-made for me by Tiffany, Young and Ellis in New York."

"Well. It's quite impressive." Mr. Blair smiled, and the knots in Nell's stomach began to slacken. Winnie crossed her arms in front of her chest, the classic pose of a sulking child. Nell would apologize to her after this transaction was made, explaining that she had no choice but to sacrifice this magnificent family heirloom. It was just a *thing*. Winnie would have to understand. "Quite impressive indeed."

He put the brooch down on the black leather inlay of his desk, slid it across to Nell, and looked up, his countenance cold. "You say you *understand* as a *merchant* about this *unfortunate* turn of events, Mrs. Starbuck, but I don't think you quite grasp the magnitude of just what is at stake here. My own neck, for starters. Because your lovely sentimental brooch doesn't even begin to account for the cost of all that lost gold."

"But—" Nell stammered.

"This is not an acceptable exchange. Think bigger. Think ninety-thousand-dollars big. And think quickly, because time is of the essence." Mr. Blair stood, signaling that the meeting was over. Nell pocketed the rejected brooch and the Starbuck women followed Mr. Blair to the double doors. "Let's have this settled by tomorrow night at my party, shall we? I know you are in mourning, but a deal is a deal, and I'd rather not have to involve Jardine's lawyers."

"Can we meet in private after the ball, Mr. Blair?" Nell asked. Her plan had failed. It had failed gloriously and now she had no idea what to do next. Ninety thousand dollars was a staggering number. It was the cost of East Brick and everything inside it. And if lawyers came after her, that's what they'd want.

Nell's most critical commodity now was time. "I would prefer to meet on Monday. I'd really rather not mix business with pleasure."

"Oh, but Mrs. Starbuck," Mr. Blair said, tilting his head sideways as if explaining something to a small child. "Here in Hong Kong, business and pleasure are one and the same."

"WHAT DO YOU mean, Joseph is *missing*?" Chin asked, his eyes wide in fright. Zander and Cowboy had rowed back with the Starbuck women, but had failed to find Joseph.

Red settled Chin back into bed after escorting him to the head, figuring now was as good a time as any to break the news. Cowboy and Zander were calling in more recruits. Red was going ashore. Cook, too, right after serving lunch.

Chin had been feeling much improved, until this news knocked the wind right out of him again. "How could you lose him?"

"I didn't personally misplace him, for the record," Red said. "Joseph did that all by himself."

"What does Winnie say about it?"

"Winnie doesn't know," Red admitted bashfully.

"Know what?" Winnie said, entering the bunkhouse.

"Nothing," Red and Chin said at the same time. They both looked extremely guilty.

"What are you up to?" Winnie asked.

Chin shut his lips tight and pointed at Red. And then Red spilled the beans.

"Well, then I'm coming with you," Winnie said.

"You can't come," Cook said, appearing at the bunkhouse door with a wooden spoon in his hand. Winnie had left the door open and Cook could hear their entire conversation from the galley.

"Why not?" Winnie asked.

"Because we believe he's in an opium den, and women are not allowed inside."

"Well, *certain* kinds of women are allowed inside . . ." Red added, trailing off. His face grew hot as he thought about those women.

Winnie grunted in frustration. What was it with men and their rules about what women could and could not do, where they could and could not go? Winnie was not going to be deterred by an edict as idiotic as that. She paced the small space and considered her options.

"Oh no," Cook said. "She's thinking."

Winnie hadn't let her father's orders stop her from sneaking on to the *Stargazer* nearly half a year ago, and she wouldn't let a man's laws prevent her now from finding Joseph and bringing him back safely to the ship.

Chin's discarded brown cap was hung on the top spindle of a small chair in the corner of the room. Winnie grabbed it and put it on her head, where it fit well over her bun. A few tendrils framed her face. "How do I look?"

"Not like Chin, if that's what you're trying for," Red said.

"Not like me . . . but definitely like a boy!" Chin exclaimed. He motioned under the bed, where his sea chest lay. "My pants will be too short for you. But I bet my shirts will fit!"

"Yes!" Winnie slid the box out and opened it.

Chin stepped gingerly out of his bed, pulling a white shirt, a vest, and a navy jacket from his belongings. "Here, three layers of tops should hide your—*kuk sin*."

"Brilliant!" Winnie cheered. From the context of the conversation, everyone in the room grasped the translation of Chin's Cantonese expression.

"I'll go change!" Winnie said.

"You have to promise me you'll find Joseph! I only have sisters and—I love him like a brother," Chin declared.

"I love him, too, Chin," Winnie said.

"Me three," Red said.

"Yeah, yeah, me, too," Cook said. "Let's hope the little bugger hasn't gotten himself into too much trouble."

AS WINNIE MADE her way to her room, she found her mother staring at her reflection in the small mirror at her father's shaving desk, lost in thought, the diamond brooch in her hand.

"I just can't believe it," her mother said, meeting her daughter's eyes in the mirror.

"I know," Winnie said. Although she had been shocked to see her mother offer the brooch as payment, she had been more upset with Mr. Blair's complete refusal of it. What would they do now?

"He was so rude to me," Nell said. She had always taken great pride in her work, in her title. Nell had never before considered that the term *she merchant* might be an insult.

Winnie stepped closer and put her hand on her mother's shoulder. "You don't have to believe him. He's just one man."

"One man bold enough to speak the truth," Nell said.

"One man stupid enough to think that gender can define—and limit—one's success. Father didn't think that."

"And yet, he made secret deals without my knowledge. So maybe he did."

Everything had suddenly been turned on its head. Without Peter, would Nell be able to continue on with their company's work? Would the hong merchants in Canton laugh at her, a widow conducting business on her own? Turn away and refuse her orders?

It wasn't just that Nell felt she had been promised a certain kind of life, expecting to be handed success and ease; it's that Nell had worked hard for it, making sacrifices great and small along the way. She had attained prominence and skill and affluence and clenched it tightly in her fist to hold on to it.

And still, it was slipping through her fingers.

"And without a loan or an item to trade with, what are we to do now?"

"I'll help you come up with a plan," Winnie said with determination. Energized by the rush she had felt in Chin's bunkroom, Winnie was certain she had the resources, ambition, and cunning to change outcomes, not just for herself but for others she loved, too.

"That's a lovely sentiment, darling. I admire your spunk. But I'm afraid this problem is just too immense for us to solve on our own." Nell sighed. She hid the jewelry away in its blue velvet box, the top snapping shut.

Nell felt hopeless. She had always been able to negotiate her way out of a difficult business situation, always. But today she had underestimated the stakes, both financial and personal. Today she had failed as both a merchant and a mother.

Nell turned in her chair. "What in the world are you wearing on your head? And why are you holding those dirty old rags?"

"It's a long story," Winnie said. "And I'm going to need to borrow a pair of Father's pants."

AFTER LUNCH, THREE search parties set out to find Joseph. Doc, the carpenter, led one group, heading east. Cowboy, Merle, Don and Harry headed west. Zander, Red, Cook, and Winnie would head south, walking into town with Victoria Peak straight ahead, an easy landmark to help them always know where they were in Hong Kong.

"Let's meet back here at sundown and regroup then," Zander said.

"Sir, what if we find him sooner?" Doc asked.

"Then row with him back to the boat and ring the bell three times to alert the others," Zander said.

"Yessir," everyone said. Several of the crew glanced at Winnie in her strange outfit, but no one dared comment. In truth, nothing about Winifred Starbuck surprised them anymore.

Winnie pulled Chin's hat down over her head and her father's pants up over her hips.

Her mother had reluctantly agreed to let Winnie join the volunteer brigade, even helping Winnie bind her chest flat with extra bandaging that the surgeon had left for Chin's wound.

"Looking good there, miss," Cook said. "Mister."

"Thanks!" Winnie said. Then, lowering her voice, she tried again. "I mean, *thanks*."

"Maybe let us do the talking," Zander suggested.

They passed rows of shops selling pottery and bolts of silk and small restaurants serving tea and noodles and all manner of foods that Winnie couldn't name. The air was fragrant with deliciousness and simultaneously ripe with sharp odors. Wearing Chin's shoes, Winnie tried to walk like a male, stooping forward slightly and aiming for a heavier gait than her own, hoping to pass for a person straddling boyhood and maturity.

Tall and dark-skinned, Zander stood out in the sea of Asians and Caucasians who made up the population. "People are staring at you, Zander," Winnie said, walking beside him.

"I prefer to call it gawking, actually," Zander said, trying to make light of it. He had traveled halfway around the world to find a city to roam in without worry, but he had yet to find a map where that place existed. "We'll let Cook and Red make the inquiries."

Not wanting to leave any stone unturned, the group entered every single storefront. They stopped anyone walking by in Western dress and asked if they'd seen Joseph. "No, sorry. No. No, I haven't met anyone matching that description." They passed small farms and fishermen's sheds, hunting everywhere.

They walked farther out, to the base of Victoria Peak, where the sloping land was too difficult to traverse on foot. Cook put his hands on his hips and looked up, squinting. There were a few homes there, but it was otherwise uncultivated. "D'ya think he went up this way?"

The consensus was no, although Winnie was loath to turn back without at least an attempt. The group was approached by sedan chairs offering rides up the hill, and Winnie hesitated.

"We can always come back, if we have to," Red said. "But it seems unlikely he's up there."

Winnie supposed so. But it felt like they'd already been everywhere but up. Could a person just disappear?

JOSEPH HAD ALL but disappeared. His body no longer existed except as a shell, and like a crab, he was ready to move on from this one and enter the next. He was voice and vapor, devoid of emotion or need. Lying in Jerry's opium den, Joseph had everything he wanted, which was nothingness.

A commotion around him stirred the air. Loud voices changed the feeling in the room, disturbing his bliss.

"I know he's in there; I can see him for myself!" a man said in a thick cockney accent. A Brit. There were lots of British people here in Hong Kong. *Hong. Kong. Rhymes with gong.* The sound reverberated in his head and Joseph laughed at his own silliness.

"See, he's the one curled up in the back corner, with the floppy hair," Red added. Joseph was alive. "And . . . is he laughing?"

"Your boy wants to stay," Jerry said, stepping in front of them and blocking their way. Two much larger men appeared from the shadows and guarded him on either side.

"Joseph!" Cook called.

"Hey, Joseph Allen!" Red joined in.

Joseph heard his name being called, pulling at him like taffy stretched thin. He picked his head up from the pillow and looked toward the sound with his eyes closed. He didn't need to open them to see. Opening his eyes was dangerous. Open eyed, he saw Samuel, reaching out to grasp Joseph's hand and just missing him as the rough current took him away. Open eyed, he saw pirates land on the deck of the *Stargazer*, the captain mortally wounded on his own ship. Open eyed, he saw a future with Winnie Starbuck, sailing the world together as husband and wife.

So he kept his eyes shut tight. Vision was an inner sight now.

"Joseph!" Cook called one last time through the dim haze before he and Red were shoved out the door and forcibly removed from the establishment.

"Here's something I never say to people who visit my opium den: don't come back." Jerry slammed the wooden door in their faces.

"What happened?" Winnie asked, standing in the street with Zander.

"He's in there," Cook said.

"Thank God!" Winnie said.

"Then—why didn't you bring him out?" Zander asked.

Cook and Red explained the problem: guards at the entry. "I think the one on the left had a knife," Red added. He may have just been imagining it, but it felt distinctly possible. "I don't know how we're going to get past them."

"I do," Winnie said.

THEY WAITED AT a restaurant across the alleyway for about thirty minutes, sipping tea at an outdoor table on the front porch and observing the establishment across the way.

"Okay, I'm going in," Winnie said, trying to keep her voice low and her pants high. They had pooled their money, so Winnie had fifty American dollars in her father's pocket. It should be more than enough.

"Just try not to talk too much," Red advised.

"Just stick to the plan," Cook said.

"Just stay safe," Zander said. "Please."

"And for God's sake don't smoke any of that stuff!" Cook added for good measure, like an extra pinch of seasoning to perfect the roast.

"I will, I will, I will, and I won't!" Winnie said, practicing her tone of voice and flashing a winning smile their way. "Enjoy your tea, boys. See you soon." She hoped that by sounding brave and confident, she'd convince herself she was.

Winnie entered the opium den, shocked at first by the lack of light and the sharp smell of vapors in the air. It was a cloud of poison, and Winnie blinked back tears.

"First time here?" the man named Jerry asked her. Winnie nodded, not only afraid to speak but unable to utter a word in the gaseous smell so strong she could practically taste it. It was not dissimilar to the stench of whale oil in barrels on Nantucket wharves in summertime, but it was distinctly worse. She handed the man a twenty-dollar bill, which seemed to please him. "Lin will take care of you."

Jerry motioned to a beautiful young woman whose black hair was pulled back into an elaborate bun at the base of her neck, a red flower tucked into one side. Winnie followed Lin into the parlor. When the woman motioned to a daybed toward the front, Winnie asked if she could sit farther back. "For privacy," she said in a low tone. If she pretended to be angry, her voice naturally dropped. Given that she was actually angry—at her father, at Mr. Blair, at the pirates, and now at Joseph, too, for getting himself and her into this mess—this strategy worked.

Smoking opium involved lots of paraphernalia and a good deal of time, which gave Winnie a moment to adjust her eyes to the gloom. Three men in British naval uniforms over here, an Asian man in a long robe lying asleep over there. Cook and Red had tried to prepare her for all of these reposed bodies, but the reality of it was quite distressing. Were they seeking happiness, or running away from pain? Was there a difference? Everything was indistinguishable in the gloom.

It was awful. The quicker Winnie could leave with Joseph, the better.

And there he was, as if just thinking of Joseph had made him appear. Two beds away from Winnie, off to the far right. "Just a few minutes," Lin said, heating a long wooden pipe over a small glass lantern. It was now or never.

"I recognize a friend," Winnie said. "Please excuse me for one minute." She handed Lin ten dollars and smiled, hoping the gratuity would keep her quiet. Then Winnie went to Joseph, sinking down on the daybed beside him.

"Hi," she said in a whisper of her regular voice. He was curled on his side with his hands tucked under his face. He looked peaceful in this position, but also depleted, empty. Like he wasn't even there. This idea sent a cold shock of fright through her.

"Joseph, wake up." She stroked his hair. Her heart was hammering in her chest. He was warm; he was breathing. He was alive, for now. "Open your eyes," she commanded in a louder voice.

"COME ON, JOSEPH," the voice said. It was familiar and pleading. It was a hurting voice. The person was stroking his hair, cradling his face. Then the person began telling him a story. A story about a pirate ship, and gold, and a captain who hadn't told his wife and daughter about a business deal that had now gone very wrong.

"We're in big trouble. And I don't know how we're going to get out of it," Winnie said matter-of-factly. "But none of that matters. *You* are the only thing that matters. You have to wake up. You have to live."

But Joseph thought he might not want to live. He didn't exactly want to die, but living was just too hard. He might have murmured this aloud.

"I know. I know living is hard. It's the hardest thing we can do. But it's the only choice we have," Winnie said.

Joseph had let Winnie down. He had killed Samuel and everyone on the *Chase*, and then he had brought devastation to the *Stargazer*. He might have said this, too.

"I don't blame you, Joseph, but also, I forgive you. Everyone forgives you. Now you have to forgive yourself."

Lin was studying Winnie curiously. "Do you want to come back to the table now?" she called. "The pipe is ready."

Winnie ignored her.

Joseph had been drowning, but now he felt himself swimming, swimming to the murky surface. Kicking, pushing away from the cold depths that had kept him underwater for the past year. He felt like he might want to breathe.

Joseph opened his eyes. "I know you," he said. "But you look different." He propped his drooping body against the wall. "You're—"

"I'm Fred," Winnie said, swallowing tears. "I'm Fred, and I'm here to take you home, Joseph. Back to the ship. Right now."

"Fred!" Joseph smiled. "Is that Chin's hat?"

"Do you think you can stand?" Winnie asked. Joseph scooted toward the edge of the bed and tried to stand, but his limbs were like jelly. He sat back down heavily. Winnie couldn't possibly carry him alone, and she cursed her three crewmates outside for not considering this part of the plan. Joseph's eyes closed again.

"How can I help?" Lin said, now at Winnie's elbow.

"You can't," Winnie said, losing her composure. "I'll return in a minute. I'm just speaking with an old colleague!" she said, her voice high-pitched under stress.

Lin looked troubled. She cast her eyes to the front of the long, dark room and then back. "Just follow me," Lin said. "Do whatever I say."

"I don't think I want to smoke—you know—anymore, actually," Winnie said, now frantic. "Thank you so much for going through the trouble of preparing it."

"I know who you are and what you are doing," Lin said. "We have met many times."

"I am sure we've never met before," Winnie said honestly.

"Over thousands of years, again and again, we have met. Because you are a woman, like me," she said, running her eyes up and down Winnie's body. "And he is the man that you love."

Winnie was speechless.

Lin reached over to Joseph's far side and hooked her arm with his. "On the count of three! Look happy, okay?" she asked Winnie.

They got Joseph to his feet and walked him to the front of the parlor without much assistance from Joseph himself, both women straining under Joseph's deadweight.

"Such special clients!" Lin said dramatically as they approached Jerry and his henchmen. "Thank you so much!" Lin practically pushed them toward the front door, holding it open for them.

Cook, Red, and Zander ran toward them in the street.

"Joseph!" Zander said, scooping him up and placing him over his shoulder like a sack of rice.

"Here," Winnie said to Lin, reaching into her pocket. She extended her last twenty dollars. "Please, take it."

Lin shook her head no, bowed deeply, then disappeared back inside.

THE OTHER SEARCH teams were waiting for them back at the docks, and the men all cheered when they saw Zander approach with Joseph over his shoulder.

Everyone got back into their dinghies and rowed back to the ship, just in time for dinner. "We're having it cold and you're all going to love it that way, like it or not!" Cook called out from his boat, which received a hearty "aye-aye" from the crew.

"Thank you for saving me again, Fred," Joseph said, his head lolling to the side, still somewhat in a stupor.

"You're welcome," Winnie said. She wanted to punch him but instead grabbed him in a tight embrace.

CHAPTER 46

October 25

By the next morning, the haze of the drug had mostly worn off and Joseph was mostly back to himself, albeit with a splitting headache and a gut roiling with mortification. He brought the chessboard up from the great cabin to Chin's bunkhouse. The ship was still with the silence of slumber, as Zander had given the crew the day off.

"I'm so sorry, Chin," Joseph said. "I feel like I let you down by wandering into that place."

"You could never let me down, Joseph," Chin said. "But maybe you let yourself down."

Joseph sighed. "After I lost my brother, I kind of lost myself."

"Did you find yourself again?"

"I'm somewhere on the map."

Chin smiled. "Good. Now be prepared to lose at chess!"

Chin and Joseph spent the morning playing quietly while Joseph gulped cups of some concoction Cook had made to alleviate some of his pain.

"I win! Again!" Chin declared.

Joseph set up the board again and again just for the enjoyment of playing the game.

"Knock, knock," Winnie said, entering through the open bunkhouse door. She was back in her feminine clothing, a simple gray cotton dress, her hair plaited and looped around her ears. "I've brought back your clothes, and—" She paused when she saw Joseph. "Oh, hello."

"Oh, hello to you, too," Joseph said sheepishly.

"Thank you, Chin. I couldn't have done it without you—and your cap." Joseph was sitting in the corner chair, so Winnie put Chin's items in a cubby hole by the door.

"I heard you were incredible, Fred!" Chin said.

"She was," Joseph said, nodding at Chin. "She is," he added, looking at Winnie.

An awkward silence followed. "I'm feeling kind of tired," Chin said, faking a dramatic yawn and scooting under his blanket. "Maybe we can play more later?"

"Of course," Joseph said, standing and leaving the bunkhouse with Winnie. They closed the door behind them and walked up to the poop deck. Winnie leaned against the railing and looked out toward Kowloon on the opposite shore.

"I want to apologize for my behavior," Joseph began.

The heat wave had broken. A soft breeze rippled the water, and sunlight made it sparkle like gold. Or perhaps diamonds, Winnie thought.

"I haven't been myself since arriving in San Francisco," Joseph added.

"What happened to the *Chase*?" Winnie asked, turning to Joseph. "And why are you so certain that it was your fault?"

Anger bubbled up inside of Joseph. "I told you, I don't want to talk about it. I'm never going to talk about it."

"Then you'll never truly be free of it," Winnie said. "And you'll never truly be mine." She brushed past him.

"Winnie, please," Joseph begged. When she reached the poop deck stairs, he called out to her again. "Fred! Wait!"

She turned. "I don't know if I want you to call me that."

He took his hands in hers. "Winnie, then. You have to understand how hard it is for me to tell this story, to relive it."

The night of her father's death flashed before her eyes. "I think I do understand," she said.

And so they sat on the top stair with their feet on the step below, and he told her about the *Chase*. About the fog that came out of nowhere. About Joseph's failure to see the rocks ahead in time and to sound the alarm. About the sinking feeling in his chest when the *Chase*'s hull struck the rock and began taking on water, slowly at first and then very rapidly. How Joseph's hands shook so badly that he had trouble untying the knots holding the dinghies in place, as the captain and first mate called out orders to abandon ship but the ship was sideways and some of the dinghies were lost to the tide, just swept away in a whirling eddy with a few men inside, and how it was hard to carefully do anything, like get in a lifeboat. How he yelled at Samuel to "hold on, hold on!" grabbing at any lines of rope they could as the ship sank under their feet and men drowned around them, pitiful final cries of distress, knowing they were dying, and how Samuel finally just slipped away while Joseph held on.

Winnie held Joseph's hand as tears rolled down her cheeks. "I'm so sorry," she said over and over.

Joseph didn't cry. Instead of emptiness, or the familiar dread conjured whenever he thought of that day, he felt filled with Winnie's understanding. Her compassion and her hopefulness and her stubborn need to help him. He had somehow weathered the yearlong storm of his loss, in large part thanks to Winnie. "You saved me from drowning."

She leaned into his side and looked up at him. "Can we start courting now?"

He answered with a soft kiss. They stayed like that for a few minutes before pulling apart.

"Last night—" Joseph began.

"Yes?" Winnie asked.

"I know this is going to sound crazy, but . . . did you tell me a wild story about your father getting involved in an opium deal, and pirates stealing gold from the ship?" Joseph shook his head. "Sorry. I probably hallucinated it."

Winnie took a deep breath and exhaled slowly. "You didn't imagine it. It's real. And my mother and I need to come up with a solution by tonight."

BY LATE AFTERNOON, Nell and Winnie still didn't have a solid plan. On the poop deck earlier in the day, Winnie had told Joseph every detail of the deal with Jardine Matheson. She had rehashed the conversation with Mr. Blair as Joseph prodded her with questions.

"Since Blair said the event was a mixture of business and pleasure," Joseph thought aloud, "maybe you can meet other merchants at the party and ask for their backing?"

"Maybe," Winnie had said. "But how will we even know whom to approach? And what if they laugh in our faces, since we're women trying to do business?" And that was as far as their brainstorming had taken them. "My mother and I think we just shouldn't go tonight, since we have nothing to offer. Make Blair come and find us on his own time."

"Hiding from your problems? That doesn't sound like your mother," Joseph said. "Or you."

"No, it doesn't," Winnie agreed. But without another option, hiding in plain sight on the largest ship in the harbor was what they would do.

AFTER LUNCH, JOSEPH returned to Chin's bunkroom and the chess games resumed. Chin beat Joseph three times in a row, which was loads of fun for Chin and incredibly frustrating for Joseph. "Why are you constantly beating me?" Joseph complained, feeling very sorry for himself.

"Because you keep making plays that help me, your opponent," Chin said. He showed him. "Like this, where you swapped your queen for mine but then left my knight in a much better position," he said, showing it on the board.

"I give up."

"No, Joseph. You can never give up! Learn from the Chinese: 'Like rowing a boat upstream, if you stop moving forward, you fall back down.'"

"That proverb doesn't help me at all," Joseph said.

"Okay, then how about what Red always says, from your War of 1812: 'Time to give up the ship!'" Chin did a fair imitation of the steward.

"That's not the expression," Joseph said, moving the pieces back into place for another game.

"Yes, it is," Chin said. "But maybe Red says it more like this: '*Time* to give *up* the *ship*!'"

"The actual saying is *don't*—" Joseph stopped. He dropped a white pawn onto the chessboard. His head snapped up. "Chin, you're a genius!" He grabbed Chin and kissed him on the temple, just like he used to when Samuel had said something particularly brilliant.

"I have been saying that all along!" Chin agreed.

"And now I've got to go!" Joseph said, excited by the revelation he'd just had. For there was a way—*one way*—for the Starbucks to really and truly extricate themselves from this situation.

"WHAT DO YOU think?" Joseph asked, having shared his idea with Winnie and Mrs. Starbuck, who sat on the blue velvet couch in their private living room while he stood before them. The Starbuck women did not look pleased.

It had been an incredibly hard few days, and now this. *How had it come to this?* Nell wondered.

Winnie stood slowly, considering the plan. Her hand lingered on the couch and then her father's desk, touching its ornate wooden roll-top. She touched the waist-high chair rail molding and then traced a sampan on the wallpaper above it. She glanced up through the sky-light, the sun shifting toward late afternoon. They were out of time. "Joseph's right, Mother. We have to do it. There's no other way."

Nell closed her eyes, then opened them. She was so very tired. But she understood and agreed with the plan. "All right. Joseph, will you come with us to the ball? It will help to have a man by our side."

DRESSED IN THEIR finest, the trio was rowed to shore by two of the newer crew members who planned to enjoy a night on the town, awaiting their return. "But we won't enjoy it too much, if you know what I mean," one of them said. "Captain's orders."

Nell, Winnie, and Joseph in particular agreed that was very wise. At the docks, they hired three sedan chairs to carry them to the home of Loren Blair, who lived on Victoria Peak.

Each chair was lifted off the ground. They were off, carried through the streets of Victoria Town with a gentle swaying motion, not unlike being in a boat during a calm day at sea.

Although Winnie couldn't see her mother or Joseph, hidden by the cane covering of the boxlike chair, she could hear each call out in an excited fright as they felt the incline of the hill shift the angle of their chairs.

The motion stopped and the chairs were lowered. Nell paid the men and thanked them.

"To think, we have to come back down at night once it is completely dark!" Winnie said, speaking aloud only one of the fears she held about the evening.

The house overlooked the entire island during that magical hour before sunset. "It's breathtaking," Winnie said. "It reminds me of Jessie Lindquist's San Francisco home, in a way."

"Wealthy people the world over seem to claim their place at the top," Joseph said. This was true even on an island without hills like Nantucket, as Orange and Fair and upper Main Streets, where the Starbucks lived, were geographically situated above the rest of the town.

The white-stone home with the red tile roof resembled the Jardine headquarters on a smaller scale. The sedan chairs kept coming as people arrived around them, in all manner of dress hailing from all around the world.

Each time the door opened, Winnie could hear violins and flutes. A concerto. "There is an orchestra inside," she said.

It was time to face the music.

INSIDE THE GRAND front hall, they waited in a small line to be formally announced. "Mr. Charles Southing, of Russel and Company," an usher in formal attire said, and a man entered the ballroom. "The Duke and Duchess of Sussex," he announced after a brief pause. "Merchants Ko Mun Wo and Chiu Shing Lam of Hong Kong."

"I've never been announced before," Joseph said, squirming uncomfortably and pulling at his cufflinks.

"Me, neither," Winnie said. Perhaps President and Mrs. Fillmore announced their guests at the White House, but no one on Nantucket ever did. Then again, everyone knew everyone else on Nantucket, making the formality unnecessary.

They inched forward until they were next in line. The man in front of them was dressed exotically, wearing a long white linen tunic over wide, white linen pants. He had a close-cropped black beard and mustache and wore a black silk turban around his hair. He spoke to the usher, sharing his name and place of work, and then was announced.

"Mr. Elias Sassoon, of Bombay and Shanghai," the usher said, and the man bowed and stepped into the room.

Nell had been traveling the world for years, but had never been invited to such an international, multilingual gathering until now. In France, she met French people, and in Italy, the Italians. Hong Kong was unique, unlike any place she'd ever been or would probably ever see again.

Joseph told the usher who they were, and they were announced. "Mr. Joseph Allen, Mrs. Nell Starbuck, and Miss Winifred Starbuck of the *Stargazer* from Nantucket, Massachusetts."

Mr. Blair nodded at her from his place at the front of the crowd in the grand, gilded ballroom. He now knew she was here. So that's why people were announced, Nell realized.

"Champagne?" a waiter said, passing by with a tray aloft.

"Oh, yes," Nell said, and she, Winnie, and Joseph all gulped down a glass.

The room was lively with music and people, with formal dancing in the center of the room. Someone bumped into Joseph from behind, knocking his empty champagne flute to the floor, where it shattered noisily.

"My apologies!" Joseph said, even though he was pretty certain the accident had been the other person's fault. Winnie, Nell, and Joseph all turned, finding that the center of the commotion was none other than Sully. Here.

He was dressed in a dark formal suit, his face contorted in rage. "You can't be sorry enough, you idiot." He pushed Joseph hard in the chest, shoving him into Nell and Winnie, who caught him from falling.

"What are you doing here, Sully?" Joseph asked.

"Oh, don't pretend you doan know. I was working for Jardine Matheson until something you said got me fired tonight!"

"I have no idea what you're talking about," Joseph said. "We just got here!"

"I believe I do," Nell said as she and Winnie exchanged a knowing glance. "Winnie and I met with Mr. Blair and we mentioned that our first mate was fired for being inadequate, among other things. Mr. Blair must have figured out who you were."

Sully wasn't going to hit a woman. Instead he knocked an entire tray of champagne flutes from a passing waiter's hand and headed for the door, leaving broken shards in his wake as onlookers gawked and whispered.

Sully may be done with the Starbucks and Jardine Matheson, but he wasn't finished. Not by a long shot. Hong Kong was a growing port city filled with new opportunities, and he'd find his way to success, come hell or high water.

"Well," Winnie said, watching Sully leave without feeling much of anything. It was a sign that it was time to let other things go, too, and move ever forward. *Semper porro.* "Shall we meet with Mr. Blair?"

MR. BLAIR SMILED warmly as they approached, as though they were all old friends reuniting after years apart. He waved off some other guests he had been talking to and ushered them to a secluded balcony outside, overlooking the dark harbor below.

Nell introduced Joseph, and the group exchanged pleasantries about the weather and the sedan chairs and the merchant's lovely home with the lovely view.

"I am glad you have been enjoying my home and my champagne and my view. But have you come up with my money?" Mr. Blair asked.

Joseph wanted to strangle the Scotsman with his black cravat.

"In a way, yes. Mr. Blair, I am prepared to give you the *Stargazer*," Nell said.

Their host barked in anger. "As we discussed previously, your diamond brooch is not sufficient."

Nell explained. "Not the jewelry. The clipper ship. That *Stargazer*."

"Well." Mr. Blair looked stupified. "I had not anticipated that."

"Nor had we. But the *Stargazer* should be *more* than sufficient in paying off our debt," Winnie said.

"The ship, of all things," Blair said, shaking his head in wondrous disbelief. "I must hand it to you Starbucks. You're back in the race, even without your captain—or your ship." He raised his glass of champagne to them, turning his attention to Joseph. "Jardine will have profits for you once the opium deal is done."

"We don't want profits from your illicit deal," Nell said. "We are walking away, buying our freedom in exchange for Peter's ship."

Joseph explained the plan. "We will sail her to the Whampoa Reach anchorage outside of Canton for you, and then she'll be yours. The ship currently has a captain who may stay on, and a crew to sail back to the States—I mean England—with afterward." He'd speak to Zander tonight, letting him decide how to tell the crew, all of whom would be free to stay on board or find other positions on other ships.

"When Jardine takes ownership of her, where will you three go?" Blair asked.

"We will disembark in Canton to conduct our business dealings with the American factories there, as planned, and then hire a ship to take us back to New England with our cargo," Nell explained.

"So as not to dirty your hands with opium," Mr. Blair said.

"Yes, there's that. Also, I cannot possibly stay on board once she's yours," Nell said.

"You will have to find another navigator, as I'm going with the Starbucks," Joseph said, taking Winnie's hand in his. "And another cabin boy, too," Joseph added, "as ours will be getting off in Canton."

Mr. Blair was excited by this turn of events in his favor. He'd have no problem replacing a few of the crew, moving them from other ships in the fleet if need be. And imagine William Matheson's face when he opened the letter from Blair, telling him about this coup. It was an achievement not only for the British company, but for the British people, who would now have a record-setting American clipper to call their own, to study and use as a template to build others just like her.

Mr. Blair stuck out his hand for Joseph to shake, but Joseph put up his hands in surrender. "I'm not the one you need to close this deal with, sir."

Nell stepped forward and put out her hand. Mr. Blair had no choice but to shake it.

CHAPTER 47

October 26–27

Sunday morning was bright and clear, reminding Zander of the day back in June when the *Stargazer* had first set sail from Nantucket. When the ship passed the Great Point lighthouse at the eastern edge of that island, catching that first true wind of possibility, he had gripped the wheel and thought, *Let's see what you can do*. He had meant it as a declaration to the ship. But maybe it had also become a maxim for himself. *Let's see what you can do, Zander Washington. Let's see what you can do.*

As helmsman, he had kept the ship on course for months, holding steady and strong even in moments when he was exhausted and had nothing left to give. He had battled a bully of a bigot and a team of pirates and had mourned the loss of his captain. Captain Starbuck had hired Zander knowing that he was a runaway slave, but never asking for more specifics, saying only "welcome aboard" and shaking Zander's hand.

And now Zander was the ship's captain.

The *Stargazer* was setting sail for Canton today, a slow, two-day journey up the Pearl River from Hong Kong. Last night, when the Starbuck women and Joseph had returned from the ball, they had called him to the dining table in the center of the officers' quarters and explained that they had sold the ship to the merchant firm Jardine Matheson. That was the first shock. The second shock was learning why they had done it.

"In all our years of marriage," Nell said, "Peter had never before conspired behind my back or acted immorally. I believe he only did it to purchase this clipper ship." For some reason, she wanted Zander in particular to know this.

Zander had nodded. "He loved this ship. He gave her everything."

"Almost everything," Nell said, hoping to salvage some of her own dignity. She explained to Zander that the ship would be used for one day in Canton to house and distribute opium like a floating warehouse. "By then, the ship will belong to Jardine Matheson, which clears the Starbuck name. And I have a way for you and your crew to avoid involvement as well. We can give everyone the night off and say that the ship is being fumigated for rats. That way, the crew cannot be held responsible for anything that happens, as you won't be there."

One could argue the fine points of whether knowing something illegal was happening and not stopping it was as bad as aiding and abetting, but Nell was in no mood to hash out further logical or moral implications.

And could a ship ever really be rid of rats, anyway? "What do you think?" she asked.

"I think we should set sail at daybreak," Zander had said.

THEY RAISED THE anchor, singing "Eliza Lee," which paid homage to another McKay clipper, one that, ironically, took passengers and goods to England. But only Joseph knew that. The rest of the crew thought it had a good beat for a capstan shanty and nothing more.

To me hey rig-a-jig in a jaunting car
Ho-way, ho, are you 'most done
With 'liza Lee all on my knee
Clear away the track an' let the bullgine run
O, we're outward bound for the West Street Pier
(Ho-way, ho, are you 'most done?)
With Galway Shale and Liverpool beer
(Clear away the track and let the bullgine run!)

"Hands aloft!" Captain Washington called.

"Aye-aye, sir!" they called back.

With the anchor raised, the fifty crew members climbed the yards and unfurled sails that had been tied down since reaching Hong Kong. It felt good to let the canvas go, Joseph thought. Cowboy, Merle, and Jonathan, working next to him along the fore topsail, grinned from ear to ear, clearly feeling the same.

"You sure you want to run off with your beau and miss all this?" Cowboy said, hanging over the lower yard.

Zander had told the crew early this morning about the new ownership of the *Stargazer*. He kept the reasons for the new arrangement private, saying only that Mrs. Starbuck was carrying out her husband's dying wish.

No one could argue with that.

Although secrets had landed them in this particular boat, protecting Captain Starbuck's legacy seemed like as good a reason as any for Zander to hold back the truth.

"What Cowboy means is, we're going to miss you, Joseph Allen," Merle said, pulling out the sails from under his body and maintaining one-handed contact at all times, just like Joseph had taught him. "From San Francisco to Canton, it's been one heck of a ride and we've been proud to call you a friend."

CHIN NOW FELT well enough to stand and walk around for longer stretches of time. For the better part of two days, he stood at the side rail and acted as the *Stargazer*'s tour guide, pointing out lands and landmarks of interest. "That's Lantau Island!" he called. And, "That one is Lintin Island!"

"Yet, he doesn't feel well enough to finish any of his duties as cabin boy," Cook complained to Red, pointing a wooden spoon at him, as if he were somehow responsible for Chin's absence from the galley each day.

"We've reached the Tiger's Mouth!" Chin called on day two, opening his jaw and growling like a tiger. The Bocca Tigris was the narrow strait where the Pearl River tapered from its greatest width of fifteen miles across to a mere two. "Just forty miles to Canton," Chin explained to Winnie. "But this part is hard to navigate. Did you hear that, Joseph? It's like a snake, this part of the Pearl River."

"Yes, Chin, I heard you," Joseph called back from the poop deck, where he stood over a barrel, consulting a chart with Zander.

"We'll arrive tomorrow," Chin said in awe, seemingly the only person on board the *Stargazer* who was looking forward to it.

IT FELT APPROPRIATE that Nell's last night aboard this ship was another sleepless one, only this time, it wasn't due to panic. The mizzenmast hadn't fallen. No fierce storms had kept Nell awake, and no one had attacked the ship, been poisoned, suffered frostbite, or perished.

Not wanting to miss a minute of the time she had left with her *Stargazer*, Nell sat vigil through the night. By the glow of her lamplight, she traveled from room to room, opening the doors to each of the passengers' cabins and remembering the people who had stayed there, the brave and dauntless souls willing to pay for a ride to California on an untested clipper ship, the trip of a lifetime. She wandered down into storage, ending up at the still-open door to the ship's hold. In her white nightgown, Nell felt like a ghost in the cavernous space. She sat on the floor and looked up through the grated skylight, where she could see the crescent of the moon. She stared so long that she watched constellations appear and shift, mapping the movement of ancient Greek and Roman heroines the way stargazers had been doing for thousands of years. Nell thought of Nantucket's very own stargazer, Maria Mitchell, who had been studying the night sky since childhood. Maria had discovered a comet four years prior, making history as a woman in astronomy.

Nell wondered if any woman in history had ever felt as she now did.

In the world record for heartache, Nell Starbuck had taken first place.

CHAPTER 48

October 28

Like a rooster crowing to announce the coming day, Chin exclaimed from the middle deck about one final landmark: the magnificent, towering nine-story pagoda at the Whampoa anchorage that signaled the clipper's final port of call. Along with all of the other international trading ships, the *Stargazer* would dock here, twelve miles downstream from Canton. The remainder of the river was too shallow for large ships to sail, so Chinese laborers with sampans and junks were hired to take passengers and cargo to and from Canton.

Nell was in familiar waters now. Gone was the sick feeling of dread in Hong Kong. Now her heart thrummed with the beat of excitement she always felt this close to the American factory where she would meet with the hong merchants. Orders placed for her wealthy clients over a year ago were nearby waiting for her approval, as were new lacquerware, silks, and furniture that Winnie and Nell would purchase with money from Starbuck & Starbuck, hoping to make a profit back in the United States.

All of this was contingent on one simple question: would her gender, which had never mattered before, impede her work in Canton now that she was a widow?

In other words, was a *she* merchant truly valued less than a merchant?

"YOU'RE REALLY LEAVING us, then," Cook said as he served Winnie breakfast in the great cabin for the final time. "And you're taking all of my favorite people with ya, too."

"And you'll be heading back to your hometown of London, which will be nice," Winnie said, trying to convince both of them that this unforeseen turn of events was for the best. "You can see your family."

"You're my family," Cook said. He had known Winnie since she was four-turning-five years old, after all. Stubborn and headstrong and full of schemes and sass. Now that Winnie was back in his life, Cook refused to get used to it without her.

Red was unable to speak as he poured her tea with his eyes red and glassy. Winnie handed him a handkerchief that he used to blow his nose. "Keep it," she said.

"Winnie, darling!" her mother called from the companionway. "It's time."

Red and Cook followed Winnie on deck, where everyone said their final goodbyes after a whole night's worth of farewells and well-wishes, following two days of the same.

From the railing, Chin started yelling, loud and frantic bursts of noise. The crew hardly listened to the cabin boy, as they had orders to follow from their captain and new first mate, Jonathan, as they pulled into port and lowered the anchor.

For the first time since revealing that she had stowed away on the ship, Winnie was just a passenger. She didn't have to pull a line or lower a sail or lift a finger. She sauntered over to the port side rail, assuming Chin was pointing out more sights. But this time, his outbursts were in Cantonese.

He called to someone below, floating by in a sampan. A woman with her hair wrapped in a silk scarf, with a black fringe of bangs on her forehead, was calling up to Chin and waving as Chin was calling back down. They talked on top of each other and they sounded so happy. Tears were rolling down Chin's cheeks.

"She heard we were coming! Other boats along the river heard about the big, fast American ship with the injured Chinese cabin boy and told her it could be me!" he said to Winnie.

"Told who?" Winnie said.

"My mama!" Chin exclaimed.

Winnie put her hand to her mouth. "Your mother? Is here?" She leaned over the rail and gazed down. Chin's mother was waving and talking and crying. She disappeared inside the small bamboo arched hut in the middle of the boat, and then emerged with four children, each one smiling and waving. "Your sisters?" Winnie asked, blinking back tears.

"Yes," Chin said. "Yes." Then he said something that made his mother look very upset. After a moment, she wagged her finger at him and laughed.

"I told her I almost died," he said, smiling. "She doesn't believe me."

As they docked the ship, the entire crew visited the port side railing to call out a hello to Chin's family.

THEY HAD WITNESSED perhaps the most incredible reunion in either American or Chinese history, and now the ship was finally docked at a mooring in the Whampoa harbor. "Mrs. Starbuck, before you go," Zander said. "The crew and I have been talking these last few days and we'd like to give you something."

"A gift is completely unnecessary," Nell said, blushing slightly at the thoughtful gesture.

"You're going to want this one," Cowboy said.

"Is it a ship?" Winnie joked.

"No, but it's the crew for one," Zander answered in all seriousness.

"What do you mean?" Nell asked, looking from Zander to Cowboy and then to all the faces of the sailors who had traveled with them.

"The *Stargazer* is an incredible ship, ma'am. And we have been lucky to sail upon her," Zander said. "But, without the Starbucks, without you, it's just a ship. Many of us—not all, but many—have decided to leave our posts in the coming days and join ranks on whatever ship you hire to return to Nantucket. Including me. We'll follow your lead. Ever forward."

"You are an incredible captain, Zander," Nell said, overcome.

"I learned from the best," he said.

"Besides, nobody wants ta go to England," Cook said. "Food's terrible!" Everyone laughed until they cried, relieved and grateful that they would be continuing on this tempestuous adventure called life together.

CHIN, NELL, AND Winnie Starbuck disembarked from the *Stargazer* and boarded Chin's mother's boat. Joseph would stay on the ship until they had a new one to call home, and planned to bring the women's trunks to Canton in a hired boat later. Chin promised he'd visit Joseph and beat him at chess every day until the crew departed for America.

Winnie looked back at the *Stargazer* at the mooring. The copper flashing on her hull still shone bright, and the brass fittings on her rigging caught the light as if showing off her beauty one last time.

Goodbye, gorgeous girl, Winnie thought. *Wishing you fair winds and following seas.*

IN THE SAMPAN, Chin prattled on while his mother stared at him as she rowed, transfixed by everything her son said. Nell knew this feeling well, for she felt it every time she returned to Winnie after a long journey. How had her child changed? What was the same, and what had altered about their appearance, mannerisms, vocabulary, entire way of carrying themselves and being in the world? What was the miracle that had allowed mother and child to live parallel existences on opposite ends of the earth, and then brought them back to one another? Nell didn't need to speak Cantonese to understand Chin's mother's love.

Chin's mother rowed them closer to Canton, and Winnie gasped.

"What is it?" Nell asked.

"The wallpaper," she said, pointing at the view before her, at the sherbet-colored sky and the soft green hills, at the neat row of impressive buildings lined up along the shore, with Dutch, French, British, and American flags waving their greetings in the gentle breeze. The wallpaper from East Brick had lived so vividly in her mind. And now the harbor at Canton had come to life.

It was just as Winnie had always imagined it. Only her father wasn't standing by her side. He wasn't here, wearing his navy captain's coat with the brass buttons. He wasn't here, calling her Fred and explaining something critical about the fluctuating price of tea or about the aerodynamics of a sampan versus a lorcha.

Winifred Starbuck had thought she knew everything when she boarded the *Stargazer*, when really she had understood nothing. A person had to traverse the globe to learn what she had, journeying far from who she thought she was in order to discover what she was really capable of. Winifred vowed to honor her father through hard work and stubbornness every day until the day she died.

"MRS. STARBUCK, WE have been eagerly awaiting your arrival," a Chinese man said, bowing to Nell and Winnie in the beautiful garden plaza in front of the American factory. Nell and Winnie bowed back. He introduced himself as Mr. Liang, a linguist who spoke fluent English and could help negotiate deals between the two countries.

It would be a perfect job for Chin, Winnie thought.

"My husband—" Nell began.

"Word has traveled from Hong Kong," he said. "I am so sorry for your loss."

"Thank you. It has been a difficult time." Nell was so new to widowhood that she didn't feel comfortable with condolences. She felt mostly like her job was to make others feel less burdened by her tragedy, sailing swiftly past the subject. "Are the hong merchants prepared to get to work? With me and my daughter?" Nell asked, unsure how to proceed.

"As long as you are comfortable doing so. Before you arrived, the merchants and I spoke about the matter, and we—"

They stood awkwardly in the silence as two hong merchants approached from a path through the trees on the other side of the square.

"Yes?" Winnie asked nervously. Should they be turned away, perhaps they could bring Joseph with them tomorrow and have him act as their proxy. He knew nothing about being a merchant, but he was a man.

Mr. Liang continued, "Forgive me for asking. But we just wanted to make sure that you were willing and able to work, even in your grief."

"Oh," Winnie said.

"Yes," Nell exhaled. "Absolutely. Yes." It wouldn't be the same without Peter. Nothing ever would be the same. But at least Nell was allowed to try.

"Excellent," Mr. Liang said. Then he turned to the hong merchants, exchanging a few words with them in Cantonese.

In the years to come, Winnie would travel the world with her mother, together becoming the new co-owners of the reimagined and much-revered company of Starbuck & Starbuck. They would see success unlike any Peter Starbuck had ever imagined, invited to ballrooms in Rome and palaces in Paris while buying up all the lace, silk, and taffeta their fleet of three ships could hold. They would return to China five more times, visiting Canton and Hong Kong and Shanghai. And on every journey, Joseph Allen was there, both as the ship's navigator and as husband to Winnie—and eventually, father to Petunia, who loved nothing more than to sail the seas with her family. She never, ever, *ever* got seasick.

But today, perched on the bow of her new life, Winnie didn't know this. She only knew that it all felt possible, in the nodding heads of the hong merchants, in the sound of the birds chirping in the garden before them, and in the whispers of the wind coming off the harbor.

Winnie heard her name being said as part of the conversation in Cantonese. "Mr. Liang," Winnie asked, "can you share with us what you just said to the merchants?"

"Of course." Mr. Liang smiled. "Please welcome to Canton Mrs. Nell and Miss Winifred Starbuck, from the *Stargazer* of Nantucket."

AUTHOR'S NOTE

My fictitious *Stargazer* and her journey to San Francisco is based in large part on the real maiden voyage of the very real *Flying Cloud*. Built by Donald McKay in East Boston, *Flying Cloud* launched from New York on June 1, 1851, and arrived in record-breaking time in San Francisco on August 31, 1851, beating *Surprise*'s time by about a week. This extreme clipper, with the tallest mast ever built at the time, surpassed her own time three years later by thirteen hours—arriving in San Francisco in eighty-nine days and eight hours—and held *that* world record for 135 years.

Aside from being the fastest ship that ever sailed the seas, what makes *Flying Cloud* particularly noteworthy in maritime history is that she was led by a husband and wife team: Captain Josiah Perkins Creesy, a hard-driving captain who refused to stop for repairs after dismasting on day six, and navigator Eleanor Creesy, who used the "Pathfinder of the Seas" Matthew Fontaine Maury's notes and charts to aid her in sailing at an exceptionally fast clip around the Horn and on to San Francisco. And, although *Flying Cloud* brought a number of passengers along for the ride of a lifetime on that first trip, she did not have a stowaway on board.

Let's discuss those characters, shall we? Joseph Starbuck was a real whaling merchant and factory owner who built the famed Three Bricks at 93, 95, and 97 Main Street on Nantucket for his sons, although Peter, as one of those sons, is my invention. Maria Mitchell was both America's first professional female librarian and astronomer, and a fictionalized version of her appears as one of the main characters in my first novel, *Daughters of Nantucket.* Winifred Starbuck, her parents, and the vast cast and crew of characters in this novel—and their subsequent stories—are my invention.

For those interested in reading more about the legacy of this phenomenal vessel, I would suggest David W. Shaw's *Flying Cloud: The True Story of America's Most Famous Clipper Ship and the Woman Who Guided Her* and *The Flying Cloud and Her First Passengers* by Margaret Lyon (a descendant of one of those first passengers) and Flora Elizabeth Reynolds.

To learn about the history of clipper ships, the China trade, and the Opium Wars, I turned to many books, including: *When America First Met China* by Eric Jay Dolin, *Barons of the Sea And Their Race to Build the World's Fastest Clipper Ship* by Steven Ujifusa, *The Opium Clippers* by Basil Lubbock, *The Clipper Ship Era* by Arthur Clark, *China Tea Clippers* by George Campbell, and *The Era of the Clipper Ships: The Legacy of Donald McKay* by Donald Gunn Ross III.

For more about the Gold Rush and the development of San Francisco, I recommend *The Age of Gold: The California Gold Rush and the New American Dream* by H. W. Brands. And for information about women at sea during the time of my novel, I turned to *Hen Frigates: Passion and Peril, Nineteenth-Century Women at Sea* by Joan Druett, *A Young Lady's Diary of Five Years in China: 1829-1834* by Harriet Low Hillard, *Pirate Women: The Princesses, Prostitutes and Privateers Who Ruled the Seven Seas* by Laura Sook Dumcombe, and *Seafaring Women: Adventures of Pirate Queens, Female Stowaways, and Sailors' Wives* by David Cordingly. Although fictional, I learned a great deal from—and loved reading—*Tai-Pan*, James Clavell's momentous saga of Hong Kong in the 1840s.

I am sure I am forgetting something. I read a lot of stuff!

If you like seafaring adventures like this one, there are plenty more to enjoy. For nautical tales both fictional and non-fictional and from historic to contemporary, I highly recommend for starters: *Two Years Before the Mast* by Richard H. Dana Jr., *The Wager* by David Grann, *Sea Wife* by Amity Gaige, *A True Account: Hannah Masury's Sojourn*

Amongst the Pyrates, Written by Herself by Katherine Howe, and *The Wide Wide Sea* by Hampton Sides.

And if you would like to journey beyond the pages of a book, I suggest visiting the extensive collection of Chinese art and artifacts at the Peabody Essex Museum in Salem, MA; hopping aboard America's oldest commercial ship still afloat, the *Charles W. Morgan*, at Mystic Seaport in Mystic, CT; learning about the Pacific Coast's maritime legacy at the Maritime National Historic Park in San Francisco; or climbing the rigging on the world's only surviving clipper ship, the *Cutty Sark*, at the Royal Museums Greenwich just outside London.

Wishing you fair winds and following seas, reader. *Semper porro!*

ACKNOWLEDGMENTS

My sincerest thanks to Allison Hunter at Trellis Literary Management for being a fierce champion from the start and for making my literary dreams come true. Allison's feedback on the first one hundred pages of this manuscript went something like, "Ohmigod, you really stepped it up!" and "Don't change a word! I'd send it to your editor today if it wasn't 4:00 p.m. on a Friday in July!" That kind of enthusiasm cannot be faked. Her excitement encouraged me to keep writing, as we both sensed that I was doing something special with *Stargazer*.

Thanks also to Natalie Edwards and the entire team at Trellis for your support.

At HarperCollins, thank you to April Osborn, who acquired this novel, and to Leah Mol, who edited it. Leah, who is also a novelist, appreciated my merry band of characters and yet found ways to streamline the story without losing the fun, sprawling adventure of it all. Thank you also to Eldes Tran for her thoughtful sensitivity read, to copy editor Greg Stephenson and production editor Terra Arnone, and to the publicity and marketing teams, especially Leah Morse and Brianna Wodabek, who positioned the novel for success in the marketplace. For everyone who picks up this book and remarks on the stunningly beautiful cover art, a hearty thank-you to Sara Loos for her art direction and creativity, to the design team who weighed in on cover concepts, and to the sales team who found the perfect title for my *Stargazer*. She is the most glorious ship that ever sailed the bookworld seas!

A big shout-out and thank-you to Ann-Marie at Get Red PR for your professionalism, can-do attitude, and friendship.

I spoke to experts in several fields as part of my research. Thank you to Mary K. Bercaw Edwards, Director of Maritime Studies at the University of Connecticut, for providing access to the Manuscript Collection at Mystic Seaport, inviting me aboard the *Charles W. Morgan* to sing a shanty while hauling lines, and for editing the nautical sections of this novel for authenticity and accuracy. We met at a *Moby Dick* conference, as one does, and she had me at "Hello, I'm a sailor and a Melville scholar." Any errors in the ship's journey are mine. Thank you also to authors, scholars, and experts in Chinese culture and history Weina Dai Randel, Lyle Goldstein, and Grant Rhode. (An important aside: readers should know that *Canton* is an outdated, Anglicized name for the city of Guangzhou, China.) Thanks to Jordan Goffin at the Providence Public Library for granting me access to your extensive collection of maritime logbooks, journals, and ephemera.

Thank you to Jim Borzilleri at the Nantucket Atheneum for regaling me with historical factoids whenever I show up at the library on a random Tuesday without warning. Jim is always game to answer historical questions on the fly and to provide an extensive list of useful sources. It is clear that he loves his work, which makes my work easier. Also, thank you to Ann Scott, the Atheneum's executive director and head librarian at the time of this writing, for championing my debut novel and for having a really good sense of humor. Thank you to Nathaniel Philbrick for sharing a list of sources about the Gold Rush, to David Billings and Beverly Hall for giving me a private tour of your extensive collection of Asian art and artifacts at your Madaket home, and to Denese Allen, Kathy Kelm, Laura Herhold, and Anne Conway for welcoming me (twice!) to the Offshore Artists Residency at the Nantucket Island School of Design and the Arts. Thank you to Tim Ehrenberg, Wendy Hudson, Cristina Blank, Maggie Hewitt, and the rest of the staff at Mitchell's Book Corner for being so good at what you do—and for always keeping a stack of my books near the front door. To the Nantucket Book Festival, thank you for enriching the lives of so many through literature. To Nancy Thayer for embracing me from the start, and to Betsy Tyler and Mary Bergman for your historical knowledge and friendship.

A huge thank-you to my writing family in Boston and beyond. Author Jenna Blum invited me into her master novel workshop in 2017 and changed my life, surrounding me with a cast of characters who always give great feedback on my work and also make me laugh really loudly. This group enriches my life in so many ways. Thank you to Trisha Blanchet, Hillary Casavant, Tom Champoux, Chuck Garabedian, Kimberly Hensle Lowrance, Edwin Hill, Alex Sunshine, Sonya Larson, Joe Moldover, Jenna Paone, Jane Roper, and Whitney Scharer. A special shout-out to Mark Cecil for being an incredible plot whisperer, usually available to talk shop within a day should I feel an emergency story crisis come on. (Readers who invite me to book clubs will hear exactly how Mark helped with a huge plot point!)

The reading community makes my job both possible and incredibly fulfilling. As a former teacher who enjoys public speaking, and as a shopaholic who loves to dress up, boy, do I love going on book tour! Thank you to everyone who buys, reads, shares, and talks about my novels, and to book groups, organizations, and festivals that invite me to speak. Thanks to every librarian and independent bookseller out there fighting the good fight and celebrating literature, including a few fave RI locals: Jennifer Massotti and the entire staff at Barrington Books (where I work), Lisa Valentino at Inkfish Books, Katie Kinnell at Books on the Square, and Michelle San Antonio at Wakefield Books. To Robin Kall Homonoff for supporting me early on and throwing the best book bashes, to A Mighty Blaze for celebrating authors far and wide, and to the amazing Annissa Armstrong and every bookstagrammer, podcaster, journalist, and reviewer who helps writers find their audience.

My list of author friends is kind of huge, so I will just say that I love you all and am so happy to get to read your work. I love the way we support and encourage one another. Being in community with you is a true highlight of my life, and you are always welcome to crash at my place while on book tour. Special thanks to the authors who agreed to write a blurb for me, because I know that's a pain in the neck. And to all of my other, non-writer friends who keep me sane and make me laugh out there in the real world, you know who you are, and thank you.

Thank you to my parents for giving me your love of history, for our Nantucket summers, and for buying so many copies of my debut that I became a bestseller for one whole day. My mother joined me on much of my first book tour, making flower crowns for my friends to wear at the Nantucket Daffodil Festival and keeping me calm when we got lost in Milwaukee. We had so much fun. Thanks a million for your support and for reading this book a million times. My dad read the final draft of *Stargazer* while we vacationed on Nantucket together, and it was a joy to get a play-by-play from him every time I came in from the beach. "Jules! I don't like that Sully!"

The novel's dedication refers to my son, Andrew Gerstenblatt, and his writing partner and best friend, Arthur Goldbart. After graduating from USC film school—where they basically majored in Storytelling—they visited RI, and I told them about a huge problem I was having with this novel. In under thirty minutes at my kitchen island, Andrew and Arthur restructured the entire thing and put the wind back in my sails. The *Stargazer* and I are enormously grateful for their wisdom and insights. *Semper porro*, guys.

To Z for growing into an exceptional adult who still enjoys cuddling on the couch with me and the dog for movie nights. Thank you for needing me as your mom, and for texting with me daily so I don't feel my empty-nestness too much.

To Brett, for understanding that my creative process involves being left alone to wander around the house in pajamas, ignoring the dirty dishes and the dog walking so that I can best attend to the characters in my head. Thanks for being the first person to read my pages and for being real at the end of every day. I love you and our children so much and am treasuring this phase of our life together.